FOREVER FIGHTING

J. SAMAN

Boston World Family Tree

This family tree is simply a reference if needed. Each book is a complete standalone.

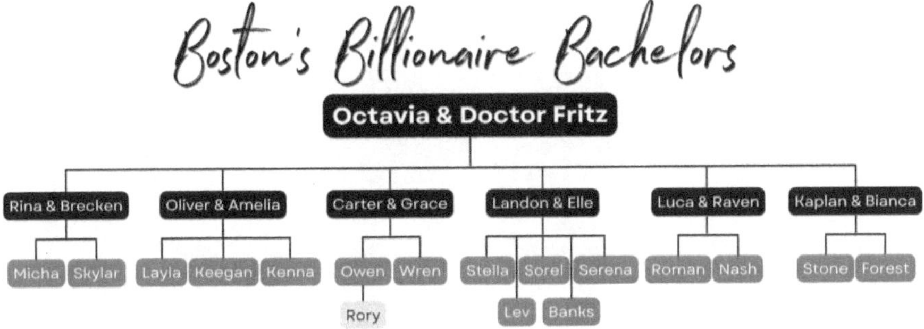

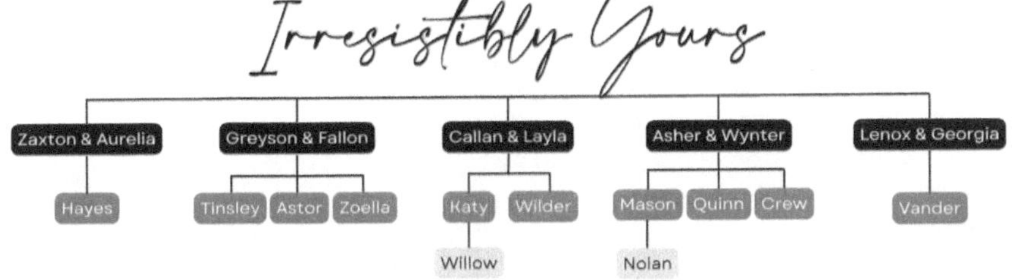

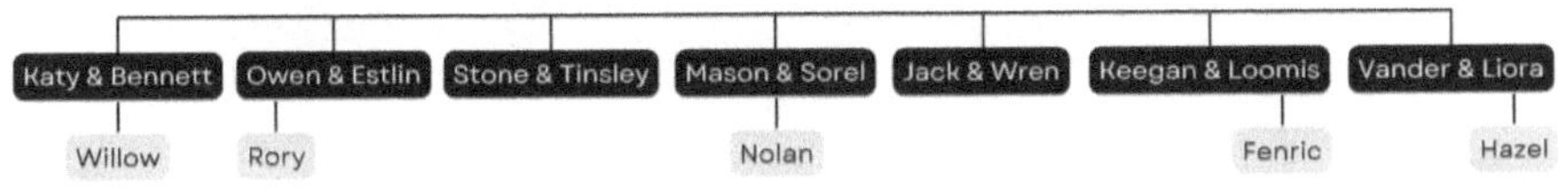

1

ROMAN

I slice the truffle with the precision of a surgeon, each paper-thin round perfect. Watching me, my sous chef, Chris, curses.

"Now you're just showing off."

I smirk at him as I finish the dish of butter-poached lobster with caramelized sweet corn, bacon, and parsnip puree with a truffle crown. The sauce only I know the recipe for takes three days to reduce and settle, which is why we only serve this dish here at South Paw on Fridays. Critics have called it transformative, and customers drop two hundred bucks to experience it.

"Showing off implies competition."

He chokes on a half-baked laugh. "God, you're such a dick. Does that come with your MICHELIN Star or your James Beard Award?"

I shrug at his sarcasm. "That's for you to decide, not me. I don't care if I'm a dick as long as the dish is perfect. Finish this up and get it out."

"Yes, Chef," he says, though there's no heat in it.

Around me, the kitchen hums with the sort of chaotic perfection I thrive on. It's a well-tuned machine where everyone knows their place and does their job without me having to bark down their throats. I own three restaurants here in Boston and bounce between all of them, but my Fridays are always spent here.

Tonight, I'm especially wired, and it has nothing to do with my restaurants or cooking. For now, I settle the adrenaline anxious to pump through my veins and focus on what I'm here to do.

"Behind," I call out as I slide past a line cook.

"Chef, the Pierce party is requesting to meet you," Eliza, the front-of-house manager, tells me. "Their daughter is with them. She's that influencer model girl everyone is obsessed with. She asked if you'd pose for pictures with her and if you're single."

I throw her a side-eye, and she tosses her hands up.

"Don't shoot the messenger. I told them I'd tell you and see what you'd say."

"Tell them I'm busy making their dinner and I don't do meet and greets, especially setups." I'm already turning my back to her as I go to taste a sauce that's simmering a bit too rapidly. She leaves it at that, knowing well enough not to argue with me. Celebrity chef status comes with annoying expectations, including appearances, glad-handing, and Instagram posts. Being a Fritz from a family of famous billionaires gets you that too, so for me, it's doubled.

I don't do any of them, and it's earned me a reputation as a dick, just as Chris said.

But as I told him, I don't care. I got into it for the food. Not the other bullshit. Europe is always better with the celebrity stuff, and it's yet another reason I'm looking forward to moving in three months.

Three hours later, the cleaning staff is doing their thing, and I've discussed inventory with both my bar and food managers. In my office, I shed my white coat and pull on a clean black T-shirt I already know I won't be wearing for long and my leather jacket.

My muscles vibrate with anticipation, and without a word to any remaining staff, I head out the back door and straight onto my motorcycle.

The old rope warehouse isn't far from South Paw, tucked in a part of South Boston that developers haven't touched yet. From the outside, it looks abandoned, dark, with crud-crusted windows and dirty brick. But anyone who knows this area knows it's anything but abandoned. Seamus O'Brien owns it and therefore no one fucks with it.

I park along the side and head over to the metal door manned by two discreetly armed men I wouldn't be excited to see in the ring.

"Roman," one greets me and steps aside to allow me entrance.

The inside space isn't all that different from the outside. The concrete floors are gritty and worn, the overhead lights dull and likely a fire hazard. The air smells of money, sweat, and expensive leather. There are two full bars, one on each side of the ring, and so far there are about a hundred people milling about and eyeing me surreptitiously.

I spot Hayes and Forest talking to two guys, but once they spot me, they head over to me. Hayes is one of my lifelong friends, and Forest is my cousin, but more of a friend as well. It's just them tonight as Crew can't be caught here or he'd be kicked off the Boston Rebels—where he plays professional football as a tight end—and his twin, Quinn, and my other friend Skylar rarely attend my fights. Typically, it's Hayes, Forest, and my best friend, Braelyn, but I don't see her yet.

"Hey, man." Forest gives me a fist bump, as does Hayes. "Supposed to be a big crowd tonight."

"The guy you're up against is also undefeated," Hayes explains. "He's also talking a lot of shit."

"They always talk shit," I say as I head into the back room to get myself ready and stay away from the anxious crowd.

"The action is heavy." Forest leans against the wall, his eyes on his phone.

"If that's so, put twenty grand down on me to knock him out before the sixth."

Hayes whistles through his teeth. "Shit. All right. We're on it."

They leave, only I'm not granted any alone time. "Winner takes fifty grand," Seamus says by way of a greeting, with a greedy gleam in his eyes. He's feeling me out. Seeing where my head is. There's no other reason for him to be in here before the fight.

I pull off my leather jacket and black T-shirt before slipping off my pants and changing into shorts. My muscles are charged, and my blood hums. I fucking love this feeling. It's the high that never gets old.

Even if the reason I do this haunts me like a never-ending nightmare.

"Roman, did you hear me?"

I don't know why he bothers to tell me the night's amount. I don't care about the money. It's not why I do this, and he knows it. All of my winnings are anonymously donated to charity anyway.

"Cool," is my only reply. He gets forty percent of that regardless of who wins. It's an easy deal for him. Even if this place is raided by cops or feds, no one in this city will go after him. The risk is all mine. I'm the one with everything to lose. But when you already know what it feels like to lose everything, you no longer have fucks to give about that threat.

"I'll go check on Biscuit and make sure he's ready to go."

Biscuit? What the fuck kind of name is that for a boxer? Without waiting for me to acknowledge him—because he knows I won't—he heads out the door, and I'm finally alone.

Only once again, my solitude doesn't last long. Not even two minutes later, the door opens and the handler announces, "It's time."

With a nod, I roll my head and crack my neck while I jog lightly in place to keep my muscles warm. I step out of the room and take in the scene before me. A couple of hundred people are crammed into the warehouse, actively making bets and shouting. Smoke curls up toward the high rafters, making the already dim lights hazy and the air reek of cigarettes and weed.

Biscuit stands beside me, a mountain of a man with a ridiculous name, and I take him in as he does with me. Neither of us speaks, but I can already see his weakness. His size. It gives him a false sense of confidence, though I have no doubt he's a bruiser when he gets going. Good. I relish that in an opponent.

Turning away from him, I scan over to the VIP area and lock in on Braelyn, who's standing there with Forest and Hayes. She rarely, if ever, misses a match. A smile curls my lips before I can stop it.

"That your woman?"

I don't answer Biscuit, and this pleases him.

"She's beautiful. She'll look even better on her knees sucking my cock after I win."

I hold in my smirk. He just put the nail in his own coffin with that.

Arnett, a henchman of Seamus's, goes through the whole welcome speech from the center of the makeshift ring. Then Biscuit and I are announced, though he refers to me as Romeo, my fighter name. We enter the ring to thunderous applause and shouts, but I ignore everyone as I head over to Braelyn and the guys. Hayes and Forest each give me a nod that I return. Braelyn doesn't say anything. She just holds out her pinkies to me, and I lock mine with hers.

We squeeze them together, and I give her a wink. It's become our thing over the years. It's our *I've got you no matter what* signal. It's for luck, and it never fails.

My head clears, and I meet Biscuit in the center of the ring, my gaze deadlocked with his as I study him one final time. He's smiling like a smug bastard, but he's already lost. He just doesn't know it yet.

"Fight!" Arnett calls and jumps out of the way. And as I suspected, Biscuit is impatient. He rears back with a mighty swing he lets fly, and I duck to the right, making him miss. It pisses him off. I bet that move has knocked a few guys out before, but that's not how I operate. He comes at me again, and when I go left this time, feeling the air displace against my cheek from his fist, I swing around and nail him dead in the ribs.

And with it, everything fades. The restaurant. The fame. The pressure. The stormy waters. The main reason I'm leaving the country.

All of it.

The violence, the blood, the sweat, the pain. It feeds the darkness of my soul.

Back and forth, we do this dance. Over and over. Round one is called. Then rounds two, three, and four. He nails a few punches, one of which manages to cut my upper lip, filling my mouth with blood, and another that slices beneath my eye. But for every hit he lands on me, I get five on him.

He's slowing. He's tired. He's big and used to relying on his size and strength, so his stamina is shit. By the time we reach round five, he's winded, hardly able to catch his breath despite the two-minute break we had. So much so that as he charges at me, I don't move. He was fun at first, but now he's starting to bore me.

I rear back and nail him right in the face. His nose shatters beneath my fist, and he tumbles to the concrete in a bloody heap.

I'm breathing hard, blood trickling down my cheek, and my knuckles are raw despite the wraps. Arnett checks him and declares a TKO, or technical knockout, and me the winner. And that's that. Match over. Cheers ring out, but after he holds my bloody fist in the air, I retreat back into the room I came from, immediately followed by Braelyn, Hayes, and Forest.

"Twenty grand," Forest tells me. "You turned that into forty. Do you want me to manage it?"

"Sure," I reply as I dry my hands with a wad of paper towels. "Along with my winnings."

"You got it."

"Come here, Hercules," Braelyn teases, her voice soft but commanding. I know what she wants, and she won't let me get away until she's examined me, ever the nurse. "He got your lip good, and you'll have a nice shiner by the end of the night. You also look tired."

And for the first time all day, I smile a genuine smile. "Says the woman who just worked a twelve-hour shift in the ER," I quip, sitting on the edge of a metal table.

"Yes, but I'm genetically blessed. You're just pretty, which requires maintenance, including sleep."

"I'll get some later," I promise her. "Where's Adam?" Adam is her fiancé and one of my closest friends, but I'm not upset he didn't join her tonight.

"Getting his beauty rest," she teases.

She removes the tape from my hands and cleans up my cuts and scrapes with a solution and then dabs them with an antibiotic ointment. Her gloved nail brushes along the underside of my left ring finger against my tattoo, and my heart gives a jerk that quickly passes as she continues her assessment.

"That cut's not too deep," she tells me, applying an antiseptic solution to my face that burns like hell. "You don't need stitches unless you decide to do something stupid before it heals."

"Define stupid," I retort, staring at her face as she places a butterfly bandage over it.

"I think you could define that better than I could."

"Probably. How was your shift?"

"Not bad. Three overdoses after a party we managed to save and a kid who stuck a Lego up his nose. No fatalities."

"How do you deal with people like that?" Forest asks, shuddering to himself.

She laughs. "Unlike the two of you"—she points at Forest and me—"I happen to like people."

"I don't hate people," I defend. "I just prefer them at a distance. Preferably separated by a kitchen door."

"Says the man who voluntarily gets into a ring and exchanges bodily fluids with strangers."

"Are you trying to make us all throw up?" Hayes grouses. "That's fucking nasty."

Braelyn shrugs as she rips off her gloves and sanitizes her hands with her travel pump. "Just saying I'd get a few extra vaccines if I were you. And I want to take a look at your eye in a couple of days to make sure it's healing well."

"I'll be fine," I assure her.

"You two sound like an old married couple," he continues. "Explain to me how it is you've never hooked up before?"

My shoulders tense reflexively. Typically, no one asks us this, but every now and then, Hayes likes to be a dick and push shit he shouldn't. Braelyn and I have been best friends since I lost my brother, who was her boyfriend at the time, when I was twenty-four and she was eighteen. It's also how I became so close with Adam, who was best friends with both of them. My friendship with Braelyn has only grown stronger over the years, and now we're all but inseparable.

But it's not like that with us. It never has been. At least not from her side.

Yet she nails me with, "I tried to kiss him once. He rejected me. Bruised my ego terribly, and I've never recovered."

"That's not how it happened," I interject, shocked she's even bringing this up when she never does. "You were trashed after party hopping. You tried to kiss me on your apartment front steps, nearly falling over in the process, and because I'm not a total fucking asshole, I didn't take advantage."

"Please," she scoffs. "I was perfectly coherent. I remember every detail, including you pushing me back and saying, and I quote, 'Not like this, Brae.'"

"Because you'd been doing so many tequila shots, you could hardly stand up."

I get an eye roll and a folding of her arms across her chest. "Three. I had three."

"It was six," I counter, standing to my full height because what the fuck? "And you threw up in the bushes of the party like twenty minutes before, which was why I was driving you home."

She tilts her head. "Oh, right. I sort of forgot that part of it."

Now it's my turn to fold my arms. "Yeah. Shocker there."

She waves me away. "Anyway, that's ancient history. Roman and I are way better like this. Bad boy Roman doesn't date, and I'm about to become an old married lady."

There's a reason bad boy Roman doesn't date, and I'm looking at it. And her becoming an old married lady is why I'm leaving the country for a while. Only Braelyn doesn't know about that yet. No one does.

"Seven weeks," Forest says, noticeably changing the subject. "You might want to schedule your next couple of matches around Brae's wedding."

"Oh my god!" Braelyn turns on me, a finger jabbed in my direction. "You freaking better. If you show up to my wedding as our best man maid of honor with a black eye and ruin my pictures, I will kick your ass. And win."

I hold up a hand in surrender. "I promise I'll be the handsome guy in the tux standing by both your sides. I'll be the best best man maid of honor ever."

"Excellent. Now I need to get home. I have a shift starting at eleven tomorrow and I promised Adam I wouldn't be home too late."

"I'll walk you out."

I toss on my T-shirt, foregoing the jeans and leather jacket because I'm still overheated. The four of us walk out together, both Forest and Hayes saying good night, knowing I'll walk Braelyn to her car. I give her a sweaty hug, and she kisses my cheek.

"Get home safely on your deathcycle."

I give her a sardonic look but smile all the same. "Yes, Nurse Albright."

She climbs into her car and starts it up but rolls down her window. "Hey, Ro?"

"Yeah, kid?"

"It was a good match tonight." She lingers on my face for a moment, then rolls up her window and drives off. I watch the taillights fade into the dark Boston night, but her words from earlier sit heavily on me, unshakable. I did reject her that night. But not because she was drunk, though she was, and not because she threw up, because oddly enough, I didn't care about that. It wasn't because I was being noble either, though I tried to be.

It was because she was twenty and I was twenty-six and we'd lost Nash only two years prior. I was in no shape to be anything good to her. Nothing that she deserved or needed from a guy. I was a fucking mess, and she was my lifeline, and I knew she'd regret it the next morning.

I was certain of it.

That was the first and only time she ever tried anything like that with me or even hinted at something. She was so trashed and likely would have kissed a garden hose if it showed interest.

But the truth is, our timing never lined up, and my guilt kept me away. After that, it was too late. Our lives perpetually diverged, only intersecting at all the wrong points. But now, with her marrying Adam in seven weeks, I can't help but wonder. What if I *had* kissed her that night?

2

———

BRAELYN

I can tell when my patient is going to code before they do. It's a sixth sense I have. A gut feeling and it's never led me astray. Not ever. And I have that feeling now as I look at my sixty-eight-year-old rule-out heart attack, or MI as we call it, who is seemingly stable except for some minor agitation she says is from arm pain.

"Hey," I say to Wren, an attending physician here in the ER. "Can you keep an eye on my patient in room eight for a minute? She's agitated, and I want to give her a bit more morphine."

Wren gives me a look. She's a new attending, but she did her medical school rotation as well as her residency here, and she's known me for our entire lives since our families are friends.

"Why?" she questions warily, squinting slightly at me.

"Because if she codes in the next five minutes, I'd like to have a doctor nearby, and you're standing here."

"Shit," she hisses. "You and these fucking intuitions. Yes, I'll watch your patient."

"Thanks. The code cart is right outside the door."

She makes a noise that's similar to a grunt and a groan, and

I head over to the Pyxis machine to pull out the morphine and draw it up. The drawer isn't even open when I hear "Code Blue, room eight. Code Blue, room eight."

Shit. I fucking knew it!

I slam the door on the machine and race back down the hall, getting caught up in the swarm of doctors and nurses as they all enter the room at once.

Wren is already doing chest compressions. "You owe me an ice cream sundae for this," she tells me.

I totally do. Damn.

A million questions shoot my way, and I explain how she's a rule-out MI waiting on troponins, but her X-ray was clear, her vitals stable, and her EKG showed sinus tachycardia with no ST-segment changes that would indicate a heart attack.

"Let's get her intubated," Jack Kincaid, Wren's husband and the chief physician in the ER, states. "Are the labs back, and do we have a shockable rhythm?"

"Checking labs now," one of the nurses tells him. "Electrolytes are normal, but troponin is 0.12."

"Pulseless V-tach on the monitor," I call out.

"Push epi and stand by with Amiodarone. Charge to two hundred," Jack orders. "Clear."

Everyone steps back, and Jack applies the paddles to the patient's chest and shocks her.

"Rhythm?" Jack throws at me.

I study the monitor. "Sinus brady at fifty-two."

"Nice. And on the first try. Let's make it the only one, but no more beta blockers until we get her out of bradycardia. Let the cath lab know that we're bringing them up a hot one. Whatever her EKG showed on admission, she's definitely having an MI now."

Great. And up until now, it had been an easy shift.

We continue to medically code my patient, gradually dragging her back from the jaws of death. Once we stabilize her, I help bring her up to the cath lab so they can unblock her coronary arteries that are causing the heart attack. As crazy as this sounds, it's all pretty standard procedure.

After I get her there and the cath team takes over, I head to the cafeteria to grab Wren her sundae and get one for myself. I don't do it with every code. Certainly not with traumas. But every now and then, you need a little ice cream to remind you that not everything in this world is as fucked and scary as it seems here in the ER.

"Ah, you're back," my mother, Margot, the chief nurse, greets me, eyeing my sundae.

"Thank you!" Wren calls out as she swoops by me and grabs hers from my hand.

"Thank you!" I call back, then turn to my mom as I dollop the first bite of vanilla with caramel sauce into my mouth. "What's up?"

"How would you like to go home early today?"

I snort a laugh and nearly choke on my ice cream. "Is that a rhetorical question, Mother Dearest?"

"We have two extra nurses on shift between three and seven, and you're on day five in a row. Go home."

"Really?" My eyes brighten, and I twist my wrist to check my watch. It's just after three in the afternoon. I could do laundry and even make Adam dinner, which in my world consists of boiling water and adding pasta to it, but whatever. It still counts.

"Yes. Go home."

"Ah! Thank you. I love you." I give my mom a wet, sticky kiss that she grimaces at and wipes away.

"You've earned it. Oh, by the way, Rina told me her wedding invitation arrived." A dazzling smile lights my mother's face, and a giddy excitement fills my belly.

"Oh yay. Did she like it?"

"She loved it. You picked beautiful ones. Only seven more weeks to your big day."

I do a small happy dance. "Seven more weeks. I'll call you tomorrow." I blow my mother a kiss and eat my sundae as I head into the locker room to grab my stuff. I'm too excited to leave to bother with changing, the taste of early freedom—and caramel—on my lips, so instead, I grab my bag of stuff and head out the door.

I call Adam, but it goes straight to voicemail. He's likely in a meeting or something. I jog up the steps for the train and see it already here at the platform. Crap. I don't want to miss it. I hightail it up the last steps and bolt for the doors as they start to close. I shove my way through, pushing the doors and managing to get on just in time.

Phew. And look at this, there's even a seat for me.

Totally my lucky day. My patient survived, I ate a delicious sundae, I got out of work early—something that rarely, if ever, happens—and I caught the train instead of having to wait for the next one.

I pop my AirPods into my ears and bop my head the entire way home, including switching trains to the green line and walking the three blocks to my apartment. The door shuts behind me, and I do a twirl as the song ends and I remove my AirPods. Only the music hasn't stopped. It's still going. But it's not Sabrina singing to me, it's freaking Harry Styles.

And he's doing it from my bedroom.

Along with the harmony of two people moaning over him.

I drop my AirPods back into my purse and set my bag down on the floor by the entryway. For a moment, I can't make myself move. I just stand here, listening to freaking Harry while staring at the trail of clothes that leads from the front door toward the bedroom.

My eyes burn and the tip of my nose stings.

It's funny. For how good my patient intuition is, clearly it sucks when it comes to myself because I never ever would have seen this coming. Knowing that when I walk into the bedroom I share with my fiancé, I'm going to find him fucking another woman in it. The bastard peppered me with hugs and kisses this morning, and we walked to the train together holding hands.

"I love you. Have a great shift," he said to me as we got on different trains.

And now this.

Releasing a breath, I force myself forward. I have to see it with my own eyes, even though I know it's going to rip me apart. I step over their clothes, wading through the sea of corporate attire until I reach the bedroom.

A woman with long blonde hair is sitting naked on top of my fiancé and faking her orgasm. Her moans are loud and exaggerated as she bounces on his lap. His face, meanwhile, is pinched up in pleasure—no faking for him. As if the gods of irony are shining down on me at this moment, the song comes to an end just as they finish. I start clapping, applauding both their efforts. It breaks through perfectly before the next song starts.

The woman screams and races to cover herself with my favorite Egyptian cotton sheets, and Adam fumbles with his phone to turn off the music as another sweeping ballad starts. She looks familiar. I can't place her, but I've seen her before.

"I didn't think you liked Harry Styles," I say to him.

He looks at me, blinking about six thousand times, and I can see his wheels spinning as he mentally questions, "What can I say that will get me out of this?" And when he realizes there's nothing, he utters, "Um. I don't."

"Oh, it must be her favorite then. How sweet of you." I look at her. "Hi. I'm Braelyn. Who are you? Other than the woman fucking my fiancé in my bed?" She opens her mouth to speak, and I wave her away. "Never mind. Totally not important." If she talks and gives me her name or says something stupid, I might kill her. "It's wild, though, because I can tell you knew about me when I knew nothing about you." I turn back to Adam. "You brought your Corporate Barbie hookup to our home? To our bed? What the absolute fuck?"

"Brae—"

I hold up my hand, stopping him from speaking because I'm about ready to kill him too. Only I decide I actually do want to kill him and race over to slap him.

"You lying, cheating, son of a bitch bastard. How could you do this?" My hands fly, hitting him repeatedly, anywhere I can get. "Our fucking wedding invitations landed in people's mailboxes today. You've been one of my best friends since we were fucking kids!"

Like the coward he is, he covers his head with his arms to prevent me from wailing on him, and I can't with this. I just can't.

"I'm sorry. Ow. Shit. Stop! It was just sex. It didn't mean—"

I punch him in the stomach, making him oomph. I'll have to thank Roman later for teaching me that move. "Don't you fucking dare say that to me!" God, why do cheating assholes always say it didn't mean anything? Like that's supposed to make it better they were sticking their dick inside another woman?

I can't be here anymore with them naked and uncomfortable like I'm the unstable one in all of this. It smells like sex, and the bastard still has the used condom on his shriveled-up dick.

"I fucking hate you!" I scream, rip my engagement ring from my finger, chuck it at his stupid head, and race for the door as the first of my tears come, pouring from my eyes like a broken faucet. He broke me. The bastard broke me because damn him! I'm not a crier!

I snatch my purse off the floor and fly out the door, slamming it shut behind me and practically tumbling down the stairs with how fast I move. My feet hit the sidewalk, early rush hour brushing past in each direction, and a car horn blares, making me jump. I don't think about where I'm going. I don't question it.

I just run because I know he'll be there, and right now, the only person I want in the world after this is Roman. Everything is always okay when I'm with him. It's his superpower. We've held each other up through the worst of the worst.

And we did it with Adam as part of that.

The March air in Boston is sharp and a little wet, but I don't care. My feet pound the pavement, and I dodge a million people giving me a million different looks.

Let them look. My fiancé cheated on me. Likely has been cheating since I highly, highly doubt that was the first time. No, Corporate Barbie wasn't shocked by me, and she wasn't mad at him. They fucked there because I wasn't supposed to be home until close to eight instead of showing up three hours early. To think I would have crawled into bed beside him after they did that there makes me sick.

Uppercut, Roman's steakhouse, is just up the block, and I breathe a sigh of relief. He has three restaurants in Boston as well as others across the world, and all have a boxing-related name to them.

I enter through the back door that leads to a back room, and I loop around toward the kitchen. It's all hustle and bustle back here. The smell of cheese, garlic, wine, and meat permeates the air. Normally, I'd be drooling, but right now, it makes me want to throw up.

I spot Roman in front of a line of metal tables, talking to another chef. He's so tall and broad and formidable. Brown hair cut short and tight to his head, palest of pale blue-green eyes that make him look almost like a wolf, and arms swirling with tattoos hidden beneath his white chef's coat but peeking out a bit on his hands.

I don't want to disturb him. He's busy, and suddenly, I think I need some time alone to process this. Before he spots me, I walk through the back area to the main dining space. The restaurant doesn't open until five, and the bartender is busy setting up. I slide onto a stool and pick up a menu when she notices me.

"I'm sorry, Miss, we're—oh. Hey, Brae. I didn't realize it was you. What can I..." She trails off when she notices my face, so I'm positive I look like ass as I always do after I cry. At least my tears have stopped. "Are you okay?"

"Oh, you know, just a shitty day. Can I get your strongest martini ever?"

She studies me for a beat, then says, "Sure. Of course. I have a bourbon that's a hundred and twenty proof."

"Sounds delicious. Add a splash of sweet vermouth and some bitters to that, along with a cherry, would ya?"

"You got it."

"Thanks."

She's still giving me that questioning, unsure look, but I don't care as long as she serves me alcohol. Right now, I'd drink antifreeze if it served my purpose, though maybe I should serve that to my ex-fiancé. Speaking of...

My phone vibrates in my purse. I don't bother checking it. I know it's him. The same way I also know this is the moment when everything starts to fall apart for me.

3

———

ROMAN

"Chef, Braelyn is sitting at the bar and looks like she's been crying," Sport, one of my weeknight bartenders, tells me, popping her head into the kitchen.

"She's here now?" I twist my wrist, check my GMT-Master II, and frown. It's not even five yet, and she had a twelve-hour shift today. I know because she was going to be off for the next two days and wanted my help tomorrow with some last-minute wedding stuff, including final say on my tux. "Wait. Did you say she's been *crying*?"

Braelyn doesn't cry. Hardly ever. The only time I ever saw her cry was when she came into the hospital and saw me for the first time after Nash died, and then again at the funeral. But that's it.

"Yep. I made her a Manhattan with the Elijah Craig Barrel Proof we just got in."

I curse under my breath. She'll be drunk in no time.

Without a word to anyone, I leave the kitchen and head through the empty restaurant, going straight for the brunette who has her back to me. She's still in scrubs, her hair up in a ponytail that looks loose, with some of her long curls tangled around each other. Alarm skitters through me, and I quicken my steps to a run until I'm by her side, turning her to me and taking her face in my hand so I can see her.

The moment our eyes meet, fresh tears form and instantly fall to her cheeks.

"What is it?" I whisper, my heart hammering so hard I can barely breathe.

Her face crumples and lands on my chest, and instinctively my arms wrap around her, holding her tightly as she cries into me. I pick her up off her seat, take her in my arms, and slide onto another stool so I can set her on my lap.

"Adam," she manages, clinging to me. "He... I found him..."

"That motherfucker," slips past my lips before I can stop it. She doesn't even have to finish that. She could have told me he's dead or something else horrible, but I know that's not what this is. He cheated. The motherfucker cheated on my girl.

Honestly, I'm shocked.

Never in a million years would I have thought Adam would cheat on Braelyn.

"Yeah." She gives a watery laugh and pulls back, wiping her face. She shifts on my lap and climbs off as she polishes off the end of her drink. "He's all that and a bag of chips. I caught him and Corporate Barbie in my bed. In my favorite sheets, no less."

"He's still at your place?"

She shrugs. "I guess. Why?"

I stand, cracking my knuckles. "I'm going to beat him to death." Fury pumping through my veins sets my feet in motion, but Braelyn stops me, pulling on the back of my coat.

"Don't go. Please. I just... I need you right now."

And just like that, my blood cools, and my heart melts, and I twist to take her pinky, squeezing it to let her know that she has me. She always has me.

"Come on. I'll take you home. To my home."

I get a shaky nod as she gets to her feet and lets me lead her toward the back.

"Chef?" someone calls out from the kitchen as we pass.

"Handle it," I reply curtly.

"Wait." Braelyn stops us. "You're working."

I kiss her forehead and meet her eyes. "You're more important."

We walk to the back room, where I take off my chef coat and slip it back into my locker. I pull out my leather jacket and drop it on Braelyn's shoulders. Dutifully, she slips her arms through the sleeves that hang on her. She pushes them up so her hands are free, and I hand her my helmet.

"Just give me your keys. I'll Uber to your place."

I smooth her hair from her face. "I'm taking you home. No more arguing with me."

"I can tell you're fuming."

I laugh mirthlessly. "Fuming isn't the right word for what I am." I'm murderous. "Come on. We'll talk more at home."

"Your eye looks good," she notes as I climb onto my bike and hold out my hand for her to climb on behind me. "It's healing nicely for only a few days in."

"Told you I'd be fine."

The engine rumbles beneath us, and I peel out into the cool Boston night. Braelyn clings tightly to me. She hates riding, but this is all I had here, and I want to make a couple of stops along the way. After I do that, I drive us over the bridge into the Seaport, where my building is. Braelyn helped me pick out my penthouse and when I bought it, she told me it was the ulti-mate bachelor pad, likely because of the open two stories, massive media and great rooms, wraparound balcony, and the custom infinity-edge pool in the sunroom with a clear acrylic bottom and a retractable glass roof that opens in the summer.

Honestly, I bought the place for the kitchen, which I love, and because of the views of the Seaport. As much as it pains me, I feel better seeing the water. Like I'm closer to him this way. Nash was at home on the water. It was his favorite place to be, and I'd go sailing or swimming or whatever it was that he wanted just to see his goofy smile.

He'd be twenty-seven this year. The amount of trouble he, Adam, and Braelyn used to get into would turn any parent's hair white. I always felt it was my job to look after them since I'm six years older. I let Nash down with that, but I won't with Braelyn now.

I walk Brae up the wraparound staircase and into one of the guest bedrooms I never use. I think she's slept in here more than anyone else.

"I'll bring you some clothes," I offer.

Her arms wrap around her chest, and she takes in the view and the furniture. There isn't much. A king bed and two end tables. Not even a dresser, though there's a large walk-in closet, and if she ends up staying, I'll buy her whatever she needs to make it her home.

"Will you bring me your Rebels hoodie?"

I smile. "You have such a thing for that hoodie."

She turns back to me. "It's my favorite."

"It's mine too, though."

She points to her chest. "Cheating fiancé."

I roll my eyes. "Fine. I'll bring it to you. But you can't burn it in effigy when you decide you hate all men."

She gasps. "I'd never. That sweatshirt is sacred."

"Fair. I'll be back."

I shut the door behind me and jog down the hall to my bedroom. I head for my closet and grab her the smallest pair of sweatpants I have that will still be ten sizes too big on her, a new pair of boxer briefs, a T-shirt, and the hoodie. Girl is lucky I love her. She's the only person I'd ever share this with. I also grab my hairbrush for her to use.

I'm tempted to text Adam and ask him what the fuck, but

I'm not ready to talk to him yet. He's lucky I didn't find him. I would have killed him. I'm not sure that's even hyperbole. I want to squeeze him and shake him because he had her and threw her away when she's all I've ever wanted. I would have held onto her forever.

I head back down the hall, knock, and when she doesn't answer, I place the items on the bed and leave. I can hear the shower going, and thankfully, I don't hear her crying. What I do hear is her phone vibrating from inside her purse. He's calling her. I bet he's not even out looking for her. Lazy shit.

I'm so tempted to pick up, but I'll deal with him in my own time.

I leave her to get herself together and head downstairs to make us an early dinner.

Braelyn and Nash were together for over a year and a half when he died. It was a big deal for them. They were best friends before he ever made his move, but he had been crazy about her since he first realized he liked girls. I can't begin to explain the guilt I've carried. The number of times I've wondered if she would have been marrying Nash in seven weeks instead of Adam.

After he died, I couldn't stay. I couldn't handle any of it, especially when Braelyn just held my hand and didn't blame me. Not once. I took the love of her life from her, and she hugged me through it.

I left for Rome, then Paris, and London, doing apprenticeships and working as a sous chef in some of the best restaurants in the world. I threw myself into cooking. Into mastering my craft. After a couple of years, I moved back stateside to Las Vegas and LA. Anything to avoid coming home. I was making a name for myself and even did some guest spots on Food Network shows.

Then I realized I couldn't keep running from it or fighting it. I loved her. It hadn't dissipated from the moment I realized it was her. This was about... three and a half years ago, I think. It was the fall, and I was twenty-eight and finally starting to feel like I could take a breath without it shredding my lungs. I moved back to Boston and opened two restaurants.

And I planned my strategy.

I made my move. Gently felt her out and tested boundaries to see if she'd respond. I didn't get much in return, and then Adam came barreling in. That was that. I never told him how I felt. I never told her either. Which is why I'm the ~~best man~~ maid of honor. The best friend. The perpetual third wheel in our not-so-triangular situation. He was good to her, and that's what I cared about the most.

So I let the dream of one day with Braelyn die. She's my best friend, and I can't live without her. The ventricle to my atria, as she once called us. I'd take her like this any day over nothing, but that didn't mean I wanted to be here while she was a newlywed with someone else.

I've signed contracts at three locations. Frankfurt, Paris, and London. I'm leaving for Europe in ten weeks and am living there for at least eighteen months. I haven't told her yet, and now this.

In the kitchen, I unpack the things I picked up on the way over here and get started on Brae's favorite dish, spicy chicken carbonara. Usually, I make this for her with homemade bucatini, but I caved and purchased packaged fresh pasta to make it easier and faster. I start boiling the water while I sauté the pancetta and grill the chicken on the griddle part of my stove.

I hear her pad into the kitchen and turn to find her looking adorable in my oversized clothes. Her brown hair is brushed back off her makeup-free face, and her milk-chocolate brown eyes are bright.

"Better?" I ask.

"Better. But I might not give you this hoodie back."

"I might not give you the option." I pull out a sauvignon

blanc that will complement the chicken and pasta and start uncorking it. She climbs up onto a stool and gratefully takes the glass when I slide it across the marble to her.

"You're making my favorite?"

"Kid, you got your heart broken tonight. Of course I'm making your favorite. I also got stuff to make pecan bars with caramel ice cream."

She rests her head on her forearm on the counter. "Thank you. Thank you for being on my side with this. I know by coming to you, I put you in a weird spot with Adam."

"There's no weird spot. I love him like a brother, but you're my Braelyn, and right now, he's just Adam."

Her eyes close, and she bites into her lip to push back her emotions. "This sucks, you know?"

I don't, but I do, so I just nod and turn back to the food so I don't burn anything.

"I got out of work early because we were overstaffed, and I walked in to find them fucking to Harry Styles."

My brows furrowed because that's just... "Harry Styles?"

She snorts a laugh as she takes a hearty sip. "I know, right? How random is that? She was also faking her orgasm. It shouldn't make me feel better that he couldn't even get her off, but somehow it does."

"How can you tell she was faking?"

She cocks an eyebrow at me, and my lips twitch up into a smirk.

I raise a hand defensively. "I've never experienced anyone faking it, so I wouldn't know. I'm simply asking."

She laughs and gives me two thumbs-up. "Okay, yeah, sure. I'm sure you're the Zeus of all sex, and no woman has ever faked it with you."

"I mean, you said it. I didn't."

She puffs out a sarcastic noise. "The arrogance of men never ceases to astound me. Haven't you ever seen *When Harry*

Met Sally? All men say that a woman has never faked with them, and yet all women have faked at one point in their lives. As Meg Ryan said in that film, you do the math."

I shrug as I whisk the eggs and yolks together before I add the parmesan and pepper to them. "Not with me, they haven't."

"Riiiight. I honestly don't want to challenge you on that. You say you hand out orgasms to women like they're M&M's, and I believe you." She takes another sip of wine. "He never made me scream. That's all I'm saying."

I toss the pasta into the salted water. "She might have been faking, but he certainly never gave you a proper orgasm then. You should have been screaming every night."

A flush spreads up her cheeks, and she stares down at the counter. I'm a fucking idiot for saying that. That wasn't helpful to her at all.

"Brae—"

She waves me away. "It's fine. I mean, it's not, but whatever. I found them like that and left. But I feel so dumb. I was going to marry him. I planned to spend my entire life with him. Mapped out our future. I've known him since I was fourteen. How long has he been cheating on me, and I was totally clueless about it?"

I finish up the pasta and slice the chicken, plating it up with a sprinkle of Italian parsley and more parmesan. "You're not dumb," I tell her adamantly as I put her bowl in front of her along with a napkin, fork, and spoon. "He's the asshole and I can't defend him even if he's my friend. Weak men cheat. Callous men cheat. I can't tell you why he did it, and I haven't talked to him to hear his side, not that it really matters or could excuse anything. I just know he's a fool for cheating on you and an arrogant prick because he didn't think he'd get caught. He's the dumb one, and now I get to kill him."

"I don't want to ask if that's hyperbole or not."

I smirk at her as I twirl the pasta around my fork with my

spoon. "Probably best if you don't. That way you can deny knowledge of anything and aren't an accomplice."

She sighs, and a tear hits her cheek that breaks my fucking heart. I hate seeing Braelyn sad. Fucking *hate* it.

"Three years of my life—hell, almost thirteen years of my life—are over, and right now, I'm riddled with a million questions and self-doubts. It's a shitty feeling. Incidentally, you likely have an invitation to my wedding waiting in your mailbox."

I got their wedding invitation this morning. I stared at that fucker for a solid ten minutes before I shoved it in a random drawer. Yes, I'm her maid of honor and his best man. Yes, I was going to stand by their side and try not to raise my hand when the pastor asked if anyone objected to this wedding. That invitation hurt. Her wedding was going to kill me, and I had plans to get very drunk that night. But I was going to kiss her cheek and tell her she was the world's most beautiful bride and shake his hand and tell him he was the luckiest son of a bitch on the planet and be there as my best friends got married.

All I want is for her to be happy, and right now she's not. I wish I knew how to fix this for her. I wish I knew how to take her hurt away.

"You can stay here as long as you want. As long as you need. Hell, you can stay forever."

Her head falls to my shoulder. "Thank you. I might take you up on that for a bit."

I kiss the top of her wet hair, leaving an imprint of moisture and the smell of my shampoo on my lips.

"You'll have the place to yourself next week."

"Huh?" She pops her head up, but recognition instantly flickers in her eyes. "Oh, right. You're going to Las Vegas for your restaurant opening and then to Mexico. What are you doing there again?"

"Overseeing the setup of a restaurant in one of the resorts

there. They need me to come in and approve the final specs and things on it."

She picks up her fork and starts twirling her pasta. "Right. Lucky you. I wish I could go to Vegas and Mexico," she mutters in an offhand way, but it sparks something big and bright and possibly insane in my head.

"Why can't you?"

Her fork stops mid-twirl, and she curiously tilts her head to me. "Why can't I what?"

"Come with me to Vegas and Mexico."

4

───────

BRAELYN

"Are you asking or offering?" I question, blinking at my friend, unsure what this odd bubbling feeling his words spurred in my stomach is all about.

He stares at me, and while I'm blinking, he's not at all. "Both," he says after a pause.

"You're serious?"

He shrugs. "Sure."

"I can't go with you."

He tilts his head and studies me. "Why not?"

"I picked out that place for my honeymoon with Adam. His imprint will be all over it. Like a freaking werewolf from *Twilight*."

He's confused, but at this point in our friendship, he knows better than to question my weirdness.

"It's a different resort than the one you picked on a different side of the country."

"Still Mexico."

"Braelyn, you can't be serious. That's like saying I planned a trip to California and ended up in Boston, but it's still the US."

"Well, it is."

He sighs. "I have to be in Vegas next week for the opening of Decision and then in Mexico for at least a week after that. I'll be in Vegas on my birthday and yours while I'm in Mexico."

"What will you do when you run out of boxing-themed titles for your restaurants?"

"Stop opening new restaurants. Braelyn, focus here. What if we went to Vegas, you attended the opening with me, and after we go on to Mexico? I work and get the restaurant where I want it to be while you relax in the sun."

Our birthdays are a week apart, except I'm very much a Pisces and he's very much an Aries. If you know anything about astrology, you're aware of the massive difference between us. I'm the dreamer. The emotional one. Always forming strong connections. Roman is all Aries. Determined and intense and action-oriented. Pretty obvious if you know him. I get what he's trying to do, and I adore him for it, but still...

"That makes no sense. Your resort is in Cancun. Vegas is in the opposite direction."

"Kid, I adore you, but you have the world's worst sense of direction. How about you leave the travel and planning to me? Just don't say no. Be open to the idea. When was the last time you had a real vacation? Or the last time I did, for that matter?"

"You'll be working in both places."

"Yes, but if you're there with me, it'll force me to take breaks and relax more than I otherwise would."

He has a point. It's a serious one too. I haven't had a vacation since I was in college and flew out to Rome to see him over spring break. No, wait, it was Paris the following year. But that was it. After that, our schedules never really aligned for me to visit him, and he came home to Boston often enough that I still got to see him. As for his last vacation... I'm not sure Roman Fritz has had a vacation since Nash died. They were on vacation at their grandparents' Martha's Vineyard estate when it happened.

"You're serious?" I question, thinking this through. So very tempted by the prospect of turning something awful into something... fun. And doing it with Roman, who is one of my favorite people in the world. Maybe my favorite now that Adam shit the bed.

"Absolutely. In fact, it's genius. Can you get the time?"

"My mother is the head RN, and when I tell her about Adam, I'm sure she'll adjust the schedule."

A strange sort of gorgeous evil smile curls up his lips. Roman Fritz is scary beautiful. The sort that puts male models and movie stars to shame because his look is effortless and his fucks to give about it are zero. The man literally has a bandaged-up cut under his eye and a fat bottom lip, and he's still hot as fuck.

I digress.

"Stop smiling at me like that."

He chuckles and takes a bite of his food before he washes it down with his wine. "Eat up, kid, and leave the details to me. But starting next week, plan to be away for the next two weeks."

"Two weeks?! I'm not sure I can be gone for that long."

"Fine. Ten days minimum but ask for two weeks. I've got you. You're living here for a while anyway. You'll be able to save the money you think you're losing with everything, and you won't have to pay any rent."

I scowl. "I hate how well you know me."

"Better than anyone. But with that, you can't get all huffy about how much money I spend on this or about where we stay. It's a business expense for me."

"Fine," I concede because really I'm not putting up much of a fight. I think I need to get away, and this is the perfect excuse and way to do it. "I'll talk to my mom about the time off. And any expenses that aren't business-related, I want to pay for."

He doesn't reply to that, and I know it'll be a fight between us, but whatever.

This sounds way better than hanging out here and dealing with this aftermath. I still have a wedding to cancel, and considering people are likely RSVPing right now, it's going to be ugly.

~

"YOUR FIANCÉ SHOWED up at my door," Skylar says through a yawn. "Is it what I think?"

I roll my eyes at myself. Of course he didn't come to Roman's. Fucking coward. He didn't come to my parents' place either. I spoke to them for over an hour after dinner about everything. I feel terrible about the money my parents are losing with this because deposits are nonrefundable. My dad won the lottery years before I was born and he's a doctor and my mom's a nurse. They're not poor, but we're not even in the same stratosphere as the Fritzes, or even the Monroes—which is what Hayes is—and the Reyeses—which is what Quinn and Crew are. Their dads were part of a very successful band called Central Square years and years ago.

I'm simply Braelyn from the block who ended up besties with a crowd of billionaires. Even Adam comes from crazy money, and his family had me sign a prenup bigger than Texas. Our condo was his, which officially makes me homeless and mooching off my best friend.

My dad told me he didn't care about the money. He just wants me to be happy and with the right man. A man who won't take me for granted. A man who will be devoted and love me endlessly. Sigh.

"Yep," I answer, lying in the giant bed in the whitest bedroom on the planet, staring out across the inky water toward the Boston skyline beyond. "I caught him fucking Corporate Barbie in our bed."

Skylar whistles through her teeth, only to yawn again.

It brings an inadvertent smile to my lips. "Tired, cupcake?"

"Dude, the first trimester of pregnancy can go fuck itself. Anyway, I slammed the door in his face and called you."

"Thanks for that. He's been blowing up my phone every five minutes or so. I'm debating blocking him, but I have to get my things from the apartment first. He can keep my Egyptian cotton sheets, though."

"That asshole. What a fucking asshole!" she yells, indignant on my behalf, and I love her for it. "I'm so sorry, Brae. I wish I had kicked him in the nuts before I shut the door on him. Are you okay or is that a dumb question?"

I release a heavy, silent breath. "Dumb question, but Roman did make me pecan bars and ice cream, so I'm not as bad as I could be. Ask me again next week and every week after until I eventually say yes."

"You will, you know. Say yes one day, that is. If I can be okay after Josh, you can be okay after Adam because we're fierce bitches like that."

I shift onto my side, propping myself up with my elbow. "Amen and hallelujah. I'm just not feeling all that fierce yet, but you keep preaching because it's good for both of us to hear."

"I'm happy now, and I'm positive you will be again with or without a guy. Should I burn your wedding invitation?"

"Go for it—" My phone beeps with an incoming call, and I laugh. "He must have gone to Quinn's too. Hold on, I'll merge her in." I don't wait for Skylar to reply as I click over to answer, except Quinn starts talking before I can.

"What the hell is happening? I came home from the hospital to find Adam at my doorstep looking like a broken-down poodle."

I cough at the description. What a loser. "Yeah. He cheated, and I walked in on it. Hold on, I'm going to merge you in with Sky."

I hit the button on my screen, and then we're all there together. "Did you slam the door in his face too?" I ask Quinn.

"No," she says. "He was outside my door. But I hip-checked him out of the way and told him if he's searching for you here, he did something very wrong, and even if I knew where you were, I wouldn't tell him."

"He's so dumb," Skylar states. "Why would he come to our places when he knows where you are?"

"Because you know he wasn't going to come here," I tell them. "He's too chickenshit and wants to protect his pretty-boy face from Roman's fist." I exhale a weary breath and climb off the bed to sit in the chair by the window. I'm restless as all hell.

"I'm glad Roman is on your side with this," Sky expresses. "I'd hate to have to kick my cousin's ass."

"He'd lose a kidney if he weren't, but yeah, me too," I agree. My voice drops as my tears threaten again. "How do I make sense of this? We were together for three years. Best friends for thirteen. We lost Nash together. We've been through thick and thin. We were planning a life together. I just can't wrap my head around it. The betrayal I feel is absolutely suffocating."

"I'm not sure you can make sense of this," Quinn says. "And I think your feelings are completely valid and spot on. I'm in shock too. We all thought you were the endgame couple. The relationship goals. Sometimes people aren't who you thought they were, and we don't know until fate steps in to show us because they've been so good at hiding it."

"I guess. I just keep thinking that if I hadn't caught that train, I would have missed it. I would have gotten home twenty minutes later and never have known."

"But you do know, and now you can start your life over again," Skylar states emphatically. "You didn't marry him. Think of the mess that would have brought."

I laugh lightly. "You mean like what you're going through?"

"Different," she tells me. "Aston and I got married out of

convenience and it turned into more. You were going to marry for love from the start."

"Whatever. Love shmuve. Saying yes to him when he proposed was the easiest thing I've ever done, and look where that got me." I pause for a moment, lick my lips, and say, "Roman wants to take me to Vegas next week for his restaurant opening and then on to Mexico after."

"What?" both say in unison. "How does that work?" Skylar finishes.

"He has to go for work, and I'd be tagging along, I guess. Roman said he'd take care of the arrangements and that it's a business expense, which is code for he won't let me pay." I brush my hair back from my face and draw my knees up to my chest on the chair. "Am I crazy if I go?"

"No," Quinn replies. "I think it's a great idea, actually. Leave town. Get away for a week or two. Get some distance and mental clarity."

"Yes," Skylar agrees. "I think it'll be good for you, honestly. I'd give anything to get out of March in Boston and go to Las Vegas, then a Mexican resort. You'll have a few drinks, relax by the pool and the beach, read some books, eat some amazing food, and chill out with Roman."

When she puts it like that... "You're right. I'm way over-thinking this."

"Then don't," Quinn retorts. "Just go with it and enjoy it. Have fun. Live a little."

I smile, thinking about that. I deserve a little fun.

"I gotta go," Quinn says. "I'll call you tomorrow. Love you both."

"Yes," Skylar jumps in. "Same. Night, Brae. You're going to be just fine."

They disconnect the call, and I sit here alone, staring out at the sparkling lights beyond the windows. My phone rings and I hit the green button without looking, wanting to get this over with. If I'm turning the page and starting a new chapter, I can't leave myself on a perpetual cliffhanger. I have to end the scene once and for all.

I put the phone back to my ear, but I can't make myself say anything. Not hi or hello or even go fuck yourself.

"Brae? You there?"

I make a noise.

"Where are you? I went everywhere searching for you."

I snort out a laugh. "Not everywhere. You know where I am. Why you bothered going to Sky's and Quinn's is beyond me."

"I was hopeful."

My eyes close, and I bite my bottom lip to the point where I taste blood. "How long?" I ask, needing to know. I rest the side of my face on my knees and put the phone on speaker.

"It doesn't matter—"

"How. Long?" I grit out. "Just be a man and tell me. The truth," I tack on.

He blows out a heavy breath and his voice drops to just above a whisper. "Three weeks."

I close my eyes. It's actually not as bad as I thought, and that's a fucked-up thought to even have.

"Why?"

"I don't know," he admits in a low tone. "The wedding was coming on fast, and she... she came on to me. Actually, she had been for a year, but I'd never reciprocated anything. I knew once we were married, I'd never sleep with anyone else again, and it just kind of happened that first time."

"And after that?"

"After that, each time I said it was going to be my last. I did. I fucking hated myself for it. I felt gross and dirty and like the lowest son of a bitch on the planet. But then she'd make a move on me, and it felt like the last breath of freedom. I was weak to it."

"How many times did you fuck her in our bed?"

"That was the first. We were going to go to a hotel, but the room wasn't ready, and she suggested my place instead."

My eyes close at the pain slicing through my chest. "Did you think about me? When you brought her into our home? When you saw my phone charger on the nightstand and my sleep shirt still on the floor? Did you even care or think about me, or was your stupid dick too hard?"

"I fucked up," he says weakly. "I did. I know I did. And I'm so, so sorry. So eternally sorry. But it truly was just sex. I don't have feelings for her. This wasn't emotional. I love you. I want to marry you. I just... I needed one last time before it was only ever you."

"Except that marriage would have been built on lies. On secrets. I would have come home and gotten into that bed beside you after you were with another woman in it. Think about that. Think about how fucking gross and horrible that is. Try to imagine the reverse. What if I had done what you did? What if I had been out fucking someone else because the thought of one dick for the rest of my life scared me? How would you feel about that?"

"I'd hate it," he answers quickly. "I'd fucking hate it." His voice cracks.

"Think of me as Braelyn, your friend, for a moment. What would you do if the guy I was with did to me what you did? What would you tell me?"

He sniffles and curses under his breath, and I hear something break in the background.

"Braelyn..." He trails off, and I can tell he's crying, which of course makes me cry.

"What would you say?" I press.

"Stop. I can't... fuck, I can't. I'm sorry. I love you. Please, I love you so much. I never wanted to hurt you. Not ever. I was going to end it. I was. I was never going to cheat on you once we were married."

Wow. That's such a lame thing to say. "But cheating on me as your fiancée was cool?"

"No! That's not how I meant it. I was never okay with it. It was just something I did, and I'm sorry. I'm so, so sorry. I love you so much. I'll say both of those a million times until you believe me. I want to be with you for the rest of my life. Please, Braelyn. Please give me a second chance to prove that to you."

I wipe my tears with the side of my hand. "You betrayed my trust. You betrayed my love. Not just as your fiancée but as your friend. I'm not the type of person who can forgive that, and even if I could, it would always be something between us. A permanent dark cloud over every sunny day."

He chokes out a noise. "This can't be it. It was a mistake. It meant nothing. I was stupid and selfish, I know. Please, this can't be it."

"I'll come over tomorrow to get my stuff. I don't want you there. I'm not ready to see you. Please respect that."

I hang up on him and throw my phone at the bed. It lands with a bounce, and I shift back to the window, a sea of opportunity ahead of me. Without thinking too much about it, or even caring that I'm only wearing Roman's T-shirt and boxer briefs, I hotfoot it out of the bedroom and down the hall to his room, where I knock on the door.

"Come in," he calls out, and I open the door to find Roman shirtless, with his tattoos all over his arms and chest beneath the blankets, holding a freaking worn Hemingway paperback in one hand, with his other tossed back behind his head. He's all muscles and ink and wolfish eyes, and for some stupid reason, my face heats. Especially when he gives me a once-over, noting me in only his shirt, and something I can't quite read crosses his features and changes his eyes ever so subtly.

I've seen Roman without his shirt a million times. The man boxes shirtless, for Christ's sake. But something about seeing him like this makes my voice squeak as I say, "The nurse dies at the end of that one."

"Thanks for the spoiler."

I laugh. I must be insane. "I'm in. I'll go with you to Vegas and then to Mexico."

5

ROMAN

Me: I don't know what to do about Adam. I'm debating if I should just kill him.

Forest: If you don't, I will, and I can get away with it, so think critically about that.

I would almost laugh or smile at that if I didn't know Forest was serious.

Me: I haven't talked to him yet and I don't know his story or why he did it but I'm not sure it matters. He cheated on Braelyn. On the flip side, he was Nash's best friend and has been one of my best friends since Nash's death. He's a good guy. A great guy actually. I don't see him hurting Brae like this.

Hayes: Can you be Switzerland and stay neutral?

Me: No. I don't know. I need to talk to him but I'm too fucking angry and full of a lot of things I shouldn't be too.

Crew: Things like you secretly love Braelyn and are conflicted because you're happy she's now single but sad because of how it happened and that she's hurting? Oh, and the fact that Adam is a close friend of yours, so there's the betrayal part of that.

Me: Are we on a daytime television show?

Crew: Tell me I'm wrong.

I can't. That's the problem, and Crew is right. I am happy and fucked up because I'm happy and conflicted as fuck because it's Adam, and going behind my friend's back with their girl isn't something I do. It's not something I'd ever do. Not that Braelyn is even interested in me for that, and there's the not-so-small issue of my leaving to live abroad in a couple of months. But the tickling along my spine is there, and I can't turn it off.

Hell, she could go back to him tomorrow for all I know. But for now...

Me: In ten weeks I'm moving to Europe for eighteen months.

Crew: What the fuck? Why didn't you tell us?

Hayes: Are you serious? Where?

Me: First Germany, then Paris and London. I haven't told anyone yet.

Forest: And this all happens right after the wedding that might not happen anymore.

I sigh.

Me: Yes.

Forest: Interesting.

Me: Not so much because everything is all fucked up now but I signed contracts and I'm needed there for what I have planned.

Crew: But you love her!

Hayes: It's all over your face, brother. I saw it the other night after the fight. It's why I brought it up.

I stare down at my phone screen, reading this. And here I thought I was so smart. They all saw it, but Braelyn hasn't. Or hasn't wanted to. I drag a hand through my hair.

Me: I can't change the move. It's happening.

But I have to try. Don't I? I can't move away not having tried.

Crew: But you have this time. You can figure out other things if you have to.

Me: Maybe. I don't know. I'm helping Brae move out of her apartment today and into mine. How soon is too soon to finally make a move?

The bubbles instantly start dancing on my screen, and I smile to myself. Here it comes.

Hayes: Motherfucking finally!! He admits it.

Me: I also somehow talked her into coming with me to Vegas next week and to Mexico after.

Crew: And you love her, or is this just some fun you're after? You never answered me.

Me: Do you honestly have to ask that? When I said make a move, I wasn't talking about sex. If for a second, I thought she'd say yes, I'd fucking propose.

Crew: Just making sure. Why have you never made a move before?

Me: Bad timing, and she wasn't interested. Before Adam swept in on her, I started to, and she never reciprocated.

Hayes: Probably because she didn't know or realize what you were doing.

Maybe. It's possible she didn't. I don't know. I didn't kiss her, and I didn't tell her how I felt, but I wasn't entirely subtle either. I'd touch her and tease her and fucking flirt. I don't flirt. So maybe that was it too. I've never had to fight for a woman. Perhaps I was doing it all wrong. Perhaps what I thought was flirting fell flat. Who knows.

All I know is she never seemed to want me back, and then she started dating Adam. The dumbest motherfucker on the planet. How he cheated on her is the mystery of the world. I hate it for her. I genuinely do. That's the best friend side of me. The guy who's never been able to get over the girl is looking at it like it's finally my time.

It always circles back to her.

But once again my life is set to diverge from hers, and I can't help but wonder if that will always be our story. If our timing will never be right.

Me: Whatever, can you help me out here? Uncharted waters and all.

Crew: Don't push anything. You don't want to be a rebound. Go slow, be patient, and feel her out (not up) to see what she's ready for. If you're serious about her, you have to be willing to put in the work.

Hayes: This *finger pointing up emoji*

Forest: Honestly? I say go for it. You can be patient, and I'm not saying to kiss her and profess your love tonight, but if you wait too long, she'll either get back together with him or you'll be gone. I say put it on the line and go for broke. But prove that you'll be different from Adam.

I think about this. About all of this.

Me: Maybe somewhere in between all of that. Thanks, gentlemen.

Hayes: Don't thank us yet. But we're happy for you, man. Truly, we are. You and Braelyn belong together.

Me: We'll see if she agrees. I already know Adam doesn't.

With that, I stare at my phone, lean my hip against the island in my kitchen, and take a sip of coffee. I pull up my chat stream with him.

Me: Tell me why I shouldn't kill you.

He doesn't reply by text. Instead, my phone rings in my hand.

"Tell me why I shouldn't kill you," I repeat as I answer.

He sighs into the phone. "I can't. I messed up."

Shit. He sounds completely broken. Fuck. My conscience is

eating at me. Hardly a new thing, but I wouldn't mind a reprieve for once.

"What were you thinking?"

He chuckles mirthlessly. "For the past few months, as the wedding drew closer, I was... panicking a bit. I've only been with four girls and Braelyn is one of them. I wasn't going to do anything about it. It was just something sticking in my head that I figured I'd get over. But there's this woman at work. She's been after me pretty aggressively since she started here a year ago."

"And you don't think that's because of your money? Or that she's seeking to blackmail you?" Adam's family owns a network in New England with nationwide syndications. Part of this network provides access to Boston Rebels games and other sports teams. They're big money and Adam is next in line.

"She's married and made it very clear her husband can never find out. Maybe she wanted to be my mistress, but I think she was just after sex. A few weeks ago, she cornered me in the garage at work and sucked me off. I felt horrible after. Like I threw up and told Brae I had a last-minute work trip because I couldn't go home and look at her."

I rub a hand across my forehead and take a sip of coffee because I don't know what to do or say. I'm furious with him, and there's no excuse for what he did.

"Why didn't you show up here for her? You knew she'd come to me."

He sighs but doesn't answer.

"You're a fucking pussy," I bite out. "Who were you more afraid of, her or me?"

"I fucked up. I didn't know what I'd say to her. What can you say to the woman you love after she walks in on you like that?"

"I don't know. But you still should have tried."

I blow out a fragmented breath. I'm his friend, and he stuck by my side during the worst time of my life. He did so without judgment or blame, and part of me feels as though I owe it to him to return the favor.

Even to my own detriment.

"But it continued with that woman?" I ask, redirecting us.

"Yeah," he says slowly. "It continued. A few more times after that, and then yesterday happened." He makes a noise and then coughs. "I'm going to lose Braelyn."

My eyes close, and everything inside me seizes up. "I don't know."

"She's moving her stuff out."

"I know. We're moving her in here."

"Where in there?"

"Fuck you, asshole." I practically slam my coffee mug down on the marble. "You have no right to ask that question. She's going into the guest room where she always sleeps."

He blows out a harsh breath. "I'm sorry. I shouldn't have asked that. I'm really fucked up with this. I can't lose her. I don't know what I'll do if that happens. I'm already going crazy."

My elbows plant into the stone, and I press my forehead into one of my hands and stare down at the gray and white.

"I'm so fucking pissed at you, man. You have no idea."

"I do actually. As pissed as you are at me, I'm a million times angrier with myself. I was selfish. I can get like that sometimes. It's the billionaire-only-child thing. I was thinking with my dick and not my heart, and now Braelyn is hurting and I might not ever get her back."

"Yeah. You might not. And you'll have to live with that. I gotta go." Without waiting for him to reply, I hang up. I grip my phone, wanting to open the balcony door and chuck it into the water. I held back because she was Nash's and it felt wrong to try to date my dead brother's girlfriend or ex-girlfriend or whatever she was after losing him. Plus, I wasn't in any state to be what she deserved. But I waited too long. Played it too cautiously.

This could be my shot but also how the fuck can this be my shot?

I have no answers, and in the absence of answers, I cook. Homemade croissants, maple-glazed ham, eggs, and gruyère. Plus the fruit plate the concierge brought up.

"Do you ever do anything simple?" comes from behind me. I turn to find her in my sweatpants and hoodie again, and fuck, her in my clothes is the best look in the world on her. "That's an egg and cheese, but it's not."

"Is that your way of saying you don't want me to make you a cappuccino to go with it?"

She squints challengingly. "Is that a threat?"

"Only if you don't eat my breakfast."

She rolls her eyes dramatically and crosses the room to climb onto one of the barstools. "Ugh. Fine," she grouses mockingly. "I'll eat your fancy, delicious breakfast."

"Way to sell it there, kid."

"There is no selling it when it smells this good. How are you still single?" she muses but pops a blueberry in her mouth, not waiting for an answer to her rhetorical question, and I don't have one I'm ready to give her yet.

We eat breakfast together, both of us quiet and introspective.

"I don't want to go there today," she finally says.

"No? Do you want me to do it?"

She shakes her head. "This will sound crazy, and I know it is, but I think I'll buy some basics and maybe in a day or two I'll do it."

"I'll help you. Whenever you're ready, if you're ever ready, I'll help you."

"Maybe tomorrow after work?" She scrunches her nose as if she's not sure. "I think I just want today."

"I'll have the concierge get you some things."

A smile curls her lips. "Fancy."

"It's what they're there for. Give me a list, and we'll have it in a few hours."

She starts to tick items off on her fingers. "Lube, butt plug, magic rabbit thing, oh, and condoms, of course."

I cough and nearly choke on my croissant. "The basics?"

She gives me a sideways look. "Am I forgetting anything?"

"Nipple clamps. Handcuffs or rope. Perhaps a flogger."

She makes a tsking sound as she sips her cappuccino. "Those don't sound basic. More like the advanced course. I'm not quite sure I'm there yet."

Perhaps you just need the right teacher, I think but definitely don't say. "Just the basics then. Got it."

"And maybe some clothes and a toothbrush."

"Obviously," I tease.

"Obviously," she parrots, rolling her eyes playfully at me, but she starts to pick apart her sandwich instead of eating it. "Can we watch a movie today? Maybe splash in your cool pool?"

"You got it."

Relief and gratitude swim in her features. She looks better for it. There's more color in her face and life in her eyes. "Thank you. I'm going to be a broken record with that, but you really are the best."

"Eat up, and I'll get you whatever you need."

I order up the clothes and things she tells me to, and we spend a quiet day in, watching old movies—her favorites— eating our way through my fridge and pantry, and hanging out in the pool. I can't remember the last time I had a day like this. A day off. A day with no work and just being lazy, with no forced agenda.

Even my emails wait—including Frankfurt housing questions from my assistant.

Today is about Braelyn. I'm her friend. Her confidant. Her safety net. The guy she goes to when she needs a shoulder to cry on. It's a role I've played well. A role I've been happy-not-so-happy to have.

She says she's coming to Vegas with me. Mexico too.

I want that more than I want anything else.

But I already know nothing with her will be easy. It never is for me.

6

BRAELYN

"Mrs. Box in room six needs a Foley started and about six milligrams of Ativan."

I pause and glance up at Wren as I take notes. "Six?"

She shrugs. "Obviously not six. But she's easily the most anxious patient I've ever encountered. Start with half a milligram, but I'll give you some room to move on that."

"Awesome. What else?"

"Mr. Tape in eight—"

I snort a laugh.

"What?" Wren shrugs as she sips her coffee. "I didn't mean to rhyme. That's the dude's name."

"Mrs. Box, Mr. Tape. I feel like we're in a game of Clue written by Dr. Seuss."

"Yes, except for instead of trying to figure out who's killing who, we're trying to save them in a hospital with a..." She tilts her head. "What rhymes with hospital?"

"Nothing that works for this. Sorry. What does Mr. Tape in eight need?"

"A chest X-ray, EKG, a CBC, CMP, renal and liver function tests, BNP, A1c, TSH, CRP, and throw in a troponin."

"CHF workup?" I ask because those are pretty standard labs when we think someone has congestive heart failure.

"Yep. It doesn't sound like afib when I listen, but I'm not ruling that out yet either. He hasn't seen a doctor since the early two thousands and is short of breath, but there's definitely fluid in his lungs, despite the fact that he's dehydrated, so let's get an IV started of LR along with twenty of Lasix IV push and see if that's enough to clear those lungs without dehydrating him more. Oh, and a cardiology consult. We're going to end up admitting him once we get him buffed up. I just don't know if it'll be on a tele floor or the CCU yet."

"You got it." I pop the end on my pen and stick my paper back in my chest pocket. "Any cardiac meds yet?"

She finishes off her coffee and throws it in a nearby trash bin. "Not yet. Let's see what the Lasix does and what his labs and X-ray show."

"On it."

"Are you okay?" Wren asks, folding her arms and tucking a piece of her blonde hair behind her ears.

"You mean because I caught my ex-fiancé cheating and called off my wedding?"

"Well, um, yeah, I mean—"

"Good morning," Katy greets us with a coffee in one hand and her other on her pregnant belly. She's a Fritz cousin and a trauma surgeon here, but considering the trauma surgeons are down here constantly, we're pretty close. "I tried calling you last night," she says to me.

"I know. I saw. Thank you. I just didn't feel like talking."

She waves me away. "No worries. I totally get it. God, why do men suck so badly?"

Wren glances up and down the hall, likely making sure Jack isn't within earshot before she turns back to us. "Seriously. It's like we all have to have a shitty ex or something. I'm so sorry you're going through that too."

"If it helps, we had our shitty exes, and now we have the good guys." Katy wags a finger between her and Wren. "You'll have yours too."

"Does this mean I get to marry a hot doctor?" I tease since both of them did.

"Not for nothing, but if I were you, I'd marry Roman."

I give Katy a look. "I'm not marrying Roman. He's my best friend."

Her hand goes to her stomach, and she grimaces. "This freaking kid loves to kick the hell out of me. Anyway, friend or not, you still should."

I place my hand on her belly because I could use a little baby kicking moment and sure enough, I get an adorable thump against my palm. "Oh my gosh! Little Braelyn is kicking so hard."

Katy laughs. "Yeah, I'm not naming my son Braelyn."

"My turn."

I move my hand so Wren can feel the baby and when she does, she sighs. "I should get pregnant." Her head swivels nervously around again. "Don't tell Jack I said that. But back to you." She nudges me with her elbow. "Please marry my cousin because then we can be cousins."

"Because your family isn't already big enough?" I quip. "How many cousins do you have?"

They both shrug. "About ten thousand or so," Katy teases. "Seriously, though, are you totally done with Adam? All moved out and everything?"

"I'm moving out today after work. I needed yesterday to think more and get myself mentally set for that. Roman's going to come and help."

"That has to be weird for him since he's so close with Adam," Wren comments, sliding her hand around on Katy's stomach like feeling another woman's body in the middle of the ER is the most normal thing ever.

"I'm sure it will be, but he offered and said it was fine." I hesitate, shifting my weight, and they catch it.

"What?" Katy questions.

"I'm going to Vegas and Mexico with Roman next week."

I get twin sets of wide eyes before they exchange glances.

"Come on. Don't give me that look. Katy, you're BFFs with Owen, and it's not like that between the two of you, nor has it ever been."

"Yes, but he's also my cousin."

"Not by blood," I counter.

She holds up a hand. "Fine. Point taken. And actually, I think it's great that you're getting away for a bit. It'll help clear your head and—"

"Delivery for you," my mother cuts in with a scowl twisting her lips as she walks a giant bouquet of purple orchids and white hydrangea toward me.

I sigh. And possibly growl. My wedding flowers.

"What a jerk face. He's not fighting fair," I mumble dryly, taking the large glass vase from her hands. I can't throw them since we're in the ER. I could throw them out but...

"At least they're beautiful." Wren leans in and smells them. "Oh, a card." She gives me a hopeful smile.

"Go for it. I don't want to read it."

"I already read it."

I throw my mother a side-eye. "Of course you did."

She shrugs unrepentantly.

Wren plucks the card from the plastic holder and pulls it out of the envelope. "Second chances lead to forever. I'm so sorry. I love you and will never hurt you again. Please forgive me," Wren reads. She waves the card across her face as if she's fanning herself. "It's handwritten too."

"Would you take him back?" I ask her. "If you walked in on

Jack fucking some chick in your bed, would you take him back?"

She snorts. "Take him back? I'd sever his balls and shove them down his throat until he choked to death and then do the same with his cock and shove it down hers. But I'm feisty like that and a bit of a psycho. Ask Katy. She's more levelheaded."

"Yeah, not really. Because if I caught Bennett in our bed with another woman, I'd..." She trails off as she tilts her head. "Wow, I have no revenge game that's better than yours." She points to Wren. "I'd have to think of something badass. I'd likely shoot him up with all of my insulin and ask Vander and Stone to hide the body. But the reality is, we can tell you what we think we'd do, but no one really knows how they'll react until they're in the moment. I have a child with Bennett and another on the way, and to that, there are women who forgive. It does happen that the guy fucks up, the woman forgives him, and they do go on to live a happy life together."

I think about this for a moment as I stare at the flowers and allow the words on a card to settle over me. I'm grateful he didn't show up here. That's likely more self-preservation than anything else. My mother works here, for starters, and you don't fuck with nurses. You just don't. Plus, I have other people here who have my back, so it's not a safe place for him.

Fine.

But right now, I don't want to see him. I don't want to look at him because all I see when I close my eyes is him inside of her in the home we made together. That's what shatters me. Perhaps if it had been a fuckup, a drunken one-night thing, I could have gotten over that. But bringing her to our home, into our bed, because their hotel room wasn't ready yet is just fucking abhorrent.

That doesn't deserve second chances.

It doesn't deserve forgiveness.

It's a slap to the face and a wakeup call.

"I've got patients to see," I announce instead of voicing any of that. I pluck an orchid from the vase along with a hydrangea and shove the rest of the bouquet at my mother to do whatever she wants with.

"What are you doing?" my mother asks.

"Mrs. Box is an anxious woman who might like some flowers." I start to walk off. "Love you, ladies. I'll see you on the flip side of Mexico."

Just before I reach the patient's room, I get a text.

> Adam: Did you get my flowers?

> Me: I did. I'm giving them to my patient at this very moment.

> Adam: I sent them for you. Not your patients.

> Me: But she needs them more than I do.

> Adam: They're the exact flowers from your bouquet.

> Me: I'm aware. I picked them out. Bye now.

> Adam: Stop! No, wait, please. I love you. Don't give up on us because I made a mistake.

> Me: You gave up on us the moment you stuck your dick into her. I'm coming by later to get my stuff. Word to the wise, don't be there. I'm feeling vengeful and have access to scalpels, needles, and drugs that kill.

I leave it at that, and after grabbing my patient's Ativan, I head into the room. "Mrs. Box, hello. I'm Braelyn and I'll be your nurse today. Someone told me you're a little nervous to be here and let me tell you, you're in the best possible hands. We're going to take excellent care of you. And I brought you flowers."

The woman on the bed eyes them suspiciously as if they're the poppies from *The Wizard of Oz* and they'll put her to sleep if she smells them.

"Where'd you get those?"

I set them down on the bedside table and pour her some water so she can take her meds. "Here. Take these. Dr. Kincaid's orders." I drop the pills into her hand and get the things I need for her Foley catheter so she'll be able to pee without retention and other issues. "These are from my very recent ex-fiancé, whom I just caught cheating on me."

She scowls at the flowers and surprises me with an appreciative lift of her chin. "I had one of those once. I met my husband, may he rest, two weeks after I left the first bastard. Don't worry, honey. Men like them are a dirty dime a dozen, and women like you are the diamond in the rough. You'll be just fine."

I believe her.

I will be just fine.

I only wish they had a miracle move-on pill that could excise him from my head and heart to make that process faster.

She unlocks the door and, for a moment, simply stands in the entryway, looking around and listening. It's quiet. I don't think Adam is home, and when she realizes that, she blows out a relieved breath.

"It's so weird how the mind and heart work. I really didn't want to see him. I asked him to respect that, and he did. But I think part of me wanted him to fight a little for it." She turns and squints up at me. "You know what I mean?"

"You wanted him here and also didn't want him here."

"Yes. Does that make me crazy or just complicated?"

"You're not complicated, kid. Someone just has to know how to read between the lines in order to get the full story."

"Would you have been here if you were him?"

I shut the door behind me. "I don't know how to answer that without hurting you more."

She nods as she slowly turns back around. "You wouldn't have cheated."

"No. I wouldn't have cheated. But in fairness to him, I would be remiss if I didn't tell you that he was a wreck on the phone yesterday morning. He knows he fucked up and is desperate to get you back."

"I'm not getting back together with him. I thought a lot about it today and yesterday and realized that if I did, it would eat at my soul. My self-esteem would tarnish and he'd own a piece of me I don't want him to take. My self-respect. But there's the part of me that wanted him to fight for me. That wanted him to be here begging me for forgiveness. And not because I'm being cruel or wanted to laugh in his face. But because I wanted him to prove to me that not everything was a lie. That there was something there that might be worth forgiving. I wanted him to change my mind about not taking him back. I wanted proof that he did love me above all else and that he had to ignore my request to stay away because he couldn't handle not seeing me." She scrunches her nose. "I'm not making sense."

"You are. You want to be someone's universe. The only one they see. The one they can't live without."

"Is that asking too much?"

"It's what everyone should have, right? What our parents have."

"You think that's why he cheated? Because he came from a broken household?"

"No. I think that's bullshit."

She considers this as she thinks about that. "Our parents are relationship goals. Especially your dad, because he's super obsessed with your mom."

I check my phone when a notification comes in, and I see several apartments I have to sort through in Frankfurt and Paris. Damn. "That's because he went four years without her and had to grovel to win her back," I mumble absently.

"You're not helping me with the groveling thing, but he never cheated, right?"

"Never. She was just too young at the time, and they were in different places in life until they weren't." Except my parents got together and with her it feels like it'll never happen.

"I love their story."

I put my phone back in my pocket. "Your parents were best friends. It's a good one too."

"It is. Enough about love. It's depressing me." She picks up a small marble ball from the entry table before she puts it back as if she changed her mind about it. "Let's get this over with. I don't want to be here anymore. All I see is her on top of him and his face as he came inside her." She makes a gagging noise. "Let's move me out."

We start with the bedroom because it has most of her stuff. The suitcases come out of the closet and one by one, they get filled. She changes her clothes out of the basic stuff we got her yesterday and continues packing. Neither of us is talking much, and occasionally, I catch Braelyn sniffling, but not a lot.

"How about some music?" I offer.

"Oh, yes. Harry Styles, please."

I roll my eyes at her and put on nineties grunge instead.

"Better. Now I'm all ragey."

I laugh, but she's not kidding. She grabs a pair of scissors and cuts up the sheets that were still on the bed and leaves them in a pile on the mattress.

"More?"

She shrugs. "I mean, that was sort of satisfying, but not really. I threw my ring at him when what I should have done was pee and leave it in the toilet for him to fish out."

I crack up. "Savage."

"Right? But I bet there's something I can do along those lines." She heads for the bathroom, and I wait out here even though she doesn't shut the door. "I'm not peeing," she calls back to me. "Get in here and do this with me. You know you want to."

I totally do, so I enter the bathroom and lean against the

wall as I watch her take his toothbrush and use it to clean the toilet.

"Why do guys always get pee on the toilet? So gross." She makes a tsking noise as she shakes her head in dismay and cleans the entire thing with his toothbrush. When she's finished, she puts it back on the charger. "Your turn."

"You took the best one."

"That was a good one. Wait, I have Nair. I'll replace his shampoo with it."

I start to lose it. "Remind me never to cross you."

Her eyebrows bounce. "Who knew I was this vindictive?"

She gets to work on his shampoo, and I dip his hairbrush in the toilet, which feels lame in comparison. I'm more of a guy who uses his fists or would perhaps mildly poison his food to make him sick all night. Then I feel like shit for doing that to his hairbrush.

"I'll bring your things down."

"Knock yourself out."

It takes me three trips, but my SUV is all packed up.

I head for the kitchen and dump an entire bottle of hot sauce into his ketchup and shake it up. He eats ketchup with everything and hates hot sauce. It's also revenge for that time he came to Round House, ordered lamb chops that were perfectly cooked, and proceeded to dump ketchup all over them.

This is more my style, and he deserves it, so I don't feel so bad about this one. Braelyn pops her head around the corner just as I'm putting the ketchup back in the fridge and hiding the empty hot sauce bottle at the bottom of the trash. She lets out an amused laugh.

"Damn. That's a good one. He'll cry like a little bitch when he eats that. I think our work here is done. Let's go see a movie."

"A movie?"

"I don't want to go home and think. I'm trying to channel

my inner badass or hard-ass or whatever women who can brush off their cheating exes and come out bright and shiny and amazing on the other side are."

I comb some of her dark curls back from her face. Her pretty brown eyes, framed by impossibly long lashes and sitting above two beds of freckles, blink up at me. I don't usually touch her like this. Not so intimately where I'm standing this close. Close enough that all I'd have to do is bend to kiss her.

"You've got this, kid. You'll get through it, but you're already bright and shiny and amazing."

"Maybe he was dulling my colors," she says, her voice a breathy whisper.

"Maybe you'll find that this was the best thing to ever happen to you."

"I think it will be. Once I get over the burn and the heartache and betrayal, I think I'll be something better than I ever imagined I could be."

I don't know where it comes from or even how it happens. But I dip down and kiss her cheek. Thankfully, not her lips, but I don't typically kiss Braelyn. Sort of how I don't usually touch her, I'm apparently breaking a lot of boundaries I shouldn't be breaking.

Instantly, I pull back, and that's when the front door opens and in walks the dickhead. He spots us hovering by the kitchen, us standing close, and instantly his expression breaks.

"Hi," he says, his gaze locked on her.

"I told you I didn't want to see you."

"I never agreed to that. I would have been here sooner, but I had a client to deal with."

"Priorities are a bitch like that. Did you see your lover?"

He looks away, shame tinting his cheeks, and that's another thing he didn't think about. The fact that he has to see this woman regularly because she works for his company.

She makes a dismissive noise. "That's what I thought. We're

done here anyway. I don't want any of the things we bought together."

"Braelyn, please don't do this. We can figure this out. Just stay here and talk to me."

She looks down at the floor. "I'm not sure what else there is to say. You told me all about her and your reasons for fucking her. The wedding is called off. Engagement over. I even returned the ring to you."

A wounded cry wrenches from the back of his throat and he covers his face with his hands. "You called off the wedding?"

"My parents are managing it."

"What about mine? They're paying for a lot of this too."

"Then you can call them and tell them what a lying, cheating bastard you are!" she screams at him. "Either way, I'm not marrying you in seven weeks. No fucking way."

Jesus. I shouldn't be here. "Do you want me to go—"

"No," she cuts me off. "I'm done with this."

"Braelyn—"

"Don't say my name like that!" She slashes the air in front of him. "You trashed three years together and over a decade of friendship because you suddenly realized you weren't going to get more pussy in your life. There is no talking yourself out of that. It's cheap and shallow, and I deserve better." She steps toward him and gets right up in his face without touching him. "I deserve better than you. A man who prioritizes his needs at the expense of the woman he claims to love isn't a man at all. Please do the honorable thing and respect my choice. We're over."

She walks out after that, and I can't stop my prideful smile.

"I can't do that," he whispers hoarsely. "I can't respect that." His gaze casts up to mine. "You have to help me with her. You have to talk to her and help me win her back."

Fuck. I stare bewilderedly at him. "Adam—"

"No," he cuts in urgently before I can argue. "You have to. I was there for you after you lost Nash in the water. I heard the whispers. I knew what people were saying. But I stood by you even though I lost my best fucking friend. So you owe me. Please. You have to help me win her back."

Motherfucker. That punch hit me as none have before.

I wince and he winces in return. He knows what he just did. But he's not backing down either. He'll do whatever it takes to win Braelyn back. That's what he's telling me.

I pick up Braelyn's purse off the counter and go to leave when he grabs my arm and stops me. "I won't lose her."

"You made your choices and now she's making hers."

I tear my arm from his grip, only to grab him by his collared shirt and hoist him up until he's on his tiptoes. His hands reflexively grab my arms and cling. I want to hit him so fucking badly. I want to pulverize him for what he's doing both to Braelyn and to me.

Instead, I shove him away, making him stagger back four steps before the wall saves him from falling on his ass. That's how I leave him.

Only I already know he's far from done with this.

8

BRAELYN

I can't believe I'm doing this. Even as the lyrics to Fergie's "Glamorous" about flying first class play through my head and I dance along. I ain't got no money and I should take my broke ass home, but Roman is leading this charge and for reasons beyond my comprehension, I'm letting him. Probably because I'm a wounded bird and hurt and fucking angry.

Over the weekend, Skylar and Quinn came over, and we took over the pool and sundeck area of Roman's place. They brought me champagne and chocolate-covered strawberries—my favorites—and we played loud music and sang and swam, and it was so great. Hayes, Forest, and Crew were also over, but they hung out with Roman in the media room as our space was a no-dick zone.

But how did this happen? How did I have a no-dick-zone party with my girls, and how am I on a flight to Las Vegas now? A week ago, I was putting the finishing details on my wedding. Now I'm descending into Sin City with Roman, running from the wreckage of my engagement.

My eyes are glued to the oval window as I finish off the last of my champagne, taking in the Vegas Strip and the jagged mountains in the distance. Roman sleeps beside me, his face slack and peaceful in a way it never is when he's awake. The cut below his eye is nearly healed, and I resist the urge to trace it with my finger to feel its rough texture.

The flight attendant glides by, murmuring about our imminent landing and how Roman needs to put his seat up. I nudge him lightly with my elbow, and his eyes briskly snap open.

"Sorry," I apologize since I clearly startled him. "We're here, and they want you to put your seat up."

He stretches, his knuckles brushing the cabin ceiling, and I try not to look when his shirt rides up. He shifts and presses the button to bring his seat up before he moves closer to me, rubbing a hand over his face and scratching at his stubble.

"Did you sleep at all?" he asks, peeking out the window as he leans half over me.

"No. Too busy enjoying the free alcohol while contemplating my life choices and debating my future."

His lips quirk up. "Come up with anything good?"

"Only that I'm going to go with the flow for once. I'm going to relax and have fun and not overthink or wallow."

"Wallowing and overthinking are overrated." He takes my empty glass and hands it to the passing attendant with a nod of thanks. "Trust me. I'm an expert."

Hard to argue that. Even if his wallowing and overthinking made him a masterclass chef, mine will likely only earn me puffy eyes and an ice cream addiction.

"Has he been calling and texting you?" I'm not sure why I ask other than when Roman met me outside the apartment after we moved me out, he was visibly troubled. The man is a tank. Solid and strong and impenetrable. Except inside is a lot of darkness, and the vulnerable, human spot he fights to keep concealed. His people are his weakness, and Adam is one of his people.

"Yes," he says simply.

"You gonna finally tell me about it?"

He angles toward me. "I'm positive you can guess. He wants you back, and he's putting pressure on me to help him do that."

I thought so. "What's your hot take on that?"

He sighs and looks out the window instead of at me. "I already told you. You're my girl. But that doesn't mean I'm not feeling a ton of guilt right now. For a lot of reasons."

I decide to let it go because he clearly doesn't want to talk about it, and as long as he's with me on this, then we're good.

We land with a few gentle bumps, and then Roman takes my hand as we exit the plane, navigating us through the terminal with familiarity. The moment we reach our baggage carousel, there's a man in a black suit holding a sign with Fritz printed in block letters.

"I would have paid for the Uber," I murmur out of the side of my mouth.

He ignores that as we greet the man. "Morning, Jordan. Good to see you." The two shake hands.

"Good morning, Mr. Fritz. Welcome back to Las Vegas."

"Thank you. This is Braelyn. I picked her up on the airplane and thought she might be fun to hang out with while I'm here," he tells him with a completely straight face. "I think we should give her the full Vegas Strip tour."

Jordan doesn't even blink. "Sounds good, sir. I'll go retrieve your bags."

The moment the driver leaves us for the conveyor belt, I smack Roman's shoulder, making him crack up.

"I am not your whore."

"Not yet, but the day is young, and you are so lovely."

"Oh my god, shut up!" Then something occurs to me. "Wait, is that something you've done before? Picked up women and kept them as pets while you were here?"

"No. You can be my first. I'll buy you a pretty diamond collar and everything." He winks at me, thoroughly amused, and an odd heat crawls over me that I immediately shake away. "Come on. Let's go tell Jordan which bag is yours."

Twenty minutes later, we're in the back of the black SUV, driving up the Strip. Massive hotels rise like fever dreams, one after the other, each more insane than the last. Vegas light hits differently. The sun is brighter here than it is at home. The sky is a more vivid blue. Then there are the giant billboards and flashing lights.

One in particular with my friend's face on it.

He's got to be at least ten stories high, wearing his white chef's coat with his name stitched in bold over his heart. The image morphs to a picture of what I'm assuming is the inside of Decision, followed by a few dishes that make my stomach growl. I shake his arm and point, making him lean over me to glance out the window, our cheeks practically touching, and his scent all over me.

Wood, leather, smoke, and gasoline.

It should be off-putting, but on him, it's anything but.

"Dude! That's so freaking cool!"

He chuckles and turns to meet my eyes, our noses somehow brushing as he does. My breath hitches, but he doesn't move away. His eyes are locked with mine and his smile slips. Suddenly my heart is pounding. I can't breathe. My mind spins. And for one moment of pure insanity and nonsensical curiosity, I think about what it would feel like if I closed the inches and pressed my lips to his. Would they be as soft and supple as they look or firm and dominating as I imagine he is in every other way?

Thankfully, the moment is broken as we turn into a long, sweeping drive that leads to a side entrance of a hotel in the center of the Strip. I make a mental note to watch it with the drinking since it has to be the champagne on the flight that had me thinking that way. Because wow. I was just thinking about kissing Roman.

Clearly, I'm a mess because I should not be thinking about how my best friend kisses or what it would feel like.

Before our doors even open, staff have materialized, opening the trunk and removing our luggage. A woman greets us, all smiles, and welcomes us as she shakes Roman's hand and then mine.

"Welcome, Mr. Fritz. We're honored to have you staying with us." She walks us into a small, marble lobby with crystal chandeliers and obscure glass pieces. "We have the two-bedroom villa your assistant requested. The suite is sixty-five hundred square feet and includes an in-suite workout facility, a massage room, a dry sauna, a private hair salon, a private kitchen, a formal dining room, a full bar stocked to your preferences, a dual gas fireplace, and a gorgeous private terrace and garden with a pool and whirlpool."

I'm trying not to have my mouth hang open, but it drops another centimeter with everything she says. Holy shit. Roman takes it all in stride, and while most of the time I don't think about the disparities in our socioeconomic situations, right now, it's impossible not to. Where most people are simply visiting or splurging on the trip of a lifetime, Roman belongs here and eases in with cool confidence and grace.

His hand meets my lower back, and he turns to catch my expression. "You okay?" he mouths.

"This is just... a lot."

He leans in and presses his lips to my forehead. "You've been on vacations with my family. You're staying in my place. You know what my grandparents' estate and megayacht are like. And Adam might not be a Fritz, but his family has money."

"I know." But those things were already in place and not for me. This feels like he's doing it for me, and that sits oddly with me.

"Don't say no, okay? I want to spoil you. Let me have some fun with it."

The woman catches his attention before I can respond, talking about reservations and tables at a club and all kinds of things I'm already lost to. An attendant leads us over to our villa and gives us a tour, informing us that our things will be unpacked and put away for us. This place is enormous. It's like three times the size of my apartment and that's not an exaggeration. Then again, it's like half the size of Roman's penthouse so maybe I should just chill out already.

The attendant leaves us with an "Enjoy your stay and please don't hesitate to reach out to us for anything we can do to make it perfect." I collapse onto a silk-embroidered sofa, my ass digging into the down cushions, and try not to choke when I watch Roman hand him a couple of hundreds.

"You tip well."

"I appreciate their help and all they did to switch up my room at the last minute."

I give him a look. "This is obscene."

"Braelyn, you've grown up with my family. What's up?"

I shrug. "I don't know. This is different. Your condo is yours. This is…" I trail off, gesturing toward the overwhelming luxury surrounding us. "You guys don't normally spend your big dollars on me and never like this."

He walks over and drops onto the sofa beside me. "You needed to get out of Boston, and I needed to come to Las Vegas. Everything in this city is over the top." He pauses, his brows pinching. "Is it too much? Did I go too far? I can call them and get us two regular rooms in the hotel."

"Are you crazy? A regular room when we have this?"

He laughs.

"Seriously, though, it's amazing, and it means everything to me. You don't act like a billionaire and sometimes I forget just how much you're worth. I'm not used to being Fritz-level spoiled, is all."

He grins. "I know. I plan to enjoy it."

"Careful. If you're too nice to me right now, I might start crying again, and then where would we be?"

"In Vegas, in a very nice villa, with plenty of alcohol to drown your sorrows. Oh, there are chocolate-covered strawberries under that metal dome."

"Now you're not fighting fair. I'm a woman on the edge."

He shifts and drops his arm around my shoulder. "Maybe you just need to hit things. Punching bags with Adam's face affixed to them. I can get you that in under an hour. I know some people."

A laugh escapes before I can stop it, half-amused, half-broken. "I bet you do." Then I sit up straighter. "Wait, are you doing a fight while we're here?"

He shakes his head. "No. I'm very careful where I do my fights and the Vegas underground scene is a different level. This is all work, with some fun mixed in. I'm glad you're here. Otherwise, it would have been all work and no fun."

He's right. We're here to have fun, which isn't something he does all that often and rarely for himself. I'm here to see my best friend's new restaurant and celebrate him, and not think about the fact that my life has fallen apart a bit and my heart has been used like a trampoline.

"Maybe it's that I feel like a cliché."

His brows furrow. "How so?"

"The jilted bride runs off to Vegas with the hot, tattooed bad boy."

A smile splits his lips. "Could be worse clichés. Imagine if I weren't hot. And it's not like you're doing anything all that crazy or extravagant. We didn't bet ten grand on one hand of roulette, and we didn't have Elvis race you down the aisle to me. It's all good and safe. You're on vacation."

I snort a laugh. "True. I haven't had random *get over my ex* sex. I didn't cut or dye my hair or even get an ill-advised tattoo."

"Ah, but once again, the day is young." He stands and

extends his hand to me. "I need to be at the restaurant soon. Do you want to shower or eat anything before we go do that?"

"I get to go with you?"

He peers at me. "Only if you want to, kid. If not, you can go shopping or to the pool or even hang out here."

"No. I want to." I do a little jump. "I want to see your greatness. Let's go."

Decision occupies a prime location in the hotel, overlooking fountains and a beautiful garden. Its entrance is marked by a sleek sign that's all hard lines and tarnished metal. The space is still closed to the public, but staff move purposefully inside, preparing for tomorrow's soft opening.

Roman places his hand on my back as we enter, and I can feel the touch of nerves and excitement in him. The interior unfolds before us with black chairs and wood floors, crimson wallpaper on accent walls, matching linens, roses on the tables, and ambient vintage lighting with burnished yellow Edison bulbs creates a cool, hip, old-world yet modern, intimate space within the larger room.

The design is distinctly Roman.

Nothing flashy, nothing unnecessary, but every detail considered and perfect and badass. It's a total vibe. "I love it."

He turns to me. "You do?"

I nod vigorously. "Yes. It's incredible."

Before he can reply, a tall woman in a tailored suit approaches with a smile that brightens when she recognizes Roman. "Chef, it's good to see you." She gives him a warm handshake.

"Lydia, this is Braelyn Albright," Roman introduces. "Brae, this is Lydia Chen, our restaurant manager and the reason I can sleep at night."

Lydia extends a hand, her grip firm. "Oh, Braelyn. I've heard so much about you. Roman mentioned you so many times, I feel as though I already know you."

Shocked by this, I raise an eyebrow at Roman, who suddenly becomes very interested in adjusting his sleeve. I return my attention to her. "All good things, I hope?"

"The best," Lydia assures me. "Though he failed to mention you'd be joining us for the opening. I'll make sure we add your name to the VIP list."

"I'm just here for moral support," I say, taking in the restaurant some more. "And to see what all the fuss is about," I tease, nudging him with my elbow in the side.

"Well, we welcome the feedback," she replies with a conspiratorial smile. "Leaf is in the kitchen if you want to check in. They're plating some test dishes now."

Roman nods, and I follow him through the restaurant toward the kitchen. As we walk, staff members acknowledge him with a mix of respect and nervousness that I find both amusing and impressive. My best friend, the intimidating culinary genius. It's still sometimes hard to reconcile this Roman with the one who reads classics and lets me beat him at Scrabble.

The kitchen is a marvel of stainless steel and precision, larger than the one at Roundhouse but with the same energy. A man with salt-and-pepper hair looks up from a plate he's examining, and his face breaks into a relieved smile.

"Chef," he says, straightening. "Just in time."

"Leaf," Roman replies, shaking his hand before panning it toward me. "This is my friend Braelyn."

"Leaf Gomez. I'm the head chef here. It's lovely to finally meet you."

Finally? I blink, surprised again at being known. "Likewise," I manage.

Roman clears his throat. "What are we tasting today?"

The redirect is obvious, but I let it slide, curious about what exactly Roman has been saying about me to his staff. Leaf leads us to a preparation table where several dishes are arranged in various stages of completion.

"Each course has a wine pairing except for the dessert, where we have a cocktail to go with it. Allow me to present roasted heirloom tomato and burrata with crispy prosciutto, topped with a pea and walnut pesto, and an aged balsamic glaze. Homemade fettuccine con fungi with shrimp, lobster, and scallops in a black truffle cream sauce. The Wagyu preparation you were concerned about, and finally the almond indulgence cake with a chocolate and coconut glaze paired with an espresso martini."

Roman examines each preparation with the intense focus I've seen him apply countless times over his own dishes. He's meticulous. A control freak through and through. He tastes, considers, and makes small adjustments. A sprinkle of salt here, a repositioning of a garnish there, a change in the wine pairing with the pasta. When he's satisfied, he turns to me.

"Your turn. And be honest."

I approach the tasting with the seriousness it deserves, though I'm hardly a foodie. I'm also spoiled by Roman's cooking. The tomato and burrata explode in my mouth, the pasta melts on my tongue, and the Wagyu is, well, it's fucking fantastic. It's cooked to a perfect medium-rare, with a crust that creates a textural contrast to the buttery interior. I legit just had a food orgasm.

"Well?" Roman asks, a touch of uncharacteristic impatience in his tone, and I notice both him and Leaf watching me intently.

"It's..." I search for words that won't sound hyperbolic. "Extraordinary. I mean, I've had your food more times than I can count, but these dishes are fun, with unique twists that take my mouth on an adventure, and the wine complements them all. And this cake and martini are scrumptious."

"Yeah? No bullshit?"

"No bullshit. I swear. This might be my favorite of your restaurants." I finish off the martini because hello, alcohol and caffeine in one.

"I've been very intentional with this menu," Roman tells me, sipping at some of the wine.

"Yes. We wanted it to be a journey," Leaf agrees. "We really stretched our creative minds with this. Sort of old and new Roman."

"Explain that to me."

"All my menus are personal," Roman states matter-of-factly. "I pick every dish on them. Some are fun for me. Some are challenging for both the chef and diner. But Decision has a journey to it. Choices I've made along the way. Things that have happened. Some I've won and some I haven't."

"You don't lose, Roman, and you fail at nothing."

His lips twist down. "That's not true, kid. I've lost plenty, and I don't always get what I want."

The weight of those words hangs between us, laden with meanings I'm not sure I'm able to fully decipher.

"But I'm excited for this," he finishes.

I beam at him. "Me too. And you're very nice to the people here."

He laughs, and so does Leaf. "I see she knows you well." Leaf turns to me. "Trust me when I say, this is a rarity, and it must be because of the company, so thank you for coming. Otherwise, we'd get Chef and not Roman."

Roman simply shrugs, unapologetic as he always is.

"Show me the rest?" I ask, gesturing to the broader kitchen. "I want to see everything." Roman takes me on a tour, showing me every last detail. When it's done, we're back where we started in the kitchen. "I think you've created something remarkable," I tell him honestly. "Not just the food, but the whole experience. It feels like you. Precise but not cold. Thoughtful but not pretentious."

His eyes move to mine for a long moment, an expression I can't quite read crossing his features. "Thank you. That means everything. Your opinion is the one I value most."

"Other than the critics," I quip.

"No. It's yours."

Heat floods me, sending sparks of pleasure across my skin.

The moment stretches between us until he suggests we take a walk, and I don't know what's happening or why my heart is beating like this today. I think of Adam, of the life I thought I was building that's now collapsed. I think of Roman, always there, always solid, even as he pursued his own dreams across the globe. I think of us, standing here in Vegas, both unmoored in different ways.

I feel a lightness I haven't experienced since finding Adam with that woman. It's not happiness exactly. I'm still too raw for that. But something adjacent to it. A reminder that even as some doors close, others stand open. That some decisions aren't as final as they feel.

I don't know where I'm going to live yet or how it will feel not to have Adam as a fixture in my life. I don't know how my heart will heal or what scars I'll carry from this.

But right now, I don't have to stress about it.

I can just be in the moment as I said I wanted to do. Vegas glitters around us, a city of second chances and new beginnings. And for the first time since I saw Adam with that woman, I'm excited to believe that both are possible.

9

ROMAN

The kitchen of Decision pulses with a controlled frenzy that sets me right at home. I move between stations, tasting, adjusting, nodding approval as Leaf oversees and executes each dish with the focus and detail I've demanded. Tonight is the soft opening, which is essentially for press, critics, and VIPs. Despite having done this dance dozens of times before, the high never gets old.

This restaurant is different somehow. It's the distillation of everything I've learned and everything I've become. It's Vegas. A place where there's no shortage of dining excellence, so this restaurant, this opening, it has to be everything. It has to be the best in town. Europe will be Europe, and I'm excited for that, but there's just something about Vegas.

I straighten my jacket and catch the healing cut beneath my eye in the ornamental mirror in the corner. It's faint now, barely noticeable. It makes me smirk and my fists buzz. My phone vibrates in my pocket and I pull it out, expecting it to be Braelyn but finding it to be my parents instead.

"Hey," I answer.

"Hi!" my mother chirps. "Happy soft opening."

I smile and laugh lightly. "Thank you. Where are you?"

"Budapest," my father answers. "Otherwise, we'd be there."

"It's fine." They were all over me about changing their plans, but that seemed ridiculous. It's not my first restaurant opening, and it won't be my last. My parents and I have a good yet strained relationship, and I know that's my fault. Their favorite son is dead because of me, and I watched them fall apart when he died. I watched their agony and devastation, and it made mine that much worse.

"We miss you," my mom says, and I rub the back of my neck that's suddenly prickling.

"I miss you," I tell them. "How are the concerts going?"

"Fabulous. They're a lot of fun, and your father is eating his way from country to country."

"Hey, I haven't had a break from the OR in how many years?"

I smile, happy to hear them like this. "Then I'm glad you're finally doing it."

"We get home right before you leave," my mother states, sadness in her voice. "I hate that you're moving, Roman."

"It's only for a year and a half. It'll give you another excuse to go to Europe."

"True," my father agrees.

"How's Braelyn?" my mother asks. "We spoke to her parents the other night. Poor girl. Is she holding up okay? She must be so heartbroken."

"She's okay. She's tough. I brought her to Vegas with me, and she'll come to Mexico too."

"Good. That's wonderful. She needs her friends right now."

Bitterness hits me, but I brush it away.

"Chef, the first guests are arriving." Lydia appears at my elbow, her iPad in her hand, her normally unflappable demeanor charged with electricity.

"I gotta go," I tell my parents. "It's showtime."

"Break a leg. You're amazing," my mom asserts.

"Have an incredible night," my father follows that up. "We love you."

"Love you." I disconnect the call and turn to Lydia. "All right. Let's do this."

I adjust my dark suit jacket and head out into the main dining area to look for her. Braelyn is waiting by the host stand, her brown eyes taking in the buzz of the restaurant while an appreciative smile tickles her lips. The sight of her stops me mid-stride. The gown of midnight blue follows the curves of her body like water, with a deep V-neckline that reveals the inner slopes of her breasts and cinches in at her waist, only to flow down along her hips to the floor. Her chestnut curls are swept up and pinned behind her, and her makeup is heavier than usual, her eyes smoky, and her lips the same deep red as the walls.

Jesus.

My typically cool and steady heart has never heated and thundered like this.

I take her distraction and run with it, studying every line, savoring every curve, waiting for the moment when her eyes finally turn to meet mine like they are now. A dazzling smile curls up her lips, and fuck, I can't breathe. It feels like an elephant is sitting on my chest. She gives me a long, approving once-over and crosses the room to me.

"You're stunning," I tell her before I can stop it, bending to kiss her cheek but somehow growing closer to the corner of her lips. She's wearing perfume. It's not something she does with any regularity, and it's light and airy, but it's making my blood thrum and my cock throb all the same.

"You clean up nicely too," she tells me, running her hand down my black shirt and suit jacket that's missing a tie because ties aren't what I do. "This is very... you."

My lips twitch. "You approve then?"

"Of you in an all-black sexy suit? What's not to approve of?"

"Did you just call me sexy?"

She laughs lightly, her tone teasing. "I called your suit sexy. You're... adequate."

"You're not. You're insanely sexy. I'll have to keep you by my side all night or I'll end up murdering someone."

A flush spreads across her cheeks, but she doesn't shift or shy away from it. "It's the dress."

"It's the best thing I've ever spent money on."

She does a twirl, giving me a nice view of her ass in the process. "Well, when a famous chef insists on buying you couture for his fancy restaurant opening, it's rude to say no and disappoint him."

"Kid, there is nothing about you that could ever disappoint me." The words come out rougher and more intense than I intend. Thankfully, Lydia comes over and interrupts us with people I unfortunately have to meet.

No hiding in the kitchen or avoiding pictures tonight.

The next hour dissolves into a series of introductions, handshakes, and literal wining and dining. Critics from every major publication circulate through the space, scribbling notes and feigning nonchalance as they sample dishes and sip on drinks. Celebrities and social media influencers position themselves strategically for photos that make them appear important.

Through it all, Braelyn stays by my side, and I hold her there, keeping her close. She's brilliant at this, always good with talking to strangers and making everyone feel like the most special person in the room. I have no doubt she's like this as a nurse, instilling care and comfort in her patients. She deflects questions about our relationship with humor, asks insightful questions about the food that makes the critics take a second bite, and charms models and actresses with wild stories about the ER.

"The secret to the pesto is the olive oil, I think," she muses, taking a taste as she chats up a critic. "Roman insists on using a specific olive oil from an orchard in Spain where the trees are older than most other countries. I'm convinced that's also why his homemade pasta is as incredible as it is."

"That's not precisely—" I begin to correct her, but the critic is already nodding appreciatively and jotting something down on his phone.

"Don't ruin my stories with facts," she murmurs when the critic moves on. "I'm playing on your mystique."

"I wasn't aware I had mystique."

I get a serious eye roll. "That's because you don't see it. But you're as elusive as they come. Quiet. Introspective. Brilliant. Annoyingly gorgeous without trying to be. And besides, it's not entirely fiction. You are ridiculously fastidious with your recipes and ingredients. It's also what makes you so good in the ring. Your attention to detail allows you to see what others miss."

I used to be more reckless. Always chasing something I couldn't quite grasp. Then my brother died, and it was my fault, and after that, I didn't want to be reckless anymore. I wanted to control everything, see every potential risk from ten miles out. But the restlessness never faded. It's why I box. Yet somehow, Braelyn manages to calm me in a similar way. Her presence has always been a balm to my unsettled, ravaged heart.

Kind of like what she's doing for me here.

I hate everything about the forced socialization and smiles, but she draws the latter effortlessly out of me.

My fingers sweep along her cheek. I shouldn't be moving as fast as I am with her. I've been testing boundaries and blurring lines. Lines I don't want to redraw. Lines I want to keep pushing. But she's not ready yet, and I have to remember that and respect it. Moreover, she's my best friend's ex. A best friend who is desperate to win her back. And I'm leaving. How can I push for something real when I won't be here to see it through?

I'm here to be her friend. The guy who helps her get over her heartache. I don't want to be a complication or a confusion.

"I'm going to grab another drink," she declares. "Do you want one?"

"Sure. Get me whatever you're having."

She snorts a laugh. "Mine is going to be girly and strong."

I smirk. "I'll take the strong part."

"You got it, Chef."

She leaves me here, lost in a mental fight I feel like I'll lose either way the decision comes. I watch her moving, her effortless smile and adorable curiosity as she people-watches. She casts a spell of fire and heat in me that I no longer know how to extinguish.

"She's beautiful," a woman says from behind us, and I turn around to find a blonde in a red dress approaching me. "Is she yours?"

I frown. "I'm sorry, I don't believe I know you."

A smile draws up her face, showing perfect white teeth. "Ah, but I know you. I'm Anne Sharpe. I'm a talent manager for Boston Nine's entertainment division."

Boston Nine. That's Adam's network. I shake her hand. "Nice to meet you, Ms. Sharpe."

"You as well, Chef Fritz. I have to admit, I've followed your career very closely. It's more than a little impressive."

"Thank you," I reply cautiously. There's something about her that doesn't sit quite right. Her smile's a little too friendly. A little too knowing. The gleam in her eye a little too calculating.

"I've got an idea I'm going to pitch to my bosses, and it involves you."

"Except I'm not interested in TV." *And I know your bosses,* which I wonder if she's aware of.

She pouts prettily and steps into me, her tits brushing against my chest ever so subtly as if that'll sway me. "You haven't heard my pitch. I can be very persuasive."

"I won't change my mind."

"It'd be a new series starring you." She tickles a flirty finger into my chest. "Half Gordon Ramsay's *Hell's Kitchen* and half *The Bear*. With your fame, good looks, and talent, I know you'd be a perfect fit for—"

"I'm flattered," I sharply interrupt, "but again, I'm not interested in television."

Anne's smile doesn't waver. If anything, she looks more dangerous at my refusal. "Perhaps we could discuss this over coffee or a drink? There are aspects of the opportunity I believe might change your mind."

Not only do I have zero interest in being the star of anything, but there are other pieces to the puzzle that come with this sort of gig. Things like dredging up Nash's death for emotional content that will pull on the heartstrings of viewers. Things like editing and spinning my interactions and personality any way they choose. Things like deeper dives into my personal life than I can afford. My boxing would come out. It wouldn't be tough to discover that the root cause of the names of my restaurants is more than simply my form of exercise or an at-home hobby as I've said in interviews in the past.

It would be exposed.

My restaurants could weather it. Hell, it might even boost them. But there are other factors like the illegality of it. The betting. The ability to continue doing it since once exposed, it would be shut down. Not to mention I could go to fucking jail. At the very least a criminal investigation would be started.

It's why I stopped doing Food Network guest spots, and those were only about cooking and not me.

"My focus is on my restaurants," I tell her firmly, shoving my hands into my pockets. "I'm not looking to diversify beyond that."

"Everyone has their price, Chef. Or incentives yet to be tapped into." She hands me a business card that I accept purely out of reflex. "When you change your mind, give me a call. As I said, I'm very interested in bringing you in for this show, and I think we could work very well together."

She glides away, and a moment later, Braelyn is back holding her pink drink and my bourbon. "This is so good. You have to taste it."

A real smile returns to my lips, and I lean in and wrap my hand around the glass she's holding. Our fingers brush, half interlocking, and I draw the pretty glass up to my lips to sip from it.

I let go of the glass and her touch, even if I can still feel it on my fingers. "Very good. What is it?"

"A bourbon Cosmo. I've never had one before, but I might be converted. It's one of your specialty drinks. Yours is straight bourbon as you can see."

"This drink was Lydia's idea. I'm glad you like it."

"She picked a good one. Who were you talking to? I only saw a lot of red and blonde."

"A TV producer looking to have me as the star of her show." For some reason, I don't mention that it's Adam's company. She said she wanted to pitch it to the higher-ups, which means he likely doesn't know about it yet, and I don't want to bring Adam up right now.

Not when we're having such a good night and she looks happy.

"She's barking up the wrong tree there, though I'm shocked you've never agreed to do your own show since you have done some guest spots on others."

I drink down half my bourbon. "That was a long time ago. Besides, I like my privacy. Come on," I say, offering her my arm. "Let's get you some dessert."

She loops her free arm through my elbow and rests her hand on my forearm. "I never say no to chocolate. How late does this event go?"

"Another hour, but I was told we have to stay for drinks after the soft opening ends, and then we might be dragged to the club to celebrate more, so it could be a long night for us. You up for a little fun and adventure Vegas style?"

"Tonight I'm up for anything."

10

BRAELYN

There's a mariachi band playing in my head, loud and intrusive, and it makes me both dizzy and nauseated.

I take mental stock of my surroundings without opening my eyes. I'm in a bed, tucked under the covers, but I'm wearing something weird. A bathrobe maybe? Why am I wearing a bathrobe?

Flashes from last night flicker through my head.

Roman's restaurant opening. Drinks with the staff after it ended. Shots. We all did a couple rounds of shots, and that was after the two cocktails I had at the opening. After that gets hazy. I stretch my mind and remember the club. We all went to the club in the hotel and had VIP access and table service.

The music pulsed through me as everything glittered gold around us. Roman had his hand on my lower back, keeping me close. Probably because I'd stumbled a few times, but it didn't matter. I'd had the best time tonight. Leaf, Lydia, as well as a few of the other chefs and bartenders, were with us as we were led by a hostess to a semi-circular booth with a high back and a view of the dance floor. Everywhere we looked, glitz and glam sparkled.

Bottles of alcohol along with mixers were ordered. Roman was stoic, taking in the scene around him with quiet introspection and an almost imperceptible grin. He was happy, and it was a good look on him. One I didn't get to see too often. It was almost as if he never allowed himself to be that way and it broke my heart.

"Cheers!" Lydia sang out, pouring a round of expensive tequila into shot glasses. "To Decision."

"Yes!" I cried, holding my glass up and nudging Roman.

"To Decision," he agreed, and we all drank down our shots.

"Come dance with me?" I asked.

I got a look. One I couldn't quite read. It felt like he wanted to, but something was holding him back. Still, he stood and held his hand out for mine, and we made our way to the dance floor. Alcohol was flowing through my veins faster than Niagara Falls. I was drunk and I knew it, the room dipping and swaying, but the current through me was as delicious as it was intoxicating.

"I'm having so much fun!" I told him, wrapping my arms around his neck for a brief moment, only to release him and start to move my hips to the beat.

He spun me around, his hands on my hips, his mouth by my ear. "I'm glad, kid. You deserve it."

I placed my hands over his and gave them a squeeze. He did this for me. He brought me out here and bought me this dress and got us this ridiculous villa. I'm so happy right now. It felt like I was floating on a cloud. All of the darkness I came to Vegas with felt like it had evaporated. Everything was new and exciting and I wanted all of it.

I lost myself in the beat, my eyes closed and my body moving.

Roman's hands stayed on my hips, trailing up and down the slope to my waist or a little lower to the crest above my ass, but always returning to my hips. He was close. His chest to my back and the two of us danced for I don't even know how long.

We took a break, more drinks pouring down my throat.

"How come you two aren't married yet?" Leaf asked as he sat back and watched a few women dancing in tiny dresses not far from us.

I snorted a laugh. "Um, because we're best friends."

"What?" Capshaw, one of the bartenders, gasped out. "No way. You're not a couple? You look so comfortable with each other. Like you've been together forever."

"Well, in a way, we have been. But I was engaged to someone else until last week," I told them.

Everyone's eyes widened.

"What happened?" Lydia pressed.

I shrug. "What always happens? He cheated, I caught him, case closed."

"But you have Roman," she said as if the fact that I had been with anyone else didn't make sense.

"Yes," a waitress, whose name I couldn't remember, agreed emphatically. "You look so good together."

"He's not my type since he's not a woman, but he's every other woman's type," another threw out.

Roman made a displeased noise. He hated being the center of attention.

I scrunched my nose teasingly. "But he's so old."

He poked me in the side, his eyes light. "Watch it, kid. I'm only six years older than you."

"But when we were kids, you seemed so much older."

His lips thinned. "And you seemed so much younger. Until suddenly you didn't."

I tilted my head at him, but Capshaw continued with, "I agree with Leaf. You two should get married. You're in Vegas. It'd be such a fun story."

Roman finished off the rest of his drink and refilled it before I snatched the bottle from him and did the same.

"Yes," Leaf continued. "Roman has talked about you enough. I think it's time he settles down. Then maybe he won't be so grumpy all the time."

Everyone laughed, but Roman wasn't laughing.

"Come on," someone else said. "We dare you."

I shift slightly under the blanket. I know there were more shots. I remember having at least one more. That's it, though. I couldn't tell you how I got back to the hotel. I don't remember going to bed. I don't remember getting undressed and into the robe. I don't remember—oh shit. Oh no. No, no, no. Please tell me no.

Because I do remember something else, and my brain frantically replays the memory.

"You're daring us?" I cackled. "How can you dare people to get married?"

They all shrugged. "I have a friend who did that with her bestie on a dare. They've been married five years now."

I leaned back in my seat and nearly fell over because I wasn't as close to the back of the booth as I thought. Oops. No one seemed to care or notice. They were all over daring us to get married.

"That wouldn't be us, though," I protested.

"How do you know until you try?" Lydia countered. "Come on. It's a fun dare."

"You can't dare me," I warned. "I never turn down a dare."

Roman leaned into my ear, clearly done with this. "Dance with me?"

I nodded and allowed him to take me back to the dance floor, ending the conversation. Except the dare wouldn't die. It tickled the back of my mind until it grew into a full-blown itch. The more I thought about it, the more I liked it.

"Maybe we should get married," I said to Roman as we danced, my arms around his neck and his face low and close to mine. I could feel his breath. Smell his cologne. It was warm and intimate, especially as I watched the different colors dance in his eyes.

A noise caught in his throat, half heavy breath, half incredulous laugh. "Yeah? You think?" he teased, holding and leading me to a slower ballad.

"I'm serious. Maybe we should." It seemed like such a brilliant idea. And fun. Getting married to Roman sounded so fun. So unlike

marrying Adam, which sounded horrible. Why did I ever say yes when he proposed? "Adam sucks. I'm sooo glad I didn't marry him. He wasn't right for me. How could he have been? My vagina is amazing. I'm incredible in bed. How could he cheat?!" I yelled, only to wince because that sounded extra loud in my ears.

Roman ran a hand up my spine that shot tingles the other way. "He was a fool."

"But you're not. You're the best person I know. You've always been right." I tilted my head, studying him from beneath my lashes. "If you know what I mean. You'd be a good husband. I should marry you. It'd be the best story ever. One we could tell our grandkids."

"Brae, how drunk are you?"

I smiled up at him. My friend was so tall. Gorgeous too. I mean, his eyes were insane. And his jawline. Woo. Roman rarely shaved, but he did tonight, and I couldn't stop myself from touching his smooth cheek with my fingers. His eyes darkened and yet appeared so clear and bright. How could that be? It felt like a contradiction, but it was exactly how he was looking at me. But that was neither here nor there. Unless he was in his underwear. I choked out a laugh at myself. Oh wait, he asked me a question. What was it?

My face twisted up as I worked my memory. "How drunk am I?"

His fingers found the delicate skin at the back of my neck, and I involuntarily shivered.

"Yes, pretty girl. How drunk are you?"

"On a scale of one to ten? I don't know. About a ten point five, so I guess I'm rounding up to eleven. What about you?"

"An eight. I'm a solid eight. So that means we're drunk and shouldn't get married."

"But this is Vegas," I whined, feeling a little hurt by his blatant rejection. Why did he always reject me?

"I don't always reject you," he said, hurt flashing in his eyes, and oops, I guess I was musing aloud. But with that, his eyes softened, and his body shifted, holding me closer. "I don't want to be your regret."

Adam was my regret. Roman was the dessert worth every calorie.

"They dared us. I've never turned down a dare in my life. I think we have to do it."

"You think we have to get married because people who work for me dared us to?"

I couldn't tell if his question was rhetorical or incredulous or genuinely asking. "Well, yeah. Right? They said we belong together. Maybe we do. I'm starting to live my new life. Let's be wild. Let's be reckless. Let's get married."

His eyes searched mine even as they swirled with color from the overhead lights. "There are a million reasons we shouldn't do this. But looking at you right now, I can't think of one."

A weird flutter rolled through me. What was I thinking? Still, I didn't want to back down.

"You honestly want to get married? Because I'll say yes and then you'll wake up married to me."

My hand moves across my body until it connects with my other. Hard metal and bumpy ridges are on my left hand. Diamonds. There are diamonds on my left hand. On my ring finger.

My eyes snap open, and I spring up, my robe falling open, but I don't care because all I can do is stare down at the row of large diamonds banded around my finger.

"Roman!" I scream as I scramble out of bed. Thankfully, I remember to close my gaping robe because I'm only in panties beneath it. "Roman!"

I fly out of my bedroom just as he comes racing into it, and we smash into each other.

"Ow!" I step back and rub my shoulder. "Do you have to have so many muscles? They hurt."

He's wearing shorts and a T-shirt and looks sweaty. How could he work out at a time like this?

"I take it you remembered that you married me last night."

I blink up at him, only to flip down to his left hand that's perched on his hip. He has a black band on it. "It's real, right?"

"Yep. We closed the place down. We were their last wedding of the night. You were so relieved we made it in time."

"Oh my god!" I cover my face with my hands. Then I laugh. Kind of loud and a lot hysterical. "Oh my god!"

"Yep."

"Did we kiss? I don't remember the ceremony. Well, not a lot of it. Some of it. I was in my blue dress, and we said our vows and... oh hell. I threw myself at you and kissed you. Didn't I?"

"You kind of missed," he tells me with some amusement in his tone. "You got more chin than lips."

My hands fall to my sides, and the room sways with it. Fuck, I'm so hungover. And when the room sways again, I hold up a finger, telling him I need a minute, and race for the bathroom. I make it just in time to lift the lid and empty everything in my stomach into the toilet. It's awful. Alcohol retching is the worst, which is why I haven't had enough alcohol to induce it since college. Ugh.

"Is this from realizing you married me or from alcohol or from my food last night?" comes from the other side of the door.

Somehow a smile manages to quirk my lips. "All three."

He chuckles. "Are you okay? Can I get you something? Some water?"

"A sports drink would be great if they have it."

"Any particular flavor?"

"Don't care. Just not red."

"How come not red?"

I sit back against the wall, sweaty and clammy and just gross. "Because I'm a nurse and vomiting red looks like blood."

"Noted. I'll be right back."

I throw up a bit more, but my stomach is already feeling better by the time I pull away from the toilet to wash my face and brush my teeth. Roman is back, hovering outside the bathroom door to give me privacy, which I appreciate.

"I got you a few different kinds."

"Awesome." I tighten my robe and take the blue bottle from his hand. "This is perfect. Thank you." I crack the top and take a few small sips.

Worry creases his brow. "You haven't thrown up like that since you tried to kiss me the last time."

"That's accurate. Ironic that you rejected me then and married me last night."

He puffs an annoyed breath. "I didn't reject you."

"You did."

He holds up a hand. "Fine. But not the way you think I did. And I wasn't drunk that night, whereas last night I definitely was."

I sigh and lean against the doorframe, taking another sip. "How are you like this? You're disgustingly chipper."

"It's professional stamina. Drinking after hours isn't a new thing in restaurants."

"Nurses can put them back too. Trust me, depending on the shift, we need it. But damn, that last tequila shot was not a good idea. What about getting married? Is that an after-hours professional thing too?"

He runs his fingers over my sweaty forehead. "That's a new one for sure."

"Does this make me a Fritz? We don't have a prenup. I'm worth billions now."

He rolls his eyes at my sardonic tone. "What's mine has always been yours, married or not."

"I wish I could say the same to you, but all I have to offer is my poor decision-making."

"Well, you're beautiful, so there's that too."

I scoff. "Especially right now. Did you put me to bed? I don't remember coming back here. That part is a total blur."

"You were half asleep by that point. I carried you back in here, and I unzipped your dress and handed you a robe. That's it. The rest you did after I left."

"So we didn't..."

He gives me a *do you even have to ask that* look. "No, Braelyn. We didn't. I didn't kiss you when you were drunk that night. Do you honestly think I'd take advantage of you when you're half blacked out and do more?"

I lean heavier into the doorway. "No. Sorry. I just had to ask."

"Trust me, kid, if we'd done anything, you'd be feeling that today as well."

Well then. A blush crawls up my face, and I cover it by taking another sip.

"So what do we do now? Other than get divorced." I bark out a laugh and shake my head. "This is so messed up. I'm sorry. I went from planning my wedding to one man to marrying another in a Vegas chapel. My family is going to kill me. Your family is going to kill me. Holy shit, Adam. He's your friend. I made you marry your best friend's ex."

"You didn't make me marry you. I was a willing participant. I didn't do it because of the dare or anything else."

"And the other stuff?"

He looks away, out toward the window on the other side of the bedroom, his expression intense and thoughtful. "I don't know what to say about Adam. I feel shitty. Very shitty. He wants me to help him win you back, and instead, I married you. Not to mention, you were engaged to him a week ago."

"I feel so stupid. I know I talked you into it. Can we not tell anyone? Can we keep it a secret?"

He turns back to me, his eyes all over my face, even as his eyebrows pull together, my question turning into understanding. "You mean get a quickie divorce and pretend like it never happened?"

I gnaw on my lip, but I don't know why I'm nervous to say yes. He didn't exactly marry me out of love and wanting forever with babies in the baby carriage. He married me after a huge professional night and a lot of alcohol and teasing from his friends. And because I thought it would be fun. And funny, which it kind of is superficially and kind of isn't logistically.

"My life is already a mess, and my engagement ending was very public, considering we had to rescind our invitation and who my fiancé was. I don't want more drama, and you're Roman Fritz. Us getting married the way we did will be mocked. It'll make the freaking news. And it'll cause issues for you with Adam. As much as I hate him right now, and I'm glad you're here with me, he's your friend, and I wouldn't ever want to come between that. Hopefully, we can get divorced, and no one will be the wiser."

His eyes search mine as he considers all of this. "If that's what you want."

Something in his voice catches me, but my head is still too muddled to think clearly. "I think it has to be that way. Let's keep it a secret. At least for now."

11

ROMAN

After I put Braelyn to bed last night, I sat on the floor outside her door, listening to her sleep. I told myself it was so I could make sure she didn't vomit on her back or anything, but the truth was, I didn't want to be far from her. I couldn't be in her bed with her. I knew that.

But I had just married her, and I had a lot of thoughts about that.

I knew it wasn't real. I knew she'd wake up this morning exactly how she did, with regrets and incredulity and wanting to brush the whole thing away like a bad dream. So I took that time last night on the floor, listening to her slow, even breaths, to come to grips with that.

I promised to love her forever, forsaking all others, in sickness and in health, for better or worse, until death did us part. And I meant it. I meant every word because there is no one else I've ever considered marrying. I had hoped that one day, I'd fall out of love with her and move on, but I never pictured marrying. I'm not really the type, I don't think. That was always Nash.

But there I was, married to my best friend, to my dead brother's ex-girlfriend, and my current best friend's ex-fiancée. Not to mention, I was planning on leaving her in less than two months for another country. Another life. As you can imagine, there was a lot to process with that. A lot of guilt to sift through because even though it's tied to some of my standard guilt, it was different.

After Nash died, I used to talk to him a lot. I'd spend my nights lying in bed, staring out the window or up at the ceiling, and I'd talk to him. A lot of it was apologizing and asking if he blamed me the way I blamed myself. That if we had returned, would he have asked Braelyn to marry him right then and there even though they were only eighteen. I'd ask him a million questions I knew would never be answered and then once I'd exhausted those, I'd talk to him about everything inside me that I didn't know what to do with.

Part of that was turning into Braelyn as our friendship grew tighter, and I started to see her a little differently than I ever had before. I'd ask him if he hated me for that, the way I hated myself. After all, she was his girl and not mine. That was one of the reasons I went to Europe the first time. To escape those feelings. All of them. To try to move on and regain any piece of my life I could.

So yeah. There was a lot in my head last night and a lot weighing down my heart, but it also felt full. Stupidly, I knew better.

"Okay. We won't tell anyone," I manage, the words cutting like a razor as they slice past my tongue.

There is as much relief in that as there is agony. I clear my throat. In fairness, I'm not sure what I'd even tell anyone. I certainly don't want more press or attention on me and there would be with that since my name is famous.

"There's food I ordered from room service. I thought we might eat by the pool if you're up for it."

"Hell yeah, I'm up for it. Food and a day by the pool sounds freaking amazing as long as I don't have to do too much and there's coffee with my sports drink."

"Always coffee."

"Perfect. Give me five and I'll meet you out there."

Without a word, I leave so she can get herself together. I do the same, methodically changing out of my sweaty gym stuff and into a clean T-shirt and swim trunks, while forcing myself not to think about the fact that she wants to pretend like last night never happened. I'm not surprised. Frankly, it's what I expected, so I don't know why I'm disappointed now.

Ten minutes later, she's walking outside to join me under the shade of an umbrella at the table by the pool. She's in an annoyingly distracting green bikini top. It's the kind that looks like a bra, and it pushes her tits up while offering me a mouth-wateringly enticing amount of cleavage that bounces as she walks.

Thankfully, she's wearing shorts over her bottoms, but I'm starting to think that hanging out by the pool wasn't my smartest move.

"Happy birthday, husband," she singsongs, making me crack up the way I only do with her. Her arm swings around from behind her back to hand me a wrapped package. "I would have wished you this earlier, but you know, hangover and remembering I was suddenly married made it difficult to focus on other things."

She's handling the marriage part better than I would have expected. Probably because it's not the least bit real to her. She's treating it as a practical joke, if anything. A stupid dare she followed through with that will magically disappear like it never happened once we return to Boston and get divorced.

I take the gift, my eyes all over the silver wrapping. "You didn't need to do this."

"What are besties and wives for? Just so you know, you're as impossible to shop for this year as you were last. I mean, what do you get the man who has everything or could buy it himself?"

I roll my eyes and get up to hug her. "Thank you. This is incredible."

"You haven't opened it yet."

She takes the seat across from me, and I waste no time tearing at the paper. There are two things, both of which might be the best gifts anyone has ever bought me. The first is a travel watch holder that can accommodate up to five watches. Watches are sort of my weakness, and I have an extensive collection, both modern and vintage. It's brown leather and engraved with my initials.

"I love it," I tell her.

"You don't already have one?"

I shake my head. "No. Really. This is perfect. But where on earth did you get this picture?"

It's a framed photograph of the two of us. It had to have been the summer Nash died, but it's me holding Braelyn above my head, *Dirty Dancing* style. She was obsessed with that movie and made us watch it at least a hundred times with her. Nash and Adam weren't as big as I was. It took us almost a week to perfect that move, and on more than one occasion, she nearly ate sand or grass when I'd drop her or fall backward. Nash thought it was hysterical.

Back then, I didn't notice Braelyn as anything more than my little brother's girl. This was all just fun, and I almost miss that time. A time when I wasn't in love with the girl I could never have. The woman I just made my wife.

"Your mom," she explains, her voice soft, and now that I think back to this picture, I know why. Nash took it. It was on his phone. My mom must have saved all of the pictures he had on there. Neither of us had our phones with us that day on the water. Maybe if we had, I might have been able to call for help when the storm came out of nowhere.

I clear my throat. "Thank you. This is my favorite gift ever."

A soft smile tickles her lips. "I'm glad. It's a small gesture and I'm not very good at saying thank you—"

"Really? You don't say?"

I get an eye roll similar to what I gave her. "Har, har. Some days I'm better at it than others. Anyway, thank you. For everything that you do for me and everything that you are. You're just... you're the perfect guy, my best friend, my ride or die, and I'd be lost without you. I hope you know that."

Warmth slithers through my veins, only to catch on three words. My best friend. I am that. I'll always be that. But I'd like to add to that title if I could. Then I think of Adam, and my insides plummet.

"Is that why you married me?"

"One of many reasons." She winks at me.

I hand Brae her food, and she immediately scarfs down her crab eggs Benedict while I pick at an omelet and sourdough toast.

"Have you checked yet?" she asks as she swallows a bite, her eyebrows bouncing.

"Obviously. Why do you think I was up before you? I couldn't sleep."

Her head tilts, and an indulgent smile curls up the corner of her lips. "Aw, you're cute, but self-doubt doesn't suit you."

It never did, but over the past week, I've been questioning everything. And imposter syndrome is real, no matter how many restaurants you open or how many awards you win.

"You're not going to tell me?"

I take a sip of my coffee, and she huffs out a breath at my evasiveness.

"Fine. I'll do the digging myself." She sets her fork and knife down, wipes her mouth with her napkin, and leans back in her seat, her phone in one hand, her coffee in her other. She types with her thumb, her eyes glued to her screen, and when she finds what she's looking for, her face lights up. "Holy shit! Oh my god!" She sets her mug down and leans halfway across the table, which makes more of her tits spill out, and I wish she'd sit back as she was. "This chick is practically composing a symphony to you. And that prickly ass from the Chronicle is weeping over how creative, original, and inspiring your dishes are. Dude, he gave you an A."

"Minus," I correct.

She flips me off, and I chuckle. "The MICHELIN guide gave you a three. Ah!" she screams. "Oh my fucking god, Roman. Seriously. This is amazing. Your restaurant hasn't even officially opened yet, and it's already a critical success. It's all over IG, with models who likely don't eat raving about the food."

She chokes up, and I shake my head at her. "Why are you crying? This week is the most I've ever seen you cry."

"I know." She wipes at her face, a self-deprecating laugh tickling her lips. "It's like Adam broke the dam open or something. But these are happy tears. I'm so, so proud of you." She gets up and comes over to me, pushing me back and parking herself on my lap. She wraps her arms around me and hugs me tightly, and because I can, I hug her back, holding her to me, breathing in the scent of her hair and skin. "Please tell me you're happy."

"I'm happy."

She pulls back and eyes me. "Do you mean that? Your voice is doing that Roman Fritz thing where it's all broody and serious and a little tense."

That's because you're sitting on my lap wearing nothing but a bikini top, tiny shorts, and my ring on your hand. I'm trying not to get hard.

"I'm happy. Seriously, I'm very happy. Thrilled even."

"And it's your birthday. This is the best. We have to celebrate this."

"Didn't we celebrate enough last night?" I hold up my left hand.

"Different celebrating. And it's not like you could marry me twice. The only thing left is to knock me up."

I choke. On nothing. Jesus, this girl.

"Gotcha with that. Please, can we celebrate you?"

"We are. This is us celebrating." My hand on her back rubs between her shoulder blades, and I will it to stay put and not wander or caress. Dancing with her last night was the same perfect torture. Then there was everything that came after.

All of that was both heaven and hell.

It's funny, I never had trouble listening before to the warning in my head that told me to hold back. I always heeded its advice because it's been a constant voice of reason for as long as I can remember. But it's as if something shifted inside of me, and now new thoughts are eclipsing all that reason.

Potential. Hope. Promise. And guilt. There is that too. Strong as fucking ever.

She climbs off my lap just as quickly as she sat down and returns to her seat.

"To your continued success and to your every wish coming true." She raises her coffee mug, and I clink mine with hers.

Right now, I only have one wish left. And I hope it finally comes true without destroying everything else.

12

BRAELYN

"Is that really called a come bet?" I ask, and Roman throws me a side-eye. "Like you're betting to come?"

"You're shouting."

"I am not."

He chuckles. "You are. But yes, it's called a come bet, and you are technically betting to come. Or at least hit a number in that field."

"And why do you have so many chips behind your first bet?"

"I'm backing up my bet. Putting all my faith in you."

"Yeesh." I wiggle my hips back and forth. "Tall order."

"Lady, are you gonna roll the dice or what?" the cowboy next to me gripes. Roman throws him a look that could flay the skin off, well, that guy.

"She will when she's ready," he answers for me. "She's learning."

"Great. Learn on someone else's time. Let's go!"

Roman is about to kill the man, but I hold up my hand and shake the dice in my other. "Come on, magic dice. Roll me a six. It's my husband's birthday, and he deserves to be a big winner."

I laugh at that. For some reason, I find the fact that Roman is my husband hilarious. I think I've officially lost it.

I blow on the dice and shoot them down the table, only to have one hit the wall and fly up and out. It knocks into the guy on the end, who is too busy flirting with the woman beside him to dodge it in time.

"Oh my god!" I cry, covering my mouth with my hand. "I'm so sorry!"

The dealers put their hands over the table, and the pit boss comes and retrieves the dice, examines them, and puts them back on the table with the others for me to choose two new dice from.

Without the same fanfare, I shoot the dice down the table and hit an eight. Everyone cheers because there's a lot of money sitting on eight, including my twenty-five-dollar chip.

"Woohoo!" I high-five the cowboy next to me, who suddenly wants to be my best friend. "See. Trust the process," I tell him.

"I will after you roll a six."

"Fine. I'll try. "I roll three more times and finally land on the six to thunderous applause. "I won!" I jump up and down, screaming like a mad woman. I jump on Roman, who catches me. "You won too!"

He beams at me, holding me securely in his arms. "Nice job, kid."

I plant a big kiss right on his lips. I don't know where it comes from. Or why I do it. It wasn't consciously thought out, and it wasn't anything like our sloppy wedding kiss that didn't even count as a kiss. It just happens in the excitement of the moment, but it surprises us both.

For a moment, we simply stare at each other, blinking. I can taste his breath against my lips, sweet from the wine at dinner, the scent of his spicy cologne coloring my vision and making everything hazy. Then his eyes dip and hold on my lips. Almost like he's not sure what to make of what I just did, though there is something darker there too.

A strange, warm flutter fills my belly and pulses across my skin. I climb out of his arms, blow out a silent breath, and get my shit together because it's still my turn to roll the damn dice.

But fuck. I just kissed Roman.

Like full-on-the-mouth kissed him.

And I didn't... hate it. It wasn't as weird or awkward as I thought it would be, and certainly not gross. Quite the opposite of gross actually. And this time, he didn't look as horrified as he did the first time I tried to kiss him, and I didn't miss his mouth and get him on the chin.

Still... that's not something that can happen again. He obviously knows that. It's not as though he tried to kiss me again or anything.

I twist my wedding band around my finger. Ugh. I'm a mess. That's all that was. Aftermath of Adam, being in Vegas, and let's not forget the fact that I married Roman on a drunken whim. It could also be the bottle of wine we split at dinner, and the vodka soda I've been nursing since. I don't drink a lot, and this is the second night in a row.

I'm gonna owe my liver an apology when I'm done with this city.

I roll the dice and of course, crap out.

"Do you want to play more or are you all done?" he asks, his lips close to my ear as he speaks.

I shiver, and what the motherfuck is my body doing?! "I think I'm done for tonight."

We have one more day here, and then we head on to Mexico. But maybe that's a bad idea. Maybe I should just go home. A week at a resort with Roman suddenly feels a little... shaky. Almost like a honeymoon even though it's not. Except what home would I return to? I'm living with Roman.

"Are you tired or should we walk for a bit?"

"Let's walk for a bit." I think that'll help clear my head.

He guides us through the casino toward an atrium that's designed to be a fairy garden. It's pretty and magical, and I'm instantly enchanted, going from set to set and taking it all in.

"Do you remember when you came to visit me in Paris, and I bought you that small tea set?"

I cough out a laugh at the memory. "Yes. And I see what you're saying because that tea set those fairies are using looks just like it."

"This time I don't think you should try to smuggle a wheel of cheese into Mexico."

"God, remember that?" I nudge his arm with my elbow. "The customs agent in Paris definitely knew. He just didn't want to deal with the paperwork. Besides, bureaucracy shouldn't stand between Americans and good dairy. He understood the assignment."

He chuckles and shakes his head as we move on to the next little house and set of fairies. "More like he was enthralled by your charms. You gave him a pretty smile and batted your lashes, and he was done for."

"Not their waiters, though. Do you remember that guy who got all upset and was going to throw me out because I kept asking what different things on the menu meant?"

"You were afraid they were horse meat or frogs."

I turn, affronted. "Yeah. That's gross. Who wants to eat a horse or a frog?"

"I've had both."

I scoff derisively. "Of course you have. Is there anything you haven't tried?"

"Probably not. No, I take that back. I haven't eaten scorpions or cockroaches."

I pretend to vomit, though my stomach protests the notion of eating bugs. "Again, gross."

He hitches up a shoulder. "Gross to you is a delicacy to others."

"Yeah, no thanks on that." I look at the magical little cottage, lit up from within. It's peaceful and sweet. "What was the name of the place in Rome? The little hole-in-the-wall where the owner kept trying to marry you off to his daughter?"

"Oh Jesus. I forgot about that." Roman rubs a hand over his head and the back of his neck. "Trattoria Del Sol."

"Right." I snap my fingers and point at him. "That was it. It was a tiny place, not as cute as these tiny places." I gesture to the cottage. "But it had the best cacio e pepe I've ever had. With the exception of yours," I amend.

"Thanks for that little nod." He rubs his forearm against mine.

"Anytime."

"The man wanted someone to take over his family business and felt a chef son-in-law was just the thing. That's what I get for you opening your mouth and telling everyone we met that I'm a chef."

"I was proud of you. It only backfired on us that night because his daughter was seventeen."

He shudders. "It's why I never went back there despite how good the food was."

We finish with the fairy garden and venture out onto the Strip, taking in the bright lights and women walking around with feathers on their backs, in thongs, with pasties over their nipples. Vegas really is an entirely different world, but the spectacle is fun.

"Want a picture with them?" I offer. "I swear not to sell it to tabloids or post it on the internet."

"You mean along with our wedding picture?"

I gasp. "We have a wedding picture?!"

He angles his head down, his lips curved up into an amused

grin, and with the lights all around us and the sensory overload, my hazy brain keeps thinking about the kiss. About Roman and what this last week has been. About the fact that I'm married to him.

"We do. It's on your phone."

Oh shit. I pull out my phone and dig through, and sure enough, I'm in my blue dress and Roman is in his suit and we're smiling—even he's smiling—and we look... wow, we look so happy. "It's actually a great shot of us."

"It's a keeper. Like my wife," he teases, putting his arm around my shoulders and guiding me around some broken glass.

But that's Roman. He's always been there when I needed him, and he's always taken care of me. I saw what happened the day Nash died rip him apart. The memories of it. The fact that his brother was gone. How it happened.

It wasn't his fault. He'll tell you the opposite. But he's the guy you go to. The one you secretly dream about. The one who will protect you and keep you safe no matter the cost. But that's nothing new.

So why am I feeling... different with him now?

It can't be because we're married, because it doesn't really count.

I don't know. It makes no sense, and I can't explain what this feeling is other than different. It's making me jittery, almost.

"Do you want to travel again?" he questions, snapping me out of my thoughts as we cross over the street via a walkway.

"We are," I quip. "Isn't that what we're doing right now? We're here, and then we're going to Mexico."

"Yes. But back to Europe. You seemed to like it there."

"I did like it there. I've always wanted to go to Greece," I admit. "See all the history and those blue domes in person."

"We'll do it then. A second honeymoon." He winks at me as

we head up toward the Venetian and walk inside, simply meandering through. "Gelato?"

"Definitely."

We get in line behind a cute couple who can't stop kissing, and if that's not bad enough, there's a bachelorette party off to the side taking pictures.

"I had no bachelorette party planned," I murmur, watching the bride pose and smile like her life is as happy as it could possibly be. I hope it is. I hope she gets the fairy tale and the happily ever after.

"I hadn't thought of it until now, but yeah, you're right. How come?"

I shrug. "Adam was going to have one. In three weeks, you guys were all going to Miami. I'm positive he would have fucked at least one woman during that weekend while I was home working."

He shifts his weight. "Likely not. As you said, I was going to be there."

I look up at him. "Why didn't I plan one?"

He angles down to me. "I don't know. Why didn't you?"

"We were going to have a night out in Boston maybe. I don't know. Nothing got planned. Not like Miami for you guys."

"I'm sorry."

"No, it's fine." I wave him away. "I didn't think about it much, and I kept brushing off the girls when they'd ask." I shift to face him as we inch forward in line. "Actually, it's not fine, is it? This trip is the first thing I've done for myself, and you had to drag me along to get me to do it. I don't put myself first enough."

"Now you can start."

I intend to. I don't mean that in a selfish, me-only way, but I should prioritize myself more than I have in the past. Then it hits me. Kind of hard. Like a bullet or blunt force trauma, only instead of bleeding out and dying, I'm coming back together. I'm living.

"I think I'm relieved."

His brows scrunch, but his eyes are intense. "How so?"

"He was cheating on me, and I discovered it. I didn't marry him and learn about it later. I keep thinking... what if I had? Would I have left him? Would my life forever be ruined? Or even worse, what if I had never learned about it, and what he did to me always remained a secret to me?"

Roman is quiet and introspective as he stares straight ahead.

"We didn't sleep together much these last few weeks, so I'm happy about that too," I continue. "I'm sad, but not the way I expected to be so soon after it happened. Maybe I'm still in shock or denial. Those are the first stages of grief, right? But I hate him more than I'm heartbroken or missing him. Losing Nash felt like the worst thing ever, but losing Adam doesn't have the same oomph. If anything, I'm mourning the idea of it all. The years of friendship. The years of a relationship. The life I had built up in my mind. The certainty and plan we had. I miss him, or at least that part of him, but I'm going to be okay. After Nash died, I didn't have the same thought. I remember thinking I was never going to be okay again. Now I know I will be." I gaze up at him. "Does that make me a terrible person? Does it mean I never truly loved Adam the way I thought I did? Was I simply with him because he was Adam, and it felt safe and smart and okay after all I went through losing Nash? Or am I still angry and headed to that stage of grief?"

His chin dips toward me. "Only you can answer that, kid." His voice is thick, and his breath is shaky, and I know it's because of what I just said about Nash. I'm not trying to hurt him, but I always thought of Nash as the love of my life, and Adam never quite fit that mold. That's all I was trying to say.

But in retrospect, I'm not sure either of them was. I have to imagine the love of my life is yet to come.

"Do you ever picture yourself getting back together with him?"

I hold up my left hand. "I am a married lady now."

He rolls his eyes. "I'm serious. Do you?"

I give this some serious consideration. "No. I don't. I'll never get that vision of him coming inside her out of my head. The betrayal is so absolute. Above friendship and love. There is no forgiveness or acceptance that could push it out. But more than that, I don't want to. He's not my one. I just didn't know it until now."

His eyes search mine before he looks away and rubs the top of his head, almost as if he doesn't know what to do with that. Finally, he says, "Then it's a good thing you didn't marry him."

"Is it a good thing I married you?"

His lips twitch. "Time will tell with that."

"You didn't like it when he and I got together, did you?"

He laughs lightly, almost as if he's shocked I knew that. But I did. I know Roman Fritz. He's the ventricle to my aorta. My heart doesn't beat or perfuse my organs without him pushing it along.

He chooses his words carefully. "I wanted you to be happy again. More than anything else in this world, I wanted that for you. He seemed to do that for you. With that, I liked you with him just fine."

"That's not an answer."

He blows out a strained breath. "No. I didn't like it when you got together with him."

"Why didn't you ever say anything to me? All those years he and I were together, I had an inkling, but you never talked about it, and anytime I'd ask or seek your thoughts, you never gave them to me about him."

He shrugs. "I was worried you'd date him, and it wouldn't

end well. Or that it would, and he'd take you from me because you'd be his and I'd lose what we had. But he came in and swept you off your feet, and you were happy. And things between us stayed as they were."

I can't imagine ever pulling away from Roman.

I wrap my arms around his chest and hug myself against him. He does the same in return, holding me and rocking us gently.

"I hate that I wasted so much time when I could have been doing a million other things. Meeting a million other people."

He draws back, and his chin dips. "You don't need to meet a million other people. All you need is to see what's in your world a little differently than you have before."

I go to question him when it's suddenly our turn to order, and decisions must be made. Important decisions because let's be real here, this is gelato, and it all looks delicious. After that, there's no more heavy talk. We eat gelato and wander from hotel to hotel, talking for hours, until it's almost dawn. When I'm too exhausted to make it back to our villa, he carries me the rest of the way and tucks me into bed.

And I refuse to think deeper about any of it, even if his words from the gelato line continue to recycle themselves through my mind.

13

ROMAN

The Yucatán heat nails us in the face like a one-two punch. Honestly, I'm shocked we got here. Yes, I had to come for work, but I thought after everything that happened in Vegas, Braelyn would have fled home. The girl continues to surprise me.

"Yeesh. Glad I didn't bother to straighten my hair," Braelyn comments, taking her curls and twisting them up on top of her head into a bun. Despite her best efforts, she has some gravity-defying wisps framing her face. "This humidity is no joke. All week I'm going to look like I've been electrocuted."

"That's different from how you regularly look?"

She smacks my arm, making me laugh. "Curly hair is both a blessing and a curse. Same with freckled skin and seeing how bright that sun is outside those doors, I'm going to have to be liberal with the SPF."

Yesterday, it was like she finally switched to vacation mode, shut off her brain, and stopped asking questions about the details. Then again, she was pretty fried after our all-night walk. She spent most of yesterday lounging by the pool while I was at the restaurant for a few hours, making sure everything was as it should be. Now we're here, and even though I'm here to work, being in Mexico and going to a resort for a week feels different than it did in Vegas.

"Come on. The car's waiting for us."

Her phone rings in her purse and she fishes it out, only to tense. Adam. She sends him to voicemail and a moment later, my phone rings. Great.

"Are you going to answer him?" she asks.

"Not right now."

"What will you tell him when you speak to him?"

"Not that we're married, don't worry." Shockingly, it's been an easier secret to keep than I anticipated. I simply removed my wedding band before I went to the restaurant yesterday and that was that. "I don't know. I'll figure that out before I call him back."

Without another word, I wheel our bags over to where the car is waiting for us. No luggage pickup here. We had to go through customs. The driver collects our things and we settle in for the drive. Thirty-five minutes later, we pull into the main building, and I get a look.

"This is very swanky."

"It's a reserve."

Her eyes are glued to the grounds and the Caribbean Ocean, playing peekaboo as we glide through toward the main building. "Not a resort?"

"It's both."

"Roman, I didn't say much about the villa in Vegas, but shit. I can't let you pay for me here, business expense or not. It has to be a couple of grand a night."

"I had my assistant get us another villa. It's all done. No arguing."

She huffs and folds her arms, but there is no getting over the azure water or the breathtaking landscape. I've never been down here before, and I'm already in love. We climb out of the car, shielding our eyes from the sun, and head into the cool lobby that feels like a breath of fresh air on our heated skin.

"Hola. Welcome," a greeter says, holding a tray of pink drinks with pretty flowers in them. "Hibiscus agua fresca?"

"Sí. Gracias." Braelyn accepts a glass despite her silent protest with me, and I take one as well, the cool sweetness welcome, even here in the air-conditioned lobby.

"Mr. Fritz, we're delighted you and Ms. Albright are here," the receptionist says to me as Braelyn meanders around the lobby, taking in the sculptures and art. Probably because she doesn't want to hear what I'm paying a night here. "We have you set up in one of our Cortes beachfront villas. It's on an upper floor, with magnificent views as well as a private terrace and plunge pool. I am sorry to inform you that we were unable to grant the request your assistant made for a room change. Unfortunately, our resort is full this week as it's also spring break in America and Europe."

Oh shit. That's going to cause a problem. For both of us.

"There are no other accommodations?"

"No, sir. I apologize. We have you in our finest villa, though."

He launches into a spiel about experiences that celebrate nature as well as soul-nourishing wellness rituals. The spa, the pools, the cabanas. I stop listening until he describes the other restaurants, and then I'm all ears. They already broke ground on my restaurant, and I have meetings lined up all week with designers, chefs, and restaurant managerial staff.

"Miguel will show you to your villa, señor. Please enjoy your stay and we are most excited to see your restaurant come to life here."

"Gracias. Brae?" I call out and wave for her. I don't know what the fuck I'm going to tell her about the villa and now my heart is starting to pound. I text my assistant, who replies instantly that she just got the notification about it an hour ago and has been working to see what else she can do. But there's nothing to do.

The resort is full. It's spring break in Cancun.

We follow Miguel, our personal attendant, through the property, a winding path that takes us past immaculate landscaped gardens full of tropical plants and flowers. The resort unfolds in levels down toward the ocean, with an endless blue horizon. It's paradise. No two ways about it.

We're led to our villa, a spacious oasis on the edge of the beach with all ocean views and a stunning living space, a magnificent private pool with an outdoor lounge as well as an eating area, an enormous bathroom with both an indoor and outdoor shower, and... one large king bed.

Braelyn notices it the moment I do, and her head swivels toward me with the speed of a meteor crashing to earth.

Miguel is prattling on about the hammock and temperature controls for the pool and the sound system and the fully stocked private bar. That's all great, but not anywhere close to where our focus is at the moment. She's going to eviscerate me.

I tip him generously and close the door behind him, waiting as silence expands, filling every corner of the suite.

Braelyn stands in the center of the living room, her arms folded, her expression a complex mixture of emotions that for once, I can't decipher.

"One bed," she finally says, and it's not a question. It's an accusation.

"Yes."

Her eyes narrow. "Did you request that?"

"No," I defend. "This is the villa I originally had for myself. I asked my assistant to change it to a two-bedroom suite in the main part of the hotel because they don't have two-bedroom villas here. They weren't able to accommodate us because it's spring break week."

"Roman..." She trails off and storms out toward the terrace

as if she doesn't know what to say. Slowly, I trail her and find her staring out at the ocean that stretches endlessly before us, an intense blue meeting the equally blue sky in a line so sharp it looks as though it was drawn using a ruler.

"Brae?"

"I'll let the money stuff go even if I'm not happy about it. But what do we do about the bed situation?"

"I'll press them a bit and see when another room or suite will become available," I offer.

"I can't ask you to pay for another suite or have you move."

My lips bounce as I catch the latter part, despite her deadpan tone. "I'd be the one moving, huh?"

"Well..." She pans her hands around. "I mean, yeah. Look at this place. I'm not switching rooms to something less. It's my non-honeymoon."

My eyebrows lift. "Your non-honeymoon?"

"I am technically a newlywed."

I gesture back toward the inside. "So this is our honeymoon suite then?"

"*Non*-honeymoon suite," she corrects. "Except I didn't intend to share the bed with my husband."

My hands meet the back of my head, my elbows butterflied out. "At least I know you didn't marry me for my money the way every other woman tries to."

I get an eye roll. "Your money is one of my least favorite things about you."

"So what's your favorite then?" I counter, giving her a challenging eyebrow.

She puffs out a small laugh. "I'll tell you later after we're done fighting about this."

"I can sleep on the sofa." Though the idea of spending seven nights on the admittedly beautiful but likely uncomfortable couch makes my back twinge preemptively.

She shakes her head. "You're too big for the sofa. You'll be in traction, and I don't want to have to nurse you back to health. I'm off-duty this week."

"I don't know what else to do, Braelyn. You're not going to fit on that sofa either."

She turns around, her hair that's escaping her bun whipping in the wind before she unexpectedly marches inside and through the suite to the bedroom. I follow and watch as she jumps backward onto the bed, her arms and legs spread wide like a starfish.

"What are you doing?"

"This bed is huge." She moves her arms and legs like she's making a snow angel. "We could probably both sleep here without knowing the other person is there."

My heart picks up a few extra beats, though I work to keep my expression neutral and the hope simmering in my stomach down. "You're okay with that? We'll have to share the bathroom too."

"Roman, I've seen you in nothing but your gym shorts with a split lip and possibly a fractured rib after those ridiculous fights. I've held your head and rubbed your back as you threw up tequila on my twenty-first birthday. I also walked in on you fucking... what was her name?"

I huff out a breath and climb onto the bed beside her. "I wasn't fucking her."

"You were both naked."

"I was twenty-three. That was a very long time ago."

"I know. I was seventeen, and I remember it. You look different shirtless now. More muscles and ink. I'll manage."

I prop myself up and stare down at her. "Are you sure?"

"We're both adults, and it's just sleeping."

Disappointment ripples through me, but it's no less than what I was expecting. Or what I'm used to fighting when it comes to wanting something I'll never have with her.

"Right," I agree with an empty laugh. "Just sleeping."

We stare at each other for a moment, no words passing, but a maelstrom of tension and emotions settles between us. She kissed me in the casino. It wasn't much of a kiss. Just a hard peck on the lips. The kind your grandmother would give you when you were a kid. But that's not how it felt to me. She was in my arms with her lips pressed to mine, and I know it was just the excitement of winning, but fuck, I wanted it to be real.

I wanted it to mean something to her.

I want all of it to. The bands on our hands and this time together.

Her phone rings again, snapping us out of the moment, and she flies off the bed to dig through her purse for it. Except when she sees who's calling her, she shakes her head.

"Just pick up," I tell her.

"What for? I know what he wants. He texted me about it all day yesterday. He's mad that I was photographed with you in Vegas and that it was stated and then commented on how beautiful your new girlfriend is." She bows and does a royal wave with her hand. "I accept the compliment from the critics on behalf of normal women everywhere."

I laugh. "Hate to break it to you, kid, you're not normal and never have been."

"Truth. But I don't want to fight with him right now. I want to enjoy my vacation without my ex ruining it. The whole point of this is to get away from him. At least the picture from our wedding hasn't surfaced or anything about that. That would be awful."

"I'll talk to him." I hold out my hand and she places her phone in it. I swipe my finger across her screen and answer. "Hey."

He's surprised I'm picking up her phone and replies with, "Uh, hey. Where's Braelyn?"

"She's here, but she doesn't want to talk."

He makes a noise. "So now you're her go-between?"

"Not exactly."

"Are you fucking her?"

No, but I am married to her. "Shut up, asshole," I bark.

Braelyn makes a noise, clearly able to hear what he's saying.

"I know. I'm sorry. I'm going crazy, though. You're supposed to be on my side. You're supposed to be helping me with her, but that's not how it looks in the media."

"I never said I was on your side with anything."

"What am I supposed to do with that? Or the fact that you're at a resort in Mexico together."

My eyebrows pinch. "How did you know we were already here?"

"I have her location on my phone."

"Argh! Shit. I forgot about that. Thanks for reminding me to turn it off," she calls out.

"Fucking hell," he yells. "I tried to get a hotel room in the area, but everything is booked solid. Please, Roman. You're my best friend. You were going to be the best man at my wedding. I love her. I love her so much. I fucked up, but everyone deserves a second chance. I gave you yours. Help me get mine."

My eyes close, and Braelyn takes the phone from me.

"Don't you dare guilt him. That's as fucked up as it gets. I don't want to talk to you, and I've asked you to stop calling and texting me. I will end up blocking you if you don't stop."

Immediately, he launches into his fight, and I catch half of it. I flop onto my back and blow out a breath, my palms on my forehead. I don't know what to do.

"Stop. Just stop! Seriously, shut up. I don't care if you say you love me. I don't care if you say you're sorry. We're over and we're never ever getting back together." She ends the call and the phone drops to the bed between us. We're silent for a long time. "I'm sorry."

I laugh, but there's no humor to it. "Why are you sorry?"

"Because he's making you feel like you owe him when you don't."

My eyes pinch tight.

"It wasn't your fault."

"Brae—"

"No." She rolls over onto her side and stares down at me. "It wasn't your fault, and you have to forgive yourself already for things that happened beyond your control. I know you've been carrying this guilt around with you that it was, and you've never listened to me before when I told you it wasn't. I wasn't out there that day with you, but you told us what happened. I spoke to Nash before you went out on the water. Sailing was his thing. Not yours. You didn't make the storm come in, and you didn't make the waves capsize your sailboat. You held on to him and did everything you could to save both of you. What happened was a tragic *accident*. I never blamed you, nor did your parents. If Adam is using that awful day and what happened to Nash against you, that makes him an absolute bastard above and beyond what he's already done. Life took Nash from all of us. You owe him nothing, Roman. Let's go walk around."

She climbs off the bed, leaving me here as she goes for her suitcase and then into the bathroom. The door clicks shut, and I blow out an uneven breath. I've worked to forgive myself. I've told myself there wasn't anything I could do to save him that day. That I tried, and he was taken from me. It's one thing to tell yourself something and another to believe it. Especially when your baby brother is gone and you couldn't save him and you wish to God it were you who was taken and not him.

Adam knew this and used it against me because he cheated and doesn't know how to live with the consequences of his own actions.

Braelyn's right.

I owe him nothing.

And as much as I hate the idea of going behind a friend's back, all's fair in true love, marriage, and war.

We both change, me into shorts and a T-shirt and her into a sundress that shows off the smooth skin of her back and neck beneath her hair that she's put up into a ponytail. We walk the grounds, and she takes a million pictures, half of them of me.

"Blackmail?" I quip after I catch her doing it for the fifth or so time.

"Evidence," she corrects, showing me the screen where she caught me smiling. "Roman Fritz on vacation, enjoying himself."

"Here. Let's do one together." I snatch her phone from her because my arms are longer, and I twist us so our backs are to the ocean and snap a selfie. I'm not exactly a selfie guy, but I want this one, and I forward it to myself when an email comes in from my business manager. At first, I expect it to be about my housing situation in Frankfurt, which I haven't quite figured out yet. But it's not.

I read through it quickly and sigh.

"What?"

"That TV woman I met in Vegas? She's reaching out to my people about the show she wants me on."

"The blonde? She's a persistent one."

I smirk at her. "Sound familiar? Your ex is worse."

"What can I say? We're both desirable entities."

I pause. I could tell her the woman is from Adam's company, but what's the point? She's in a good mood, having a good time, and I don't want to ruin that. Plus, I'm not taking the show, so it doesn't matter which company she works for.

"I think it's margarita time," I announce.

"Along with chips and salsa time."

"Absolutely."

Afternoon flows into evening, and we head to one of the resort's restaurants surrounded by gardens.

"Chef Fritz, we're honored to have you and your guest dining with us," the waiter says. "Our executive chef would be delighted to prepare a special tasting menu, if you'd allow it."

I glance at Braelyn, who nods excitedly. I turn back to him. "Sure. We'd love that."

"Excellent. To start, we have an amuse-bouche of grilled octopus, roasted tomatoes, cactus, lime, and cilantro. We've paired it with our house tequila. Enjoy."

The moment he's gone, Brae leans across the table to me. "Does this happen everywhere you go now? All this special treatment?"

"Only in nice restaurants or if I'm recognized, which happens way more in Boston than anywhere else," I admit. "Otherwise, it's usually only if they've been warned I'm coming."

"Warned?" Her eyebrows rise.

"I'm opening a restaurant here. It's a chef-to-chef thing. Especially chefs with certain public personas." I shrug, uncomfortable as always when this sort of thing happens to me. "It's just business. They want to be able to say I dined here and loved it."

"And will you? Love it, I mean."

"That depends on what they serve us." I hold up my small glass of tequila to her. "Cheers."

"Cheers." She takes a sip and we both taste our octopus, which is excellent. Course by course, we're wined and dined and spoiled by the chef, who comes out and chats with us for five or so minutes. She's very gracious, and she and Braelyn hit it off. She's also much better at this part than I am. I rarely leave the kitchen to talk to anyone.

By the time we finish, it's dark and we're both quiet and tired. The walk back to the suite is silent as we listen to the waves now bathed in blackness and the sound of music from a distant bar and the occasional laughter that carries on the breeze. It's comfortable and peaceful, and I know this is only our first day here, but I already don't want us to go home.

Something happened to me this afternoon. I've been fighting it. Forcing myself to hold back and not allow the thought or hope of more with her. It's too soon. I know that. Adam is very much still in the air and lingering in her heart despite what she says. But this time with her can build on what we already have. It might even allow her to start seeing me in a different way than she ever has before.

And maybe, if I'm seriously fucking lucky, it'll start to turn her heart in my direction.

I don't know what that'll mean for the plans I already have in place, but that's a later Roman problem.

We head out to the terrace and Braelyn goes straight for the hammock, kicking off her sandals and settling in with ease.

"I'm claiming this as my territory for the remainder of the trip. You can have that lounger over there." She points lazily in the direction of a chaise.

I sit on the edge of the pool and drip my feet in. It's cool but not cold, and it feels good against the pervasive humidity. "Very generous of you."

"Actually, it's you who's generous," she counters, rocking ever so slightly. "This is all very you. You have a way of taking something that would have been one thing and turning it into something extraordinary. You were right. This trip is exactly what I needed and if I had stayed home, everything would have been Adam and my canceled wedding and a lot of tears and moping."

"I have my moments."

She gives me a serious look. "No. It's you. You make everything... better. Special. Honestly, I think you're the best thing to ever happen to me."

My heart thumps painfully in my chest, and I return her look with one of my own. "You are to me," I tell her, wondering if she can hear it in my voice. The fucking hope I feel right now simply being with her and hearing her say that.

"Thank you, Roman. For everything."

I grin. "Anytime, kid."

"I'm going to take a shower and get to bed. I'm fried."

"Go ahead. I'll wait out here before I take my turn."

She disappears into the suite, and I'm out here alone, lost in my thoughts, stuck somewhere between what Hayes and Crew said and what Forest said. Patience versus going for it. I've maintained boundaries with her since I was twenty-five and came to see her as something more than my best friend or my brother's girl. It was never our time, but now our lines are blurring, and all I can think about is erasing them completely.

When I finally enter the bedroom, Braelyn is already under the covers on the far side of the bed, her damp hair spread across her pillow as she reads on her e-reader.

"Bathroom's all yours," she murmurs without looking up.

"Thanks."

I take my time in the shower, using the space to compose

myself. I'm going to share a bed with her tonight, and my stupid dick is nothing short of excited. I jerk off twice for good measure, and by the time I get into bed, the room is dark and cool. But with that, I'm hyperaware of the space between us. Of her soft breathing and sweet scent.

"Night, kid."

"Night, Ro." Then a pause. "This is weird, right?"

I laugh quietly, putting my hands behind my head, my elbows out across the pillow. "A little, yeah."

"But not bad weird?"

"No," I answer easily. "Not bad weird."

She shifts slightly and the mattress dips with her movement. "Good, because I'm really glad we're here. Together, I mean."

My heart pounds painfully against my ribs. "Me too." I close my eyes, willing my body to relax. And when I'm positive she's asleep, her breathing deep and heavy, I whisper, "This is just our start, kid. I'm gonna make you fall so hard for me. I dare you."

"You know I'm not really a massage or spa kind of guy, right?" I say to Braelyn as she drags me along the stone path from our suite toward the spa.

"It'll be good for you," she explains. "We have an appointment with the sensei for a wellness consultation too."

I give her my best *what the fuck does that mean* look. "Braelyn, I'm not sure I even have words for that."

"It's for our mind-body wellness. When the concierge called the room this morning and offered it to us, I jumped."

I sigh. "They want us to post about it online or something. They likely saw the pictures from Vegas."

She gasps and covers her mouth with her hand.

"Not the wedding picture. The picture from the soft opening. If anything, people think you're my girlfriend, not my wife. I'm not a travel blogger. I'm a chef. One who doesn't particularly like the limelight or people I don't know."

She snorts. "And yet you're like one of the most famous chefs out there so..." She trails off with a shrug.

"Not by choice."

"Bro, you just opened another restaurant in Vegas and are going to do the same here at this fancy resort."

And three more in Europe, but who's counting?

"Bro? Did you just bro me?"

She beams at me, and why is that look so fucking irresistible? I'm already melting at it, my resistance for a sensei and a wellness consultation pooling at my feet in a lame-ass puddle.

"I did. Come on. It might be just the thing to relax all those tense muscles. And think about your forehead. If you keep scowling and furrowing at everyone, the amount of Botox you'll need will deplete your trust fund."

I roll my eyes. "You're very funny."

I get a cheeky wink. "I have my moments. Come on. We get a couple's massage and body scrub out of this."

"Couples?"

"Yeah, that's just what they offered me. They think we're an item. Besides, they have a hydrotherapy room and a beachfront pool." She pats the large tote bag on her shoulder. "I brought my swim stuff, and you're already in trunks. It's perfect."

"*We* have a beachfront pool."

"Are you always this much of a downer on vacation?"

My lips reluctantly twitch. "I can't remember."

"I want to be scrubbed and rubbed and come out like a shiny new coin on the other side."

I open my mouth, only to immediately close it. That talk of getting scrubbed and rubbed suddenly has my stupid dick getting chub. Maybe it'll be hot. A couple's massage sounds like that, but it also sounds like torture.

"You'd better have a female masseuse," I mutter, but of course, she doesn't. We meet with the sensei, who asks us a million questions about our health routine and goals and blah, blah, fucking blah. Not my thing. Braelyn, ever the nurse, is loving it, so I play along.

After we're done with him and he's tailored our treatments to our health needs, we're each brought to a gender-specific side of the spa and given robes to change into. I leave my briefs on, not knowing if I'm supposed to get fully naked, especially when I know Brae will be in the room with me. Then again, I'm now thinking about Braelyn getting fully naked, and once again, my stupid dick is acting like an eager-beaver high school kid.

Not an uncommon thing with me when it comes to her, but I had it better in check until we shared a bed last night. I woke up hard as a rock and have pretty much been in varying stages of that since this trip began.

"Señor Fritz," the attendant calls. "This way, please." I'm led down a hall that smells of rosemary and citrus into a treatment room. There are two beds about three feet apart, a large shower with a glass door, shiny green glass tiles, and multiple shower-heads. I don't understand the shower, but then again, I don't exactly find myself in spas, well, ever. Instead, I focus on the two beds when Braelyn walks in wearing a similar robe to mine.

My throat dries. "Hi."

"Hi." She licks her lips and shifts her weight, looking at me and then looking away.

"Are we supposed to get on the table?" I ask.

She shrugs. "My attendant told me to wait for our technicians."

Before I can respond, the door opens, and a man and a woman enter, each holding two glasses filled with an orangish-pink liquid.

"It's our antioxidant, purifying cooler," the woman explains and hands one to each of us. Brae and I exchange looks, but both drink it down. It's tart as fuck but oddly delicious and refreshing. "We'll leave the room, and you can both remove your robes and get onto the tables face up to start. There are towels to cover yourselves."

Then they leave, and I blink at Braelyn, blood already pulsing loudly through my ears, making my brain slower than perhaps I otherwise might be.

"I'm only in my briefs."

She laughs, but it's strained. "I'm in nothing but a thong."

I choke and cover my face with my hands, breathing out slowly so I don't collapse. "Jesus, fuck, Brae."

"Clearly, I didn't think all this through when I agreed. Turn around, and I'll get on the table first, and then you can. I've seen you in your briefs."

"Yeah, well, I haven't seen you in only a thong." I turn around, trying not to listen as she gets undressed and onto the table, but I have bigger problems at the moment, and yes, once again I'm talking about my dick. Because I'm going to embarrass myself when I'm lying on a table and pitching a fucking tent under the towel.

I adjust myself, but it's useless. There is no hiding it, and when she says, "I'm ready," all I can think is, *I am too.*

Keeping my back to her, I remove my robe, hang it on the hook beside hers, remove my uncomfortable flip-flops, and climb onto the bed. I don't look at her. I don't. But it's like my peripheral vision is running the show, and I catch flashes of her with two towels covering her tits and pussy.

The bed is heated, which isn't great, considering I'm already sweating. I stare up at the ceiling and think about how to make croquembouche, a complex French dessert that is a test of time and patience.

It works for a bit, especially since neither of us is talking now, but then the attendants walk back in and the guy goes for Braelyn and the woman for me, and I hate this. All of this. He's going to touch her when she's practically naked, and I'm not. Adding to that, the woman snaps on gloves before she dollops a cold, goopy salt concoction onto my body and starts scrubbing the hell out of my skin.

The only good thing about it is that it gets rid of my hard-on because it fucking hurts. By the time she's done, I'll be completely raw, bleeding, and lucky if my tattoos are still visible.

After the longest fifteen minutes of my life, she tells me to roll over and does the same torture to my backside.

"Now you can both shower," the technician tells us. "Just press the button on the wall when you're done, and we'll be in five minutes after that. Make sure you dry off before you get back onto the bed, face down to start."

They leave us alone, and I blow out a harsh breath.

"You are so grounded."

She laughs. "Do you remember how often our parents used to say that to us?"

I don't reply. I'm trying to figure out how this will work without me showering essentially naked with my best friend. Because while she's my best friend, I'm also seriously in love with her and seriously attracted to her. To where I don't even see other women at this point.

It's all her.

She's the most beautiful. The funniest. The smartest. The sexiest. Other women are gray, while Braelyn is painted in every color.

"Braelyn... I can't shower with you like that." *I'll touch you. I'll touch you everywhere. I'll fuck you in the goddamn shower, spa technicians and a lifetime of friendship be damned.*

"No. Agreed. Do you wanna go first?"

"This was supposed to be fun and relaxing, right? This is the opposite of that. You owe me... I don't know. I'll think of something, but my skin feels like a tuna."

She giggles. "A tuna?"

I climb off the bed and head for the shower, keeping the towel around my waist, forcing myself not to look at the bed beside mine. "Yes. A tuna. I just had my skin flayed off me and now it feels like my flesh is being seared. Is it supposed to burn?"

Suddenly, it's like my skin is on fire while someone is taking pins dipped in acid and stabbing me with them.

"Ah! I don't know. Hurry up. Because it's totally burning me now too."

"Shit. You go first."

Her hands wave frantically through the air. "No. Just do it fast."

"That's the first time a woman has ever said that to me."

She laughs, but it's pained. "Not funny."

I start the water to cold instead of hot. "Get in the shower with me."

"But..."

"I won't look. I'll keep my eyes closed. But we have to get this salt off us now."

She screeches, and I hear her moving, but I drop the towel and get my ass in the shower. Immediately, I start to rub the scrub off, pumping copious amounts of bodywash onto my hands and lathering it everywhere I can.

"Wash your body, kid. It's helping."

The shower door bangs behind her, and then she's pushing into one of the streams.

"Oh my god! I thought this was supposed to be pleasurable. It's horrible."

I stand with my back to her, refusing to move from the cold water of my stream. Lucky for me, between the burning on my skin and the ice water dumping down on me, I'm not exactly thinking about her being naked.

"Are you okay? Is your skin burned or anything?" I ask, peeking open my eyes to take in my chest, which shockingly isn't even red.

"No." Then she laughs incredulously. "Actually, it's softer than a baby's ass. Feel."

"Is that meant to be a joke?"

More giggling. "I meant feel your skin." Then her hand is on my back, and what the actual fuck is she trying to do to me? "Oh, yours is too. Maybe we just didn't move fast enough into the shower."

I feel my arms and abs, and yeah, they're soft and there's no burning or even redness. It's like magic but magic I don't want to ever have done to me again.

"I'll get out first," she offers. "There are heated towels on the rack right beside the shower. I'll cover the girls and my ass, and once I'm back on the table, I'll call out for you."

"I don't want him touching you." My eyes close. I don't know why I said that, but now that my skin isn't on fire anymore, I don't want to spend the next hour on a bed where I'm subjected to another man touching her.

She's silent for a minute, and when she speaks, her voice is soft and apologetic. "Do you want to skip the massage and go hang out by the pool instead?"

I inwardly sigh and press my forehead into the wall as I shut off the cold water. "No. You want the massage. I'm just..." Being childish, I guess. A caveman.

I want to pick her up and drag her back to my lair and keep her there, where no man can ever see her or touch her again. Not exactly rational. She's not mine, and who knows if she'll ever be, and it's not the first time I've had to stand on the side-lines with her and watch her with another man. I've done it throughout her entire relationship with Adam.

I get out of the shower and wrap a towel around my waist. "You know what? I think I'll go to the gym and burn off some of this energy. I'll meet you at the pool after. Enjoy your massage."

"But—"

"No, really. Please, stay and relax and enjoy it. You deserve it. I'm going to go for a run or hit a bag or something."

Her hands plant onto my shoulder blades, and I shudder. "Are you okay?"

No. And I don't know why. I love being here with her, and I love this time together, but I'm starting to struggle in ways I never have before, and it's pissing me off. I want her to have the best time, and I'm being moody.

"I just need to get my shit back in line, and I think a run or something will help."

"Your shit back in line?"

I shake my head, my fist clenching. What the fuck is wrong with me right now?!

"Enjoy your massage, kid. I'll see you at the pool in an hour."

Without waiting for her to say anything and definitely without looking, I grab my robe and flip-flops and get the fuck out of here. In the locker room, I change back into my clothes and head to the gym, which is right next door to the spa. No punching bag, not that I expected one. Rarely do I ever find them in gyms that don't have training for boxers.

Instead, I pop in my AirPods and hit the trail that winds around the resort. I feel bad that I bailed on her, but there's only so much a man can take, and after sharing a bed with her and knowing she was essentially naked and another man was going to touch her—even if in a non-sexual way—I'm just done.

I'm not in the mood for music. Instead, I call Forest.

"Hey," he answers after the second ring. "How's it going in Mexico?"

I haven't talked to my friends much since I left Boston. I haven't updated them except in our text chat, and I've been vague because frankly there hasn't been much to say. I launch into an account of everything that's been going on, omitting the wedding part because Brae asked me to keep it a secret, and then he's patching Crew and Hayes into this.

Hayes is in Paris, and I hear him say something to a woman in the background. So naturally, we all ask, "Who's that?"

"It's nothing," he replies quickly. "Just work. Tell me what's going on in Mexico."

Except Paris is six hours ahead of me, and it's late into the night there. Hayes is keeping something—or more like someone—from us. And it better not be who I think it is because I don't want to see him get hurt again. Still, I launch into yet another rendition of the saga of Roman and Braelyn while my friends listen intently. I had two sets of friends growing up. Nash and Braelyn, even though they're six years younger than me, and eventually Adam once they started high school, and these guys along with Skylar and Quinn. Braelyn is also friends with my friends, and so was Nash, which is likely why it all flowed together so well.

Only Adam never really became friends with them. Nash and then Braelyn were his connections. But this is when having a female on the line, like Skylar or Quinn, would help, but they're Braelyn's besties and therefore, that's a no.

"What if you just tell her?" Crew asks. "Oh, or you should go back into that massage room, kick that dude straight out of the room, and do the massage on her yourself."

"Right. That'll go over well." I shake my head as I pick up my pace, my feet pounding the stone path while sweat streaks down my body against the hot sun and humid air, but I revel in it.

"Maybe it would," Hayes suggests. "She set up a *couple's* spa appointment for you both."

"I think the resort did all of that," I tell them.

"Except she didn't say no, we're not a couple, and we'd prefer separate treatment rooms and spaces," Forest protests. "She went in there only wearing a robe and a thong, knowing you'd both be in the same room. Women don't do that with men they solely consider friends."

I come to a screeching halt, nearly toppling over with how fast my feet stop moving even if my momentum doesn't. "What do you mean?"

"What he means is that Brae would never do that with me," Crew jumps in. "Never in a million years would she do a couples massage and be naked beneath her robe if I were in the room. Think about it, brother. Could you picture Quinn doing that? No. Not ever. And I'd kill you if she ever did, but that's a different matter."

My lips bounce at that. It's not like he could use Skylar in that inference because she's my cousin. Still...

"You're saying..."

"We're saying whether she's aware of it or not, she's starting to think of you as more than simply her best friend," Hayes states flatly.

"Yes," Forest agrees. "She's testing boundaries. So maybe you should start testing some back."

My massage was amazing even if Roman didn't stay for it. I don't know what happened in that shower or why he fled like that. It's not like I was going to jump him naked or anything, though I'll be honest, Roman Fritz in nothing but skin-tight black boxer briefs is a sight to behold. One I've ignored throughout our friendship, but him in the shower with water running down his muscles...

And I need to stop that now.

I think sharing a bed with him has scrambled my brain. You know, like everything freaking else in my life at the moment.

The sun is hot and the spa pool isn't very crowded. It's quiet and peaceful, and I've parked myself on a chaise under an umbrella while I wait for Roman. I slink down on the towel, a happy smile on my relaxed face. I could live like this forever.

On the flip side of that, I can't live with Roman forever. That's something I'm going to have to figure out. My apartment was Adam's and now I'm essentially homeless and need to find something new that I can afford on my nursing salary. I could stay at Roman's as long as I need to. I know this. But honestly, the sooner I can move out of his place, the better.

I'm starting to... well, I don't know. Things feel a little different between us, and I can't tell if my thoughts or even some of the feelings I'm having are real or rebound or bitterness or what.

I need to find my own place and start a new life by myself. I need to get myself back to a place where it doesn't feel like the earth beneath my feet is constantly moving. I'm in an emotionally precarious place. Obviously since I freaking married Roman on a drunken dare and a whim.

I don't want to do anything that can't be undone or that I'll regret.

Right now it's not such a big deal. We'll get a divorce when we get back, and that'll be that. But... the way I feel with him lately isn't as easy to abolish.

My eyes close and I try to relax, but it's not happening. I've taken all my chill and washed it away. Now I'm unsettled and jittery with it. Slipping off my chair, I pull the brim of my Rebels hat lower on my head and slide into the cool water of the pool. It only goes up to my waist and I dip down lower until it meets my chin. Then I pace, back and forth, my arms moving like a wave, propelling me along.

I don't know how many times I do this, but a tingling awareness, like someone is watching me, prickles the back of my neck. I glance up to find I was right. Roman is leaning against a stone pillar in the shade, with his arms folded over his sweaty shirt and his sea glass eyes on me, fitted with an unreadable expression.

My heart gives a thump, and a weird, fluttery kind of nerves tickle my belly.

This is what I'm talking about. This reaction to him. What the fuck is it, and how do I make it stop?

"How long have you been watching me?" I ask, standing back up to my full height and letting the sun bake off the drops of water clinging to my upper half.

His eyes do a quick sweep of me. "Not too long."

"Did you have a good run?"

"I did actually. It was enlightening. You seem a bit unsettled."

"Just thinking about having to get a place now that I moved out of Adam's."

He frowns. "There's no rush on that."

I swallow and nod, my hands running along the top of the water, making swirly patterns with it. "I'm just glad he and I never bought a place together as we had talked about. It'll make moving on easier. Hopefully, for both of us."

"I doubt he's moving on that easily. You're impossible to let go of."

He steps out of the shadow, toes off his sneakers, pulls off his sweaty T-shirt, and comes straight into the pool. He goes under, only to immediately pop back up, and my eyes land on his nipples that harden, the goose bumps on his tanned skin, and the way rivers of water flow over his ink. My face heats, and I turn away.

Cold, wet fingers on my shoulder startle me, and my head snaps over.

"You're getting more freckles," he explains.

My breath hiccups at his touch, and I can feel my own nipples hardening in my bathing suit. Something he could very easily see if he looked.

"I freckle the moment I set foot in the sun. That's not new." I pull away from him and push through to one of the built-in loungers they have in the water and climb on it.

"How was your massage?" he asks.

"Good. It was nice. You could have stayed."

He sighs and sinks back down into the water, but his gaze hasn't left mine. "No, kid, I couldn't. I was already struggling enough with you being naked beside me in there."

Guilt gnaws at me. I didn't mean to make him uncomfortable. "I didn't realize it would be that big of a deal. I figured we'd be in the dark and have robes and drapes over us. It's not like you saw anything." A memory flickers through my head, and I start laughing. "Do you remember when I came to your grandparents' compound for brunch, and you accidentally walked into the bathroom as I was pulling up my underwear?"

The first smile I've seen on him all day hits his lips. My heart feels lighter for it as some of the tension and strain I was feeling evaporate.

"You mean when you yelled at me before slamming the door in my face because I barely caught a flash of your pussy?"

"Yes." I laugh a bit harder. "That was horrifying."

"You didn't talk to me the rest of the day."

I splash water at him. "I was embarrassed. I was only nineteen or twenty."

"You were twenty. I was twenty-six. I was home visiting from Paris." He splashes me back. "That was a rough day. I felt like such a pervert because I got hard over seeing you like that."

I gasp and sit up straight on the sunbed, the plastic crinkling beneath my ass. "You what?"

He shrugs.

"You never told me that!"

He laughs at my reaction and sits on the curved end of the sunbed, lifting my feet and dropping them on his lap. "Damn right I never told you that. You never would have talked to me again."

"Oh my god! That's crazy. Have you gotten hard over me other times besides that?"

He gives me a stern look. "Braelyn, do not ask me that unless you truly want the answer and the repercussions with it."

I hold up my hands. "Fine. I'm changing the subject."

The waiter interrupts us. "Good afternoon. Can I get you anything to eat or drink?"

"We'll each have a frozen margarita, and we'll share a chicken quesadilla and an order of chips with guacamole, please."

"Very good, señor."

The guy leaves us, and I shift to my friend. "Truth or dare?"

He chokes. "What? Are we teenagers again?"

"You were never really a teenager when I was."

"You never really acted like every other teenage girl," he parries. "It's why I could handle being friends with you."

I preen a bit. "Nash helped with that. Maybe Skylar too, because I never hung out with other teenage girls much because they were all such bitches to her. But it got me thinking. Come on. Play with me."

He cocks an eyebrow, and I arch one in return, not backing down despite the bold innuendo.

"Fine. Truth."

I snicker. "Wimp."

He flicks water at me again. "If you're going to be judgy, I won't play. Besides, I think we've gotten into enough trouble from dares on this trip."

"Ugh. So temperamental, husband." I roll my eyes, feigning annoyance. "Fine. What's the biggest turn-on for you?" I ask because now I'm curious. Him telling me I made him hard that afternoon is something I never expected to hear.

"Confidence," he answers easily.

I lean back on the sun chair but splash him. "That's such a job interview reply."

He tosses his hands up. "You can't rate my answers, kid. If I said sexy nurses with pretty brown eyes and tons of curls, you'd hit me."

That earns more water on his chest. "Now you're teasing me."

Something flickers across his face, and he shakes his head ever so slightly. "What about you?"

"Honesty." My answer comes just as fast.

"Now who's giving generic answers?"

I give him a meaningful look. "I think right now I'm entitled to mine. You saying confidence is lame, considering you don't do girlfriends. You just fuck your way around." Then something hits me because now that I think about it, I can't remember the last time I saw him with anyone. "When was the last time you went on a date?"

He laughs. "Nice try. My turn to ask. Truth or dare?"

"Dare."

Our food and drinks are delivered and set on a table by the edge of the pool. He hands me my drink, but for a moment, our food is left untouched.

"Tell me something that'll make me hard."

Instead, it makes me blush and my breath quicken. "How will I know if I do?"

He smirks. "I could show you. But perhaps maybe I'll just tell you."

"You're sitting in the cold pool."

"Then it seems like you have your work cut out for you."

Shit. "No way! This is a bad idea."

He tilts his head and takes a sip of his drink. "You started this, kid."

Oh my god, I so did. "Fine." I bring my glass up to my lips and intentionally drag my tongue up the side of it and through the ring of salt before I take a sip from my straw, pointedly sucking hard on it. "Mmm." I lick my lips. "That tastes so good," I say in my best porn star voice. Then I give him a long once-over and lean in toward him, ignoring the smell and heat of his skin as I get closer to his ear. "I bet you'd taste better. Would you like me to find out?"

He shivers, his breath hitching, and hell, his reaction and the thought of making him hard are riling me up. I instantly pull back and take another sip of my drink until I give myself a freaking brain freeze. Anything to stop this reaction.

"Nicely done," he tells me before glancing down into the water at his dick in his trunks.

"Why, thank you." I bat my eyelashes at him, ignoring the static tension now prickling between us or how much I like the idea that I just made him hard. "Your turn."

"To make you wet?"

I roll my eyes but mentally think, too late. Ugh. This is bad. "Truth or dare?"

"Truth."

I squint at him. "You look way too pleased with yourself right now."

"Oh, I am. Pleased, that is."

I smack his shoulder. "No more innuendo."

"That's the entire point of this game. Anyone who argues that is a liar. I'm going with truth again."

And I'm steering us away from all the sexy stuff. "Damn you. Fine. What's something you've never told me before because you thought it would be weird?"

He's silent for a very long moment, his eyes blinking slowly as he thinks. He drags a thumb across his bottom lip and looks down at the water where his left hand that's sporting his wedding band, which he rarely takes off except at work, despite the risk of getting found out, is.

"That you're the only woman I could ever picture falling in love with or marrying."

My heart thunders, and now I'm staring down at the water. I know it's likely because Roman isn't the type of man who falls in love, and I'm not sure I could picture him settling down and getting married to anyone. Not for real. But still. It's hitting me, and it's hitting hard. I don't know how to reply to that.

"Truth or dare?" he asks, saving me from having to try.

"Dare."

"Show me your favorite place to be kissed and let me kiss you there."

Holy fuck. If I thought my heart was racing before. I should stop this now. I know I should. Hell, I never should have started it and I certainly hadn't meant for it to go this way this fast.

But I actually go with the truth and it's that truth right now that will save me. Save us.

I point to my forehead, and a smile curls up his lips as if he already knew I was going to say that. Without hesitation, he lifts up from the curve of the sunbed and comes straight for me, his eyes on mine, and I inhale a shaky breath and hold it. My hand clutches my drink, my other hand balling into a fist.

He lifts the brim of my hat, and just as he reaches my forehead, my eyes close. His lips are soft and firm as they feather along my skin. Then he's pressing them deeper into the center, and his hand comes around to hold the back of my head. He kisses my forehead, his lips holding still for the longest minute of my life, my body filling with a sweet ache and a sense of... longing?

Is that what this is? I don't know. How can that be? I hate feeling this confusion. This unsettled, *I don't know what's happening or even how I feel about it*, sensation.

Then he pulls away and retakes his seat as if none of that happened.

"Truth or dare?" I whisper.

"Truth."

I knew he was going to say that. And because we're doing this and I've always wondered and I doubt he'd tell me otherwise, I ask, "Do you ever wonder what would have happened after if we'd kissed that night? If you hadn't stopped me?" Or if I hadn't been drunk or his dead brother's ex.

His eyes pierce into mine. "I know exactly what would have happened. You just weren't ready for it."

17

BRAELYN

The schooner cuts through the water that glitters like melted sapphires in the late afternoon sun. I lean against the railing, sipping a delicious margarita, letting the salt mist spray my face and frizz the fuck out of my hair. We've been at the resort for three days now, and Roman hasn't been in the ocean once. Honestly, I'm shocked he suggested this. To the best of my knowledge, this is the first time he's been on a sailboat since his capsized off the coast of Martha's Vineyard, and Nash was swallowed by a freak storm and rough tides.

Roman worked all day at his restaurant. I didn't join him. I needed a bit of space this morning, and I spent that time talking to my parents and even searching for apartments while I hung around on the beach.

Roman stands beside me, his profile sharp against the impossibly blue horizon. He's a beast of a man. All tall and broad, with dark lines. His short hair gently rustles against his forehead in the wind, and his pale blue-green eyes look almost colorless against the sun and water. Then there's his ink, vivid against tanned skin and sunshine.

Our game of truth or dare in the spa pool yesterday ended after he answered my question about the kiss. He ended it, I should say, by getting up and sitting under an umbrella and eating lunch. I joined him, and we morphed into regular conversation, and that was that. But it's been sitting with me, and I can't shake it.

But I'm trying to. I'm desperate to return to us as we've been since I was a kid.

So far, this boat ride is living up to the hype. The catamaran is sleek and spacious, carrying maybe twenty other guests who scatter themselves across the various seating options, sipping complimentary margaritas and taking photos against the spectacular backdrop. The sun is starting to hang low, beginning its descent toward the horizon.

"What's that?" I ask, noting the underside of his hand as he rests his wrists on the railing.

"What?" he replies, turning from the water to glance down at me.

I take a sip of my drink because damn do these people know how to do a margarita, but I use my other hand to tap his left ring finger just beneath his knuckle. "It looks like a sideways teardrop or something."

I've never noticed it before. Then again, I don't regularly study his ink and it's on his palmar side. I know he has his brother's name and date of death on his arm. I know he has a chef's knife on his forearm with the words *live by the sword* beneath it. I know he has a raven for his mom, whose name is Raven, and a bunch of other things. But I never really paid attention to the tattoos on his hands, even when I'm cleaning them up after his fights. Probably because I'm more concerned about the cuts and abrasions than I am anything else.

"It's nothing. Just something I did one night a few years back," is his flippant response, which naturally makes me study it closer. Still, I legit can't figure it out.

"Okay." I pause and nudge him with my elbow. "You're quiet. Why are we doing this? Sunset cruises aren't exactly your style."

"Do you remember that day?"

Shit. My head bows, and my insides tumble straight into the sea. "Yes, I remember that day." I didn't go with them to the Vineyard, but I talked to Nash a few times that morning. It was two weeks after our two-year anniversary. We were eighteen and planning to go to school together in Boston. Then I got the call, and I think I died that day along with him. Nash was my first everything. The guy I gave my heart to and loved with everything I had.

Maybe that's why I'm not more broken up over Adam. Maybe I simply tried to transfer what I felt for Nash over to him. I don't know anymore. Everything is so confusing. I digress.

Roman completely shut down. Lost himself. Went somewhere so dark, I'm not sure how he returned. Actually, I'm not sure he fully did. And there were whispers. Roman was the adult, and Nash was still a kid. Why didn't they have life jackets on? How could Roman let go of Nash's hand? All the things they said, and Roman blamed himself harder than anyone could.

Roman and I had been close before that. But that brought our friendship to the next level. I stayed by his side, and I've been here ever since.

My head falls to his shoulder, and I step closer to him, needing the contact but also sensing he does too. As if proving my point, his hand wraps around my waist, and he holds me.

"I live above the water, and I stare out at it every day, thinking about Nash. About where he'd be and what he'd been doing and how his life would look. If he'd be married to you and if you'd have children. But this is the first time I've been back on the water. I know it's not possible that he's here. We were off the coast of New England, and likely a whale or shark or something ate him—"

I gasp and sob at once, but he presses on.

"—but still. I like the idea that he's down there looking up at us and smiling that smile." He looks down at me. "Do you remember that smile?"

Tears are all over my face, but I manage a nod because I do remember that smile. It could light up remote villages at midnight.

"So you brought us on a booze cruise to make me cry?"

He smiles at my attempt at humor and wipes my tears with his hand. "I don't talk about him a lot and I've been thinking that's not the healthiest approach. If you don't talk about him, then it's like he never existed. Like he never happened."

"Like documenting."

"Huh?"

My lips curl up on one side. "I had a nursing school professor who told me that if you don't document something, it didn't happen."

"Where do you think he'd be if he hadn't died?"

This might be the first time Roman has ever said that in a way that didn't imply that he killed him. It was a freak accident. The two of them were out in the water sailing around when a rainstorm blew in out of nowhere. Not uncommon off the coast of New England, but it brought rough waves with the rain, and one capsized their small boat. They were holding hands over the hull when another wave came and tore Nash from Roman's hands.

Roman dove into the water and searched for him, but he never found him, no matter how many attempts he made. Roman was in that water for three hours before he was rescued by the Coast Guard, clinging to the boat and screaming for his brother. They never wore lifejackets. Maybe that's stupid, but

Nash was a professional sailor, and from the time he was sixteen on, he stopped wearing one.

Since then, darkness has lived inside of Roman. A perpetual anger. A need for control. An unsettled quietness that if you don't know him or why he's this way, seems elusive and makes him mysterious and a bit of a dick. It's sexy to women and alluring to men, but he shies away from all of that. He's just Roman. Quiet and soulful and deep and broken, but with the heart of a lion.

"I like to think he would have become a doctor as he said he wanted to. I think he would have worked with your father as a neurosurgeon. He would have settled down and gotten married and had a dozen kids."

"With you, you mean."

I smile up at him. "Maybe. Who knows. We were kids back then and had a lot of growing up to do."

His fingers graze along my cheek and his hand on my waist tightens. "I always felt like I robbed you of your future with him."

"You didn't rob me of anything. Life took him. Not you."

His eyes dance about my face, and a soft smile hits his lips. "You're so fucking beautiful."

He holds my eyes and inches in ever so slightly. My heart starts a drumroll, and I grip my drink so hard I'm shocked I'm not cracking the plastic. My belly tightens with an uncontrollable flutter. Because it feels like... like he's going to kiss me. Like he *wants* to kiss me, and I don't know what to do. If I want him to kiss me or not. I don't know what happens to us, to me, if I let him.

Would it be just a kiss or would it turn into sex? Just a vacation thing?

Or would it be the start of something else? We're technically married, and that complicates this further. I can't sleep with my fake husband.

Am I even ready for that with anyone?

He dips again, his thumb dragging along my cheek. "Brae," he whispers, and I don't know what comes over me, but I shift toward him and put my hand on his chest. His heart is pounding beneath my palm, but before he can do something crazy like kiss me, a woman screams across the boat, and we break apart.

"Help! My son! He was leaning over to see a fish and fell overboard."

There's a flurry of gasps and cries for help, but before anyone can respond, Roman is racing across the boat and without stopping, flips himself over the railing and dives straight into the ocean.

Panic seizes me, and I run, my stomach slamming into the railing as I frantically search the choppy blue water. The sails are lowered, and the boat slows to a crawl. A horn wails through the air, and two attendants are armed with life rafts, searching the water as I am.

"There!" a woman cries, pointing to the left behind the boat about twenty yards back. "There they are. He has him."

Relief like I've never felt before slams through me, settling some of the adrenaline that had taken over. My knees threaten to buckle beneath me and more tears spring to my eyes.

Two life rafts are tossed right at them. Roman grabs one of them and secures the boy onto it by wrapping the strap around his chest and making sure he's holding on tight so they can haul him in before he does the same for himself with the other raft.

I run to the back of the ship where they're lowering a platform for them. An attendant waves me back. "Señorita, please stand back."

"I'm a nurse. I can help."

He reads the expression on my face that tells him I'm not going anywhere because he lets me stay. They pull the boy, who isn't much older than twelve or thirteen, up onto the ship and his mother all but dives on him, holding him tightly. He's obviously soaking wet, but his color is good and doesn't appear to have swallowed or breathed in too much water.

"I'm fine," the boy tells her, sitting up and removing the strap from his body. "He saved me. I didn't go under for long. He found me right away."

Roman is next, and the moment he's on the dry dock, I launch myself at him the way that mother threw herself on her son.

"Oh my god!" I wrap my arms around him and check his face and body. "Are you okay?"

He nods. "I'm okay."

I'm shaking, gasping for control as he pulls the life raft away from his body. The moment he's clear, I climb on his lap and wrap my arms around him, hugging his wet body fiercely.

"You can't ever do that to me again," I tell him, half-sobbing against him.

He hugs me back, his face in my neck. "I'm okay, baby. I swear, I'm fine."

My eyes pinch shut. He just called me baby, and he's never done that before. I don't know what it means or why he said it, but right now, I don't care because he's alive.

"Señor, you're bleeding."

"What?" I pull back and shift, noting the attendant's face before glancing down at Roman. Sure enough, he's bleeding from a large laceration on his hand.

"I think it's from the rope," he tells me. "It's not that bad."

I give him a *who the fuck are you kidding* look and take his hand onto my lap so I can examine it. Blood is oozing continuously from the wound and dripping down his wrist and all over my lap.

"You need stitches."

He's not amused.

"What? You do. You know you do."

"I've had worse cuts in the kitchen." He flexes his hand and winces slightly, more blood pouring out. "Shit. Fine. Can you do them?"

"With what? Fishing wire and a hook? I'm not freaking MacGyver, and it needs to be cleaned out. Especially if the rope sliced it. Those things are dirty as hell. I don't want to think about the microbes living on that."

The attendant hands him a clean washcloth to put over his wound to help with the bleeding.

He sighs, and I smack his shoulder. "What was that for?" he asks.

"For giving me a heart attack. Now that you're okay, I can hit you for it."

His lips twitch, but the mother and son come over, and I climb off his lap so they can thank him. They're both a mess, hugging Roman and showering him with praise and gratitude that he brushes off because that's Roman. Once everything is secured, the sailboat turns around and uses the engine to bring us back into port.

The sunset booze cruise is over.

When we arrive back on dry land, we're handed towels and offered tokens of appreciation, including free robes and drinks, and a complimentary spa treatment, but told that for stitches, he needs to go to the local ER. We do a quick change, and the resort has a driver take us thirty minutes away to a hospital.

Roman throws me a look when we enter the overcrowded ER, teeming with people.

"Ah, home sweet home," I drawl.

He rolls his eyes at me, but we go and check in. Roman and I both speak Spanish, though his is way better than mine. They inform us it'll be a six-hour wait, give or take.

"No," he tells me flatly. "Abso-fucking-lutely not. I'm going to purchase the supplies that I'm positive they'll sell me with cash, then we'll go back, and you'll do it."

"Fine. Let's do that."

"Fantastic, I'll be right back."

Roman walks off, and I let him do his thing, watching as he goes up to the counter and talks with someone, only to remember he has no clue all the things I'll need. I head in his direction, but now he's speaking with a crying woman holding a crying baby.

I don't catch every word. As I said, my Spanish is decent but not amazing. Roman is fluent. But from what I'm gathering, the woman's baby is sick and needs special imaging, and she's from Nicaragua, not Mexico, and therefore isn't eligible for country-funded care and doesn't have the money to pay for getting her child treatment.

Roman listens intently before he turns back to the nurse he was speaking with prior. "Add whatever the baby needs onto my bill," he says in Spanish.

And much like when he ran and jumped into the water, he's not doing this for fanfare or for Instagram likes or for any notoriety at all. He's doing this because that's the sort of human he is. The woman tries to argue, but her attempt is half-assed. After all, her baby is sick and needs help.

"Please," Roman says to her in Spanish. "I can do this. It's okay. Let me help you."

She thanks him profusely and says something about repayment.

He shakes his head. "No. No repayment. Take care of your girl."

He must catch me out of the corner of his eye because he turns, and if Roman Fritz could blush, I swear he would be now. He didn't want me to know he was doing this for her, and I can't describe the rush I'm suddenly feeling. It's the nurse in me, but it's more than that.

It's him. This man. This incredible fucking man.

The same one who can scare the shit out of men with a simple look. Who can reduce line cooks to tears over an improperly cooked sauce. Who fights strangers for money in warehouses because he can't handle the anger inside of himself but donates every cent of his winnings to charity. Who has an emotional barrier between himself and the world, never revealing too much. His heart is a secret. A beautiful, magical place.

And I get to see it.

He's been my best friend forever, but somehow, it's like I haven't truly seen him until now. It's all these things, the giant and the tiny, but they all add up to something I'm finding harder and harder to ignore or deny.

It's Roman.

At least that's what my heart is trying to scream at me.

But what happens to us if I listen?

18

———

ROMAN

Braelyn is quiet as we sit in the back of the taxi, the bag of supplies I purchased without issue on her lap since she made me hold a clean pad of gauze over my cut. She's not mad at me. I don't think it's that, but she's... I don't know. I don't know what this is, and I can typically read her pretty well.

"What's up?" I ask, no longer able to handle the suspense. Our driver is yelling at someone on his phone in Spanish while blasting music, so it's just us back here.

She turns her head and looks up at me. "You're a good man, Roman Fritz."

My insides shift, and not in a fun way. "I'm really not. Ask anyone who works for me."

"I'm not talking about being nice. I'm talking about being *good*. There's a difference."

I don't know what to say to that, so I don't say anything. I don't feel like a good man. Or maybe it's that I don't feel like a deserving man. Nash was the good one. Always smiling and happy. He wanted to be a pediatric neurosurgeon. He wanted to save lives and make a difference. I cook food. Expensive food that not many can afford. I slam my fists into people and revel when I make them bleed or break bones.

That's not good. There's a certain amount of evil in a man who does that.

I have more money than I'll ever be able to spend in ten lifetimes, and I spread it around. It's my way of evening the karmic scales, but I already know they'll never be tipped in my favor.

"You're a nurse and have the kindest, most honest and pure heart I've ever experienced in anyone. You see the best in everyone."

"Roman, you're a good man," she tells me firmly. "At some point, you need to start accepting that. What happened that awful day wasn't your fault. You saved two lives today, and that's everything."

She lets it end there, and it does because now we're back at the resort, then in our suite. She sits me down at the dining room table, a towel beneath my hand, where she has me soaking it in a basin of Betadine as she sets everything else up.

"Dude, there's no lidocaine."

"What?"

"Numbing agent."

"Oh." I shrug. "I guess they forgot to include it. It's fine."

Her lips form a flat line. "It's going to hurt."

I try not to smirk, but it happens anyway. "Kid, I'm a boxer and a chef. A little pain doesn't scare me. Hell, I like it."

She shakes her head and rolls her eyes. "Yes, you're a tough guy, but I'm going to be poking around at your wound, and it will sting like a bastard. Plus, the Dermabond can burn when applied."

"I'll be fine, Nurse Albright. I promise."

She huffs, so very annoyed with me as she opens a sterile drape and sets it down on the table. "You do know I've never glued or sutured anyone, right? Typically, the interns or second-year residents do that."

"How many have you seen?"

She throws me a look. "About a million."

"See a million, do one."

"You have a lot of faith in me. Sit back."

"Why?"

Without answering me, she drops herself onto my lap, stealing the breath from my lungs as she settles back and inadvertently nudges my dick.

"Do this with all of your patients?" I tease, trying for a levity I don't feel.

"Only the hot, married ones," she quips.

"Funny."

"It's the best angle, and if you want me to do this so you have a functioning hand, let me work."

She holds my hand over the basin and proceeds to squirt it with sterile saline from a syringe. And yes, that does burn. When she's satisfied, she pulls my hand away from the basin and sets it on top of the sterile drape and starts to dab it with sterile gauze to dry it. She opens all of the supplies, dropping them from the packaging onto the drape before she puts sterile gloves on and gets down to business.

"Touch each of your fingertips to your thumb for me."

I can't help my smile. Luckily, she can't see it because her back is to me and she's hyper-focused. I do as she says and she continues her examination.

"Any numbness or tingling in your fingers or fingertips?"

"No."

She pokes at me with the tip of the tweezers around my hand. "You feel that?"

"Yes."

She sighs in relief. "If this were any deeper, you'd have been in big trouble, and I wouldn't be able to close it. Hold still. This will hurt despite what you think."

She examines the wound using tweezers and cleans it with more antiseptic, and yeah, that doesn't feel great either, but it's nothing terrible. Still, she's in my lap and I wrap my other hand around her waist, holding her to me. Then I drop my face into her neck, breathing in the scent of her.

I nearly kissed her on the boat. I was inches away. I wouldn't have stopped.

She clears her throat and shifts ever so slightly on my thighs, and silence descends, thick and heavy and charged with electricity. The woman literally has a sharp implement in an open wound on my hand, but all I can think about is the feel of her. Her ass on my dick, her hair tickling my face, her soft skin against my cheek and lips.

Right now, she could stab me with those tweezers, and I wouldn't notice.

"This..." She clears her throat again. "This will burn."

I nod against her, my grip on her waist tightening as she opens the Dermabond and starts to glue up my hand. She gets to work, tweezing and pulling and gluing as more dense silence holds us hostage, only broken up by the sound of our breathing. But she feels me. I know she does. Her breathing has changed, and her body is still, almost afraid to move an inch.

"You're, um, distracting me with your..."

"I know. I'm sorry. I can't help it. You're in my lap and I..." Fuck. My eyes close and my heart thunders. "I want you."

"You do?"

I would laugh at that question if there were anything humorous about it. She doesn't know because I haven't told her, and I haven't told her because she wasn't ready to know. Maybe I wasn't ready to push it, afraid of where it would take us, and the fact that I felt wrong about it because she was Nash's for so long and I didn't feel as though I deserved any piece of her because of that. But now, I can't think about anything else but her and what we could be. What this incredible friendship could grow into.

I don't know what to do about Europe, but if I'm lucky enough to get to a place where I have to figure something out, I will then. I don't know what that could possibly be, but hopefully something.

"Braelyn, you don't know how much." My lips glide gently along the slope of her neck, and her breath hitches.

"But..." Her voice wavers with fear and uncertainty.

"I know." She doesn't have to say anything. I can read her thoughts clearly. "You're the most important person in the world to me, so if you tell me no, I get it and it's okay because you're worth more to me than that."

"But you..."

"Yes. More than anything." I want to tell her. I want to say the words and bare my soul, but I can't. They won't come out. *Not yet. It's too soon. She's not ready for that. Not yet.*

She doesn't say anything. Just continues to glue up my hand, and when she's done, her tone is clinical. "You don't need a bandage. The Dermabond is a waterproof seal. Just keep it clean and dry, and pat it gently with a towel after the shower or washing your hands. No creams or anything on it. It should peel off in five to ten days, but no sooner. Keep a watch for signs of infection, including increased redness, pain, warmth to touch, or drainage from the wound."

"Okay."

She removes her gloves with a snap and wraps everything up in the sterile drape before she climbs off my lap to throw it all away. I stare down at my fixed hand, unable to move, my heart in my feet.

A hand on my shoulder pushing me back startles me, and I lock eyes with Braelyn as she climbs onto my lap again, this time facing me. Her arms sling around my shoulders, and she shifts until we're practically nose to nose. Instinctively, my hands find her hips, and I hold her steady.

"Don't let this become the worst decision we've ever made."

With that, her hands meet the back of my head, and she brings my mouth to hers so she can kiss me. The effect is instant. There is no hesitation.

I tilt my head and kiss her back, fueled by years of pent-up hunger and need. I groan into her, already losing my mind. I don't know how to hold back. I can't go slow.

My good hand is in her hair, and my bad one slides to her lower back. I urge her forward until we're flush, her legs spread on either side of mine, tucked against the arms of the chair. There isn't enough room on here, and I can't get her as close as I need her.

Things ping-pong through my mind. Things like hard limits and safe words. Things like NDAs. Things that are typically brokered and discussed like the business transactions they've been. This isn't that. She'll never be that. I married her, and that makes her my wife even if she doesn't think of herself that way.

But I'm not focusing on any of that. Instead, I'm leaping into this blind and with abandon, not caring about anything other than the feel of her lips on mine. The way she tastes and the sounds she makes.

I breathe hard against her mouth, dizzy in my frenzy while trying to mentally talk myself into chilling the fuck out. It feels impossible. I'm eager and excited and nervous in a way I've never been with anyone before.

Braelyn whimpers against me as I bite her lip and suck it between my lips, only to switch up the angle and devour her mouth in an entirely new way, taking her in a new direction. Something I plan to do tirelessly.

But this chair sucks.

My good hand scoops her ass, and I stand, taking her with

me, only to immediately drop her onto the table she was just using to glue my hand. She makes a small, surprised sound that dies and turns into a moan as she wraps her legs around my waist and feels my straining erection.

This isn't a gentle brush against her. This is hard and right against her pussy. This is no fucking around and no going back territory. All the times I've thought about her and gotten myself off to this very thing have paled in comparison. She is delicious and perfect, and her mouth was made to only kiss mine.

I know it now, and I'm going to fucking prove it to her.

My hands tear at her shirt, yanking down the collar, only to rip it over her head. She's still in her bikini top with her golden skin flashing against the pink cups. I shove one down and duck against her breast, nuzzling and biting and sucking her, utterly mindless.

"Roman," she rasps, pulling on my hair, followed by my shirt when she realizes I don't have a lot of hair for her to pull on. At least not at the back of my head.

Without breaking my kiss on her nipple, I reach back and pull my shirt over my head. It gets tossed somewhere, and then I'm back on her chest, cupping and squeezing and holy shit, her tits are so fucking pretty. I have to see all of them.

"Take this off," I demand harshly. "I want to see you." My voice has the low, deep timbre I use when I expect to be obeyed, and with it, I almost assume she'll balk. But she surprises me yet again. Angling up, she reaches awkwardly behind her back and unhooks the clasp, making the cups fall away. My mouth is back on hers, and I'm lost.

I kiss her and kiss her, my hands in her hair, on her tits, on her waist. My cock grinds against her, digging and searching, hating my shorts and her shorts for keeping me from being inside of her.

Her nails scratch down my back, our bare chests brushing, the heat so fucking exquisite we both moan. She goes for the belt of my shorts, and I work the button and zipper of hers. I don't care about my hand. I don't notice the pain. We're fumbling and pulling, kissing awkwardly in between forced breaks to get this or that undone or off.

Pushing her back, she arches into me, the unforgiving table beneath her, and I drag my cock, only covered in my briefs, up her slit over her bikini bottoms that are still adorably tied at her hips as if that will stop me from anything. I draw back and meet her eyes, dark and glazed over, her cheeks flushed, her lips swollen, and her tits heaving as she tries to get control of her breathing.

She's so fucking gorgeous like this. Turned on for me. All mine.

I do it again, dragging roughly up and down her cunt while I look at her. It's the first time I've slowed down since we started, but feeling her like this, I know I'll either come or lose control with her in another second. She's awoken a desperation in me I constantly fight to overcome. The kind of desperation that only has one way of being sated, and even then, I'm not sure I'll ever be able to quiet this beast again.

I pull her up to me by the back of her head and crash my lips to hers, kissing her with fire and licking the flames. My lips glide down her neck, biting and sucking, marking her as I go. I swirl my tongue around one nipple, followed by the other. She whimpers as my teeth sink into the side of her breast, but her body rocks in counterpoint to me as I do.

"Lower," she demands, pushing my head. "Do that lower."

I smile and play with her belly, dipping my tongue into her navel and tickling her with my lips. I love that she just asked for that. That she pushed and isn't afraid to show me exactly what she wants. I wasn't lying when I said confidence turns me on.

I reach the top of her bottoms and graze them with my teeth while I take her feet and rest them on the arms of the chair so I can sit back down. Gripping her hips, I drag her to me and bury my face in her center. She squeals, even though this is what she wanted.

"If you expected gentle, you've got the wrong man, Braelyn."

My nose presses against the damp spot covering her cunt, and I groan as I suck in a breath, inhaling and tasting her scent. Her hand finds the top of my head, and she gasps loudly as I pull on the strings on either side of her hips until the bottoms fall away, and she's bare beneath me.

A kiss to her inner thighs, a tremulous breath, and my mouth is on her pussy. One hand swoops under her ass so I can lift it to my mouth, my other holding her open for my tongue. But much like kissing her, I don't know how to take this slow. I don't know how to go easy. I'm fucking ravenous for her, and there's no way to hold that back or hide it. The number of times I've dreamed of doing this very thing...

I circle her entrance, then fuck my tongue straight into her, groaning at how fucking good that is.

"Holy fuck," she cries out.

"You taste so good," I growl as I do it again, thrusting my tongue in deeper, harder, faster. "I've wanted this so badly for so long." My tongue slides up to her clit, and I plunge two fingers straight into her, twisting my wrist so I bang her with them as I work her clit. She squirms, as what I'm doing is hard and intense, and half-heartedly pushes at me. It makes me chuckle against her skin. "Baby, you're not going anywhere until I let you. Learn how to take it because this is only the start."

My cock throbs painfully with the need to fuck her, but right now, all I want to do is make her scream my fucking name.

Her pussy grinds against me, my tongue and lips all over her clit, playing with it, rolling it, sucking on it. She's so wet. So perfectly, deliciously wet, I can't get enough of her. I'm beyond high. I'm in fucking heaven with her splayed out on a table for me to devour. My hand slides up her chest until it's around her neck, collaring her without applying pressure. My ring stares back at me from around her neck, and it's the sexiest fucking thing ever.

I'm collaring my wife.

It sparks something primal in me. Something so possessive and finite.

Shocked, she props herself up, her elbows digging into the table, and her eyes meet mine as I eat her cunt with abandon. I give her neck a small squeeze, only to immediately relax it. *Trust me*, this says. *Let me own you.*

And something about that is all it takes because a second later, her head falls back, and she absolutely loses it as she starts to come. Her cunt clenches my fingers, holding them tight and deep inside of her. I rub her front wall as I suck on her clit, not slowing, not easing up. I increase the intensity until her hand is ripping at my hair and she's screaming, writhing, arching against my hand on her neck, at the very brink of what she can take with this.

"Oh my god! It's... I can't... Ah! Jesus fuck, Roman! Oh my god."

She hasn't even felt what I have planned for her next.

19

BRAELYN

I can't breathe. Like seriously, I can't breathe. It's not even from Roman's hand on my neck, though who knew that would turn me into a puddle of whore at his feet? Because holy shit! Never in my life has anyone gone down on me like that. But like really, what the fuck am I doing? This is Roman.

Roman Fritz. My best friend. My lifeline. My safety net. The one person I don't think I could ever live without. And yes, I'm married to him. I do realize that. So technically, in that regard, we're not doing anything wrong. And obviously I've been curious. I mean, hello, he's insanely fucking gorgeous and he's an incredible man and I think that's only natural.

He rejected me when I tried to kiss him that one time, and after that, I told myself he wasn't interested. That it would never be like that between us, and I was better off for it.

But now...

He gives my pussy one final kiss and a lick before he climbs up my body, his hand still around my neck as his face hovers above mine. And it's his eyes that do it for me. It was the fire and raw need in them that threw me over the edge. For a moment, he simply looks at me, both of us silent. Then his mouth descends on mine, and he's kissing me in such a way that he's all I know, and the racing thoughts in my head have no choice but to quiet.

"Do you want this?" he murmurs against my lips, his hand leaving my neck and trailing up and into my hair.

"Don't give me time to reconsider."

He pulls back and meets my eyes. "No. That's not how this will be between us. If we're doing this, it's real. It's not some rebound moment or a *we'll pretend it never happened* thing. We won't do this and divorce from it later. I won't be your regret. It's why I didn't kiss you that night all those years ago."

I blink at him, but before I can question that, he sits me up and shifts me until my legs are dangling.

The truth is, I want him. I do. I know I do. I want him to fuck me hard. I want him to take me to the edge and push me over it so I can see if I fall or fly. But I'm also scared, and frankly, I need a minute to figure this shit out since it all just kind of came on me quickly. And no, that's not a pun.

I rise to my feet, and he steps back, knocking the chair and causing it to slide across the tile floor until the back feet catch on the grout line and it stops. I'm completely naked, and he's very much aware of that as his eyes dip and seek and smolder. I've never been shy and I'm not all that self-conscious either, but having Roman's eyes on me is an experience I wasn't prepared for, and I can feel my face heating. I take a step forward, but because this is Roman, he doesn't step back. He's a wall. Strong, formidable, protective.

I touch his chest, his skin hot and his muscles unyielding. But beneath them is his heart, and there's something so oddly sexy and human about it that it has me smiling. Pushing him back, I force him to take three steps back until he's sitting in the chair. He's quiet—as he often gets when he's thinking seriously about something—but his gaze casts up to mine.

"What are you doing?"

I shake my head and stand here, waiting on... I don't know. Something.

A sexy smirk curls up his lips, and he quirks a finger at me. "Come here, kid."

It's a weird nickname. He started calling me it after I forced him to watch Casablanca one night. *"Here's looking at you, kid,"* he'd said to me, quoting the film, and after that, it stuck. I actually love it. I always have. It makes me feel special. Like his.

With my heart in my throat and my body tingly and filled with nerves, I lower myself to the cold tile floor. It's about as uncomfortable as the table was, but it also grounds me. I crawl to him, and the effect is immediate. His eyes darken to midnight and his lips part on a silent breath.

"Jesus, Brae. You really know how to get me."

He sits back in the chair, his hands going to the arms, clutching the wood as he watches me. I reach his thighs and climb up them, my fingers immediately tracking to the band on his boxer briefs.

He brushes some of my curls back from my face. "What are you thinking right now, beautiful?"

"That you got to taste me, and I want to know what you taste like."

His fingers trickle down my cheek even as he shifts to allow me to remove his briefs. His cock, thick and long and angry-looking, bounces out, the tip gleaming with pre-cum.

"You're stalling," he accuses.

"I am now that I see how big you are. No way that'll fit where you want it to go."

His lips bounce, but he still gives me a look that tells me he's waiting for an answer.

"I'm stalling," I agree while I grip his cock and give it a firm stroke that makes him grunt and his eyes momentarily close.

"You know my brain better than I do. Let me do this because it's what I need right now. I want to do this. I just…"

"I know. Okay." He swallows and pulls my hair back into a makeshift ponytail. "If I get too rough, raise your hand or tap my thigh twice."

Holy crap. So much for giving him a simple blow job while I mentally work through the fact that we crossed the line of no return. Though I should have known. Roman isn't simple. He's the most complex person I've ever known. I've heard rumors. The guys joking around with him.

"Do I get a safe word?" I tease.

"Not yet. We'll get there."

Oh. Now my heart starts to pound, but a thrill also runs through me like a current, and my empty core clenches. Why is that thought hot?

"Yes, sir," I quip, but I've read it in books, and I like it. The idea of it all.

But before he can respond, I grip his cock tighter and take him all the way down my throat until I gag. He makes a strangled sort of noise and secures his grip in my hair. The fact that I can affect him like this drives me wild. We are talking about Roman Fritz after all. Yes, he's my best friend, but I'm not stupid or blind. I see the way women follow and track him. Billionaire. Famous chef. Impossible to catch. And let's not even get into the bad boy boxing thing because the man has groupies he doesn't even cast a second glance at.

It only adds to the mystery and desire.

"Remember what I said if you need to tap out."

I won't tap out. I already know that. My pussy pulses at the thought of him fucking my face. I don't know where it comes from or even why it turns me on, but it totally freaking does, and it makes me feel bolder. Sexier. Like even though he's going to be the one in control, it's actually me who is.

I flatten my tongue and glide it up his shaft, giving myself a second to catch my breath as I lick around his head, tasting him and giving him a few jerks. He releases a shaky breath and lets me play and experiment with him for a minute. I lick and tease and test and see what makes his breath hitch or him move differently or even tug harder on my hair.

Then I get cocky. Pun intended this time. I take him deep again, and he swats my hand away and holds me down on his cock, using my hair to keep me in place. His cock is huge. That part actually wasn't a joke. Him fitting inside me is a legit concern. Especially given how big he feels in my mouth, how stretched my lips are around him. I choke, tears instantly stinging my eyes, but his other hand strokes my face, and his words calm me.

"Breathe through your nose. That's it. That feels so good. *Fuck*, Brae. Your hot little mouth on my cock is incredible. Remember what I said about your hands. If you need me to stop, I will."

My eyes close and I force myself to relax, breathing through my nose as he instructs. Then he uses the hand in my hair and on my face to start pumping in and out of my mouth. His cock slams into the back of my throat over and over, and I swallow reflexively, making him moan low and long.

He goes five or six times before he pulls back so I can breathe, but he never leaves my mouth. He just slows his pace. My eyes open and he's right there watching me. Something about his heat and lust and intensity has me putting my hands behind my back, my fingers intertwining, gripping, so I can allow him to lead.

It sets him off with a loud, "Fuck," followed by a "You perfect girl."

Then that's exactly what he's doing. He's fucking my face. Repeatedly. I can't control it. I just work to keep my tongue flat and try to shield my teeth, but I definitely scrape him with them. It's impossible not to. It doesn't bother him. If anything, he gets off on the flash of pain. It's a pounding, relentless pace. Pump, pump, pump, breathe. One hand, he keeps in my hair to work his dick. The other cups my throat again, feeling the muscles move. And while this should be the ultimate turn-off, a man taking his pleasure from me like this, it's the opposite.

I feel owned and sacred to him. Like a fucking goddess.

Probably because of how he's reacting. How much he loves it. The filthy and incredible things he's saying to make me wetter and wetter. But also because this is Roman and I know he'd rather die than hurt me. He'd never do anything I was uncomfortable with. If I raised my hand or patted his leg, he would stop in a second.

That's power.

"Yes. Like that. So fucking good. Damn. You have no clue. No fucking clue how many times I've dreamed of you on your knees for me."

I don't know why that surprises me, but it does. Like everything about this encounter with him, I'm shocked stupid and silent. I can't make sense of it. It feels like a contradiction, but at the same time, one I'm happy about. And we won't discuss my knees because I wouldn't be shocked if I have bruises on them from the tile.

That thought is only magnified when he hits a brutal pace, going deeper until he's literally down my throat, and breathing through my nose doesn't mean shit because oxygen won't move past his cock in my trachea. I gag and sputter and drool and swallow. My hands grip each other, and I fight the need to tap out.

"Holy shit. Ah! Fuck. Holy shit."

It's that. The way he's losing himself somehow keeps me going, and I swallow again, managing a bit of oxygen as I do. But the swallowing is driving him headfirst to the edge of reason, and that's exactly where I want him.

"Braelyn, I'm gonna..." A grunt. "If you don't want me to..."

He can't even finish that. But I don't care because I know he's trying to warn me, and I want it. He fucks my face, and I swallow and swallow until his head flies back and with a roar, he comes with a jerky thrust and a tight vise in my hair. He comes straight down my throat, and there is no choice but to swallow that too.

The moment he's done, I'm suddenly pulled up into his arms and he's holding me and kissing me and praising me in a way no one ever has. No one's ever kissed me after they've come down my throat either, and I love that he's unafraid to do that.

His forehead presses to mine, and he holds my face.

"We both need a shower. I dove into the ocean today."

"I'm sitting naked on you."

He smiles and pecks my lips. "I noticed that."

"I can tell. You're already getting hard again."

His fingers trace along my face. "A magnificent feat, considering how hard you just made me come."

"I didn't tap out."

He wraps his arms around me and holds me against him, kissing my hair and face and lips. "You have to promise me that if you need to, you will. I don't want you to do something for me that doesn't make you feel good in return."

"I won't."

He kisses my forehead. "You were incredible."

"I know."

His lips twitch against me. "So confident."

I smile. "I've been told it's a turn-on."

He shrugs. "Everything about you is to me." He kisses my lips.

"So we're..." I trail off. "Not quite fucking each other, but likely will be soon?" I drop my forehead to his shoulder. I'm a mess.

His fingers glide down my hair. "That's one way to put it. I already told you I want you, and I do. I can't half-ass this. Yes, we're married, but I know that doesn't mean much to you. That said, if you want to talk about this on a deeper level, I'd be happy to."

"Not yet."

His hands are all over my face as he lifts it back up, and for a beat, he just stares into my eyes. "I'm going to be forever fighting for you, aren't I?" He sighs and without following that up or explaining it further, he lifts me and walks us into our bedroom and straight into the bathroom, right toward the outdoor shower.

He turns on the faucet without setting me down, but his mouth is back on mine, filling my jumbled mind with deep swirling kisses, and I have a choice to make.

Have sex with my best friend and fake husband. Or not. Either way, things are about to get very complicated and confusing between us.

20

ROMAN

I shift Braelyn in my hands, cool water gently falling on us from the rain showerhead above. The shower is outdoors but protected by a wall. Still, we can hear the ocean waves and smell the salt. The heat and humidity are with it, but it's pretty cool out here. Like a secret garden with rocks and plants. She wiggles in my hands and reluctantly, I set her down.

Wordlessly, she goes for the shampoo pump that's attached to the wall and I put my back to her, closing my eyes and tilting my face up to the stream. It's dark out here and my stomach grumbles, reminding me we missed dinner with all that's happened this evening.

I haven't even been inside of her yet, and that was already the best sex of my life. It was simply incredible, and it was with her. My Braelyn. Now it's like I don't know how to talk to her or what to say. I'm terrified I went too fast. Too rough. That even though she's out here with me and still naked, our moment is over and will never be found again.

But worse is the thought that she'll pull away from me because of it.

I was already afraid the marriage piece would cause that

and so far it hasn't. But this upped the ante, and she's not ready for all that I come with.

Hands in my hair startle me, and I start to turn, only to have her hold me still. "If you turn, I'll get shampoo on your face. Hold still. And maybe squat a little. You're annoyingly tall."

I smile and step out of the stream to let Braelyn wash my hair. The scent of flowers and eucalyptus surrounds me while her fingers massage my scalp. It's heaven. My eyes close and a rustling breath empties from my lungs.

Once she's satisfied with her handiwork, she pushes me back under the stream and I rinse the suds from my hair while she takes my hand in hers.

"It looks good despite our shenanigans. Does it hurt?"

"No," I tell her, opening my eyes and watching as she examines me.

"Good."

We continue to wash up, moving around each other and not touching all that much. I had other plans for this shower, but it's obvious they don't line up with hers.

"You pushed me away," she says, her voice barely above a whisper, and between the slapping sound of water on stone and the ocean beyond the wall, I have to strain to hear her.

"That night?"

"Yes."

"You were drunk."

She looks up at me with those big brown eyes I'm always lost in. "Is that the only reason? Because the things you said yesterday..." She trails off, and I stare at her, hardly able to form the words.

"I was battling a lot of guilt. You had been Nash's, and I felt wrong wanting to kiss you the way I did. Like I was betraying him after it was my fault he was gone. Yes, you were drunk. And that was an easy excuse because the rest was far more complicated."

She absorbs that. "I don't know..." She audibly swallows. "I don't know what we're doing, and it scares me. We're technically married, and now we're fooling around, and it feels like everything is out of order and we're doing it all wrong."

I comb some wet strands back from her face. "What do you want this to be?"

"I broke up with Adam not even two weeks ago."

I get that. I truly do. She loved him and was going to marry him. This trip was for her to reset and escape the heartache, and here I am, making a move when I told myself I wasn't going to do that this soon. That I was going to be patient and wait for her to be ready.

"I didn't kiss you that night because I knew that when I finally did, I wasn't going to be a regret. I was going to be your forever. We'll do this your way, not mine."

Her eyes search mine, her brow pinched ever so subtly. "You've always been my forever. That's what we are to each other."

She either doesn't get it or is intentionally being obtuse. Either way, I have my answer. So I do the only thing I can do. I fucking nod. And it kills me because it feels like the hope I had been starting to cling to just died.

Being in unrequited love with Braelyn for as long as I have has become part of my personality. A character trait or flaw in this case. It's just who I am at this point. Like how I don't like bananas because I can't stand how they smell or that my eyes change colors depending on the lighting or what I'm wearing or that I'm better at listening than speaking, and sometimes it makes me seem like more of a dick, which I'm fine with.

And because of that, I was able to manage it. It was kept in a nice, tidy place. The place where you hide the quirks you'd rather others not know about or see. But I got stupid and let it out of that place, and now it's grown and festered and taken over, and I wish I could put it back and continue to live with it simply as background noise instead of the only fucking thing I hear.

Maybe it's better I'm moving away. Soon, in fact. Less than two months and I'm gone.

Her hand rests over my heart, and I wish we weren't doing this naked. I already feel too exposed.

"I don't want to have sex with you out here."

I blink and tilt my head because she just said she doesn't want to have sex with me, but finished it with... "Out here?"

"You'd have to hold me the entire time, and that wall is rough with all those stones in it. It'd hurt. Plus it's not good for the cut on your hand."

I run my hands up my face and through my hair to clear the water away. "I don't think I'm following—"

"Roman, it's not that complicated. This outdoor shower, while very cool, is probably one of the worst places to have sex unless we do it completely standing up, but like, meh. You're a lot taller than I am, and the mechanics of that are just all wrong."

I laugh. Like a full-on belly laugh, which isn't something I do often, if ever. "You're right. It would be a lot of fumbling and awkward angles."

"Exactly. I'm thinking the bed is better."

Right or wrong, stupid or not, I scoop my best friend, my wife, back up into my arms and walk our wet bodies inside. She laughs at my reaction, but I cut her off with a kiss because she's taking a chance, and this chance will lead to more. I will make damn sure of it. She has to get there. That's what all that was. She's not yet, and that's fine. I can manage that. But she's going to try, and that's more than I can ask for.

The air conditioner hits us, and we shiver, goose bumps breaking out across both of us. I snatch a fresh towel from the towel warmer, and Brae helps me by wrapping it around us.

She rubs my hair with it and blots hers, and we both look a little wild, but who cares?

I slip and slide, but then we're at the bed, and I bring her down sideways across it, falling on top of her and kissing her. I take her wrists in my hand and pin them above her head, forcing her body to stretch out and her tits to angle up into me. A bolt of desire sizzles straight through me and tightens my chest with an unfamiliar excitement.

I've never had sex with anyone I cared about emotionally. Yes, I know that's as fucked up as it sounds—but I'm about to be inside of Braelyn.

In fact, I can hardly catch my breath with it.

"I don't have condoms in here. I have two in my wallet."

"I was tested after Adam."

I pull back. "You were?"

She rolls her eyes at me. "Um, yeah, I freaking was. Wren did it at the hospital."

"I'm sorry you had to go through that."

"Me too, but it was necessary and everything came out negative."

I stare down at her, our bodies flush, and my heart is hammering. "I've been tested too. And I've never not used a condom before."

Her fingers trickle along my jaw, up to my temple. "I get to be your first, then."

And I plan to be your last.

"What about birth control?" Though the thought of knocking up Braelyn, of having my baby inside of her, makes me harder than steel. That's a new fucking kink for me and I already have a long list.

"I have an IUD."

My lips slam back down on hers, and I kiss her and kiss her and kiss her. My lips trail along her jaw and down the slope of her neck, where my teeth graze her thrumming carotid. She whimpers and squirms, and I pinch her nipple with my other hand in warning.

"You're going to have to hold still."

"I'm not sure I can."

"Try for me." The multitude of ways I mean that are likely clear in my tone.

She stops squirming, and the pleasure that ripples through me is intense. I continue down her body, kissing and sucking, even biting because I want to see her skin redden from me. I want her marked. I want her to feel that too. Sucking a nipple into my mouth, I release her hands and my cock throbs when I see she's left them there. I rub it against her thigh so she feels it. So she knows how happy and hard she's made me. Then I thrust up her tits and scrape my teeth along the tight peaks.

"Ah," she cries, twitching left and right. I let it go and continue to lick and suck at her tits while my hand slides between her thighs, one finger slipping inside of her.

"So wet for me."

"Roman, please," she whines. "I want you inside of me."

I want to be inside of her too. That's all there is to this. Everything else fades, and I climb back up her, my face above hers, our eyes locked. I lift her thigh and place it on my hip and settle between her legs. Her cunt is so warm, and I drag the head of my cock up and down her slit, watching her face as I do. As I touch her like this.

Her cheeks flush red, and her hands lose the battle with staying above her head and come to my shoulders. I line up with her entrance and push inside of her. It's unlike anything I've ever experienced before. A wave of euphoria intoxicates me, creating a haze around everything. She's so goddamn tight stars are already dancing behind my eyes.

My neck arches back and my eyes close. I'm positive I groan a long, "Fuuuck," because it can't be helped.

Her nails dig into my shoulders. "Wait. Don't move."

My head snaps down, and I take her in. "What's wrong?"

"Big."

I try not to smile. I truly do. But... "Oh."

"Don't *oh* me. Just give me a moment."

"Baby, I'll give you a lifetime." I dip and kiss her, and with that, I roll us so she's on top of me. My cock is still inside her, but now I'm propped up on a pillow with her straddling me. "Better?"

She nods. "Yes."

I'll be honest. It's a hell of a view with her like this. Her slightly smaller than a handful tits and her smooth, creamy stomach, and dark, curly hair all around her.

"Christ, you're so beautiful." I reach up and play with her tits. "So fucking beautiful, Braelyn."

"You are too, you know." She bends to kiss me, but sits up again, her hands on my chest as she rocks forward and backward like a pendulum, testing, adjusting, and taking me in. It's killing me not to thrust up, but her expression right now makes it worth it. She lifts onto her knees and allows me to slip partially out along the way before she pushes back down. My eyes roll back in my head, and my hands grip her tighter.

"Fucking hell, that's so good." Understatement. Holy hell, that's an understatement. Nothing has ever been better than this. "Keep moving. I want you to fuck me until you come, but you're getting more than one. One you'll take, one I'll give you."

"Oh god." She moans loudly and starts to bounce on me, her tits moving with her. I join her, finally thrusting up into her now that she's ready for me. I pound, one hand on her hip, the other finding her clit. I rub her in hard, tight circles before I test her a bit and pinch it.

Her head flies back along with her hands that meet my calves, and she squeals. But she's also grinding harder, deeper, opening herself up for me to continue to touch her like this, and I do. I'm so hard for her. Harder than I've ever been in my life. I pull on her nipple and roll her clit, and my girl is fucking me so hard now. She's absolutely incredible, and I tell her that.

She's getting close. I can see it all over her, and I help her get there. I jab into her, but she's doing most of the work. This one is hers, as I said, and when she comes, it takes everything in me not to come with her. I clench my jaw and my ass cheeks and hold my breath and watch as she comes all over my cock, squeezing it tight and making me so slick I can hardly stand how good it feels.

The moment she settles down, her movements slowing, I spin her around on me and bring her down to the bed until she's on her stomach and I'm behind her. I push her legs closed so it's an even tighter fit, one she'll feel like an ache in her belly, and I thrust back into her.

"Now the one I'm going to take," I rasp in her ear and force her hands above her head. I hold her wrists with one hand, my other pushed into her back between her shoulder blades, so all she can do is lie here and take what I'm giving her.

We don't have a safe word, and I have to be cautious, but having her pinned beneath me sets off the fractured, depraved part of my mind, and I pull out, only to press right back into her, hitting her front wall with the head of my cock and gliding along it with the rest of my shaft.

I'm intentionally deep. Intentionally slow. And she's losing her mind with it, her cunt still swollen and sensitive inside. She rubs against the bed as I continue to fuck her like this, and I slap her ass, making her buck and moan.

I bend and speak into her ear. "You little cheat. You're rubbing your clit on the blanket, aren't you?"

Her eyes are closed, but a saucy fucking smirk curls up her lips.

"I didn't give you permission for that." I spank her ass again, then spread her cheeks as I fuck into her, digging deeper.

"Oh god! Oh fuck. What are you doing?"

"Breathe," I tell her because she's not breathing. She's holding her breath with what I'm doing, and she'll pass out if she does that.

She's squirming again, this time back and forth, trying to free my hands from holding her open like this. "Roman, what are you doing?"

In and out, in and out, I saw back and forth, watching my cock get swallowed by her pussy but also staring at her asshole. I want it the way I want the rest of her, completely and obsessively. Her eyes are pinched shut and her lips are parted to accommodate her ragged breaths. I don't stop. I keep fucking into her, rolling my hips and slicing repeatedly into her while keeping her locked in place.

"I'm going to play with your ass," I tell her with a strangled groan, my cock throbbing with the need to come. "If you don't like it, or truly want me to stop, and not from modesty because I think it's so fucking hot and I'm so fucking hard from it—you can feel that, I know you can—then say my middle name and I'll stop."

"Your middle name? If I say Fletcher, you'll stop?" She's incredulous.

"Yes. You say that and I stop. That's your power, and it's absolute, but I also want you to trust me to see how far I can take you." Then I spit, and it drips straight onto her ass. She makes a shocked noise but also moans. My thumb dips down by my cock, and I gather some of her cum that's coating me and bring it up to mix with my spit. And as I pump in and out of her cunt, I ring her asshole with my thumb.

"Holy shit!"

"Just relax and feel it. Allow yourself to feel it, baby, and trust me."

By some miracle, she does. She lets me hold her down and fuck her and play with her ass. And when my thumb starts to fuck her in time with my thrusts, she's having trouble controlling herself. She's moaning and writhing beneath me and squirming and even fucking back into me.

"My sexy girl, you're doing such a good job taking me like this."

I pick up my pace, using my hand on her wrists for better leverage and angle, and I seriously start fucking her, both her cunt and her ass. I told her after that dickhead Adam cheated on her that he never fucked her properly if she wasn't screaming for him, and I'm going to prove that to her now. I'm going to make her come so hard she screams.

My feet dig into the blanket, and I thrust in and out of her. She's so tight like this and I can't help myself from grunting and groaning, my balls drawing up, my body on a hairpin trigger, needing to come, anxious to do it inside of her without anything between us.

"Fuck!" That notion nearly pushes me over the edge, but then Braelyn is coming.

Her cunt crushes my cock, and she screams as I knew she would. I fuck her harder, slamming my body into hers, making sure I get her G-spot and keeping my thumb in her asshole. Her release forces my own, and I bellow out a savage growl as I still, my muscles seizing as my cock jerks and empties into her until there's nothing left of me.

I collapse, my thumb sliding out of her ass and my grip on her wrists slackening. I kiss a trail up her neck and move the wet hair sticking to her face.

"Are you okay?"

Her eyes are sleepy, but she's smiling. "I'm more than okay."

My chest thumps, and I lean in and kiss her, the words *I love you* on my tongue, and I swallow them down. She's not ready and I don't want the moment after we've both come to be when I tell her. When I say the words, I want her to know it's real and not question the moment or motive.

"Good. Don't move. I'm going to get a towel to clean you up, and after we'll order in dinner."

"Sounds good, but I'll get myself cleaned up. You order the food." She rolls away from me and slips out of bed, walks to the bathroom, and shuts the door behind her.

That's that.

I flop back onto the bed and stare up at the rattan fan above me. I'm not known for overthinking. It's not something I do, and I've never worried about what a woman is thinking when she's with me.

Until now.

Braelyn is within my grasp, but I can already feel her slipping through my fingers.

21

———

BRAELYN

I'm crying and I don't know why. In the last two weeks, I think I've cried more than I ever have in my life, and that's a whole other thing that's freaking me out. I'm sitting on the toilet with my face in my hands, trying desperately to hide my sobbing, and when that fails, I get in the shower—the inside one this time—and cry in here.

I don't have my phone with me, but I could really use a phone-a-friend moment. One where I freak out and they listen and tell me it's going to be okay. That life changes on a dime for all of us and that I have to believe the course it's charting now will take me somewhere incredible.

I have to believe that because otherwise I'll never stop crying.

Him calling me "my sexy girl." His finger in my ass. Safe words. Being spanked. His hand on my throat. All the things we just did replay through my head, and I can't... Jesus, I don't know how to make sense of it.

Maybe it's the *what did I just do* thing or the odd cocktail of endorphins and happiness when that happiness absolutely terrifies me. I thought I was happy with Adam. I thought things were great between us. I would have blindly and dumbly married him. How could I have felt so absolute with that two weeks ago and now have everything feel different?

How can I trust myself after that? It's not even how can I trust men because I trust Roman. Maybe that scares me too because I just had the best, most intense sexual experience of my life with my best friend, but how can he still be my best friend after we did all that? How can I suddenly start to see him differently than I ever have before when I've known him liter-ally my entire life?

Is it some strange form of grief or rebound? Or am I finally opening my eyes and looking at what's been right in front of me all along? Then I almost laugh. Roman doesn't date women. He doesn't get serious. Not with anyone.

Is this different?

Am I ready to ask that question and learn his answer, whether it's yes or not?

I wish I hadn't married him. I glance down at the sparkling ring still on my finger. I haven't taken it off. I'm worried I'll lose it, and he hasn't taken his off. I don't know what any of that means. I wish we could have a fresh start and it wouldn't be complicated from the start.

Ugh. I'm a mess. Again.

Just fucking fabulous.

I give myself a quick wash and step out of the shower so I can brush my hair and get my shit back on straight. My stomach rumbles, and I have no clue what time it is. It could be seven or midnight.

I get into my robe and leave the bathroom to find the bedroom dark and empty. I throw on clean undies and a soft, wireless bra, along with a pair of cotton shorts and my favorite old college T-shirt. Then I woman up and go in search of Roman. And food, let's be real.

He's out on the patio, on the edge between the rock garden

full of flowering plants and the dark wall of sand and ocean beyond it. His short hair is barely rustling in the breeze, and his profile is bothered. Food sits untouched on the table with metal covers on the plates. My friend is troubled. Unsettled. It's not something he wears well. He buries it deep within himself like an artifact after a sandstorm.

My heart thunders. I have a choice. Embrace the possibility or pretend everything we just shared didn't happen. Only I know I can't do the latter. Because I am seeing Roman in an entirely different way and it began before tonight. He's a rare and special gem. The kind you only uncover once in a lifetime and only see all the facets if you look closely enough.

Otherwise, you see what everyone else sees. The gorgeous face. The tall, muscular body. The tattoos. The brilliance in the kitchen. The broodiness. The fierce boxer.

But he's Roman. The soft-hearted, will protect you with his life and will do whatever it takes to make you smile while he dominates your ass until you're screaming for him guy.

All that aside, I don't know if I'm ready for what this could be.

Sucking in the shakiest of shaky breaths, I cross the stone patio, past the pool that's glowing until I'm behind him. I know he hears me because his shoulders tense, but I shock the hell out of him by wrapping my arms around his chest from behind and resting the side of my face against his back.

I don't say anything. I'm not quite up for that. This is still new, and I'm still raw, and I'm still afraid of, well, everything, if we're being honest. But his body relaxes into mine in a way that draws a smile to my lips and a skip to my heart.

His hands cover mine that are pressed against his chest, our rings clinking against each other, and he releases a tense breath. The kind I wish didn't ever find its way to his lungs.

"You were crying."

I lean deeper into him. "I wish you hadn't heard that."

"Did I push you too far? Was it too much? Did I hurt you?"

His question almost makes me laugh, though the panic and torment in his voice shatter any mirth before it can form. "No. Not even close."

"Braelyn, I went easy."

"I figured."

He threads his fingers through mine, squeezing them. "But you were still crying."

"Not from that. I mean, not in that way. I'm overwhelmed. That's what those tears were."

"Baby..."

Oh god. Him calling me that.

"Do you regret it?"

"No. Absolutely not. I want more."

He takes a heavy breath in and releases it slowly. "I want to go harder and deeper with you."

That rolls through my head and my nipples tighten and my pussy clenches. They say bring it on because we're ready to roll with it. "Okay."

He laughs, but there's no humor there. "Okay? Do you have any clue what you're agreeing to?"

"No," I tell him honestly. "But I liked what we did today, and I'd like to do more."

He's trembling. This guy. His heart is guarded by an army, and yet it's the softest, most beautiful thing when you breach its defenses.

"You don't know what you're saying. Where my mind or even my heart is with this."

"Will you hurt me?"

"Not the way you think and never your heart. It's the thing I value most in this world. Above all else. And if you tell me you don't like this or don't want it to be like this, that you want it to be more of a typical vanilla thing, I'm fine with that. I swear it."

I close my eyes and think about this. I have to focus on the physical. I'm not ready to talk about relationships even if we're married. So... sex. Sex with possibility. It's something I can work with. For some reason, that takes a lot of the pressure off my chest while also making my insides squirm. Fuck, I'm a contradiction, but I think it's safer this way.

"If I ask you to stop or tell you I don't like something or say 'Fletcher', which still feels kind of weird?"

"I stop." He's almost hurt by the question. "We'd have boundaries. Safe words. One you pick. Braelyn, I'm not a sadist or anything. I just... I'm physical and dominant, and I like to make sure my partners feel safe in that space. What I want the most is your trust because you already know I'd never hurt you."

I do know that. And I do trust him. More than anyone, really. And the idea of somehow giving myself over to him in that way doesn't feel awful or demeaning. It ironically feels empowering. Sexy. Fierce.

But... "Roman, it's more than the sex that has me afraid."

"I know. Me too." He squeezes my hands. "But it's still us, Brae. Me and you. Married or not, it's as you said, we're forever. At least, that's my hope. Are you hungry?"

I smile at that. And relax. "Famished."

"Let's eat then."

He spins around and his hand is somehow on my cheek, with his blue-green oceanic eyes on mine. It's like I'm looking at him for the first time. He's Roman, but he's also someone new and it's all these things.

He dips down and kisses me. Just a sweet pressing of his lips before it's over just as fast and he's leading me to the table.

"Tequila *and* wine?"

He laughs. "I had no clue what you'd be up for."

"You ordered one of everything on the menu, didn't you?"

"Not the ceviche."

I shiver. "I hate anything raw."

He smirks. "You seemed to love it this evening."

I smack his shoulder and laugh. "Not yet! I have to have carbs in my stomach before I can handle your brand of sexing me up."

He laughs and kisses my forehead. "I got you a cheeseburger and fries."

"Thank god." We sit down and it's not strained anymore. It's us. It's us chatting and laughing and telling stories and me checking his hand and us drinking and eating.

And when it's time for us to go to sleep, there is no tension. It's not awkward. We each take turns in the bathroom and once we settle into bed, he simply wraps his arms around me, lets out a contented sigh, and that's that.

He's not pushing me, I realize. He's giving me time to acclimate. Acclimate to what, I'm still not sure, but I'm choosing not to overthink anything.

Instead, I fall into the blissful abandon of sleep.

I STIR, chasing the tail end of my dream, not wanting to wake up just yet. Everything is that delicious sort of heavy, the sweet grogginess that comes after a good night's sleep and an incredible dream. I don't get these often. Hardly ever, actually.

Working in the ER, you see the worst of the worst. No one comes to you on their best day and sometimes you save a life and sometimes you lose one. Or it's just fucking sad. You have to teach yourself to disassociate, but even when you do, there are remnants you can't fully excise. A patient who sticks with you.

So to sleep the way I slept last night while dreaming of stars and the ocean feels like a gift. One I'm not ready to let go of just yet.

Until I hear a sound in the other room. A voice. Roman talking.

"No, she's still asleep," he says. "How are you feeling? How's the pregnancy?"

Skylar. He's talking to Sky.

"Good." A grunt. "He better fucking be or you'll have to let me kill him finally." He's silent for a beat, though I know he was talking about her ex. "I know. I spoke to Crew." He laughs. "Quinn sees hockey players, not football. No way she'll work for the Rebels unless forced. She doesn't want to work with her brothers or parents." More silence followed by, "Things are... good. The restaurant is coming along. The resort is incredible and we're having a good time. No, I won't elaborate on what that means, and my voice does not sound funny." He huffs. "Stop fishing, Sky." The doorbell rings. "Our breakfast is here. I'll have her call you when she gets up. Bye. Love you too."

I hear him move around and answer the door, speaking in Spanish to whoever is there. More noise, then the room service guy is gone, and I hear Roman head toward the bedroom. For a moment, I lie here, debating if I want to be a child and pretend to be asleep still.

He chuckles by the entryway. "You're the worst faker."

Busted.

"I wasn't giving it my all. I was still undecided," I admit as I roll over and open my eyes to see him. He's shirtless, damn him, in only a pair of track shorts. He's also sweaty like he went for a run or worked out. "What time did you wake up?"

He smirks. "Dawn."

"You didn't wake me."

"If I woke you, I would have fucked you or had my mouth between your legs. You looked like you needed the sleep, so I went for a run and to the restaurant for a bit."

I belt out an incredulous laugh and flop onto my back, my hands on my face. "Roman! You can't say that to me."

"But I thought it was our honeymoon."

"Oh my god! Shut up."

He chuckles. "Come on. Get up. Breakfast just got here."

"Your love language is feeding me."

"My love language is food. Feeding you is a bonus. Come join me. Unless you want me to join you."

"I do, which is why I'll get up."

"I figured. It's why I gave you space this morning and will wait till you tell me you're ready for more. But, Braelyn, I want more. So go have your freak-out, and after that, we can eat and talk if you want. Then I might kiss you and see where that goes."

Without another word, the man leaves me here to have my freak-out. Which I do. I smother a squeal and an oh my god, what the fuck am I doing? Then I pull myself together, use the bathroom, wash up, and follow the smell of coffee and bacon into the living area. Roman is sitting at the table with his phone in his hand and a mug of coffee in his other.

"In case you didn't hear before, Skylar called."

"I heard." I take the seat opposite him, pour myself some coffee, and make myself a plate of food. "She sounded like she's suspicious."

He sets his phone down and scoops up a bite of omelet. "It's Skylar. I think that says it all."

"You didn't tell her."

He smirks as he slides his fork from his lips and chews. "About the marriage or the sex?"

"Yes."

"I figured I'd let you have the honors. Or not if you're not ready to share."

I change the subject, because yeah, not ready. "How's your hand? Any signs of infection?"

He glances down, then holds up his palm for me to see.

No extra redness, drainage, or swelling. "Looks good."

"Feels good. I have a good nurse. One I get to spend the next five days with."

He watches my expression, and I hide it behind my coffee.

"Then we go home. Back to life."

"Could be a new life," he counters. "Even if you want a divorce, it could still be a new life."

I lean back in my seat, taking a croissant with me and nibbling on it as I stare past the floor-to-ceiling windows at the ocean. "Roman, is that what you want? I'm honestly scared to ask, but I think I have to know all the same." I turn back to him. "Is this just some vacation fun for us? Or are you asking for *more*?"

His intense gaze holds mine. "I'm afraid to answer because I'm not sure you're ready to hear what I have to say about it. And things are... complicated in my life right now. It's things we'd have to talk seriously about."

My heart sputters in my chest. Complicated. Meaning he doesn't date. He doesn't get involved with women. But he's talking about a new life with us. Meaning... friends with benefits? Is that what he wants? Is that what we are right now? Ugh.

He's right. I don't think I'm ready for this discussion.

"We have five days here together. Can we have these five days?" I ask.

"Absolutely," he agrees and continues to eat. "We can figure the specifics out later."

I swallow and smile a little at that. Five days of sun, water, and Roman. I can handle that.

22

ROMAN

"We're narrowed down to two potential sites in London, and the architect in Frankfurt needs an hour with you," my assistant, Katie, says. "Also, the supply company is giving us some grief on the fridge and freezer pricing."

I rub a hand across my forehead and pace by the window in the restaurant that overlooks the ocean. "What kind of grief?" I swear, it's always something.

"Oh, you know, that they want to double the initial quote because they're swearing we never told them we'd want stand-alone units instead of side-by-sides."

"Yes, we did tell them that, and that's what they quoted us at. Tell them that if they can't meet their quoted price, we'll go with someone else. I know for a fact that they're not the only restaurant supply company in Germany."

"On it. Have you had a chance to review the housing options I sent you?"

I stop pacing and instead get lost in the waves as they roll in. Braelyn doesn't want to talk about anything serious. She doesn't want to talk about what we're doing or what we are or what we could be. Fine. She's been single all of like three weeks. Not even that. Before she was engaged and nearly married.

I get that she needs time. The last thing I want to do is push her. If I do, she'll retreat. Hell, she already hid in the bathroom and cried because she was overwhelmed. That nearly killed me. I thought I had fucked up. Seriously, irrevocably fucked up.

I keep reminding myself to be patient. To remember that she's in my bed with me. That she needs time and space to work this out because that's how she operates. It's why I came into the restaurant after breakfast, when what I really wanted to do was stay there with her. There's all the time in the world for this to build between us, except there's not because I have a very real and looming deadline on my head.

"I haven't really looked yet," I admit.

"Roman, it's a six-month rental and those aren't all that easy to come by, especially for the type of place you want. I know you're in Mexico and working on stuff there, but we need to get these places figured out."

My eyes close and I release a silent breath. I'm so fucking torn. How do I continue to plan the future I have set in place when the future I always dreamed of but never thought possible is now within my reach?

I have to go to Europe.

The restaurants I'm opening there aren't like this or even the one in Vegas. They're not part of some resort that takes care of the heavy lifting and I don't have the same managerial and chef presence. They're being built from the ground up, from scratch, and need my constant input and my fingerprint all over them. It's exactly how I did it when I first moved back to Boston and opened Roundhouse and South Paw and then Uppercut after them.

But...

Braelyn doesn't want to be with me. She wants her fun. Her fling. It'll be five days of this and after we'll go home and life will return to normal as she said. We'll get a divorce and I'll have to move on and leave because she won't want me to stay. Friendship ruined. Heart TKOd.

Fuck.

The thought cuts the air from my lungs and has my insides seizing.

"I'll take a look this evening and let you know."

"Good." Katie exhales a relieved breath. "Great. I'll send you some Paris options as well. There isn't much in London yet, but I'm keeping my eyes on it."

"Sounds good, Katie. Thanks."

"You got it. Let me know if you need anything else."

We disconnect the call and I slide my phone into my pocket and put my hands on top of my head. I need to tell Braelyn about Europe. I didn't want to put it on her before the wedding because she had enough on her plate, and I figured I'd tell her after it.

The day after Adam proposed, she came over and was so happy. She showed off her ring and asked if I'd be her maid of honor. Of course I said yes.

Even as I felt like I was dying.

The next day, I decided I couldn't stick around after she was married. That I needed the distance to finally get over her. It was easy. A no-brainer. Setting up restaurants keeps me busy like nothing else, and I'd already thought about the type of places these would be.

I wanted five-star dining but at an affordable price.

I was tired of only serving to a particular clientele. When I mentioned this to Katie, she went running with it, and before I knew it, things were falling into place. Contracts were being signed. Now the wheels are in motion and can't be stopped.

But if I tell Braelyn now, she'll use it as her reason why we can't be together for real. She'll shut her mind down to the possibility.

I can't have that.

All of this might be for naught, but I can't go backward. I can't have her like this and then pretend we're only friends after. I can't pretend that she's not all I think about. All I dream about. All I want.

Except I might not have a choice.

I'm at her mercy with this.

My hand dives into my pocket and I finger the ring in there. I take it off whenever I come in here. I'm Chef Fritz in this building and a wedding band on my hand will garner questions. Questions my wife doesn't want me to answer.

My wife.

I nearly laugh at that.

I'm married to the love of my life and to her it's fake.

Then there's the Adam factor, but right now, I don't have it in me to care about his bullshit.

The fire alarm going off interrupts my thoughts. Only it's not just the alarm. It's lights flashing, things breaking, people screaming, and chaos.

Then there's the smell of smoke.

"Oh my god!" someone cries out in Spanish. "The stove is on fire."

Fuck. Seriously?

"Why is it hooked up?" I call out, also in Spanish as I walk briskly toward the kitchen. "And can someone turn off the fucking alarm and laser light show?"

"Laser light show?" the designer questions.

"The lights." I point up at the strobes.

"Oh." She laughs. "I think you might want to get the stove under control first."

I give her my most scathing look as I plow past her.

I enter the kitchen and sure enough, the stove—the brand-new, top-of-the-line, expensive-as-fuck—stove is on fire. Four of sixteen burners are shooting flames high into the air, with black smoke rising from them.

All I know is, thank god the sprinkler system isn't hooked up yet or this entire kitchen would be flooded.

The plumber is staring at the flames like he has no clue what to do. Not exactly reassuring. Two guys are running around, there are broken pieces of something on the floor, and another guy is working on the lights, but the bigger question to that is why are the lights going on along with the smoke alarm?

"I started the burners to test the gas," the plumber tells me.

"Turn off the burner."

"Oh. Smart idea."

"Ya think?" I can't stop my sarcasm, but this is literally what the man does. He doesn't even hear me over the blaring siren. "The grates are clearly not on right," I shout. "Turn it off!"

The smoke is a problem. There shouldn't be black smoke from a gas stove. Then I notice that the plastic is still covering the grates and that's what caught on fire and caused the smoke.

He tested the gas with the plastic still on.

Also, while the alarm has been going off, he didn't turn off the gas or the burners. If he ruined my new stove, I'll quickly earn my reputation for being a dick all over again.

"Just the burners or the gas?" he asks, still mesmerized by the fire and I can't with this. I just can't.

I push him aside and twist the knobs on the burners. Just like that, the fire is gone.

Unfortunately, the alarm and lights won't budge. It's like a rave in here and if I ever did acid, I'd be having a flashback for sure.

I don a thermal glove and go for my stove while the electricians hopefully fix the alarm. Plastic is stuck to the cast-iron grates, crinkled and charred. Piece by piece, I peel it back and by some miracle, my stove isn't ruined.

"How about next time you don't test out a stove while it's still covered in plastic."

The plumber looks at me with a sheepish expression and this is really not what I needed today.

"Chef Fritz, the fitness center called and informed us that they got you a punching bag."

I don't know who's talking to me. I don't care.

"Great. Take care of this. It better be back to normal by the time I return." I'm talking to everyone, but this is why I have to be on site during the construction of a restaurant.

I'm likely not coming back today, but they don't need to know that. I need everything working before Brae's birthday in a couple of days because I have a lot planned for that and I need my kitchen operational.

I start out at a jog, taking the trail back up to the villa, the echo of the alarm still ringing through my ears.

"Brae?" I call out.

"Out here," she mumbles, sounding sleepy.

I find her on the hammock, swinging gently as she reads whatever it is she's reading while looking cozy and adorable. "Hey, kid. You move today?"

I get a middle finger that makes me laugh.

"Good stuff. The gym called. They got me a bag. You cool if I go work out?"

I get a hand wave this time.

"Wanna come with me?"

Another middle finger.

Life would be so much easier if I weren't so fucking in love with this woman.

"I could teach you how to box."

"Ro, in all the years of our friendship and all your attempts to teach me to box, have I ever taken you up on that offer?"

"No, my beautiful wife, but you also never thought it would be fun to marry me before either and now look at us."

"Ha. So funny."

I lean against the wall and fold my arms as I watch her. "You just don't want to see me shirtless and sweaty. You're afraid it'll turn you on and make you wet."

I don't even get a spare glance. "You're quite full of yourself."

"Yes, but think, you could be full of me too."

An eye roll. "Go box."

I'm so screwed. Especially when my phone vibrates in my pocket and I see it's an email from Katie with a revised contract from the supplier, along with a resend of the email with the rental listings she wants me to pick through. Rentals I don't have it in me to look at. Not yet.

Boxing. That I can do. That will fix everything as it always does.

I change into gym shorts, sneakers, and a different shirt before I hit the trail and run all the way across the resort to the gym. It's empty at this hour of the day, but when I get there, the attendant leads me to a separate room where they have yoga mats and balls.

"We got you a big bag and a little one," he tells me.

He means a heavy bag and a speed bag. I'm in fucking heaven.

"Muchas gracias." I'll have to remember to heavily tip the manager. They even have tape here for me. I can't believe they did this.

I wrap my hands up and pop in my AirPods, setting my phone to my workout mix. It's a heavy metal, angry as all fuck kind of anthem, and I start off on the heavy bag, working side lunges and punches one after another. I go hard, working my muscles and quieting my mind.

After that, it's the speed bag with rolling wrists and alternating hands. Punch, punch, punch, dip-sway, dip-sway the other direction, punch, punch, punch. My muscles vibrate. My body hums. I block everything out. The restaurants. Europe. Adam. Guilt.

But no matter how hard I try, there is no blocking her out. All I want is to be with her. Except if I've learned one thing, life doesn't care about what I want. Not when it comes to Braelyn.

23

—————

BRAELYN

The hammock sways gently, my eyes half-closed as I lazily read the book Wren suggested. Roman and I had breakfast, but then he went to his restaurant, and I couldn't muster the energy to do much. After sitting in the pool for an hour, followed by the beach under an umbrella for a bit, I found myself back here. It's been the best lazy day ever.

The gym procured Roman a punching bag to work out with. I could see the excitement in his eyes. Sometimes it's good to be a Fritz.

I shooed him away since I know he was anxious to go train or whatever. That's where he's been for the last couple of hours until maybe fifteen minutes ago, when I heard him return and the water running in the shower.

"I see you've moved," he quips, standing on the edge of the doorway.

"Ha. You're very funny. I did get up twice, believe it or not. Did you have fun?"

He comes over and climbs on the hammock with me since it's made for two, making it swing wildly back and forth before he settles in and manages to still us. "I did. It was great actually and my hand didn't bother me. You should have come."

"You and your humor today. What fun things did they get for you?"

"A speed bag and a heavy bag, so I worked out with both." He kisses my hairline and groans. "You smell good. How do you always smell this good?"

"Good genetics. You should go pro with your boxing. Make it less illegal," I tell him with a yawn as he rolls me over so my face is tucked against him.

"Why are you so sleepy?" More kisses, these against my neck, and I arch to give him better access.

I crack an eye at him. "Vacation mode. Answer me."

He cuddles me, wrapping his arms around me and moving us so I'm half on top of him, half beside him. We haven't touched, at least not like this since last night when we fell asleep. He's given me space to work my mental craziness out and I've appreciated that.

"Never wanted to. Cooking is my passion professionally and boxing is a sport I love doing, but more than that, it allows me to release all the built-up tension I can never seem to let go of. I like the rush of it. The dirt and grime. Plus, I'm in my thirties, which makes me officially too old."

"You could get caught. Or hurt."

"I could," he agrees.

"Then what?"

"What are you worried about?" he counters, his finger trickling along my jaw and cheek.

"I just said it. You getting caught. You getting in trouble. You getting hurt. You losing everything you've worked so hard to build and possibly even going to prison."

"Baby, the Irish mob in Boston runs this. Unless I'm physically apprehended, there is no evidence of me in those rings. And I don't mind getting hit. I like the sting and adrenaline."

I don't like any of it, even if the fights are exciting and I agree with him on the adrenaline of it. He's not only a Fritz but also a famous chef. His face is everywhere all the time. Who is Roman Fritz dating now? It's all anyone cares about, and I've never explored or read those headlines. They were bullshit and I always hated reading them. But he's gorgeous and insanely wealthy and mysterious because of his bad boy vibe and his elusive and asshole chef presence.

The press loves him. They want him. And I worry that in their hot pursuit of him, he'll get busted. Then again, he hasn't yet and he's been doing this for years, so maybe I need to let it go.

"If you say so, I believe you," I tell him.

"I do. You read, I'll catch up on emails and maybe nap."

"Works for me."

The hammock sways gently as I roll slightly so I can tap my e-reader and resume where I left off. I haven't read a book in way too long, but Katy, along with Wren, sent me a list of books I had to get and I downloaded a few of them.

Roman simply holds me, his focus on his phone above my head, and I read, tucked against his chest. For a few minutes, that's how this goes. Except he's not reading emails on his phone. He's just good at playing that part. He was watching me instead.

"What are you reading that's making you blush?"

"I'm not blushing," I protest adamantly. Too adamantly. And the blush on my cheeks isn't helping my cause. "It's just hot out here. And you're too close."

"Right." He sets his phone down on the side table. "Let me see then."

"It's nothing." I try to angle the screen away so I can turn it off or change the book, but he's faster, his ninja boxing skills and dexterity snatching my e-reader in a half-second. Damn him! Again! I didn't want him to see this. Of course this has to be the scene I was reading. Ugh.

He holds my e-reader and starts to read.

"Are you wet?"

Her eyes blaze into mine. "Yes."

Fuck! I can't stop my groan, my hand stuck to my lower abdomen, hovering so near the hem of my briefs that my fingers twitch with the need to take myself in hand. "Good girl. Slip two fingers inside and pump them in and out slowly. I want the butt of your palm to rub your clit as you do. Put your other hand on your breasts and play with your hard nipples under your shirt." I pause, licking my lips. "If you're quiet, sweetheart, I won't put my tongue where you need me to." She lets out a breathy moan, her eyes falling back in her head as she finger fucks herself to my command. She's moving on the bed, grinding against her hand, and I don't think I've ever seen anything sexier in my entire life. "Does that feel good? Your fingers in your warm, tight pussy, stroking you just the way you like it?"

He stops reading and pulls the e-reader away, his eyebrow cocked, and I want the ground to open up and swallow me. "A little light reading?"

"It's a good story," I defend.

"I'll say. Damn, kid." He looks at me, his eyes wide, and now his cheeks are flushed.

I shrug like it's nothing. "Katy and Wren sent me suggestions for fun beach reads. This is the first one I downloaded. I just happened to be at that scene."

"Is it working? Is it making you wet along with her?"

"Knock it off," I bark, almost annoyed but not really, because I'm just being defensive.

He grins. "Do you like that? Do you envision yourself in a place where you give yourself over to the other person and allow them to take total control? Where you allow them to tell you exactly what to do and you do it because there's nothing you want more?"

"Cut it out." I snatch the e-reader back from him and fight a smile. "Some of us enjoy literature that isn't considered a classic or involves cooking techniques."

"No joke. Clearly, I've been reading the wrong stuff."

"Clearly," I mock. "I need to start reading more. I've been all work and no play."

"The more play part I agree with. Read me some more," he challenges, leaning back but keeping me close, and I have to say, our proximity isn't helping. Because he's hard. I mean, there is no denying that. We're on a freaking hammock together, side by side, but I can see he's hard.

"I can't read more."

"You're a nurse. Are you telling me you haven't had sex conversations with your patients?"

"Um, I don't exactly get explicit like this."

"Are you nervous?"

"A little," I admit. "It's not every day I read spicy sex aloud."

"Read it to me." And his voice changes when he says that. It's his dominant voice. The one that commands that dark part of me that doesn't know how to—or simply doesn't want to—say no. He's not making a move. He simply wants me to read him more smut, which is kind of hot. Fuck it.

I bring the e-reader back up so I can see it and start reading. *"What do you want? My cock or my mouth?" She lets out that breathy hum again, and I swear, that's my favorite sound ever. "I'm dying to taste you. I'll need to give you both. I'm going to fuck you slowly. So slowly you'll claw at my back, wild with desperation. And just when I start to get you so worked up and needy, my cock will slip out and I'll bury my face into you, licking you, devouring your sweet pussy in a way no one ever has before." Her eyes pinch shut as she bites her lip, trying to hide her sounds from me. But I can't have that. "That's right, sweetheart. Let me hear it. Let me hear how good I make you feel." She moans loudly, her face turning away from me, pressing into her pillow. Even though I'm dying to watch her face, I'll let her have that if she feels she needs it. If it gets her to come for me. "And just when you get close..." I trail off and she groans, her back arching and her tits peeking high into the air under her too-thin shirt. "I'm close," she cries."*

"You stop before she comes?" Roman gripes incredulously. "That's cruel."

"To her or to you?" I quip.

"Did it turn you on?"

"Yes," I admit. It turned him on too. His eyes are black, ringed in green.

He shifts, and his hand glides over my body, along my tits and down to my pussy. He cups me over my shorts. "I think this scene lacks a certain something."

"What's that?" I manage, already feeling winded.

"He's watching her touch herself. That isn't nearly as good as being able to touch her." He rubs his hand up and down. "I mean, you're so warm like this. And the way you smell." His face ducks into my neck and he takes a deep inhale as he starts to suck on my neck. "This woman doesn't know what it feels like when he touches her here." He cups me harder. "Or kisses her like this." His lips drag along my jaw, and I'm already gone to him. "But worse, the poor bastard doesn't know if his touch will make her breath hitch the way yours just did."

He's right. My breath did hitch and his eyes flashed with excitement.

"The book can't convey how it would feel if he did this." In one motion, he rolls us, forcing the hammock to cradle our weight even as it rocks wickedly. Suddenly, I find myself beneath him, my head tilted back, throat exposed, the world literally turned upside down. My e-reader is gone from my hands. It's just him. Just us.

And he's all over me.

"This is better than reading, I think. Less imagination required. More accurate."

"I don't know," I tease. "In my experience, fiction is often better than reality."

His smile is dangerous. "Challenge accepted. Though I might take certain artistic liberties. Any complaints?"

I shake my head, so ready for all of his artistic liberties.

"Good." His mouth drops to mine, and he kisses me hard, his tongue swirling into my mouth. His hand fists my hair and trickles through the curls to the ends, where he gives a rough tug that has me grinding against him. He wraps his arms around me and lifts me off the hammock to carry me over to the couch out here. He sits down with me straddled over him, his eyes on my face.

The sun behind our building creates weird shadows and odd light.

Feeling bold, I slip off his lap and stand before him so I can peel off my clothes piece by piece until I'm only in my bra and panties. His gaze smolders, his hands reaching for my hips so he can bring me back to his lap. His hard cock lines up perfectly with my pussy and I grind against him, moaning.

His hands take my wrists and lock them behind my back, forcing my tits to thrust out toward him. The slide of his mouth moves against me, his tongue seeking contact as it swirls with mine, familiar and new and exciting. He grunts into me as I grind down on him, needy and anxious for contact, my body remembering how he possessed it.

Twisting his head the other way, he switches his position and dives deeper, exploring every inch of my mouth. His fingers glide under the strap of my bra before he lets it fall off one shoulder, then does the same with the other. The cups slip lower and my nipples pop free. He pulls away to see, smiles, and dips his head to take one in his mouth, using his hands on my wrist to angle and arch me up higher for him.

"Braelyn, you have sexy fucking underwear."

I almost laugh. "I bought them for my wedding night along with a few other pieces."

He grins against me and bites my nipple until I squirm in his lap. "And you felt like you wanted to wear your wedding night lingerie for me? Your new husband?"

"It made me feel bold and sexy."

His eyes meet mine. "You are. You always have been."

I fight my smile. I like the way he talks to me. I like the way he looks at me. Actually, I love both because they feel natural, but I know for him, it isn't. Roman Fritz holds so much of himself back and only opens up, or talks even, to a select few. He trusts no one. He's a lot broken on the inside. So having this side of him as mine has always felt like a treasure and now this part of him is kind of killing me in the best and worst way.

He releases my hands. "Unhook it for me."

"Yes, sir." I give him a cheeky wink but without hesitation, reach behind my back and unclasp my bra. It slips from my chest and arms, and I set it down on the sofa beside us because it was expensive and I don't want it to get dirty on the ground. It is white after all but has delicate blue ribbons woven through the cups.

"You're so beautiful." He gives an incredulous head shake. "Braelyn, no one has ever affected me the way you do. You make me shake."

My eyes close and I loop my arms around his neck so I can kiss him. His hand slides down my back over my ass and he cups my pussy from behind, rubbing over my panties and opening without fully getting to my clit. It's delicious and frustrating all at once.

He lifts me again and sets me down on the sofa that's deep, meant for lazy lounging by the pool, but he's taking full advantage of this perk. He moves to the valley between my thighs, his eyes roving over me before he presses himself down on me and devours my mouth. His hands are all over me, playing with my tits, touching them, pinching and pulling on my nipples until I give him the desired noise he was after.

He kisses me like a man possessed. All lips and teeth and tongue. It's as if his control snapped, and I'm the air that's sustaining life. I reach for his shirt and pull it up and over his head, our mouths only breaking for that moment. His skin is hot and still slightly damp from his shower, and I want him. I want him like crazy. I don't know what's happening and what's not. I don't know if this will end after five days or if it's the start of something else.

But right now, I don't want to stop. I want more and more and more.

My hands drag impatiently along Roman's skin, hot and hard beneath my touch. Shifting back, he removes his shorts and I watch, his tattoos and muscles a feast for my eyes. He's got his locked on me too. On my tits, swollen and wet from his mouth, down the slope of my stomach to my pussy covered in virginal white lace.

Faster than I can anticipate, his hands grab the sides of my panties, and he shreds them from my hips. I gasp and jerk back to the end of the sofa, against the wicker arm.

"What the hell?"

"You bought these for another man. Did you honestly think I'd let them survive?"

"But, but…" I sputter.

"I'll buy you new ones."

I smack his shoulder. "I don't want you to buy me new ones."

"I know." He smirks. "That's what makes it so fun for me to do."

"Ugh."

"Now back that to that scene. I believe he mentioned something about face fucking her cunt."

"I believe he used a less crude term."

"That's literature. This is real life, and I'm going to make you fuck my face." With his eyes still on mine, he grasps my hips and in a move I can't even comprehend, he's got me straddling his face as he lies down on the chaise part of the sofa. My hands plant into the wall behind the sofa and my chin drops to meet his eyes.

I get a taunting eyebrow while his tongue comes out and circles my clit before it slips lower, straight up into me, as deep as he can go.

"Oh!" I cry out, my head flinging back and my eyes closing. Shit. He smacks my ass. Once. Twice. The third time is the hardest, making me squeal, but then he's clutching my hips and pulling me down on his face. His nose rubs my clit and he takes a deep inhale.

"Goddamn delicious." Like a man possessed, he growls into me, dragging the rough stubble on his chin along the most sensitive parts of me. Swirls and deep, grinding fucks make my clit pulse and my pussy drip. He's sinful. Depraved. And it makes me high. High on this. High on *him*.

"Roman," I moan, rocking against him.

"Did you buy those panties and think about him doing this? Him licking your cunt and making you come?" His voice is pure fucking gravel, coarse and stone and unrefined. Around and around, his tongue swirls, and I can't think.

My eyes pinch shut, and when I don't answer him, he smacks my ass so hard I yelp and I know there's a handprint there.

"Answer me, Braelyn."

Fuck. "Yes. I wanted him to do this to me."

He flips me over until I'm on my back and his face is hovering over mine. Two fingers pound straight into me while he uses the heel of his hand to rub my clit. "But who's doing it to you now?"

Oh god. "You are."

His hand slides up to my neck in a possessive collar while he finger fucks me like no one ever has before. It's almost brutal how deep and hard he's going. The sound of it, how ridiculously wet he has me, only turns me on more.

"Damn fucking right. Only me, Braelyn. Never him again. No one fucking else but me."

Jesus.

His hand squeezes my neck before he eases up, before he slides back down my body and puts his mouth on my pussy. French kissing me with flicks of his tongue that twist my body and bend my mind.

"Fuck!" I yell and pull at his hair, ripping and annoyed that I can't get a tighter grip on it.

He blows cool air on my throbbing clit and uses his wet fingers to slap it. My opening. My ass. Blood thrums through my body, making my clit pulse before he puts his fingers back inside me, curling them, quirking them, and thrusting them in and out while rubbing that spot that has me seeing sparkles of light behind my eyes.

With one final flick of his tongue and pounding of his fingers, he has me tightening around him and spasms taking hold within my core, intensifying until I'm screaming and undulating against him, fucking his face and fingers with everything I have, and begging him to never stop.

My mind frazzles and those sparks of light I had behind my eyes turn into fireworks and parades and marching bands. My orgasm is so intense it splinters me from the inside out and causes my toes to cramp from how tightly they've curled.

I have no clue if anyone nearby can hear me. Actually, I'm positive they could, but I don't care. I want him inside me this second. I need to feel him. To feel that fullness. And I must tell him because he growls into me, his tongue giving me one final lick that has me whimpering and pushing against him.

I fall flat against the sofa, my eyes closed while I pant for my life.

He shifts and I hear him moving. I quirk an eye open and watch as he licks his fingers to clean off my cum. I don't get a second to take that in before his wet fingers smack my breast, making it jiggle. But then he's kissing me again, swallowing my heavy breaths and framing my face with his hands.

I taste myself on him. Salty and clean, but he's there underneath it. Reaching down, I tug on his boxer briefs, using my feet to push them down the rest of the way. He kicks them off once they reach his ankles, his mouth never leaving mine.

One knee gets dropped onto his shoulder, the other butterflied out, suspended off the edge of the couch. Then he plunges straight into me all the way to the hilt and I'm calling out his name like it's a prayer and a plea and a fuck you. Because holy shit, I feel him in my uterus. No matter how many times we end up doing this, I'm positive he'll always feel this big on that first thrust. There is no getting used to that.

The walls of my pussy clench as I somehow grow more sensitive than I was before.

"Fuck." His forehead falls to mine. "Fuck, baby, nothing feels better than being inside you. Your cunt is fucking incredible."

He lowers himself onto me, stretching me with my knee on his shoulder, but his hands come under my shoulder blades and he holds me against him, keeping our foreheads locked. His cock pistons in and out of me with upward thrusts and heavy rocks that brush my clit. My breath scrambles from my lungs as he picks up his pace. The friction is otherworldly, but with my body like this and him holding me as tightly as he is, he controls my movements.

I have no choice but to take what he's giving me even as my

hands claw at his back with each pound. I quake with how good this feels. How deep inside of me he is. How big he feels, filling me so that he's all I know.

Rough teeth scrape along my jaw as his lips trickle up to mine. He holds me tighter against him, his hips pistoning and pounding, his cock slicing in and out of me so fast I can't catch my breath. My orgasm is rapidly building, with no way to slow or stop it. He's dragging it from the depth of my body, commanding I give it to him when he declares so.

I'm tight and swollen. His cock thick and hard. All of it making me crave more.

"Mine," he grunts, biting my lip. "No one else's. Not ever."

He hasn't stopped fucking me. He hasn't slowed. He's covered in sweat and I am too and the way he's fucking me, hitting my front wall on the inside and my clit on the outside has me digging my nails into his shoulders. I'm marking him. I'm positive of it and he must realize that too because he changes the angle and swivels his hips.

He licks my neck and sucks on my flesh. "My sexy girl. You don't know how I crave you. How I can't get enough. Braelyn, I'll never get enough."

"Roman... I..."

"Give it to me, baby. Come all over my cock. Then I'm going to fill you up." He moans as he feels me start to come. "Yes. Oh hell, yes, that's so good."

I shatter. Absolutely fall apart. My eyes close and my face buries in his neck, and I hold on as he fucks me through my orgasm. I grind against him, my body shaking as he comes inside of me with a feral roar. The sound and feel of him coming inside me like this take me to the next level.

He collapses on top of me. Releasing my leg from his shoulder, he drops his weight over me, and wraps his arms around me. For a few moments, we simply hold each other and work to slow our breathing. His weight is heavy against me, but it feels perfect. Slowly, he rocks into me, his lips trickling along my neck.

My fingers glide along the slopes and planes of his back, memorizing them.

"Let's go for a walk," he murmurs against me.

I can't help but giggle. "You expect my legs to work after that?"

I can feel him smile against me. "We could get in the pool and I could fuck you in there next."

I cackle. I have no clue where it comes from.

His head pops up and he eyes me. "You okay?"

"I have no clue what I am. I'm a lot. That's all I know."

"I can't argue that."

"Maybe a walk would be good. I haven't moved much today."

"That I can argue." He winks and slowly pulls out of me. I'm sore. Definitely sore, but in that pleasure-pain kind of way. Like after you've had a hell of a workout but are vibing on all the endorphins.

He slips back on his briefs and shorts, his eyes all over me as he dresses.

"I'll be back in a minute."

He clasps my jaw and holds me still before I can escape. "No more tears or hiding from me."

"You ripped my panties. I need new ones."

He shrugs. "Not really. You can go without them."

I scrunch my nose. "I'm leaking your cum."

He groans, his forehead back on mine. "You have no idea how hot that is to me." He reaches down and rubs my pussy, feeling his cum and pushing it back inside me with two fingers. He starts to pump in and out, and holy Christmas, how can I possibly be responding to him when my vagina is simultaneously yelling at me?

"Ah. No. My pussy needs a break before the next happy hour."

He laughs and kisses me, withdrawing his fingers from me. "Are we good?"

"You're checking in with me a lot."

His thumb drags back and forth along my cheek and his soulful eyes dance about my face. "I don't want to mess this up. This feels like the most important week of my life, and I want to get it right."

My heart gives a floppy thump, and something inside me shifts. It says, *What the fuck are you doing, you idiot, and why are you holding back from this incredible man?*

I don't have an answer. It's right. I'm just not ready yet. Maybe that's crazy, but so is blindly jumping into something when if I hadn't caught the train home that day, I'd likely still be engaged to another man. Instead of being married to this one. Oy.

I don't answer him with words. Instead, I tilt up and kiss him. I hold his face in my hands, feeling my ring shift against his cheek. It's been the most chaotic almost three weeks of my life. It scares me. Everything has changed with us, and it'll never go back to how it used to be.

There is fear with that uncertainty.

But also... that voice is back. The one whispering how nothing has ever felt more right than Roman. Despite the madness in my head and my heart, I know I don't want to let go of this because I'm afraid and have been burned.

Roman won't burn me.

He's the guy who burns down the world for you.

I just have to hope I won't need him to.

25

ROMAN

Braelyn is hunting for sea creatures. We're on the stretch of beach on the other side of the grassy area from our suite. It's a long stretch of not a whole lot except sand and ocean, with a few ships offshore dotting the cloudy horizon. An attendant asked if we wanted chairs and umbrellas set up for us, but we declined.

I have an obvious love-hate relationship with the ocean.

I spent my life sailing on it with my brother, and now I live above it, but I haven't been back in it since that day. No, we're not counting me diving in to save the kid. That was different. Even being on the beach right now isn't my favorite, but watching Braelyn's happy smile and excited movements as she chases tiny crabs and unearths shells from the sand is making it tolerable.

I told her I didn't want to mess this up, that this was the most important week of my life and she kissed me. But that's okay because she's mine. She is. In Braelyn language, her kissing me is her way of saying okay without overthinking it. So even though I wanted to take a walk on the path and maybe get an ice cream or something, I allowed her to take me down here.

I've never been the sort of guy who would have thought I'd ever be pussy-whipped, but this girl has me, and she clearly knows it because here we are.

"Come on, little guy." She holds out her hands, hoping he'll crawl into them. "I won't hurt you."

"But I will. I will legit take that crab and cook the fuck out of him."

Braelyn throws me a menacing glare from where I'm standing ten feet from the water while she's got her toes in the wake. She drops her chin back to the crab and starts to give chase as it scurries back into the sand. "No, wait! Don't go. He didn't mean it."

"I did. You should save yourself."

"You're evil."

"You know you ate crab two nights ago at dinner, right? And at breakfast in Vegas."

She peers up at me. "Crap. I totally did. Do you think it was his friend?"

"Absolutely. His best friend. Since birth. You're a crab killer. A destroyer of crab lives and legacies. Worse than the birds that eat them."

She flips me off. "Thank you for that daytime drama take on it." She stands, no longer caring about the crabs in the sand. "Do you remember when Nash dared me to dive naked into the ocean by your grandparents' place on the Vineyard?"

"You mean the summer he made us watch *Jaws* and wanted to recreate the opening scene?"

"Yes." She laughs at my scowl. "He told me there wouldn't actually be a great white waiting for us."

"He just wanted to see you naked."

She purses her lips. "Now that I think about it, maybe."

"Definitely."

"I made everyone turn around and stripped down, then ran into the water, only to run back out two minutes later. I don't think I've ever been more afraid of anything than I was in that moment."

"Considering there are great whites in that area, it was likely smart you ran back out."

She shudders and comes over to me, her arms wrapping around my neck, and she pulls up onto her tiptoes to kiss the corner of my lips. My arms band around her, and my hands land on her ass over her tiny shorts. I give her a squeeze as I tilt my head and deepen the kiss. I'm starting to get scared and scared isn't something I do well.

"You know, you could say no to a dare once in your life."

She scrunches her nose. "I think I'd regret not doing it and taking the chance more than I would turning it down."

"But now you're married to me."

"Now I'm married to you. Think of the millions of hearts that'll break when they realize you're officially off the market."

She's laughing, but I'm serious when I ask, "Am I? Off the market, that is?"

"At least until we get divorced."

She's still teasing, but it pisses me the fuck off. Regardless, I don't press it.

I'm at the point where I won't be able to go back. I won't be able to let her go. I've had her and I get to hold her and kiss her and tease her and touch her and be inside of her. I want this forever and I don't know how I'll recover if I lose it. I can't just be her friend anymore and that feeling fills me with dread because being her friend is the best part of who I am. She called me a good man, but the truth is, without her, I'm not sure I would be.

If she hadn't been there after Nash died, I'm positive I would have gone down a very dark and different path. She's held me firmly in the light. She's made me want to be better. A man who deserves her even when I feel like I'll never live up to that quest.

I lift her into my arms and kiss her harder. Until we're both breathless and smiling and the wind hugs us together.

"Let's go in the water."

I stiffen. "Or not."

She pulls back and meets my eyes, her body tangled around mine as I hold her up by her ass. "Just our feet."

"Braelyn—" I cut myself off as I think about this. About what I was just saying about fear. "All right."

Her eyes round. "For real?"

"For real."

She wiggles out of my arms and takes my hand, instantly walking through the hot sand to the cool water. The moment it hits my feet, a shock rolls through me. Yes, it's cold in comparison to the sand, but it's more than that. It's visceral. Like the first hit in a match, it awakens my senses and gets my blood thrumming. It's fight or flight and I always choose the former and never the latter.

I pull my phone from my pocket and take a picture of my feet and send it to my parents like a little kid showing off a stick-figure art project. But I don't care. They'll know what this is for me. In the last six years, I've pulled away from them. Maybe it's time I changed that. Maybe it's okay to live again.

Two nights later, it's Braelyn's birthday. She spent the day doing sunrise yoga, getting a massage and a facial, and lounging by the ocean. Unfortunately, I had to work for most of it. One of the major produce vendors was here and that was how it went. Braelyn said she didn't care. That she was happy to have the time and spent most of the morning chatting with friends and family.

Friends and family whom she didn't tell that she was married.

I tried not to let it burn me. After all, she asked for this time here to simply be and explore where we could go. She's not ready for the interrogation both of us would undoubtedly receive, and that's fine.

Since she wouldn't let me buy her a birthday gift, claiming that Vegas and the resort were already her gifts, I decided to do something special with her.

"Where are you taking me?" she asks, one hand gripping my forearm like I'm about to toss her blindfolded ass off a cliff, the other outstretched like if I don't throw her off a cliff, I'm going to smash her into a wall.

"Are you always this annoying with surprises?"

"Yes. In fact, I officially don't like surprises after walking in on my ex in flagrante delicto."

I cough out a laugh. "You sound like my grandmother saying it that way."

"Your grandmother is very wise. Oh! I just realized. Now that we're married, Octavia is my grandmother too. Yay! That's so cool." She does a little happy skip in the air and claps her hands. "I've always wanted her as my grandmother. She's the freaking best."

I sigh. "So you married me for my family?"

"And your money. Don't forget that. No prenup, baby."

"Right. How could I forget? Don't move." I stop her so I can unlock the door to the restaurant.

"Is this the moment before you throw me off the cliff? Because I can hear the ocean and feel the breeze."

See. This is how well I know my girl.

"In a minute. First I have to smash you into a bunch of walls."

"Ha. You're very funny. Seriously, what is all this?"

"Your birthday present."

She groans and sags dramatically. "Roman," she whines my name. "No more gifts or money spent on me."

"I thought you just said you married me for my money."

"And you know that was a lie. I hate your stupid money and I don't like this."

After I open the door, I kiss her temple. "Trust me," I whisper against her skin, retake her hand, and guide her over the threshold. I peel the sleep mask I was using as a blindfold back from her eyes and flip on the lights. Lights that are no longer working as a club effect.

Clinch unfolds before her eyes, most of the decor not yet finished. The restaurant itself sits up on stilts, some of it partially hanging over a wetland and the ocean. The wide-plank natural wood floors are covered in paper and there's no furniture or light fixtures yet. Just some industrial lighting, but the framework is here, as is the most important part.

The kitchen.

"Oh my god," she whispers, her hand covering her lips. She hasn't seen it yet and whenever she'd ask if she could, I'd blow her off, intending that tonight would be her reveal even if it's not finished yet. "Roman..."

My name trails off as she slowly enters the space, taking in the one-hundred-eighty-degree floor-to-ceiling—and the ceilings are twenty-five feet tall—windows that overlook the grounds of the hotel, the wetlands, and the ocean. There's a rectangular bar in the center of the room and the granite my designer picked out isn't here yet, but the dark wood is and it was freshly varnished today.

"This is stunning. Wow. I'm speechless with this."

I come in behind her, resting my chin on her shoulder. "You haven't seen my favorite part yet."

"I'm positive I already know what that is, but I can't imagine there's anything better than this view."

"Depends on your angle. Come with me, kid." I lead her through the swinging door to the spacious kitchen. Like the restaurant, it's not finished either, but it does have what I need for tonight set up and waiting, not on fire or covered in plastic, along with a chilled bottle of champagne.

"What's all this?"

"I'm making you dinner tonight."

A smile lights up her face. "Can I help?"

"Sure. Let's get you in an apron."

Braelyn isn't much of a cook, but she follows orders exceptionally well as I already knew. She's also a huge lover of all things Italian food, so I'm making her some dishes I know she loves like arancini with buffalo mozzarella, pecorino, peas and prosciutto, a wild boar pappardelle made with homemade pasta, cocoa, cognac, and parmesan, grilled rosemary focaccia, pork loin with polenta, Swiss chard, and roasted carrots, and for dessert I already made the batter for a molten chocolate cake that I'll serve her along with homemade ice cream that's in the freezer.

I pop the champagne and we get to work on preparing the dishes along with the items I've already prepped. We listen to music and sip on champagne and chat and as weird as it sounds, I haven't had this much fun in the kitchen in a long time. Usually, it's work, and though I love everything about my job, it's still exactly that. A job.

I've never cooked for pleasure like this alongside someone.

There isn't a great place to sit since the dining room isn't set up, but I created a table in the corner of the kitchen for us and put a tablecloth over it and some flowers the resort gave me for her. I've already set up our wine pairings, but Brae is a champagne girl and doesn't want to part with her glass.

"Cheers," I say, holding up my glass to toast her. "To my best friend. My favorite person in the world. The woman who never fails to see light through the dark and make everything shiny and bright. I..." I pause. I want to say it, but I also want her to enjoy her special dinner. "I'm so happy you're here with me, my wife." I wink at her. "Happy birthday."

"Cheers, husband. This is incredible."

We clink glasses, and even though she's joking as she calls me *husband*, I still can't stop the way my pulse quickens every time she says it.

Course by course, we eat, and when we reach dessert, I make her an espresso martini and drop a candle in the cake.

"Make a wish."

She closes her eyes and with a smile tickling her lips, she leans forward and blows out the candle. Her eyes open slowly, dark against the trickle of smoke that rises from the extinguished candle.

"This has been the best birthday I've ever had."

My chest pinches. "Yeah?"

"Without a doubt."

She rises from her seat and comes around the table to me. I lean back, and she climbs right onto my lap. She leans in and shocks me with a kiss, tasting like chocolate and coffee and everything decadent I love.

"Have you ever fucked anyone in one of your kitchens, Chef?"

I smirk against her lips before I trail down her neck. "I'm about to."

26

ROMAN

I shift Braelyn around on my lap and lift her up into my arms. She makes a surprised noise, she likely thought I was going to lift up her dress, push her thong to the side, and slip inside of her. But that's not how I work. Or how I want her birthday to end. I want to give my wife something special. A night she'll never forget, regardless of where things go for us when we leave Mexico.

I walk her over to the prep area we did a lot of our cooking in earlier. I don't have to worry about health inspectors or sanitation. The restaurant isn't open yet, and everything will get a deep clean before then. So tonight, this is going to be a fantasy for both of us.

Me fucking Braelyn in one of my kitchens. And what I'm going to do to her in it.

I shove aside some of the empty prep dishes and utensils and set her down on the metal table. Her dress isn't long. It hits her mid-thigh, which is why she shivers and screeches a little at the cold of the metal.

"Don't move," I warn her, and go over to get the sleep mask she wore here.

She spots the black satin in my hand and her breath hitches. Braelyn likes to play. She also likes me pushing her. She won't need a safe word tonight, though I will remind her she has one. There will be no punishments or rough play. But I do intend to test her limits.

"Lift your arms."

Without hesitation, she does as she's told, and my cock pulses at her obedience.

I lift her dress over her head, and once again, my little vixen is wearing seriously sexy fucking lingerie for me. I don't even care that she bought it for him. I'm the one who gets to see it. I'm the one who gets to remove it from her body.

"What's your safe word?" I ask as I set her dress over to the side so it stays clean.

Now she's breathing heavily. "Arrest."

It's the one she made the other night.

"Good. Keep it close. We're not going to go too far, and this will be all pleasure and no pain, but I won't listen to the word no because I have a feeling you're going to say that more than once to me tonight and not fully mean it."

"Oh." Her lips form an O, and a blush scorches her cheeks. "Well then, sir."

I smile. She has a thing with that. She teases me with it, but I know part of her likes calling me that otherwise she wouldn't. It's not as though I've asked her to, though there's no denying how much I like it.

Braelyn's eyelashes flutter and a small breath leaves her as I place the blindfold over her eyes. She's still and quiet, which tells me she's listening for me, trying to figure out what I'm up to.

I dip my finger in the bowl and bring it up to her lips to paint them with chocolate. She starts ever so subtly, but her curious tongue juts out, tasting the rich sauce.

"You never had your dessert," I admonish. She licks her lips, humming lightly, and I retrieve the cake though now the center is likely ruined. I'll have to get over that. I fork a bite and bring it to her mouth. "Open."

Once again, she obeys and I feed her the cake, watching as she hums contentedly and chews eagerly. She's so fucking cute. And I know that's not always the right thought to have about a woman. She's sexy and fierce and stunningly beautiful. But sometimes, like right now, she's also so cute I can barely handle it. Something about that hits my heart differently than her in any other way, and I can't help but chase it. I cup her face with my hand and eagerly kiss her, licking into her mouth with a playful intensity as I steal some of her cake for myself.

"Gross!" She laughs when I'm done.

"Not gross. Delicious. Here. You try." I take a bite of the cake and when I've chewed a bit, I kiss her so she can taste it. It tastes like me and like the chocolate and like the wine and champagne we've been drinking all night, exactly as hers tasted. It's the most intimate thing I've ever done with anyone.

She pulls away, licking at her lips. She's getting it now. Feeling it too.

I return to the chocolate sauce, painting her lips once more but intentionally dribbling some onto her chin and allowing it to roll down until it drips onto her tits above her bra.

"Clean me while I clean you." She squirms on the counter as I slip my chocolate-covered finger into her mouth so she can suck it while I suck on her skin. A moan tickles my finger as I ravish her tits, licking and sucking and biting at them over the expensive fabric as I pump it in and out of her mouth the way I will inside her pussy.

Slipping the digit out, I feed her another bite of cake, followed by a sip of the champagne we didn't finish.

"Good?" I question.

"Mmm. Yummy."

"I can't wait to find out."

With the flat of my hand on the center of her chest, I push her back. Her back arches against the cold, but I force her down, holding her still.

I'm between her parted thighs, and the marathon of things I want to do to her in here is running circuits through my head. I take one of the strawberries we never sliced up for the cake, plunge it into the chocolate, and put everything I am on the line.

I draw swirls that in cursive, spell out *I love you* on her belly with the tip of the strawberry. It's impossible to decipher with all the curls and twists, but before she can question me, I feed her the berry. When she's done, I lean across her and lick the chocolate and strawberry juice that's ringed around her lips before I trail down her and erase my confession with my tongue.

I tip the glass of champagne and pour a little on her belly to clean the rest of the chocolate, drinking it as I go.

"You're so sexy like this," I murmur against her skin. "So sweet, my beautiful wife."

"Oh, god. Roman—"

"Shh. Tonight isn't about that. I simply want to make you feel good. Understood?"

On a shaky breath, she utters, "Yes, sir," and my world stops and starts all at once.

"Perfect," I praise and return to her skin, kissing her, worshiping her. There's a large pillar in the center of the kitchen, and it's the reason I placed her over here. "Braelyn, this is where you're going to have to trust me and keep your safe word handy."

"Um…"

I grab her wrists and begin to bind them with thick kitchen twine. Around and around, I loop the soft rope, twisting and knotting as I go.

"Um…" she repeats a bit more urgently. "Roman… I…"

"Do you have a word for me?"

"No. But I'm not sure... shit. Oh my god!" she squeals as I force her hands to hold on to the pillar while I tie her to it. "What are you doing? Stop."

"Braelyn, if that's really what you want, you need to say *arrest*."

She bites her lip. "I don't know."

I glide my hand up and down her sticky stomach and chest. "Then go with it for now and trust that I have you, that I'll protect you and keep you safe, and that I'm trussing you up like this so I can eat your cunt and ass while I have you at my full disposal."

"Shit."

Reaching behind her, I remove her bra, followed by her panties. She is a goddess like this, tied up and blindfolded and already panting for me.

"Fuck. What if someone walks in here?"

"They won't. It's off-limits for the night." I bend over her and kiss her lips. "It's just us, baby. I swear it. But if you're uncomfortable with this, I'll untie you now."

I can practically feel her battle. Then she shocks me with, "No. I trust you. I'm just insanely nervous."

"I've got you. I've always got you." I kiss her, thrusting my tongue in her mouth as my fingers find her pussy and I ring her clit. Her cunt is hot and aching, and she rocks up, seeking more of my hand. "I'm going to make this feel good. So good."

"Yes." She sighs, her head dropping back as I increase the pressure on her clit. "Like that?"

"Better," I mumble against her neck as I trail down her while I drag my finger lower and join it with another to slip inside her. "So fucking good. So fucking tight."

"Oh god," she moans as I pump in and out of her, hitting her front wall and getting her clit with my palm.

"Can you take more?" I ask without really asking because

I'm not giving her the choice but to do so. I pull away from her skin as I slip my fingers out of her so I can shift her knees up to my shoulders. Then I stand to my full height, lifting her ass and back off the table and forcing her arms to extend and her hands to clutch the pillar tighter.

With her ass and pussy open to me like this, I hold her body up to my face and I lick from her tight ring of muscles in the back straight up to her clit. She cries out, fighting and squirming against me, unsure how to handle what I'm doing to her. Using one hand to hold her to me, I slap her ass with my other hand. Hard. A warning, but one that has her moaning and grinding into my mouth.

And I devour her. I eat her cunt like I've been waiting forever to. It feels like that. The notion of having Braelyn this way was always a dream and just out of reach. But not anymore. There will be hell to pay for this. A reckoning. I'm sure of it. But my blood thrums and my body breathes fire for her. That's the simple and not-so-simple truth of it.

I will lose Adam over this.

And he will make me pay. He's that kind of guy.

I don't care. I'll face anything to keep her.

My tongue plunges inside her as my lips rub against her clit. I groan, unable to handle how much I love the smell and taste of her. I set her back down on the table because I know she doesn't like being fully suspended in the air, especially blindfolded as she is, but I keep her ass and legs elevated, crouching so I can eat her better. I hold her against me, my grip on her ass and upper thighs secure. But I don't give her room to move. She still has to hold on and take what I'm offering.

It needs to be more.

And more.

And more...

More of my mouth on her cunt. More of my hands on her skin. More of my cock hungry, ready to be inside her. I'm desperate. And I hate this feeling because it's never brought me anywhere good. It always leads me back to the water. Back to that day. But Braelyn is my lighthouse. She's the beacon that guides me home.

My fingers dive inside of her and rub against her front wall while my tongue and lips work her clit. And because I'm feeling like being a bit of a cagey asshole, I spell out *I love you* on her cunt with my tongue the same way I did with my finger on her belly.

Her thighs clamp against my head, stuck on my shoulders, and her hands twist and fight, gripping the post but also needing to move. "Ah. Roman. This is so much."

"I know, baby. I've been waiting for you for so long. You are too fucking beautiful like this." Another swirl of my tongue. Another hard suck on her clit. Another hard thrust inside of her. "You're amazing. Look at you."

She's gripping the pole like it's her lifeline, her eyes closed and her chest expanding while I hold her tight. Yet she's starting to fuck my face the way my face is fucking her. She's making noises that are no longer fear but desire. *Desperation.* They're screams mixed with thrashes. Insanity mixed with depravity. Magic mixed with forever.

I'm doing this because I want my girl to fall. Not just for me, but into another realm. A realm I think her body will grow and thrive in. Where ultimately, she'll be found.

It's with this notion that I eat her cunt until she comes. Until I can barely hold her up with how her body moves. I play with her pussy through it, licking her cum and tasting her as deeply as I can. I don't want to stop, but her noises, harsh protests, and wiggles tell me I need to or she'll kill me when I untie her. I lower her back to the table and swirl my tongue around from her opening to her clit once more before I trail up her body until I reach her mouth where I hover. I can't see her eyes, but her limbs are heavy. Even her grip on the pole is challenged.

Because it's her birthday, I ask, "Do you want me to untie you or fuck you like this?"

"Untie me."

That's all it takes. Carefully, I use a pair of kitchen shears and free her, drawing her body up into mine and holding her close. I remove her blindfold and massage her wrists, while I check her for marks. There are a few red indentations, but nothing that will bruise.

"You okay? Did you hate that?"

"No. It was intense and very different and pushed me hard, but I definitely didn't hate it."

I kiss her hairline. "I'm so proud of you. You did such a good job."

She emits a sigh and sags into me, her head heavy against my chest, especially as I continue to massage the marks until they're gone. Only then do I adjust her hips, shifting us until I'm on top of her, and slide straight in.

"Tell me if it's too much."

She shakes her head and grips my ass, urging me in deeper.

"No. I want to feel you. Please, I want you to fuck me till you come in me."

Jesus hell. No woman has ever begged me for that, and it happens to be my woman who is. There will never be another moment for me like this moment with her.

I lean forward and scoop her up into my arms until she's sitting up, and we're pressed together, and my forehead is against hers.

"I love you," I breathe inaudibly, knowing she can't hear it as I start to push into her.

It's not a pounding. It's not a brutal force or a hard fuck. It's feeling her. It's letting her feel me, as she said she wanted. It's push and pull and thrust and draw and give and take. It's breath and sweat and eyes and air and a stirring that can only happen when two people are so joined there is nothing else but them and the moment.

I'm fucking her. Yes, of course I am. But it's so much more than that. I'm pushing my cock in and out of her cunt, forcing moans and swiveling hips until I have it just right for her. Her pussy feels so good. So fucking good. Like a glove or a hug or something just as cosmic and intimate.

All I know is that being inside her like this is like nothing else.

Her pussy flutters around me, and she begs me to take her harder, deeper, more aggressively. Her thighs are around my hips, and I lean her back down on the table so I can give her what she needs. I miss her contact and bend forward, taking her lips and kissing her sloppily while I hold her body and fuck her relentlessly.

She clings to me, holding on as she takes the pounding my cock is now delivering. Side swipes and roundhouses and below-the-belt and perfect jabs.

It's gloves off, toe-to-toe, mindless, *exquisite* pleasure.

I fuck her like I ate her. With total command and without mercy. With ownership. With lines fractured and boundaries crossed and lives irrevocably altered. And when we come, this time we do it together. No words or warning. It's a connection, and it pulses between us as it electrifies from within.

I kiss her and hold her and tell her a million things about how incredible she is. Braelyn doesn't talk much. She's quiet and introspective, which isn't like her, but I don't press her. I think I pushed her into subspace a bit from all the endorphins, and with that, I give her some soothing aftercare.

I hold her and caress her and kiss her softly. Gently.

Once we're dressed, it takes us forever to clean up, but Braelyn is back to being herself. Our hands touch, our smiles are dopey, our minds are calm. We return to our villa, unable to stop touching, and I take her again in the shower. This time it's fast and all kisses as we chase an exhausted release.

We fall asleep with reckless abandon, our bodies twisted around each other like vines. And for one blissful moment, everything is perfect. Except I should have known better. Nothing stays that way for long.

27

BRAELYN

"I don't know if I should be a nurse," I said quietly, the grains of sand beneath my bare feet digging themselves between my toes. It was cold out here, but I didn't mind it, and Nash didn't seem to either.

"How come?" he asked softly, his eyes cast toward the choppy water.

"Because I'm scared I'll kill someone."

He released a breath. "I am too. I'm hoping that fear will make me a better doctor and keep me from getting complacent. But chances are, I will kill someone at some point."

I shuddered. "I could never be a doctor because of that."

"Being a nurse is heart and being a doctor is science. I think you're going to be an incredible nurse. I think your patients will be lucky to have you and will remember you long after you forget them."

I shifted until my head was resting against his shoulder, but he moved to wrap his arm around me and I tucked into the crook under his chin.

"I think you're going to be an incredible doctor. You have science, Nash, but you also have heart. The world needs more of that."

"I don't have the intuition you have. You see things before they happen."

Not always, I thought, though I didn't actually think that. Not then. That thought came later. I tried to hug closer to him, but he wasn't there. It was just the darkness and ice gathered in my soul.

"Nash?" I called out. I didn't want him to go. Not yet. I loved my dreams about him even when they made me sad afterward. Suddenly, I wasn't on the beach anymore. I was somewhere else. The hospital but not exactly that. There were waves of light. Of yellow. Then...

"Systolic is dropping. Is dopamine on board?"

"Yes," I replied.

"We're losing him. BP is crashing and he's in V-fib. Push epi and charge the paddles. Let's go!"

Except I couldn't. My limbs were heavy and my body was sluggish. It felt like I was running through water or sludge or sand.

"I think losing a patient is inevitable."

"I have lost patients," I told Nash, grateful I was out of the trauma room. That was a horrible shift. A horrible death. "He didn't make it. He was so young."

"It wasn't your fault."

"Doesn't make it any easier to manage."

"It wasn't Roman's fault either."

I held in my sob and clung to him. I loved Nash. He was everything perfect a first love should be. A best friend. A confidant. Gentle. Sweet.

"You need to tell him that," I whispered.

He kissed my hair. "You need to tell him that for me. And make sure he believes it."

"I've tried. I'll keep trying."

"It's okay to love him."

"Charge to two hundred. Clear!"

I jolt awake, covered in sweat as my dream fractures into pieces and dissolves around me. All I'm left with is that feeling.

That awful, icky, prickly feeling you get after a bad dream. Except... Nash. I was with Nash on the beach. It was the week after we got our acceptance letters to college. We were at his grandparents' Martha's Vineyard home, and not even three months later, he was gone.

I went to BC without him. Skylar started the following year, and we were in the same program. But I didn't have Nash and that first year was the hardest and worst of my life.

But there's more. Something else I can't quite remember from the dream but is what's making my insides squirm and feel all wrong.

I roll over and face Roman, who is sound asleep on his side, facing me, his eyelashes fluttering as if he's dreaming. I hope whatever he's dreaming about is better than whatever I was just dreaming.

Last night was incredible. He's incredible. But that's nothing new. It's everything else that he's doing. Everything else that I'm afraid to analyze and think about and obsess over and feel. Because where will that lead me? Roman isn't the type of man who dates. He's never had a girlfriend. Not one that I can remember.

Yes, he's called me his. Yes, he's hinted that this runs deeper, but is that because it's me and it's us? I release a breath. I could ask him. I *should* ask him. But when he answers, I'll have to be ready for that answer either way. It's a slippery slope I'm toying with. An edge I can't seem to get my bearings on.

Then it hits me. Why I've been holding myself back when everything else inside me is telling me to run blindly toward him and never look back. I couldn't figure it out. But now it makes so much sense.

I've loved and lost more than once. They were obviously different, and yes, those losses hit differently too. Losing Nash was devastating. I clung to Roman because it felt like holding onto Nash. We had a shared grief and that grief was consuming. Our friendship became a lifeline for both of us. I didn't date anyone until Adam. I fooled around in between and of course, tried to kiss my ex-boyfriend's older brother.

But the only two men I ever gave my heart to broke it one way or another. I've had to grieve them both. Live through the loss. So my fear is real. It's valid. It's a byproduct of deep, penetrating scars.

Even if I want to leap blindly at Roman, those scars are what's holding me back. Not him. Not necessarily. But I also don't want to run from this. I want to see where I end up. Where we could end up. Even if it's just us walking out of here as best friends and nothing more.

He looks so peaceful. So perfect. My heart gives a thump.

Something is making me antsy, though. The part of my dream I can't quite remember. It pulls me out of bed. I use the bathroom and pace around a little in there, but there's no way I'm falling back to sleep now. Quietly, I pad back into the bedroom. Roman stirs, rolling onto his back, and I freeze.

He mumbles something unintelligible in his sleep that makes me smile, but he's still out. I snatch my phone from my nightstand and head outside onto the terrace, the warm ocean breeze kicking at my face and whipping my hair behind me.

I'm twenty-seven now.

I'm young and yet I don't feel that way. I've experienced so much. Seen so much. Both in life and in the ER. I've had sleepless nights at the hand of the ER before. It's an uncomfortable anxiety that stirs the pit of your stomach and rattles your mind. Did I miss something? Did I kill anyone? Will that patient be okay? Will their families?

I set my phone down on the side of the stone, get undressed, and slip into the pool. I don't even know what I'm after or what answers I'm seeking. I just know I don't feel right.

I'd call Skylar, but she's sleeping and has been exhausted during her first trimester, and I don't want to bother her. But I do need to talk to someone, and while I could call Wren or even Katy, they're cousins of Roman.

I unlock my phone and dial Quinn.

She picks up after the third ring. "Hey, first-time caller, long-time listener, welcome to the ortho all-night party line."

I snicker. "How long have you been awake?"

"If we're asking, I'm on hour sixteen, but in fairness, it's been a hell of a shift, and I was supposed to take an hour and a half nap two hours ago."

"But you didn't?"

"I tried. This is what happens when you graduate early, and everyone thinks you're a prodigy when you're actually not. They throw a million things at you and ask you all the questions because they think you have all the answers. I'm fourth year, not a freaking attending."

"Yeah, but you're the age of second years, and you're a gold medalist."

"Pshft. Like that matters. Where are you and why are you calling me in the wee hours of the morning?"

I put my phone on speaker and rest my forearms on the edge of the pool so I can kick my legs out behind me. "I'm still in Mexico, awake in the middle of the night, on the terrace because my bed buddy is sleeping. I heard a rumor you're possibly doing some of your residency with the Rebels."

I hear her moving around in the background and then a door closing. "Never repeat rumors. But I will give that a maybe in the hopes of never. Unfortunately, I am at the will of my attendings. Working with my brothers and father sounds horrible, and I prefer hockey over football."

"Is that because of your ex or your brothers?"

"Ha! You're very funny."

"I have my moments."

"You don't sound good. What's up?"

I blow out a breath and stare out into the darkness, toward the water I can't quite see but can hear. "I had a horrible dream I can't fully remember. I know Nash was in it, but that's not the horrible part. It woke me up. I think it was a work dream."

"Ah. One of those. Ghosts of ER patients past?"

"Something like that." I sigh. "I'm keeping a secret from you. From all of you."

"And does this secret include your sleeping bed buddy?"

"Roman and I... we're—"

"Ahhhhh!" she screams, and I wince as she's on speakerphone. "Oh my god!"

"A little louder," I deadpan. "I don't think everyone in the hospital and at the resort here heard you. For that matter, I have you on speaker and I don't want you to wake up Roman while I'm talking about him."

"Yeah, but I don't care. Tell me everything. Are you okay? What does this mean? Are you together? Is this just for fun? Has he told you how he feels about you? Have you told him?"

"Whoa, slow down, Nancy Drew. We'll get to the end of the mystery soon enough. It's not just that we're sleeping together. We're... married."

A beat of silence and then. "I'm sorry, what? Did you say you're *married* to Roman Fritz?"

"Yep. It happened in Vegas."

She snorts a laugh. "You sound like Mason and Sorel."

Right. I kind of forgot about them. Mason is Quinn's older brother, and his wife is Sorel Fritz. "Sorel was a runaway bride, and she married Mason as revenge. Mine wasn't that. Adam didn't even cross my mind that night while we were doing it. How weird is that?"

"Weird, but also kind of awesome. Is this a quickie wedding

followed by a quickie divorce or is this a lifetime of love and making babies?"

I kick my feet up and down beneath the water surface. "It started out as the former, and I'm not saying we're staying married or want to be married because we don't. It's not like that. Honestly, I don't know what it is now that we're having sex. How can we do this and yet be married and get divorced?"

"It's you and Roman. Except you're calling in the middle of the night because you don't know what's happening."

"No clue," I agree, chagrined. "I'm scared. The only two guys I've ever loved…" I trail off, swallow, and mumble, "They didn't turn out well for me. I'm two for two, with broken hearts to show for it."

Quinn sighs. "Yeah. But life goes on. And Nash is still there. You know that. You feel that. Hell, you told me you dreamed about him tonight."

I blink back tears. "I don't remember what he said or the rest of the dream, though I know it wasn't good."

"Losing Nash and getting dicked over by Adam doesn't equate to a lifetime of hurt. Our future love isn't dictated by our pasts. At least I hope not."

"I bet you don't."

"My ex chose to follow his dreams, and I chose mine. They didn't align. I like to imagine the next guy I find will be a better situation. Roman is different, Brae. He's not the type of guy to risk you or your friendship unless he's invested. He's not going anywhere."

I think about this for a moment. About what that means.

"But am I ready?"

"Only you can answer that. But on the flip side, I can't imagine you'd risk what you and Roman have if you weren't. The marriage piece aside, you're there with him, sharing a bed, and having sex. You wouldn't be scared if it didn't mean something to you. More than the fact that he's your best friend."

I take that and let it settle over me. I hold it against my skin, against my chest, against my mind.

"I hope not. I hope this becomes our best decision instead of turning into our worst mistake."

"It's all any of us can hope for."

28

BRAELYN

The sound of our phones ringing wakes us from a dead sleep with a jolt. It's the second time I've been startled awake in the last five hours, and it's not a fun way to wake up. The minute one stops ringing, it instantly starts again, as does the other. Roman and I exchange panicked looks and dive for our phones to answer.

"Hello?"

"You're married to Roman, and you didn't tell me?!" my mother screeches into the phone.

Her words don't fully register. "What?"

"Don't what me, Braelyn. It's all over the damn internet. A copy of your marriage license from Vegas *a week ago* as well as pictures of the two of you kissing on the beach."

"Oh shit." Oh shit, oh shit, oh shit.

My head flips over to Roman, who has an equally impressive oh shit look on his face.

"Yes," he says to whomever he's on the phone with. "Stop. I can't change that. Do we know who leaked it?"

"Braelyn!" my mother yells, calling my attention back to her.

I jolt. "Crap. Sorry."

"Tell us what's going on."

I rub a hand up and down my face, trying to calm myself and gather my thoughts. Because my oh shit is turning into a lot more than that as my mind goes wild. "We got drunk in Vegas and his friends dared us to get married. I don't know. I don't remember everything, but I'm pretty sure I talked Roman into it. Something I'm sure he regrets right now. It wasn't our finest moment."

"And the kissing?" she presses.

I close my eyes and rest my forehead in my palm. "Um, well, Roman and I are, well, we're..." I trail off. God, what a mess. "We haven't figured that out yet."

"Jesus Christ, Braelyn. You're sleeping with your best friend, who happens to be your accidental husband? Are we living out our best *Days of Our Lives* self?"

"Ha. You're very funny."

"Don't listen to her, Brae. I think it's awesome," my dad calls out from the background. "You and Roman are like your mother and I were. It's all going to be fine. Are you okay, though?"

I blink and stare down at the white blanket resting on my lap, swarming with unease. "I have no idea what I am. You said this was all over the internet?"

"Yes, it's—"

She gets cut off when a call comes in. I pull the phone away to see that it's Skylar.

"Mom, Sky is calling."

"Fine. Go rally the Fritzes, but this conversation isn't over. You were engaged to Adam and now you're married to Roman. This is a very big deal and the Boston media as well as the world are now interested in it."

"Fabulous. I'll call you back."

I rub a weary hand over my forehead as I flip over to Sky.

"Oh my god!" she screams into the phone before I can so much as say hi. "What on earth is going on?"

"I don't know what's going on yet," I admit, my voice tremulous. "I woke up to a zillion phone calls and my mother screaming in my ear. Sort of like how you are." I climb out of bed because Roman is still talking to whoever the hell he's talking to, locate my robe, and go to the living room where there's a coffee maker I can use because I need serious caffeine stat.

"Are you married to Roman? Is this true or some messed-up AI thing?"

I sigh as I fill the coffee maker with water and set in the large pod. "Yes, it's true."

"Why didn't you tell me?" She's hurt, and I hate that. Skylar trusted me with her biggest secret, and I didn't do that in return. I should have. I just... I never wanted anyone to get hurt with anything, but now it seems that's how it's going to be for everyone. I told Quinn overnight but not her.

My eyes close in regret. "I'm sorry. I should have. We didn't tell anyone, but that was my decision. I called Quinn overnight and told her, but I didn't want to wake you. Roman and I got drunk in Vegas, and I don't know. We just did it. We didn't think much about it until the next morning when we woke up with hangovers and rings on our fingers. Our plan was to get a quickie divorce and have no one be the wiser."

I hit start, and the coffee maker makes a loud bubbling and churning noise as it fills the mug with magic.

"Okay, well, that's a bullshit notion and I'm pissed you didn't tell me."

I sag my hip into the counter. "I know. You have every right to be. It was shitty. It wasn't meant to be, though. I just felt like it was something we didn't want a lot of voices on at the moment given everything."

She releases a heavy breath into the phone. "Fine. I get that. But I'm even more pissed that I had to learn that you're making out with your bestie on a freaking Mexican beach through the internet. Are you sleeping together? I mean, I had a feeling you were."

"Your intuition is as good as mine."

"Only about other people and not myself."

"Truth. That's so fair." I add sugar to my coffee and stir it in as I reply. "Yes, we're sleeping together. But we weren't when we got married. The sex part started here."

"Holy crap! Braelyn, you're having sex with Roman! I can't believe it and yet I can."

"You sound like my mother."

"I already spoke to your mother. She called me at first light. This is huge. Oh, hold on. Quinn is calling, I'll merge her in."

"Girl, I'm on twenty-something hours of no sleep and now this? How am I supposed to go home and sleep when this is all over my phone?"

"Uh, yeah, I'm not helpful with that. I'm waking up to this, so my day is just about to start."

"I'm about to get on the T to head home, but I keep getting alerts on my phone."

"Lovely," I mutter.

Roman saunters out of the bedroom wearing boxer briefs and a scowl. I lift the coffee to my lips and take a sip before I hand him the mug.

"Who is that?" he mouths.

"Quinn and Sky," I reply silently.

He nods and blows off some of the steam so he can take a sip.

"Brae, are you even listening?" Quinn asks.

"What do you want me to say?" I reply, leaning against the buffet and turning out toward the water so I don't have to look at Roman. "I don't know what to say. I haven't seen the pictures yet, and I'm not excited to."

"You realize someone has been following us," Roman jumps in, and my head flips back to him, my eyes wide. Because shit. He's right. How did I miss that?

He takes the phone from my hand and sets it to speakerphone.

"Yes," Quinn agrees. "That's exactly what it means. That's seriously scary stuff."

I blink at Roman, my suddenly trembling hand covering my lips. He draws me into his side and kisses the top of my head. "Hey, it's okay," he whispers, but it's not okay. Not even close.

"The kissing pictures look like they were shot from far away," Skylar notes and Roman pulls out his phone for me to see what we're dealing with. "Like, I don't think someone is there beside you getting these."

He hands me his phone and I scroll through the article.

"Likely from one of the boats we saw offshore," Roman agrees.

"Roman Fritz!" Skylar yells at her cousin. "I cannot believe you married my best friend. Your best friend. You'd better be good to her or you'll have to deal with me and I'm pregnant, so you know my hormones are not to be trifled with."

He chuckles. "Promise."

"Good. Now back to this. They knew exactly where you were and when you were going to be there or at the very least, they were stalking the beach."

I flip through photos on various sites before I can't handle it anymore and hand it back to him. "It's the beach right in front of our villa," I whisper, completely shaken by this. "That's where we were. Do we know who it is? Who started this? The pics I just saw were on freaking IG and TikTok."

"*Intertainment* and shortly after *Boston Nine* posted it," Quinn informs me, her voice the equivalent of a grimace.

Boston Nine. As in Adam's company.

"Fuck," I hiss, momentarily closing my eyes. I look up at Roman. "I'm so sorry," I tell him.

"Listen, you know Forest is already on this," Sky states. "I don't want to know how, but he'll dig and get you info, and in the meantime, you two have stuff to figure out."

"Thank you, ladies. I love you, and I'm sorry I didn't tell you. Don't be mad at Roman. That was all me. I'll call you later, okay. He and I need to talk."

"Bye. Love you!" they sing out, and I disconnect the call and set my phone down just as it rings again. Adam. Naturally. I decline the call and take my coffee back from Roman, who is quietly observing me.

"Freak-out on a scale of one to ten?"

I laugh. "Oh, you know, about ten thousand. Tell me how bad this is?" I ask.

"Depends on your definition of bad. Forest is looking into it, but someone obtained our marriage license. Either it was leaked from them or someone found it since it's a public record. They somehow knew where we were and followed us here. That's the fucked-up part, but it's not uncommon. My name is all over this place with my restaurant being here and us meeting with that other chef the first night. I don't know if they're at the resort or offshore in a boat or what, but it seems like they were offshore, going by the pictures."

"Fabulous. But Adam's company got it right after *Intertainment*?"

"Yes. He called me too, but I was on with my assistant and my PR staff."

I scrunch my nose. "You have PR staff?"

"For the restaurants, yeah."

"Right. Of course." I blow out a breath. "This is all my fault. I plunged you into a scandal all because I was stupid and drunk and thought it would be so funny if we got married."

He shrugs. "I don't care that much. Not my first scandal and definitely not the first time people are talking about me. I never cared about what people thought of me, and I doubt it'll impact my restaurants. Scandal brings people in, actually."

I take a sip of coffee, wishing it were spiked with something stronger. "I suppose that's good. Don't they say there's no such thing as bad PR?"

"Something like that." He runs a hand over the top of his head. "What I care about is how this will impact you and about Adam learning about us this way. I'm positive he's furious his network pushed the story. I honestly can't believe they did. It makes him look bad. Regardless, it's not how I wanted him to find out about us."

"You mean like walking into your bedroom and finding him fucking another woman in your bed, finding out?"

His hand cups my cheek. "You already know my loyalty is to you. He cheated and hid it. You have every right to your anger and resentment. But it's not why I'm here with you. What he did to you was unforgivable, but I want to be a better man than that, and I was going to tell him when we got home."

"You were?"

"He deserved to hear it from me, but now that ship has sailed."

I swallow thickly. We haven't talked about this, and again, that's my fault. But I need to stop running. I need to put my faith in Roman. But more than that, I have to take the leap and trust that when I fall, it'll be him catching me.

"What were you going to tell him?" I place my hand over his steady heart. "We haven't talked about this, and again, I know that's on me. I also know this is likely the worst time ever to have this conversation. But... is this more than fun for you? It feels like it is. It feels like you're fighting for something with me instead of simply enjoying whatever it is we've been doing."

He inches in until we're practically chest to chest. He takes the coffee from my other hand and sets it down as he searches my eyes. His fingers glide along my cheek, and he gives me a sad sort of smile.

"I'm forever fighting for you because winning you has been impossible. Braelyn, I'm in love with you. I have been for years. This entire week, I've been losing sleep thinking about the life we could have together and how to get you to not only see that but want it despite all you've been through."

Emotion rushes over me like a geyser. "You have been?"

His eyes glitter, and his fingers are soft on my skin. "God, baby, the way my heart beats for you." He covers my other hand on his chest and presses it in. "You have to feel that. I know you do."

"But... what does that mean? You're my best friend."

"It worked for your parents. For you and Nash."

"I know, but—"

"Did you ever think that I could be your best friend and the love of your life? That they're not mutually exclusive but build on one another? I am your best friend. Your friendship means everything to me. But I'm also in love with you, and that's been the plight of my life."

I stare up into his clear blue-green eyes, my skin hot and itchy. "You never told me. Never hinted."

He gives me a rueful smile. "I tried to hint at it before you got together with Adam. When I moved back to Boston, I tried. At least I should say, I thought I tried, but clearly, I wasn't direct enough because you missed all of it."

I choke out a half-sob, half-laugh and drop my forehead to his chest, breathing in the scent of him. "Yeah. I missed it. Completely. Shit."

"I should have kissed you." His lips peck the top of my head as he runs his hands down my hair. "I should have told you."

I look up at him, pressing my chin on his sternum. "After you rejected my kiss, I thought you had no interest in me, and I pushed my curiosity about it away. As you said, my parents were best friends, and so were Nash and I, and after all that, I wondered about it. I let go of it because I thought that would never be us. That you didn't want that with me or anyone really since you never had girlfriends."

"I know you just broke up with Adam. I know you just canceled your wedding, and things are still in upheaval from all of that. I know the world now knows that we're married, and that was the last thing you wanted to come out. I don't want to pressure you or have us move faster than you'd like us to. Despite all that, I'd like to try for something real."

"You better be sure," I warn. "Because I'm going to fall so in love with you. I've been holding myself back. You know that, right? Like I'm going to be fangirl obsessed and I won't make it if you break my heart. I won't. I survived Adam and came out better on the other side, but surviving you won't be the same."

His forehead meets mine. "I want you obsessed because that's how I've been for the last six or so years."

"Since after Nash?"

He looks between us for a beat before his gaze returns to mine. "You're the only reason I made it through that and along that journey, I started to see you differently than I ever had before. I fell in love." He shrugs. "As wrong as it was and as wrong as it felt, I did. I decided having you however I could get you was better than not having you at all, and at the time, I wasn't in a place to be more to you. I had to get myself right and I wasn't. Then Adam came along. But now that we've had this time together, I can't go back." His lips bounce, and he throws my words back at me. "I won't make it if you break my heart. I won't survive losing you."

"Then I guess we're doing this."

A smile lights up his face, making this serious bad boy look almost boyish if such a thing were possible. "I guess we are."

"I have no clue how we'll explain this to anyone, but whatever."

"I don't care how things look. Bonus of being an asshole to the world. You're a sweet little nurse, so you're the one who'll have it worse than I will. Sorry. Sucks to be you, I guess."

I pinch his nipple brutally hard, making him jump and swat my hand away.

"We have two more days here before we return home."

I sag. "Yeah. That kind of sucks, but—"

I'm cut off when my phone rings again. Adam.

"I'm going to answer it," he tells me.

I wince. "This won't be pretty."

"It was never going to be since I made you mine." He winks at me and slides my phone across the counter to answer it, instantly putting it on speakerphone. "Hey."

"Hey?" Adam barks indignantly. "That's how you answer *her* phone? Hey?"

Roman picks up my coffee and drinks half of it down. If it burned his mouth, he doesn't register it. "What do you want me to say?"

"That everything my fucking network is reporting is bullshit."

He meets my eyes as he says, "It's not. I married Braelyn in Vegas. I knew what I was doing even if she was a bit too drunk to know. I would have married her sober if she'd asked me to."

"You motherfucker! How could you do this to me? I believed you were on my side. You're supposed to be my best friend, and you betrayed me."

"I did," Roman admits. "I wish it weren't like that. And this wasn't me getting even with you for betraying Braelyn, which you did. I love her. That's all there is to it."

"I can't believe this. It can't be real. Braelyn was going to marry me. She doesn't love you. There's no fucking way."

He grins at me. "Whether she does or doesn't, this is the situation."

"Nash would fucking hate you for this. You're a traitor—"

"Nash would fucking hate you for what you did to Braelyn," Roman cuts him off, his jaw locked tight and his voice colder than death. "Don't you dare call me a traitor." He shifts his weight and glares furiously down at the phone as if he wants to reach into it, pluck Adam from the other side, and strangle the life from him. "It's funny, all this time I was tainted by your friendship with Nash and our friendship over the last six years. I was plagued with guilt over this. But these last few weeks have really shown what an unremorseful, selfish piece of shit you are. You don't deserve her."

"You don't either, and you know it. You're the selfish one. Not me. I believed you were helping me win *my* girl back."

I roll my eyes. I kept my mouth shut, biting my tongue, but that's my breaking point.

"That's so lame," I smart. "I'm not your girl. You lost the privilege of calling me that when you decided to start sticking your dick into Corporate Barbie. You knew the risk. You knew what fucking someone else could bring down on you and yet didn't do it once or even twice. You did it again and again over weeks and then brought your side piece into our apartment and our bed. So fuck you, Adam. You have no right to try to win me back and you sure as shit have no right to comment or be angry about what you let go of. Roman and I were a long time coming. I think you already knew that, which is why you're not shocked, just pissed. So take your sanctimonious anger, wad it up into a ball, and shove it up your ass because you can go fuck yourself with it."

I hit end on the call and Roman stands here for a minute, giving me a look. "You just totally handled him like a boss."

I preen at that. "That's because I am a boss."

His lips twitch and all that ice has melted into fire. "A sexy fucking boss. That was insanely hot. Nice job. But you know he's not done with this."

That gives me a moment of pause because I do know that. Our marriage and whatever pictures of us kissing on the beach coming out embarrass Adam. And if I know one thing about him, he doesn't like to appear the fool. Especially not in front of others, let alone the world.

29

———————

BRAELYN

We didn't end up staying the extra two days. The resort felt tainted. Anytime we left our villa, we were paranoid, always looking over our shoulder and keeping our heads down, fearful of being photographed.

Boston won't be better. If anything, it'll be worse, but it somehow feels better than being here. Roman finished up everything he had to do in the restaurant yesterday and this morning, one day after our marriage made headlines, we left for the airport, but instead of flying home commercially, Roman had the Fritz jet come pick us up.

I didn't argue it. Everything has spiraled out of control.

Adam and I used to be photographed, especially when we first started dating. We'd go to a charity dinner or out on a date and inevitably, our faces would end up somewhere online. It was annoying, but it wasn't that big of a deal and it fizzled out quickly. Even when we got engaged, there was some press with it, but not a ton. Boston isn't like New York or LA with that and I'm not a celebrity.

I'm a normal girl who happens to have wealthy and famous friends.

But as the Boston skyline grows bigger out of the oval windows, I have a feeling this will be different. Thus far, the press hasn't been all that flattering about me and neither have the comments. It's been painted to look like I left Adam and ran off with his best friend. Adam's infidelity hits at like the second paragraph of whatever snippet article, if it even shows up at all. It's all reading as if I were going behind Adam's back and not the other way around.

So now I'm the bad guy.

The harlot who broke a devastated billionaire's heart to chase another's. The woman who metaphorically left one guy at the altar so I could marry another.

I'm trying not to care. I truly am. I'm also trying not to go on any social media. But it's eating at me. The lies being spread. The hateful comments by strangers.

Roman hasn't said much since we left the resort. He's been on his phone a lot, texting and occasionally getting up to go to the bedroom in the back to make a phone call he doesn't want me to hear. There is nothing more isolating than becoming the center of attention.

I have no home. No sanctuary. I'm staying with Roman, and I want to be with him, but now everything feels tainted. Like it's falling apart before it could even start.

Typically, I'm a glass-half-full kind of girl, but right now, that glass feels empty. I feel empty. I just want to crawl under the sheets until all this blows over. It'll make going back to work hell. It'll make simply trying to be with Roman hell. How can a relationship start and build when it's under a microscope? When everyone wants us to fail?

Ugh.

Roman takes the seat beside me and buckles up as we get ready to land. His hand meets my thigh, but my focus stays out the window.

"There's press outside my building," he says quietly, his

words carrying just loud enough to be heard over the hum of the engine.

"Lovely."

"Adam has also come out as the tearful ex, making a statement about how he's brokenhearted by everything and loves you and feels endlessly betrayed by our actions."

My eyes close. "What an asshole. Let me guess, he never mentioned Corporate Barbie."

"No."

I bluster out an annoyed breath and shake my head. "You know, in all the years I've known Adam, never did I ever think he was capable of anything like this. The cheating and lying and manipulation. The morning of the day I caught him, if you had asked me if he'd do any of this, I would have sworn under oath that he wouldn't."

"I never saw this coming with him either. Anytime we ever spoke about you, it was always him telling me how he couldn't wait to get married and how much he loved you. Despite how I feel about you, it's honestly why I had so much guilt other than the fact that he is—*was*—my friend. People make mistakes and second chances are sometimes warranted, but not in this case. Not with him."

"I just want to be a nurse."

"I just want to be a chef."

I rest the back of my head against his shoulder. "We can't get a divorce now. It'll look so bad and keep all of this in the press longer than it hopefully otherwise will be."

He kisses my hair. "I don't particularly want a divorce anyway. As far as I'm concerned, you and I are meant to be."

"You're the silver lining."

"You might change your mind about that. The only reason people care about this is because I'm Roman Fritz."

〜

HE'S RIGHT, of course. The press lining the front of his residence proves that. Thankfully, the Fritz security team takes us into the underground garage of the building and we don't have to wade through them. The doors of his penthouse open and we drag our suitcases inside, but before I can even release a relieved breath, I'm practically body slammed by a pregnant woman.

"You're here. You made it!" Skylar gives me a fierce hug. "This is so insane but thank you for taking the heat off my wedding to Aston."

I cackle a bit at that. Skylar Fritz Davenport and Aston Hughes got into a marriage of convenience for a multitude of reasons. But she's a Fritz and he's a Hughes—another big billionaire name in this city—and with that, their fake wedding made front-page headlines about a month or so ago. It seems mine has now eclipsed all of that.

"Happy to help."

She pulls back and puts her hands on my shoulders. "Don't stress it. We're all here and we'll get to the bottom of it."

"Everyone's here?"

Roman throws me a wink and we leave our suitcases in the foyer for the time being as we go and meet our people in his living room. Hayes, Quinn, Crew, Forest, Aston, and obviously Skylar are all set up with food and various types of drinks and even laptops set up. It's like a UN summit but better.

Forest is on the phone, leaning against the glass wall with a serious expression on his face. None of us asks a lot of questions about what Forest does for work. He's an attorney and for years worked for his mom's stepdad in LA. But he's more than that, and his job out there consisted of more than that. He doesn't talk about it, but we know what he is.

A fixer.

I just don't know how you fix this. Not when it's already out of control like it is.

"Come sit and eat something," Crew instructs around a mouthful of pizza as he points to another box. "We got your favorite."

"Hot honey pepperoni with mushrooms?"

"Yep."

I could cry. I almost do, and I don't know what's up with all these tears, but I'm so over it. Who cries over pizza?

I come and sit beside him and help myself to two huge slices even though I ate a little on the plane. He pours me a glass of wine to go with it, and I think I'm going to be okay. I have this. I have my people. Even Katy and Wren texted this morning to make sure I was okay and asked if I needed anything.

It would have been us here with Adam before. That's what's still getting me. He wasn't as close with everyone else as he was with Roman and me, but still. He was part of us, and now he's so removed, and I have to accept that. People surprise you. Sometimes in the worst of ways. That's what Adam did, but watching Roman talk to Forest, noting the intense look on his face, I have to believe Roman will only surprise me in the best of ways.

"So... you and my guy?" Crew quips.

"I didn't know you had a thing for Roman?"

His lips curl up into a sardonic smile. "Nice deflection, babe. I guess I can throw that back at you."

I shrug as I take a bite of pizza. "I didn't know I had one either."

"But you do?" he persists. "Because Skylar told us she gave him the warning, but now it's my turn to give it to you. He loves you. He's ready to blow shit up for you. Don't break his heart."

I smile at my friend. "I won't."

He nudges me with his elbow and takes a bite of his slice. "This won't hold," he tells me. "You know that. Between Roman and Forest, they'll handle it."

"And that means Adam," Hayes throws in, testing my reaction.

"I could just come out and tell the truth about it," I suggest, and everyone pauses to look over at me. "What? Do Fritzes and Central Square people never do that? I realize I'm on the outside of that and have the least public persona out of all of us but..." I trail off, leaving it hanging at that. I don't exactly want to do that. I don't want more attention on me or this. Maybe it's a dumb idea. But I can't let my name or Roman's be tarnished either.

Forest and Roman exchange glances.

"Who would we send it to?" Forest asks, considering this.

"I don't care." I take a sip of my wine and glance over at Skylar and Quinn, who are whispering to each other. "Who should I tell it to?"

"*Intertainment*," Skylar suggests, and Quinn nods.

"They broke the story." She agrees.

"Yes, but that's a bit of a red herring," Forest states.

"How so?" Hayes questions.

"I just got off the phone with my LA guy. They were fed the story from an anonymous source, except that the anonymous source created the email account using real information, and my guy was able to trace it."

Roman looks like he's going to murder someone when he says, "It's Anne Sharpe."

I scrunch my nose. "Who?" But something about that name is sticking to me, tickling a recessed part of my brain.

"She's the TV person who came to me in Vegas about doing the show. She works for Boston Nine."

I stare at him for a minute. "You never mentioned she worked for Adam's company."

He tosses his hands up but comes over and takes the seat on the other side of me. "We were having a really good night at the soft opening, and I didn't want to bring any of that down by mentioning Adam. Plus, I knew I wasn't going to do the show, so I didn't think it was all that important."

"Why would Adam send—"

"He didn't," he cuts me off. "She told me she wanted to lock me in for the show so she could pitch it to the higher-ups."

My brows furrow. "Does she know about your friendship with Adam?"

He shakes his head bewilderedly. "No clue, and I didn't say anything. All I told her was that I wasn't interested. She emailed my people, and my people told her again that I wasn't interested and that was that. Until this."

I frown and look sightlessly across the room as I think this through. "She was in Vegas when we got married. So either she was following us or digging into you and came across our marriage license. Are you saying she followed us to Mexico?"

"It looks that way," Forest states.

My hands cover my face, and I think and think and then... My hands drop to my lap and I look at Roman. "The woman Adam cheated on me with was blonde. I mean, I realize there are millions of blondes in this world, but..."

Forest comes over, working something on his phone before he hands it to me.

It's a picture of her from the Boston Nine corporate site. Anne Sharpe. Again, there is something familiar about her that I can't quite place.

"This is Adam's Corporate Barbie." I sigh bitterly. "Nothing like trying to fuck your way to get what you want. She likely seduced Adam to get a show out of him, and that show was going to star his best friend. She must have thought it was a no-brainer and would make her career and when you said no, this was her retaliation."

"Something like that," Roman agrees.

"Fabulous. Can I out her publicly?"

"I wouldn't do that with a vengeful woman especially when

you don't know all of her motives." Skylar throws her hands up. "But that's just me."

"I agree," Aston says, tucking Skylar in by his side. "You don't want to provoke her into more action. What she did is already done. Focus on your story."

"Let's write the statement," Hayes comes in, ever the CEO. "Then once you're good with it, we'll put it out there and see what happens."

30

ROMAN

Braelyn's statement went out two hours ago, and it's completely taken over everything. We won't fully know how it's going to be taken likely until tomorrow. But for now, it's done. *Boston Nine* isn't posting it and I'm not surprised. It makes Adam look like a cheating asshole. It makes Braelyn and me look like two friends who got a little careless one night in Vegas, but from it something real and unexpected has spawned.

Except Braelyn didn't write it.

Hayes wrote most of it and we signed off on it.

Since we got back here, even on the plane before that, she's been a little distant. I can't get a full read on her. I need to tell her about Europe, but I still can't find the right words. I'm trying to figure this out. Like what if I don't go for the entire time? What if I do a week or two, then I'm home for a bit and repeat? Or maybe sometimes I take Braelyn with me for a few days here and there or something.

I can make it work. I know I can. I just have to figure out a way that makes sense and until I do, I'm not sure what to say.

Now that everyone has left and it's just us and I don't know how to proceed. The statement was the right thing to do, but for some reason, it still doesn't feel finished. Like this was just round one of the fight and not the knockout.

It was easier in Mexico. Just us in the small villa with one bed, but now we're back at my place, and she has her own room here. As if proving my point, that's exactly where she heads after she reaches the landing at the top of the stairs.

For a moment, all I can do is watch her go. She enters her room, the door shutting behind her, and she did all of that without a word to me. I'm left standing here in the hall with my stupid fucking heart in my hand, and she shut the door on me.

So there's that.

I had been wondering how she'd be when we got back here, and I guess I have my answer. *Fuck!*

I want to go after her and demand answers. I want to call her out on her bullshit and tell her to get the fuck over it already. But how can I do that? I've already put myself on the line with this, and her going in there and shutting the door tells me everything I never wanted to hear.

I head for my bedroom, anxious to change out of these clothes and punch the fuck out of a bag. I have a fight in two weeks and I'm not ready for it. Usually, I train daily. Running, weights, drills, bag work. Considering I don't do this professionally or even legally, I work very hard to stay at the top of my game.

But more than that, it releases the tension I can never seem to shake from my muscles and bones. Tension that tells me even though the marriage stuff is out there, I still have secrets I'm keeping. Big secrets. Secrets that could shake everything I'm fighting to build and hold on to.

I toss off my clothes one by one and quickly throw on a pair of shorts and sneakers. A minute later, I'm jogging down the stairs, refusing to look at her door as I go to my gym. I run five miles on the treadmill, do fifty pushups, a hundred crunches, and beat the ever-loving fuck out of my heavy bag.

I don't know how long I'm in here, but by the time I head back upstairs, my muscles ache and my mind is too tired to fight.

Braelyn's door is still closed and for a moment, I hesitate, only to say fuck it and go to her room. I knock on the door, but she doesn't answer and in my anger and frustration at her ignoring me, I twist the knob, storm in, and come to a screeching halt.

Empty. Her room is empty and dark, as is her bathroom. And closet. Holy shit, all of her clothes are gone. She left. Braelyn not only left me, but she snuck out, and what the motherfuck am I supposed to do with that?

"Shit!" I pace her empty room, my fists balled up on top of my head. The mind-twisting furious need to put my fist through the wall is compelling, but I manage to hold myself back. Just barely, but I do. I need to call her. This isn't what we do. This isn't who we are. We don't ignore each other. We don't walk out on each other. Lovers or not, she's my best fucking friend, and you don't do that.

Goddammit, Braelyn.

I race down the hall to my bedroom, anxious to get my phone, when I come to another screeching halt. Braelyn is on my bed in only my favorite Rebels hoodie and a pair of knee-high black fuzzy socks with her e-reader in her hand as if nothing is amiss in the slightest.

She glances up at me, and the smile she had slips instantly. Her e-reader hits the bed, and she sits up, alarm all over her face. "What's wrong?"

"What are you doing in here?"

She blinks at me, confusion and uncertainty replacing the

concern. "Um... well, I just thought..." She glances around the room, shifting uncomfortably. "I mean, in Mexico, we were sharing a bed and you said you loved me and that you wanted..." She trails off and releases a shaky breath. "I should have talked to you about it before I moved in, I guess. I'm sorry. You're right. I totally took liberties moving my stuff in here, but you were in the gym after I'd packed up my suitcase and I didn't want to bother you. You looked like you were training hard."

"You came down to the gym?"

She chews nervously on her lip and looks up at me through her lashes. "I didn't know where you were, so I went to look for you and found you there. I figured you needed the workout, so I put my stuff in your closet. You only use the large one, and the smaller one was empty. But if that's not—"

Before she can finish, I cross the bedroom and my hands are in her hair and my lips are fused with hers. I kiss her and kiss her and kiss her because holy shit. Holy fucking shit, she wasn't ignoring me. She wasn't pulling away. She didn't leave. She moved her stuff into my room because she's mine and she knows it and she wants that too.

I pull back, kiss her forehead, then press mine to hers. "I thought you left me. You came upstairs after everyone left and were really quiet and then you shut the door to your room. I thought you were pulling away from me, so I went to work out because I didn't know what else to do. When I came back up, I went into your room and found you gone and it empty."

One hand covers mine on the side of her head, the other rests on my sweaty cheek. She doesn't seem to care about the fact that I'm dripping in sweat.

"I'm so sorry. When we came upstairs, I was lost in my thoughts with everything that had happened today and over the last couple of days. I didn't really think about it. I just kind of went on autopilot, and when I snapped out of it, you were working out so hard, I figured we'd talk when you came back up."

I blow out a breath. "The way I love you scares me. I can't lose you, kid. Not ever. This just proved it to me."

"You won't." She swallows, licks her lips, and meets my eyes. "I love you too. I didn't think it was possible to say this to someone so soon, and I certainly didn't think it was possible to mean it, but I do. I love you." She licks her lips. "So much."

"You're sure?"

She smiles and laughs lightly. "I'm positive, Roman. I know what you're asking and why, but the way I feel about you is nothing like how I felt about Adam. The thoughts I have about you, the way I think about us, all of it is so different. Being with him was a transference of how I felt about Nash. I didn't know it wasn't right until it ended, but I don't think I would have known *you* were right unless I had gone through all of that first." She kisses my lips. "I lost so I'd know what I never want to lose again. And that's you. I never want to lose you. Not ever. You're the love of my life."

In a flash, I cover my mouth with hers, my hands on her hips as I drag her to the very edge of the bed. But I'm tall and bent in half and she's sitting and wearing only my sweatshirt, which is a damn sexy look, but not as sexy as her naked. I grasp the hem of the hoodie and rip it up and over her head, our kiss only breaking for a second.

She's so beautiful. And tastes so sweet. Her tits fill up my hands perfectly with just enough space that I can squeeze and play with them. She was made for me. *Meant* for me. All our moments, the good and the bad are what brought us here.

Braelyn's hands drag along my back and a giggle tickles my lips.

"What?" I ask, trailing down her neck to her tits where I take a nipple in my mouth.

"You're so sweaty."

I release her nipple with a wet pop. I pull off her fuzzy socks that are both ridiculous and adorable. She's only in her thong now, which works nicely for me.

I stand, extending my hand to her. "Then come shower with me."

She takes my hand, her eyes dragging up and down my chest before she shakes her head.

"What? What's that look for?"

"I don't know. Just a random thought."

"What is it?" I chide as we head toward my bathroom.

"I was just thinking back to high school. To all the girls who were so obsessed with Nash's sexy and mysterious and older brother."

My lips bounce. "Sexy?"

She rolls her eyes at me. "Riiight. You're going to play it that you don't know what you look like."

"You thought I was sexy?"

"No. I thought you were smelly and gross. Sort of like you are now."

I scoop her up and drop her over my shoulder, fireman-style before I swat her ass hard. She makes an *eep* noise and squirms on my shoulder and I smack her ass again to get her to be still. I keep her like this, pulling her panties to the side so I can rub her cunt.

"Oh my god! Roman, put me down!"

I chuckle and push two fingers into her as I start the shower with my other hand. She squeals when the cold water hits the back of her thighs and squirms some more. I give her pussy two pumps and pull out, letting her slide down my body as I slip those digits into my mouth so I can taste her.

"Take off your panties."

With her eyes on mine, she shifts around until they meet the shower floor before she kicks them to the corner. The water is heating now, steam surrounding us, and I stare into her eyes.

"Braelyn." It's a whisper. A prayer. I've spent years of my life running. Hiding. Hibernating. Existing without living at all. She's woken me up. She's brought me back to life.

Roughly, I cup her jaw, my thumb scraping along her bottom lip before I kiss her again, harder this time, more urgently. I have to be inside her. I can't wait. I'll make her come a million times after this, but I have to be inside her.

Lifting her up in my arms, I walk her to the shower wall and hold her ass tight. I line myself up and push inside her in one powerful thrust.

She sucks in a breath, her nails digging into my back. My lungs empty at the tight, hot feel of her. Her cunt clenches me in a vise-like grip and I have to force myself to take a breath so I don't come this instant.

With my eyes trained on hers, I slide back, practically slipping almost all the way out before I fuck back in harder and deeper, all the way to the hilt. Using the shower wall for leverage, I hold her up with one hand while my other wraps around her neck.

Her eyes close and her head tilts back and my mouth takes advantage, sucking and licking at her wet skin just above my fingers. I pound into her, loving how she takes me so well. The tops of her tits jiggle and bounce with the force of my thrusts, partially crushed against my chest.

I work myself in and out of her, forcing her to take every inch, feeling her stretch and glide up and down my shaft. I fuck her with everything I am. All my wicked desires. My silent torment. My undying love. All of them I give to her.

"Braelyn," I rasp, grunting and groaning mindlessly. "Fuck, baby. You feel so fucking good."

"Harder," she demands. "I want it harder."

I squeeze her neck before releasing it and give her exactly what she wants. I ram into her and her eyes roll back in her head. "Yes. Oh! That."

I smile and bite her lip. "Is that hard enough or can you take more?"

"More. Don't stop. Don't hold back."

I don't. Not for a second. I slam into her, her grip on me tightening. A loud cry flees her lips as her body trembles against mine. But I'm not done with her. I'll never be done with her.

"This is only the start, baby. I'm fucking you rough now but after this, I'm going to fuck you sweet and slow. Then when you're exhausted and a little sore, I'm going to eat your cunt in our bed."

She bucks against me, her clit rubbing along my pelvic bone, and just when I don't think I can take another second, she comes. I watch her stunning face twisted up in pleasure while I swallow her moans and desperate cries. It pushes me over the edge and with a low growl, I still and come inside her with hard, jerking thrusts. For a few moments, we're quiet, clinging and trying to catch our breath.

I set her feet down and hold her steady while I kiss her like a man possessed. Obsessed. Because that's what I am. She owns me.

Our kiss is sweet and unhurried, and when she has her bearings back, I lead her over into the water that's shooting out at us from above and the sides. I wash her hair and body, touching and toying, pulling on her nipples and rubbing her pussy. Once she's clean, I wash myself quickly, but I'm not ready to get out yet.

I detach the overhead sprayer and bring it down to her, her expression twisting from confusion to realization when she sees what I intend to do with it.

"Put your foot on the bench."

If possible, I think she's blushing, and Braelyn isn't much of a blusher.

My obedient girl does exactly as I ask with a "Yes, sir" that instantly makes me harder than steel. I reward her by rubbing her tits and kissing her neck, and running the sprayer up and down her legs.

"You know what I'm going to do with this."

I get a shaky, "Yes."

"Good. Now turn around, hands on the wall, foot back up on the bench."

I pull back and stand to my full height, waiting for her to comply. She does, her eyes dark with fire and lust as she turns, presenting me with her perfect ass and a hint of her sweet cunt as she lifts her leg.

I adjust the pressure on the sprayer, making it more concentrated, then my arm bands around the front of her. Twisting my wrist, I angle the sprayer up and move it in so I hit her clit with the jet of water.

"Oh fuck!" she cries out, her head flinging back and meeting my chest. "Shit, Roman. That's intense."

I bet it is. It's essentially a high-pressure water vibrator.

With even back and forth flicks of my wrist, I work her clit and play with her tits, pinching and pulling on her nipples. She can barely hold herself up, her hands planting harder into the wall, her breathing all over the place. She's already close, and I make a mental note to buy her every fucking toy I can find.

I rub my cock between her ass cheeks, playing with the seam.

And just before she comes, I push the sprayer up right against her clit, line my cock up with her opening, and thrust right in.

"Fuck!" she screams and comes instantly. I don't pound into her. I fuck her slowly through it, pushing and sliding and rubbing her inner walls exactly where she needs it. Her orgasm goes on until she gets too sensitive, and I release the sprayer, letting it dangle by the metal cord and shower the walls.

My hands find her tits, my chest to her back, my mouth

against her neck, and I fuck her like this. Smooth and deep and slow. I murmur a million things in her ear. I tell her how beautiful she is, how good she feels, how much I love her, how I'm never letting her go.

Not ever. No matter what happens next.

31

BRAELYN

Morning comes with a stirring to an indistinct noise that tickles my senses and wakes me. Rolling over, I reach for Roman, only to find his side of the bed empty. I keep moving, shifting, and sliding until I locate what woke me. My phone.

Picking it up, I see it's Katy calling and answer with a smile.

"Good morning, sunshine," I chirp brightly. "How's it going?"

"Oh, Braelyn," a familiar voice that's not Katy's replies. "Good morning. And congratulations on your marriage."

My brow scrunches, and I pull back the phone. "Oh my gosh! Katie! Hi. I'm so sorry. I didn't realize this was Roman's phone. Our phone cases are nearly identical. I saw the name and I thought it was my friend Katy."

She laughs. "No worries at all. It's a very common name and an easy mistake. Is he there?"

"I don't see him, but I can go find him if you need."

"No, no. Enjoy the relaxation time. I'm so excited he's married to you. You have no idea how happy that makes me.

You're the only woman he's ever talked about, so it makes sense."

A smile curls my lips, and I roll onto my back. We haven't quite figured out the marriage stuff yet, but for now, especially after last night, I'm trying to roll with it.

"Thanks. It's good. Weird, but good." I've known Katie for a long time. She's worked for Roman for years and years. "Do you want me to pass along a message or have him call you?"

"He's been dragging his heels, but I really need him to pick out a place in Frankfurt ASAP. He—well, I guess both of you—will be moving there so soon and these places won't keep for long. We need to get the contracts signed on the residences. But while I'm thinking about it and before he signs anything, is there something specific you'll need while you're there? I'm happy to email you the places so you can see if there's one you like or don't like."

I blink about sixty thousand times. "I'm sorry. Frankfurt?"

"Yes. But I also sent him some places for Paris even though that's six months after Germany. The sooner we get these locked up the better. London is still in flux a bit for housing, but it'll come together. Are you leaving the hospital permanently or just taking a leave of absence?"

"Wait." I sit up, rubbing my eyes, positive I'm missing something vital. "Are you telling me Roman is moving to Europe? To Frankfurt, Paris, and London?"

She's silent for a very long beat. "Um. Well. I'm not sure—"

"Katie. Please."

"Braelyn, I can't give you the specifics. I'm so sorry. I thought you knew. Otherwise, I wouldn't have said anything. It's my fault. Completely."

I would laugh at that if there were anything remotely funny about it. "It's not your fault he didn't tell me he's moving to Europe. It's his. I'll have him call you and I'll make sure he picks a place and signs the contract on it ASAP."

"Uh, okay. I'm sorry."

"Really. It's fine." I disconnect the call because it's not fine. Not at all. I told Roman I loved him last night. I moved myself into his room. I'm in his fucking bed. I'm married to him. I mean, technically, we're married.

But he didn't tell me he's moving to Europe. To Germany, France, and the UK.

All this time we've spent together over the last week. Endless hours and limitless conversations and he didn't mention it. Not even a hint.

I can't wrap my head around that. The betrayal of it. He's telling me he's fighting for me, for us all the while he's planning a completely different life and future that doesn't include me.

What am I supposed to do with that?

Other than leave.

I need to go. I've had it with men lying. With men hiding things from me. With men who I thought I could trust with anything betraying that and disappointing me. Wow. I never saw Adam cheating on me coming and I never ever saw Roman offering me forever, only for it to be a lie.

What did he expect? Me to leave my job and move with him? He had to know that would never happen. Not that he asked me to.

A tear hits my cheek, followed by another. All I can do is sit here, staring at my hands. I'm pulverized by this. All the things he said last night. I told him I loved him! It felt like everything was finally coming together. That we fit in place. I couldn't help but fall for him. He made it effortless despite everything I'd been through and now this.

I force myself up and use the bathroom before I go into the closet to get dressed. I'm on autopilot even as my tears won't stop. They won't slow. I keep trying to rationalize this, but there is no explanation. Every step feels like I have lead in my feet.

My limbs are heavy and my heart is so broken I don't think it'll ever be able to heal.

I gasp out a sob, my shoes in my hand. I can't do this again. I don't know how to do this. Not with Roman. That's not who we are to each other. We don't lie. We don't hide things. We don't betray.

But that's what he did, and nothing makes sense to me anymore.

I'll put on my shoes, grab my purse, and go, though I don't know where my phone is. He must have grabbed mine this morning thinking it was his. But I'll find it and I'll leave.

Exiting the closet, I stop short when I see Roman walking in, his eyes on the phone in his hand, which is clearly my phone.

"Hey. You're up. Good. I grabbed your phone by accident and Sky called."

I chuck one of the shoes in my hand at him, the sneaker rotating end over end as it sails through the air. Unfortunately, he sees it coming and ducks to the side with his annoying catlike reflexes. Ugh.

"What the hell?"

"What the hell?!" I fire back indignantly. "Are you kidding me? You're moving to fucking Europe, and you didn't tell me and you have the nerve to ask me what the hell?!" I chuck my other shoe at him and thankfully, this time he doesn't duck. It nails him straight in the chest, except it's not nearly as dramatic as I was hoping. It simply hits him and drops to the floor.

Boo.

"How did you find out?"

"That's another good one. How did I find out?! You son of a bitch, I should have found out from you!" I point at him. "Katie called and I thought it was my phone and my Katy, so I picked up. Oh, she wanted me to mention that you really need to get on picking a place in Frankfurt. You know, because you're moving there so soon!"

He holds his hands out defensively to me like I'm a cornered animal. "It's not what it seems."

"Not what it seems?" My arms flail about me. "Please tell me you didn't just say that."

He sighs. "Fine. It is what it seems, but not the way you think."

"Roman, I swear to god, I am at my wits' end with everything male right now." My hands go to the top of my head. I'm broken and dejected. I can hardly stand to be in my own skin. I hold my breath so I don't sob and break down completely as I utter, "Why didn't you tell me you were moving?"

"I was going to tell you after the wedding."

I shake my head, nothing making sense. "After the wedding? When are you supposed to move?"

"In a couple of months."

That rips me apart, and I spin around, unable to look at him.

"Roman, I called off my wedding three weeks ago. And you said nothing in all that time."

"You got engaged to Adam, and I knew I wasn't going to be able to sit around and watch you as the happy new bride with him. I made plans to open three restaurants, one in Frankfurt, one in Paris, and one in London. I was going to leave for about a year and a half to work the miracle of falling out of love with you."

My eyes close and I collapse to the bed, my elbows meeting my thighs and my face planting into my hands.

"When you ended things with Adam, it felt like it was finally my shot with you," he continues. I hear him moving closer to me, but I can't look at him. "I knew if I told you about Europe, you'd use that as an excuse for why we couldn't be together, so I didn't say anything as I worked through options on how to make everything work."

"You should have told me. You hid it from me. Do you have any idea how that feels?"

He moves in front of me and crouches until he's at my feet. "What would you have done if I'd told you? What would you have said?"

"If you told me you were moving to Europe for a year and a half? I don't know."

He pries my hands from my face and I jerk them free of his grip. He looks as broken as I feel, but I've seen that face on another man who was hiding things from me recently, so it's not doing much to thaw me.

"Yes, you do. If I had told you before we got together, you would have told me that you were happy for me and that you'd come visit me, and that would have been that."

A tear rolls down my cheek. He's right. I likely would have said that.

"I couldn't have that. I couldn't have you brush me off. Not before I made you mine. Not before I figured out how to fix this."

"There is no fixing this. You hid this from me. You're moving away for a year and a half."

"I'm sorry I hid it from you, but I didn't know what else to do. I was going to tell you. I was. I know you don't believe that, and you have no reason to, but I swear, I was going to talk to you about it today or tomorrow. Because I'm not moving away. I can't."

I search his face. "What about your restaurants?"

"I've already signed contracts at the locations. They're going to happen. I think what I'll do is I'll go for the first few weeks at each location and after go back and forth as needed. It will mean a lot of travel and some time when we're not together. I was hoping we could work it out so that maybe you come with me sometimes, and when you can't, I'll try to make it so that I'm not gone very long."

"Roman, I don't know what to do with this."

"I know." He blows out a breath and inches in on me until he's up against my knees. "I know you're mad, and you have every right to be. I know you feel like I betrayed you after you've already been betrayed by someone you loved. I know all of this, and I'm so, so sorry for causing you more hurt and stress. You're entitled to all of it, and if you want to throw more shoes or whatever you need to do to let me feel your anger and frustration, that's fine. Be as mad as you want. Just please don't walk away."

"You keeping that from me is not a small thing. You did it with intent. How do I know you won't do something like this again or keep other things from me?"

He takes my pinkies with his and squeezes them tight, his eyes locked on mine and nowhere else. "I'll never do anything like this again. I swear. I'll talk to you. I'll plan everything with you. No more hiding or withholding. Not ever. I only did it this way so I could keep you. So I wouldn't lose you."

I bite my lip and shake my head when he forces his forehead to mine.

"I'm not gonna tell you I love you or that I'm sorry. I did that and you know I meant it and I won't be him. I won't fucking be him, Brae. I'm going to be me. The guy you know. Your ride or die. The one who will never stop fighting for you or for us. I fucked up. I was scared. I was scared and so I didn't tell you what was happening because I was positive you'd bug out on me and I'd be left without you. I knew I'd figure it out and I think I have if you're willing to bend a bit with me. If you know it won't be perfect and we'll have some weeks where we're apart very long distances. But the way I love you won't ever change. And how I'll obsessively miss you will be the thing that gives you peace because there won't be a minute of any day that you doubt me or us."

"I can't do this again," I tell him, my hand coming up to his cheek. "I can't get a call like this and be blindsided. I can't have another woman know more about you and your life than I do."

"It'll never happen again. And Katie doesn't know more than you do. You know more than she does because I'm telling you the plan I have for the next eighteen months."

"I'm still mad."

"Be mad. Just don't go."

I think about this. About everything he's saying. The things he's telling me and promising. He's rewriting everything for me. All of it was written because of me. I don't want to go. I don't want to run. I want to believe this is the moment that makes us.

"I'll stay." I press my forehead deeper into his and repeat the words I said to him in Mexico. "Don't let this become the worst decision we've ever made."

32

BRAELYN

"There's something I want to do today," he tells me as if it's the most important thing ever.

"What's that?" I ask, my mind still heavy with everything even as we're back to lying in bed, his arms around me, his steady heart by my ear. He dragged me down and held me and told me every detail about the restaurants in Europe. We talked it out and figured out a tentative plan. I'm still pissed he hid it from me, but I don't want it to be the thing that tears us apart either.

"I want to get a tattoo."

I giggle. I don't know why that's funny. The man has a million tattoos, and I can't imagine how getting one today requires the level of seriousness he's exuding.

"Good stuff. I think I want to get one too," I whisper, and I don't know why I'm whispering. It feels like a nervous secret for me. I'm a tattoo virgin after all.

"What would you get?" he mumbles, shifting closer to me and kissing the top of my head.

"I was thinking I'd have *lick this* put above my pubic bone with an arrow pointing down."

He chuckles and flips me over so he can crawl down my body. "Right here?" He taps the space above my mound.

"That's the spot."

"Hmm. I think I already understand the assignment, and I don't want anyone else touching you here, so that's a no."

I peer down at him. "I wasn't asking for your permission. You're still in the doghouse a bit, guy."

He kisses my pussy over my clothes and climbs up me until he's hovering over me, his hands planted into the mattress. "What else you got, kid?"

"I want a heartbeat on my wrist with a heart on the end, but I think I want the waveform to be abnormal. Maybe tachycardic or V-tach." I blow out a breath and meet his eyes. "And I want Nash's name on my back left shoulder because I feel like he's my guardian angel and always with me and I want his name there."

A smile lights up his face. "I love that. Let's do it."

"Yeah?"

"Yep. It's a long drive, though."

I tilt my head. "Why?"

"The place I go to is in Maine."

"I thought you had your last one done in Boston."

"Lenox was in Boston that day and fit me in. He's the only guy I go to."

"Then let's get a move on."

"Do you forgive me yet?"

"Pfft." I roll my eyes. "Absolutely not."

I get a deep, plunging kiss. "I'll make it up to you." Then he climbs off me and helps me out of bed.

The drive up to Maine is a long one, but Roman called ahead and secured us spots and now I'm nervouscited, which is nervous and excited in one. At least that's what one of my patients told me once. It's a thought that's been brewing for a while.

The dream I had about Nash back in Mexico won't leave me. I still can't remember the details of it, but I can't seem to shake the feeling. It's both hope and dread, but I know Nash is the hope part.

It's funny, every guy I've loved has been my best friend. Maybe that's what made them so perfect for me at the time. But Nash was the piece that connected it all and I wouldn't be the person I am today if I hadn't loved him the way I did. And I wouldn't have Roman—best friend or lover—without Nash as well.

I can't think about what-ifs. I can't dwell on questions I'll never have answers to.

Life moves. It adjusts and adapts. It changes in the blink of an eye. I came to realize yesterday when all of that madness was happening with the media and Adam that I don't want to focus on the journey. I want to focus on the path ahead.

That's why I made that statement.

I also think the press will grow bored of us now.

Regardless, I feel vindicated, no matter what the world thinks about my relationship with Roman. I told him I loved him, and I meant it. I don't think there was any other option for me with him. I was always going to fall for him, which is likely why I never allowed myself to consider the idea of more with him.

I don't know what will happen with the whole Europe thing. I work here and I love my job and it's not realistic for me to bounce around Europe as a nurse, nor am I simply going to follow the guy around. That's not who I am. There will be a lot of this that requires faith. Faith in him and faith in us.

Roman has his eclectic play mix going that has everything from rap to R&B to hip hop to old-school rock to eighties elec-tronic to grunge. It's so much fun, and I love his reaction every time I sing horribly off-key at the top of my lungs. Like I'm doing now to Tom Petty's "Free Fallin'."

That is until he turns the volume down as we get off the highway and drive into town.

Lavender Lake, Maine, is an adorable, quintessential small town with cute shops and New England flair. At the very end of the strip is a nondescript building that I know to be Lenox Moore's shop. Lenox is best friends with Quinn and Crew's father, and they basically grew up with his family since they're all Central Square people.

It's no surprise to me that this is who Roman trusts with his tattoos. But man is it a schlep up here.

The air is chilly as we step out of Roman's SUV, and I tuck my hands into my pockets. Roman wraps his arm around my shoulder and leads me toward the door but stops before he opens it, his hands on my shoulders and his expression wary.

"I have to tell you something."

"Okay," I reply cautiously since his tone is uncertain, if not a little cryptic.

"You might freak out a bit."

I cock an eyebrow at him. "You mean more than I already have today?"

"Yes."

"Great. Just what my heart needed to hear. You're scaring me, and I'm already nervous. Plus, I'll be honest, I'm not sure how much more I can take."

He releases a breath and turns toward the street, watching the people come and go as they shop, and now my heart is really going haywire.

"Do you have a secret kid I know nothing about or are going to prison or actually moving to Europe forever?"

A smile hits his lips, but he doesn't respond and what the fuck?

I tug on his shirt, drawing him back to me. "What? Just tell me."

"The tattoo you saw in Mexico? The one I didn't tell you about?"

"Yeah?"

His eyes hold mine. "It's half of an infinity symbol."

My eyebrows draw together. "Okaaay. Why didn't you just tell me that?" I don't get the big deal with this. He's scaring the shit out of me over a half an infinity symbol?

"Because I had half of it inked when I came back to Boston and had decided I was finally ready to make my move on you. I told myself I'd get the other half done when I had made you mine."

My lips form a giant O and my eyes are bulging out of my head cartoon-style.

"You got an infinity tattoo for me?"

"Half of one. Today I plan to get the other half."

Jesus. Way to knock the wind out of me.

"It's on your left ring finger."

His fingers trickle along my cheek. "Brae, you're my forever. How I feel about you is infinite. After the morning we had together, it's even more important that I prove that to you. My words only go so far. My actions are what you need."

"Wow. I don't even know what to say."

He studies me. "Are you against it?"

"No. It's not that." I hug him, pressing my cheek to his chest over his heart. "All this time you felt like this, and I didn't know."

"Baby, I don't just love you one way. I love you all the ways there are. It's my certainty. The one thing I'm always sure of and have never wavered on. Not once. No matter how difficult or painful it got. You said we're each other's forever, and that's unchanged. It's why I had half of it done. But the other half is for all the things we'll be and what our future will look like together."

"God, Roman. How do you have a heart like this, and how am I the one who gets to own it?"

"You're just lucky, I guess."

I laugh lightly. "Always so humble, Chef Fritz."

He is actually. That's kind of what makes him even better.

I look up at him, studying the too-handsome-to-be-real lines of him. "My kids are going to have your face one day, aren't they?"

"If I'm lucky, they'll have yours."

"I want them to be lovers, not fighters."

"I want them to be both, but how they choose to fight can be up to them."

I guess I can live with that.

My nose scrunches. "You know we're already married, right? Like how weird is that? We're dating and married and you're moving to Europe and we're talking about babies. We skipped a million steps."

"I don't think best friends can ever simply date. They know the other person inside and out, so it's not trying something on to see if it fits. It already fits or we wouldn't be here and have risked everything for it."

"Wow. I seriously love that. Kind of like how I love you."

A smile splits his lips and makes the corners of his eyes crinkle. "Come on. Let's go get inked."

I give him a cheeky smirk. "Yes, sir. Incidentally, I'm going to need you to hold my hand because I may be a nurse, but needles aren't my favorites when they're aimed at me."

"I got you, kid." He kisses my forehead and leads me inside where it's warm and very cool. There are awesome photographs on the walls, but not of tattoos. Lenox Moore is sitting behind a long counter, his face on a tablet that he sets down when we enter.

"Hey, man," he says to Roman as he gets up. The two shake hands.

"Lenox, this is Braelyn. I'm not sure if you've met before."

"I don't think we have. Nice to meet you." He shakes my hand.

"You too. Your shop is amazing."

"Thanks. Roman told me what you're interested in. How about you go over it more with me before we get started?"

I launch into exactly what I picture in my head, and he listens as he sketches stuff on a piece of paper. He doesn't talk or input opinions. He just draws, and when he's done, I squeal in delight at what he's come up with.

I'm led down the hall to a room with a movable bed and given a gown that's open in the back, and I remove my shirt and bra and put it on. Roman is quiet and it's making me more nervous than I was before, but I know that when this is done, I'll be so happy I did it.

When I'm ready, Lenox returns. "I'm going to stencil what we came up with on your skin, and after you give me the final approval, we'll get started. It might be uncomfortable and even painful at times. You can't move, so if you need a break, just let me know. I'm also going to put some glide gel on to help reduce friction. Does all that sound okay?"

"Let's do it."

He has me lying flat on my stomach on the table and Roman is in a chair by the head of it. He's holding the pinky of the hand on the side that's not being tattooed and when the machine buzzes, I close my eyes, bite my lip, and squeeze his pinky. The needle burns, but it's not intolerable. It's not pleasant either, don't get me wrong. I can't wait till it's done.

"How have you done this a bazillion times?" I ask Roman, but it makes Lenox chuckle. "That question goes to you, too."

"I'm a sadist and a masochist," Lenox answers, and I start to laugh, only to have him give me a reprimanding look.

"Right. Sorry. No moving. Then don't be funny."

"I'm rarely funny. Just ask my wife."

"I think I met your wife once. She was lovely."

"She is," he agrees.

"Now you answer," I prompt Roman.

"You already know I like pain. It's awakening in a way." He kisses the tip of my nose. "It reminds you you're alive and fighting."

"I experience pain differently than that," I say in a soft voice. "When I see pain, it's typically someone's worst day. My job is to try to take that pain away or make it better for them."

Only it doesn't always work out that way.

Way too many hours later, I have Nash's name on my back, a rapid heartbeat with a heart on my wrist, and a promise of forever on the inside of Roman's left ring finger. It's late and we're exhausted by the time we get back to Boston. Roman doesn't like eating in his restaurants. He says it makes him feel weird, but the thought of going out to a regular restaurant isn't high on my list right now.

I convince him to take me to Roundhouse because I'm craving a bacon cheeseburger and duck fat truffle fries—they sound gross, but they're so freaking good. We sit at the bar, sipping martinis and chowing down on grease. There are people taking pictures of us. I know it. I don't look, but I know it and so does Roman.

I'm married to a Fritz in Boston. I might as well have a sign on my head that says take my picture. I can only hope it doesn't stay this way and things return to normal for us. Roman's phone buzzes and after he checks it and replies, he orders us both another round.

"What's up?" I ask because I wasn't going to have a second martini tonight, but here it is in front of me.

"I think we'll need this. Trust the process."

I tilt my head. "Who were you texting?"

"If I tell you, you'll run."

I give him a very distinct arched eyebrow. "Roman..." I trail off because a flash of black catches my eye a second before I'm fiercely hugged by a squealing woman.

"Ah! I'm so happy to be hugging you right now!"

"Oh my god!" I fly out of my chair and practically tackle Raven Fritz, Roman's mother. "I can't believe you're here." We both jump up and down as we hug.

"We flew home when we saw the press stuff," Luca, Roman's dad, tells us as he peels his wife off me and gives me a hug. And yeah, if I thought we were getting photographed before, damn. But it's all good because these people are like my second parents.

I hug Luca, who gives me a squeeze for the ages. Then I smack Roman's shoulder. "You said I'd run if you told me who was texting you."

"Did I say you'd run? I meant that more for myself."

"Ha. You're so funny." His mother looks at me. "He's making jokes now. That's all you, you know."

They sit down with us, ordering their own drinks and telling us all about their overseas travel.

"So you married my son," Luca quips after their food is delivered.

"I'm a Fritz. At least for now."

Roman holds up his taped-up finger at me, and I give him an eye roll.

"You know what I mean. That's not a wedding band. It's different."

"You're right. I had to take off my wedding band in order to get the ink done. You're wearing mine."

"We skipped over parts," I argue. "Over the dating and getting serious stuff. We did this backward."

"You already said that to me today."

"I know." But I can't shake the feeling. It's like we forgot or are missing something. Like when you leave your house for a trip or go into work and can't remember if you turned off the stove or the curling iron. I haven't been able to shake this sensation loose. It's been with me since Mexico.

"We got serious in a heartbeat," Raven says, gesturing to Luca. "Our timing wasn't right. I was too young, and our worlds didn't line up."

"Until they did and I forced her to see me again," Luca continues with a love-struck smile for his wife. "The steps aren't important as long as you're where you both want to be in the end."

Raven takes a sip of her drink, her expression pensive. "I think our own doubts and the external voices we allow to feed them become our worst enemies. Especially with things like these. You're married and that's all over the internet. But you're also working to start something new. I get it."

"There will always be those who love to feed that doubt and destroy the happiness of others," I agree. "People who love to hurt because they can." As I say the words, that feeling of foreboding drops into my gut.

My odd sense of intuition tells me I'm missing something. The angel of death is anxious to take her next victim. And that not everyone can be saved.

33

———————

BRAELYN

"My patient in room three is going to code," I tell Katy's husband, Bennett, when he comes down to evaluate our latest trauma patient, who we stabilized and got into his own room.

Bennett pauses and twists to face me. "You sure?"

"No." I mean, that's my answer because I'm not sure. Over the last couple of weeks, I've had this premonition at least eight other times and I've been wrong fifty percent of those, which isn't how I typically roll. Normally, I'm a hundred percent girl, so my confidence is a bit iffy at the moment.

It's that dream I can't shake. The one I've had a few times since the original but can't replicate upon awakening. It's just a feeling. One that hasn't gotten me far but has made me out of sorts. Other than this stuff, everything else has been great. Things with Roman are amazing. My tattoos are completely healed. The press has died off.

And I haven't heard from Adam.

As far as I know, he's faded back into his life and subsequently left me the hell alone.

But I haven't been settled. I haven't felt... *right.*

"I think so. This one I'm giving like a sixty-seven point five percent rating."

"Is the CT back?"

"I was actually about to check, and then you showed up—"

"Code blue, room three. Code blue, room three."

"Shit," Bennett hisses. "Seems you were right this time."

"Ugh."

We race down the hall back to my patient's room to find a backboard being slid under him and epi being pushed through the IV.

"BP is crashing," someone shouts. "Fifty over palp. I think he's having a MI, and my guess is hypovolemic despite the unit of blood going in."

A shudder rolls through me.

"Charge the paddles. Let's go!" Bennett is all over it. "Can someone read me the CT results? I have a feeling he's bleeding from a liver lac if the location of his ecchymosis is any indication. Let's also get another unit of type-specific up. I want rapid transfusion. Two hundred. Clear!"

We all jump back and a flash of something hits my memory, but it's gone just as quickly as we work to save our trauma patient for a second time tonight. Somehow we manage to pry this guy back from the jaws of death and I help with transport upstairs to the surgical floor.

"Hey!" Katy greets me in the hall outside the surgical suite. "Are we all on for drinks tomorrow night?"

Bennett throws her a side-eye and she rolls her eyes at him.

"Obviously mine will be a mocktail."

"A sugar-free one," he tacks on.

"Braelyn, do me a favor. When you marry—oh wait, you already are. Never mind that. When Roman decides to get all high-handed on your adult, educated, brilliant ass, remind him that you've been taking care of yourself and your type I diabetes without his input for a long time and that you already know to request a sugar-free mocktail."

I can't help my smile. "I'm not involved in your domestic stuff, nor do I have diabetes as you know, but yes, we're totally on for—"

My words cut off as an intern runs at full speed down the hall, not paying attention to anything, and in the process of wherever the hell they're going at top speed, plows into Katy from behind. Her large belly slams into the rail of the gurney, which then jostles the patient, causing the IV machine to crash into the wall—narrowly missing Bennett—and snaps off one of the pumps.

"Sorry!" the kid calls over his shoulder, but he doesn't stop. Not to make sure Katy's okay, which she's not, or that the patient is, which he's not now that his dobutamine drip is failing after his cardiogenic shock.

"We need help!" Bennett calls out, and a nurse from down the hall races over, helping Bennett reattach the pump and get the IV going again. "Katy?"

"I've got her," I tell him as I bring her down to the floor. Her face is ashen, having lost all its blood flow.

"My belly hurts," she murmurs to me before her eyes track right, indicating she doesn't want Bennett to hear. "I'm getting spasms."

"I've got you," I promise.

"Are you in pain? Any bleeding or fluid?" he presses.

Katy gives me a troubled look. "I'm okay." She doesn't mean it. I know she doesn't. I can tell. Because of her type 1 diabetes, she had trouble with her first pregnancy at this point, but to get hit in the stomach is just scary no matter what your other health conditions are.

"Page Dr. Iverson," Bennett demands. "He can do this surgery for me. Katy, let's go straight to labor and delivery."

"He left ten minutes ago," the nurse tells him. "It's only you and the other Dr. Lawson on this evening for trauma."

"Fuck!" Bennett yells.

Katy looks like she's about to break down, but ever the trauma surgeon, she forces me to help her stand. "You have to get him into surgery. You have to see him through this."

Bennett shakes his head, his eyes pleading even when he knows it's the right call. "I can't."

"It's not a choice. Find a general surgeon to assist, but you have to start. He's going to code again if you don't. You can't let him die."

That triggers more shudders. More thoughts.

"Katy!"

"I've got her," I promise again. "I'm going to take her straight over to L&D."

"Keegan is on," Katy tells him, and that's that. She grips my hand like the jaws of a lion chomping down on a zebra and nudges me on. Keegan is her cousin and best friend and an OB in this hospital.

"Braelyn, I want constant updates. Real updates. My wife won't give me them."

"I will. You go scrub in. I'll take care of her."

The nurse takes the patient into the OR and Bennett comes around, one hand on Katy's belly, the other on her cheek. "I love you. Nothing risky. Take care of you and I'll be there as soon as I can be."

"I know. I love you too. It'll be fine." She gives him a weak smile no one is believing, but she forces herself to walk away, head high and back straight until Bennett is gone. Then her façade cracks. "I'm cramping," she tells me as we get to the elevator. "It's too soon. They weren't going to induce me for another month."

"Let's get you to Keegan."

She nods, biting deep into her lip and squeezing my hand.

"Contraction?" I ask as we step onto the elevator.

"Yes! Oh god!" She releases me and grips the railing, holding on tight as whatever pain she's in rolls through her. I pull out my phone and text Keegan to tell her we'll be there in a minute and that she needs the team ready and possibly the OR and NICU teams. Then I text my charge nurse tonight and let her know what's happening and that she'll have to cover me because I'm not leaving Katy.

I just fucking won't.

The elevator doors open and clearly Keegan got the message because she's here.

"What happened?" she asks, her red hair on top of her head and her green eyes fire and nothing short of intense. I relay a quick version of what happened upstairs, though Katy hasn't moved from the railing.

"Katy?" I question.

"My underwear and scrubs are wet. I can't look down. I can't do it. Red or clear?"

Keegan looks like she's about to lose her shit right here. "Red."

Katy sobs, but that's it. That's the only sound. "Get me to the OR and get my baby out safely. I don't care about the cost. I think I might also need some dextrose because I'm shaking and I can't tell if it's low blood sugar or adrenaline. Or blood loss, for that matter."

"We'll check you. Can you get to the wheelchair?" I question, placing my hand on her back.

Katy nods and takes a step back, her eyes pinched shut as if she can't stand to look down. I help her into the wheelchair, and then we're off, heading down to the OR while Keegan rapid-fires questions.

"When was the last time you ate? When did you feel the baby move last? Are you feeling him move now? Where is Bennett and what do you want me to do about him?"

Katy answers every question, but the moment we get into the OR, I'm told to gown and glove up while they get Katy onto a gurney and do a stat ultrasound.

Keegan talks to Katy as she scans her. "Baby looks good and his heart rate is strong, but you're absolutely in labor, and your placenta is tearing from the uterine wall. I know it's early, but I'm going to do a C-section to get him out because while he's okay now, if we don't act, he won't stay that way for long. The tear is too great to heal on its own. I'm going to scrub in and get your little man out. We have everything we need for both of you. Get that epidural in now," she barks at the person standing off to the side.

Anesthesia places an epidural in Katy, the room uncomfortably silent as everyone works.

Katy bites her lip as tears streak down her face while the nurses put a mesh cap over her head, and I place one over mine. I sit on a stool by her head because I'm absolutely no help here. I've seen C-sections, but I've never assisted, and this isn't my place. My place is here with her.

"Bennett has to do the surgery," Katy tells me, her eyes beseeching. "But I need him here."

I press my forehead to the side of hers. "I know. What do you want me to tell him?"

"Nothing yet. It'll distract him."

Katy's arms are winged out beside her, and I grip the one closest to me as Keegan returns, is gowned up, does a quick time out, and says, "Ten blade. Baby out in ninety seconds, and the NICU team along with pediatrics are standing by. What's mom's blood sugar?"

"Ninety-three," one of the nurses calls out.

"Good. You hear that, Katy? Your blood sugar is fine, and you will be too."

That's it. Then Keegan is all work and a giant blue drape is the only thing separating us from Katy delivering her baby. Katy is crying and I'm crying along with her.

> Me: Give me updates on where you are with the surgery.

> Bennett: Jessica texting for Dr. Lawson.
> Patient has a grade three liver laceration and a small bowel perf and continues to dance in and out of V-tach with evidence of an MI. We have cardiac and general surgery on the way.
> Dr. Lawson is asking for an update on the other Dr. Lawson.

"Bennett wants an update," I whisper to Katy. "He's operating right now, and reinforcements are on the way, but he's still lead."

She sniffles. "I don't know what to say. The trauma surgeon in me wants you to tell him I'm fine so he can focus on the patient. But the mother and wife in me wants him here."

"Baby is out," Keegan declares, though we don't hear a cry. "Time of delivery seventeen thirty-three."

"Keegan!" Katy cries.

"NICU and peds are on it. I'm on you."

Katy gives me a harried look, and I stand, watching the teams work. "They're bagging him and inserting an umbilical central line. Epi is going in. No chest compressions." I glance down at her. "That's good. He has a heartbeat. I can't see the monitor, but I know he has one that's strong enough."

Katy can hardly hold it together. "I need more."

"Give it a minute, Katy. They're working on him."

It's the longest minute of my life. Maybe two or three. Katy is sobbing. Keegan is barely holding it together and doing everything she can not to cry as she works to close Katy up. I'm holding my tears back too because they won't help any of us right now.

"Ah! There it is." I practically jump. "He's pinking up. They're still bagging him, no intubation yet, and he's pinking up."

Then we hear it. The softest, tiniest, weakest cry. It's not even a cry so much as a noise, but it's there and Katy hears it, which makes her cry even harder.

"Katy, we're going to put him on BiPAP and will hold off on intubation," the NICU doctor tells her. "Sats are good for now, as is his heart rate. He's a strong kid. A total fighter."

"Can I see him before you take him up?" They wheel the incubator by her bed, and she emits a sob. "I'll see you soon. I love you," she tells him before they wheel him out to the NICU.

"Mom's blood sugar is now seventy-two," the scrub nurse states.

"What do we have her on?" Keegan questions.

"D10."

"Increase to D40. Jesus, Katy. Tell me you ate today. Why is your blood sugar dropping this fast?"

Katy makes a noise. "I had lunch but nothing since about eleven. I was going to make freaking orgasm chicken tonight."

The whole room falls silent. "What is orgasm chicken?" I ask.

"It's chicken in a garlic cream sauce." Then she makes another noise, this one more of a snort. "Your husband made it years ago on one of his Food Network drop-ins."

I can't help it. I sputter a laugh before my hands drop to my knees and I crack up like I've never laughed before. The nurses, other doctors, and even Keegan join me even as they work and do their jobs.

My hands scrub up and down my face. "Oh my god, I so needed that."

"Me too," Katy agrees, though she's not laughing. Not yet.

"Sounds amazing. I'll have to ask Roman to make it for me sometime." Not tonight. He has a fight tonight.

"Blood sugar is back up in the nineties."

"Now we're talking," Katy crows. "Keegan, finish up. I need to go see my baby."

A second later, the OR doors burst open, and there's Bennett, sweating and harried as he practically dives on Katy. "You didn't tell me."

"You had a life to save."

His hands are all over her face, his lips following their trail. "Are you okay?"

"I am now."

Bennett nods but keeps his face against hers. "I saw him. I saw them in the hall with him. He's so small. But he's so beautiful, Katy. So perfect."

Her hand wraps around the back of his head. "Go be with him. I need you to be with him."

"Callan," Bennett declares, wiping her tears with his thumbs. "I want to name him Callan."

Callan is her uncle, who adopted her as a kid when her parents died. He was also the chief of the ER before Jack took over, so I know him pretty well. "He'll love that," Katy rasps, her voice hoarse with emotion.

"I'm going to head out," I announce, feeling like an interloper on their moment. "You and Bennett need your time together and to go see little Callan."

Katy's head twists to me. "Thank you, Brae. I have no words beyond that but thank you so freaking much."

"I'd say anytime, but let's not do this again."

I get a watery smile from her.

"Do you want me to let people know for you?"

I get a nod from both Bennett and Katy and that's that.

I walk myself out of the OR. Bennett is here and Baby Callan is doing okay and so is Katy. But fuck was that scary. As ridiculous as this sounds, I want to get to the fight, watch Roman beat whomever he's hopefully going to beat, maybe have a glass of wine or eight, then go home, snuggle in bed, have hot sex, and sleep this shift and day away.

I text everyone I can think of, all of Katy's closest friends and even my Fritz people since Katy is technically a Fritz, to let them know what happened tonight. I think about how they named their baby after her uncle, who took her in when she lost her parents, and wonder how Roman would feel about naming a baby Nash when—if—we ever have one.

It's so odd to me to even think that way. I never did with Adam. I never thought about our children, which in retrospect, maybe is an odd thing. I was going to marry him. Kids, if you want them, sort of goes with that. But it didn't with Adam, and it is with Roman, so there you have it.

I head down to the ER and finish out my shift, answering questions about Katy and Bennett and Baby Callan. I check in on Katy and Bennett in the NICU, and everyone seems to be about as good as they can be. When my shift is finally over, I grab my stuff from the locker room. I want to go home, shower, and eat something before I need to go to Roman's fight. Except I'm met with the last person I ever thought I'd see here.

I come to a halt, my eyes wide and my blood cold. "What are you doing here?"

34

My heart pumps faster as I take in the lines of Anne Sharpe standing in the hall of the patient area outside the women's locker room. It's just past change of shift, the night nurses and doctors are hard at work, and the day staff are already gone. But all that means is that no one is back in this part of the floor.

Except for us.

"How did you get back here?" I press since she didn't answer my first question.

"I requested you as my nurse, but they told me you were busy with other patients." She gives me a disdainful once-over. "You don't look busy."

I swallow thickly. "I'm off for the night now. And you shouldn't be over here."

She makes a sardonic noise. "What is it with you medical people always wanting to kick patients and their loved ones out? I got discharged to follow up with a cardiologist. This hospital is such a waste of time. I could have died. I could be having a heart attack right now."

"Except you're not, so how about you tell me why you're here?"

She shrugs, pushing her blonde hair back over her shoulder. "I told them I was having chest pains." She takes a step toward me. "That gets you in the door quickly. Whether they keep you here or kill you is another matter."

"Are you here for me?"

"Yes," she answers, her tone neutral. Almost conversational. But her eyes tell a different story. Reflexively, I take a step back toward the locker room.

She doesn't seem to care about my uneasiness. "You don't recognize me, do you?"

The way she's saying that I know she's not talking about how I found her faking her orgasm on top of my ex-fiancé.

She takes my moment of hesitation and continues. "I think that's part of what's so frustrating for me about you. No matter what I do, I can't seem to catch your attention. To you, he was just another patient, and I was simply the wife. To me, you're the monster who said my husband was going to die minutes before he did. It was like you knew it was going to happen and made it so. You're the angel of death."

I blink at her, studying her face, and it comes racing back to me. The dreams I've been having. The feeling I haven't been able to shake. It was her who triggered it. I knew she looked familiar when I saw her with Adam, but I was a bit too preoccupied at the time to try to place it. When she showed up in Vegas, I never saw her face. She talked to Roman, and that was that. But perhaps subconsciously, I recognized it was the same woman. Who knows.

"Your husband was a patient here a year ago, Christmas. He had a heart attack. He was only thirty-four."

"Thirty-three," she corrects, her posture so still it's eerie. "Do you remember his name?"

"I don't," I admit. "I'm sorry."

Her lips twist, and her expression turns mocking. "You're sorry? That's laughable. You told me it didn't matter what my name was."

The urge to cock an eyebrow or be a bitch is pervasive, but I tuck it in. "That's because you were fucking my fiancé."

"Because you killed my husband. I had to make you hurt somehow."

I glance to my left and see the ER way down the hall moving around as it always is on a Friday night. Busy as hell. I'm technically not alone in this hall, and if I needed help, I'd have it. There's a button on the wall not too far from me, and even a good old-fashioned scream will get attention. There should be comfort in that, but right now, there's none.

I shift my focus back to her. "Why are you here? Why now?"

Her weight shifts to her other foot. She's in a designer dress and heels, with her hair and makeup done to perfection. She's not in a gown, and I wonder how long she's been hanging out back here waiting for me.

"After Pete died—that's my husband's name—every attorney I went to told me I had no case to sue you. That there was no malpractice. Pete simply had what's called a widow-maker and that was that. But that wasn't enough for me. How was I supposed to take that? He was so young. Too young. Men in their thirties don't die from heart attacks. I heard you tell one of the doctors that Pete was going to code and you weren't even in the room. You were at some machine when they called out the code blue. You knew he was going to die and you weren't even in the room. Did you poison him?"

"What?" I gasp out, beyond disgusted by the accusation. "No. His vitals weren't looking good, and neither was his EKG. I was getting meds from that machine to try to help him and I told the doctor I thought he was going to code so they'd be in there when he did and start ACLS, which is advanced cardiac life support, immediately."

She shakes her head, her hands going to her hips and her face turning away. She thinks I'm lying.

"You wouldn't let me be in the room with him. You told me I had to wait outside. I never got to say goodbye. That's also your fault," she spits, turning back to me with venom glowing in her eyes. "You said he was going to die so easily, so cavalier, just another moment in your life, while it was the worst of mine."

"Nothing I ever do with my patients is easy or cavalier," I defend harshly. "I think you should go."

"You can't dismiss me again," she hisses. "Not this time. I tried to ruin your life the way you ruined mine. I got a job working at your fiancé's company and seduced him." She snorts and gives me a feigned pitying look. "Not that it was difficult to. It was pathetically easy actually. I'd already had pictures taken of us, and I was going to have them sent to you the night before your wedding, but when the hotel room wasn't ready, he agreed when I suggested fucking at your place. It was too good to pass up. I was planning to leave something behind in your bed. Something you'd find. But then you came home."

I tilt my head, utterly gobsmacked by this, even as my brain fights the adrenaline telling me to get the fuck out of here.

"You seduced Adam to get back at me? I thought it was so you could coerce or even blackmail a show out of him."

"The show idea was how I got my boss to let me fly out to Vegas. I would have fucked your new boyfriend"—she holds up a hand and rolls her eyes—"oh, excuse me, *husband*, too by the time I was done. You jumped so quickly into his bed after Adam's. I was pissed. It was like all my hard work was for naught. You hardly even cared that I ruined your relationship and stole the man who was supposed to be the love of your life from you the way you did mine."

"Wow. Okay then." I take another step away, this time toward the nurse's station. I need to create distance between us. I need to actually get the hell out of here and likely make a police report for my psycho stalker friend and get a restraining order going. I feel horrible about her husband, but her grief has twisted things in her mind.

"I watched you at the club with Roman that night. I followed you to the wedding place. I saw it all. You looked so stupid and drunk and happy, it made me furious. I had just ruined your life by fucking your fiancé and there you were, not even two weeks later, with Roman Fritz. I leaked your wedding. I leaked your photos from Mexico. You'd be shocked if I told you how much *Intertainment* paid me for them."

Another step back, but now she's giving chase, keeping close, the sound of her heels on the floor like fingernails on a chalkboard. "That's great," I tell her. "Super happy for you. I'm going to have security escort you out, and I think it's time you leave me and Roman, for that matter, alone. I understand with grief it's easy to blame others for things beyond our control, but this isn't the way to do it."

She digs into her expensive purse and tosses papers at me. Except they're not paper. They're photographs that slip and slide on the floor in front of me, hitting my feet and colliding into the wall right behind me. I glance down and see most of them are of her and Adam, which isn't great to see, but whatever. That's not new.

Except there are three other pictures, large and glossy, of a redhead hugging and kissing Roman this morning. I know it's this morning because he was wearing that shirt under his leather jacket when I left the apartment.

"It's sad how easy it is to get a man to cheat. My PI didn't even have to follow your husband more than a few times to catch this. My PI heard everything. She's one of his waitresses and they used to meet up at the coffee shop a few days a week before they went back to one of their places. This morning, it was her place since you're living at his now. I guess they had been an on-again, off-again thing for a while before you came into the picture." She taps her toe toward the pictures at my feet. "Clearly, it's back on again."

She smiles the most malevolent smile.

"It hurts when you lose the thing you love most, doesn't it? We're not quite even, but this is good enough for now. Your face says it all. Just so you know, I'm going public with those. All of those."

Before I can reply, movement catches my attention, and I find yet another person I didn't expect to see. Someone I'm not too excited about at the moment.

"What are you doing here?" Seriously, what is with this night and these people?

Adam comes in beside me, his shoulder practically touching mine. "I came to see you," he says. "I was worried about you. I was on my way out to meet up with some friends and I got a notification from my PI that Anne was here and you never left at the end of your shift."

My eyebrows shoot up to my hairline. Does everyone and their grandmother have a PI? "I'm sorry. What the fuck now? What's with all this PI stuff and following me around?"

"I tried to fire her two weeks ago and she blackmailed me," he explains, looking at Anne scathingly. "She had these pictures of us." He points to the ground. "And said she'd publish them and accuse me of coercing her into sex. I hired a PI to follow her around and earlier this week, he found the information on her husband and how he related to you. He also discovered that she was having you and Roman followed. I don't give two shits about Roman, but I had my PI simply keep an eye on you. I wasn't doing it to cause harm but to keep you safe until I could find a way to get her taken care of."

I shake my head, more than a little burned out after the day I've had.

At the pictures still sitting at my feet that I can't even comprehend yet.

"You'll all deserve what you get. I have no regrets," Anne states.

"Except I have evidence of everything you've done, including stalking with malicious intent. I have the garage video of you following me out and pushing yourself onto me before you got on your knees, and I was shaking my head and saying no. I have receipts you charged to the network for your Vegas trip, followed by your Mexico trip, the latter of which wasn't solicited by us. I have records of the payments you received from *Intertainment* and the emails you were stupid enough to send from your work computer telling your PI to, and I quote, ruthlessly follow Braelyn and Roman and to find anything he could that would hurt you."

I'm not breathing. Or I'm hyperventilating. Or both. All I know is I'm a half-beat from passing out. Holy shit. I can't believe this. My trembling hand covers my lips as I absorb what's happening before my eyes.

"Sorry to end your revenge scheme," Adam continues. "If you leave Braelyn alone, I won't press charges, though you're obviously fired. If you go near her again, I'll ruin you to within an inch of your life and make sure you go to jail. Don't test me on this. I have a longer list of your crimes than I stated."

Anne looks like she's about to use her red talons and scratch Adam's face off. Instead, she kicks the photographs at me. "It doesn't matter. I already ruined her life again. The pictures don't lie." She gives the cruelest smile in the history of the world and saunters down the hall to the back employee entrance.

One of the night nurses catches some of this, but I wave her away, letting her know everything is fine. She looks at Adam and back at me but doesn't press it. She knows about what happened with him and with Roman and me, for that matter, as everyone in Boston does. But she and I aren't close and instead she turns and goes back to work.

"Are you okay?" Adam asks, his hand going to my shoulder.

"Am I okay?" I laugh. That's actually a good one. "No, I'm not okay. A woman plotted an entire revenge scheme for me and cornered me in my hospital, and you showed up because your PI, who's been tailing me, tipped you off about it." And I'm looking at pictures of my husband kissing another woman. So there's that. "This isn't exactly fucking Candy Land, Adam."

His expression softens, his eyes all over me. "Braelyn, I'm sorry. About all of this. She seduced me. It was never my idea, and I never went after her. You have to believe me."

I scrub my hands up my face and blow out the harshest breath of my life. "Adam, I seriously don't have the bandwidth for another one of these conversations."

He holds his hands out, placating me. "Fine. I get it. But she's out of your life now. I'll make sure of it."

"Thank you." It's all I've got. It feels like someone was tenderizing my insides with a hammer. It's as gruesome and painful as it sounds.

"I'd do anything for you." He grasps my chin until I'm forced to look at him. "I still love you. Despite everything, I love you and I want to be with you. I tried to stay away these last couple of weeks. I fired her and I tried to clean everything up. But I can't get over you."

My face pinches up. "Adam, please..."

He bends and picks up all the photographs, keeping the ones of him and Anne but forcing the ones of Roman with the woman into my hand.

"Roman's a loser. He's damaged goods. You'll see. When you're ready, I'll be waiting and I'll see you tonight at the fight."

"Why are you going? You never go to his fights."

"The bachelor party I'm attending wants to."

That catches me strangely, but my head is too full to do much with it. He kisses my cheek and leaves me standing here. I fall back against the wall, trying to make sense of everything. Corporate Barbie and all the things she did simply because she heard me say her husband was going to code. Yet another instance of my intuition being a serious motherfucker. Then Adam showing up and stepping in like that.

Now these.

The redhead has her arms around Roman's neck and she's pressing the side of her face against his chest. His arms are out as if he's in the process of hugging her back, but her expression is one of pure contentment. Of happiness and love. His isn't much of anything, and in the next picture, his eyes are closed and his hands are on her shoulders as they kiss.

And he is kissing her. I can see that. Their lips are pressed together and he's holding her tightly.

"Hey," a voice comes from my side. Quinn. "I thought you'd be gone by now."

I don't respond. I'm still staring at the picture of my husband kissing another woman. I mean, I realize I never call him my husband unless I'm teasing him, but that's technically what he is. Boyfriend sounds dumb in my head because it's Roman, but he's that too. Or was, I guess.

No. Roman isn't this guy.

"Are you okay? You're—what are those?"

"Pictures," I manage, though my voice isn't my own.

"I see that. Is that…"

"Yes. That's Roman kissing another woman."

Quinn takes the photos from my hand, but instead of lighting them on fire for me like a good friend would, she's holding them up and inspecting them.

"Are these new?"

"He was wearing that shirt this morning. That's all I know."

I drop into a squat and blow out a breath because legit, my vision is hazy and I don't want to pass out in my ER. I have to think and I can't think that well right now because my brain is all fucked up.

"Braelyn, what the fuck?"

I cover my face with my hands and breathe through my fingers because I don't have a paper bag handy.

"It was the woman I caught with Adam."

"In these pictures? I thought she was blonde."

"Not the woman in the pictures. The woman who gave me the pictures." I launch into an account of what just happened, and by the time I'm done, Quinn's hand is locked on my shoulder in a ninja grip.

"Braelyn, Jesus. I've had some patients and their families do crazy shit, but that's up there. Are you okay? From her, I mean."

"I have no clue what I am from her. Adam says he's taking care of it, but I'll have to double that up and likely file a report or something. I don't know. I'm not a Fritz. Not really. Forest will help me with this."

"I realize you've recently been cheated on, but Roman wouldn't cheat."

"I never thought Adam would cheat either. Seriously. If someone had asked me if he was cheating, I would have replied never in a million years."

"Babe, think about this for a moment. We're talking about Roman Fritz. The man who tattooed an infinity symbol on his ring finger for you. A man who married you and didn't even blink twice about it when he doesn't even date. He's forever fighting for you, planning your future, and reworking his entire European situation around you. It's *Roman*."

I sigh and stand. "I know. I do. My head knows this. But my heart is so tired. It's been through so much, and it doesn't know what to believe. You're literally holding a picture of a woman kissing him. His eyes are closed. His hands are on her. It doesn't make sense to me, but visual evidence is telling me something else. Or honestly, I'm too messed up after everything that happened with Katy and then this for me to figure it out."

"Go to his fight, bring the pictures, and talk to him."

I nod because that's all I can do. I have to believe there's an explanation for this. Even if right now it doesn't feel like that's possible.

35

ROMAN

"Chef, one of the patrons at the bachelor party pinched the waitress's ass after they all got belligerent with her when she cut them off from ordering more alcohol. They also ordered two tomahawk steaks, ate them, and complained that they weren't cooked right so they shouldn't have to pay for them. What do you want me to do?"

I glance up from the plate I'm finishing to take in Eliza, my manager. It's been like this all fucking day. One thing after another. My motorcycle had a flat this morning. Then a woman came up to me in my local coffee shop and all but attacked me. She hugged and kissed me before I was able to pry her away. It was the most ridiculous thing ever, and in the process of her doing this, she spilled not only her coffee on me but mine—thankfully, I didn't get burned. The owner of the shop had to kick her out. I've never had that happen before.

On top of that insanity, the restaurant at the resort in Mexico is set to open in two weeks, and there was a problem with the flooring, so now everything might have to be pushed back. And now this fucking bachelor party.

Grown-ass men acting like drunken babies.

"I'll handle it," I tell her, and her eyes round because most of the time, I stay back here in the kitchen and rarely go out front.

"I can handle it," she assures me. "I just didn't know what you wanted—"

"It'll be fun," I tell her as I wipe my hands with a clean dish towel.

"O-okay. Thanks."

She steps back and allows me to pass her but stays hot on my heels since she's the manager as I coast through the restaurant, ignoring the photographs and whispers as I pass. I get a few hellos and I nod in return, but as I reach the private room where the bachelor party is six drunken assholes deep, I'm reminded why I don't like people other than my people.

Except that all comes to a screeching halt when I see who one of the drunken assholes is. Adam.

"What are you doing here?"

He gives me a cocky smile despite the dollop of steak sauce he has on the side of his mouth, his eyes glazed, and he looks more than a little drunk. The three empty bottles of wine on the table along with empty shot glasses, explain that.

"You know you're not the first person to say that to me today. I was a hero."

I fold my arms, far from impressed. "Good for you. Answer me."

"It's a good thing you didn't say yes to the show, though I would have enjoyed canceling you before you even began."

I narrow my eyes. "What show? The one your girlfriend wanted me to do?"

"Not my girlfriend. She's a vindictive, backstabbing whore. Sort of like you." He points at me, and I'm lost.

"Adam, what is this bullshit?"

"I'm here for a bachelor party since I didn't get to go to mine." His smile stays glued to his lips, but there's something extra about him I'm trying to figure out.

I glance around at the other guys who have gone quiet since I entered the room, their eyes dancing back and forth between Adam and me. I know two of them. They were supposed to attend Adam's bachelor party. They're guys he went to college with that I never liked much. Adam has a lot of douchey friends and looking at him now, thinking about who he is, I realize if it weren't for his friendship with Nash and his 'sticking by me' after the incident, I never would have bothered with him.

"That's great, but why are you and your friends assaulting my employees, generally being assholes, and griping about food you clearly finished?" I gesture to the two massive Fred Flintstone-sized bones void of meat on the otherwise empty plates.

He wipes his mouth with his napkin and tosses it on the table. "Because we can, and you'll take care of it. You owe me a hell of a lot more than that."

I didn't get to hit him after he hurt Braelyn.

I was still stuck on the he's my friend train and wasn't quite sure what to do with him, but now I'm regretting that I didn't break his nose or his jaw or his orbital bone. Jaw is the worst of those three. Trust me. Nothing like needing your jaw wired shut or limiting your ability to talk or eat.

That would drive him wild.

Motherfucker lives for those.

Except I got the girl, and he's busy making a fool out of himself because he's got nothing left except his ridiculous pride, which clearly isn't serving him well.

"You're right. I will take care of it. Eliza, can you call the police?" I ask my manager.

"As you know, we have a zero-tolerance policy on sexual

assault, harassment, or disorderly conduct here. I'm positive their waitress would like to press charges. We'll also be able to tack on theft since they're trying to steal their meals after they've eaten them. Considering the cost of their steaks, the charges will be felony grand larceny."

"Whoa! Hold up now!" Jason, one of Adam's college buddies, cries out. "That's not necessary."

"I beg to differ," I tell him.

"Wait. Hold on, man," one of them says, his hands up in the air. "I didn't agree to any of this."

"You didn't stop your friend either," I counter dryly.

"Shit." Another friend starts to nervously shift and lean across the table in Adam's direction. "This is not how I want to spend my bachelor party. Laura will kill me if I get arrested. Let's just pay the bill and get out of here."

"Yeah," they all agree. "No harm, man. We'll pay and be on our way."

Adam looks murderous.

"And my waitress?" I ask coolly without removing my eyes from him.

"Adam, fucking apologize to the woman so we can get out of here," another friend who clearly wants no part of this jumps in.

So Adam was the dick who got handsy with their waitress. What a piece of shit.

"It got him in here, didn't it? That was the point."

I honestly have zero patience for this. "You waited till the end of the night, till shortly before we close to do this? You wanted to see me, so you assaulted a woman instead of being a man and coming to talk to me? What a sad little sack of shit you are," I say to him. "You cheat on your fiancée, and over a month later, you throw a temper tantrum in a public restaurant and bring your friends along for your ride of shame? What did you think I'd do? Just roll over and take it because we were friends until I got the girl you were dumb enough to let go of? Did you think I'd throw a punch and you could sue me?"

His jaw locks, and yep, I can see it. That's exactly what he thought.

"Grow up, Adam. Learn how to be a man and take responsibility for your actions." Jesus. I can't believe I just said it that way. "And fuck you for making me sound like my grandfathers." I point at him, followed by his crew. "My manager is going to charge someone's card right now for the full dinner amount, and I expect a generous tip for your waitress along with an apology. That said, if she wants to press charges for people putting their hands on her without her permission, that's her right, and I'll support it."

The guys race to their feet, reaching for their credit cards. "Here." One of them hands Eliza their card. "Put a fifty percent tip on for her. We're sorry. No harm, no foul."

"Yeah. Truly, we're sorry."

The guys continue to go one by one, apologizing up, down, and sideways for being twats and following Adam's lead.

Meanwhile, Adam doesn't move. He has a look on his face. A gleam in his eyes. I've seen the same thing on the faces of my opponents when they think they have something on me. An upper hand that will let them beat me.

I walk around the table until I'm standing above him. "Do you have a problem with that?"

"Whatever you say, Chef," he replies evenly as he stands, but he's not as tall as I am and not nearly as in shape. He's sure as hell not a boxer, and he knows I could crush him with my pinky.

Everyone falls silent again, waiting to see what I'll do. But I'm not a hothead. I never throw the first punch. I don't lose my cool for anyone, not even this guy.

I put my hands on my hips, making sure my wedding band

is visible. His gaze drops to my hand, and he sees it. What he doesn't see is the tattoo I have beneath it, but that's not for him.

He smiles, complete with full teeth. "Still married, I see."

I don't reply. It was rhetorical anyway.

"She told me about the show. When I went to fire her, and she tried to blackmail me, she told me about the show."

I have whiplash with him, but it takes me a second to realize he's talking about his girlfriend and not Braelyn.

"It was never about me or even you," he continues. "It was always about her. She would have done anything to hurt her, and I was the hero. Not only that, she ruined you, and I didn't even have to lift a finger. You're finished. You don't even know it yet, but you are. Don't be shocked when Braelyn comes crying and begging me to take her back. I'll have the pleasure of saying I told you so first."

Without explaining further, he shoves past me, jabbing his shoulder into mine like the tough guy he's not, and he and his friends shuffle out. I hear them apologize to the waitress, who tells Adam to learn some manners and respect.

That's how it ends, and I get myself back to work, finishing off the night since it's already close to closing.

I check my phone, anxious to message Brae about this, but see a text as part of a group message with my other cousins and some of her closest friends informing us that Katy had her baby. What happened is terrifying, and I'm more than a little relieved to know that both she and Baby Callan are doing well now. My cousin Keegan posted a picture of the baby in the NICU with Bennett, who is giving a thumbs-up.

I reply back and after I text Braelyn, except she doesn't reply.

Just as she has intuition, I do too.

And no matter what, I'm unsettled even as everything goes smoothly here. I can't make heads or tails of what Adam said. It could have been drunk musing. Or not.

An hour later, everything is shut down and the cleaning staff is taking over. I head to my locker, change out of my white coat, into a clean shirt and my leather jacket, grab my bag, and head out the back door.

Only I'm greeted by the last person I ever expected to see. "What are you doing here?" I ask for the second time tonight.

36

———

ROMAN

Liam, Seamus O'Brien's bodyguard, is standing in the dark, his eyes fixed on mine with an indecipherable expression.

"You need to come with me."

Shit. That's not good. Not good at all.

"What for?" I ask, leaning against the side of my building, trying for unaffected and feeling anything but. He's armed. I know he's armed because he's always packing.

"Seamus needs a word." His Irish brogue is as thick as his beard, and I glance to the side of him and see a black Mercedes sedan, nearly hidden in the shadows.

I shift back to him. "What about my bike?"

"You won't need it tonight. We'll drop you off back here later."

"You mean if I'm still alive."

He's not amused, likely not taking kindly to me pointing out his particular line of work, but I'm not kidding, nor am I asking it like a question. In all the years I've been boxing at one of Seamus's warehouses, he's never sent any of his men for me. Not once.

But it seems I don't exactly have a choice.

I shove off from the wall and walk toward the car. He opens the back door for me, and I slide inside to find I'm not alone back here. Seamus is seated by the other window, his face all but invisible in the darkness. He doesn't say anything, and I don't bother greeting him or asking him what this is all about. I assume he'll get there.

Liam climbs in and starts the car, pulling out of the alleyway behind Uppercut and off into Southie. He's driving us in the general direction of the warehouse, but I haven't removed my gaze from the windshield, which gives me a good peripheral shot of Seamus.

"Do you know why I have you here?"

"No," I tell him truthfully.

"I got a visit from someone a couple of weeks ago about you. I'd seen you with him in the past. It's your new girl's ex. The television guy."

"Adam," I supply, and he nods.

"Yes. He came to me and asked to make a deal. I have one of my guys rough ye up a bit before your fight, crack a few ribs or fuck up a kidney, something not so visible, and we place heavy bets on you losing."

Wow. That's so incredibly sick and fucked up I hardly have words.

"I brushed him off. I had no problem with ye, and if he did that was on him. But then he came back again the other day, offering me the same deal and sweetening it with a bonus for me. A hundred grand if I do it, plus whatever I win on betting against ye."

"Jesus," slips out, and I lean back against the seat. "Sounds like quite the offer."

"He said you stole his girl."

I almost crack a smile at that. Maybe I would if my heart weren't pounding so hard, shooting ice-cold blood through my limbs and ears. "I didn't steal anything from him. He cheated on her, and I've been in love with Braelyn for years. Things between her and me just happened."

"Do you believe in loyalty?" he asks, and I rub a hand over the top of my head, angry and annoyed all over again.

"Yes. I believe in loyalty to those who deserve it and have shown loyalty in return. Adam threw my past in my face and tried to use it against me for his advantage after he ruthlessly cheated and hurt his fiancée, who is my best friend. Maybe me making a move on Braelyn breaks some guy code, but from where I'm sitting, especially right now, he can go fuck himself."

"I believe in loyalty," he continues as if I didn't say any of that and I'm regretting my outburst. It's not who I am, and I need to get my shit back in control. "That said, I did consider his offer because I also believe in money."

That's fair and nothing less than I would have expected.

"You don't do this for the money," he follows that up. A statement and not a question, but I answer him all the same.

"No."

"Ye give it all away. Even yer betting money."

"Yes." And now Adam's words about me going down make sense. He went to the freaking Irish mob to do it.

"A man who fights like that isn't fighting to win. He's fighting to get rid of his demons."

I twist to look at his profile. "You know this about me, Seamus. You did your research on me. I know you did. What fucking difference does it make if that's why I'm fighting or not? I still fight to win. So if you're going to take Adam's money and rough me up and force me to fight so I lose and you and Adam win, so be it. But if it goes beyond that, if you try to hurt my wife or my family, I have no qualms about responding to that."

A smile cracks his lips. "He's having the police arrest ye after the match. That's his angle."

"So not only am I to be broken and lose, but then arrested?"

"He doesn't know I'm aware of that part. He's arranged things with the chief of police and the DA."

Holy shit. I bark out a laugh. "They come to my matches."

"Your old friend Adam doesn't very often, so he never saw them there. He used his connections through the network and his daddy for this. His plan is to have them arrest ye outside the warehouse, but not have them enter."

I rub my jaw. "I see. And what would that do to you?"

"Likely nothing since neither the DA nor the chief of police wants to be involved with me in that way. Regardless, he and his friends are coming to yer fight tonight so he can see it all unfold. He asked I place them in the VIP area."

Lovely. Brae will be there. And Adam is expecting me to lose and then get arrested and have all of that happen in front of her. The irony is, this was going to be my last fight. Braelyn hates it and I don't have the same... need for it anymore. I'll still box and train, but no more fights.

Now the decision might no longer be mine.

Tonight is going to end badly, and I can't simply pull out and walk away.

Seamus wouldn't let that stand. He's the guy who doesn't just take you out—he takes your family out, and that means Braelyn. This goes however he says it does.

The car turns into the parking lot for the warehouse and drives around back to a part I've never been to. It's completely empty back here, save for one dingy overhead light. The car stops, and I have no idea what's coming next.

"You realize outside of the illegal gambling, the boxing isn't considered much of a crime. So he'll have to get me on the gambling side of it as well."

He gives me a pitying look. "That's the plan."

"Got it." My heart starts to pound, and adrenaline hits and hits hard. I look out the window. No cameras. "I take it this is where you fuck up my ribs or kidneys."

Sweat pours down my forehead, chest, and back. I finish getting taped up while the sound of the crowd leaks through the door. Typically, I love this moment before the fight. It's when I get my mind set. My mental game straight. And my body ready. Except tonight nothing is happening as planned.

There's a knock on the door, and it opens before I can answer. Seamus comes in and gives me a once-over. "Ye look like shit."

I'd chuckle if it were funny. I don't bother responding.

"It's time. Did ye take care of what you needed to?"

"Yes," I answer as I stand. "It's all set."

He gives me a firm nod, and that's that. Show time.

I follow after him to the outskirts of the ring. There are easily three hundred people here tonight, and a moment later, my opponent is beside me. I've fought him before. Fought and beat him. And while that should give me confidence, he's bulked up in the last year.

He doesn't say anything to me, and I don't bother with him. My focus is across the room on my girl standing at the edge of the VIP area flanked by Hayes and Forest. Forest's eyes meet mine, and he gives me an almost imperceptible nod.

Meanwhile Braelyn looks nervous. Annoyed perhaps. Or maybe upset? She doesn't look right, and with that, I walk over to her, ignoring the protocol of the match. Adam and his douche friends are off to the side, but I don't bother to acknowledge them. Motherfucker is trying to play a game he doesn't understand, and with that, I no longer have remorse where he's concerned.

"Hey," I say to her, sticking out my pinkies. She eyes them harshly before slowly looking up at me. "What's wrong?"

She shakes her head. "Nothing."

"You're lying. Is it Adam?"

"He's one of many things." Her brows crease as she takes me in. "Are you okay? You're... sweating. A lot. And really red."

I cup her jaw since she didn't take my pinky, but I don't answer her as I ask, "Baby, what is it?" She can hardly meet my eyes.

"Roman, I really don't want to have this conversation right now. Everything's fine. We'll talk after you win."

After I win. She has no clue what tonight's about, and I can't tell her. That's also a conversation that'll have to wait.

"I love you." I dip my head and kiss her lips. She kisses me back. Sorta. Only to rip her mouth away before I can deepen it. Something isn't right. Something is very wrong, in fact.

"You already look beat. Something got you down?" Adam howls with raucous laughter. "Guess she's another thing you're losing tonight, *Romeo*." My boxing name is practically spat at me. If he did something else, if he tainted her thoughts, he's a dead man.

I look back at her. "Whatever he said that has you pissed at me, he's lying."

Braelyn releases a breath, gives me a small nod, and holds out her pinkies for me. I lock mine with hers but flip our left hands over. I'm not wearing my band since I'm fighting, but I shift her hand until her fingers touch where my tattoo is.

These past couple of weeks since we returned from Mexico have been great for us. Now it feels like she's yet another thing I have no control over about to slip through my hands.

"Don't give up on me yet, kid."

The lights dim and the announcer gets started with his spiel. That's my cue and I wipe the sweat on my brow and running down my back. Adam is shouting about something behind me, but I block him and everything else out.

I have to get through this. I don't have a choice.

This can only go one way for me. If it doesn't, shit will go down and it won't be good.

"Fight!" The announcer jumps out of the way, and Curtis, my opponent, immediately comes at me. Except he doesn't go for my face. He ducks and loops around me and goes for my back. For my kidney.

He gets a blow in that has me staggering three steps. The crowd goes nuts. I never get hit like that. Not so soon and never a hit that hard on my backside. Searing pain radiates up through my spine and down into the back of my legs. I hear him coming at me again and I spin around a second before he lands another shot to the same spot and slam my fist straight into his face.

His nose shatters, and blood spurts out everywhere. He had that coming for being part of this.

He doesn't go down, but he does stumble back, only to regroup and come straight for me. He lands a punch to my ribs, followed by my face. This continues. Him wailing on me, and me throwing random, but effective punches. The guy is a bruiser. Heavy yet agile. If he were fighting fair, it might actually be a good match.

But he's not.

He's fighting me with intelligence he shouldn't have except for the fact that he was tipped off by my ex-best friend.

Round one ends, and I slink over to the corner instead of joining Brae, Forest, and Hayes as I typically do. We don't do trainers here, but I take a sip of water while physically taking stock of my injuries.

Round two starts, going exactly as round one did. I hit the ground this time, my lungs on fire, my muscles screaming, and my bones aching in a way they never have before. I can't look at Braelyn, but I hear her screaming out and gasping, and I hate that she's having to see this. This is the thing she feared the most, and it's happening right in front of her and I can't protect her from it.

The rounds continue, one after the other, filled with blood and sweat.

By the fifth round, I'm wrecked. Curtis isn't great, but he's not as bad off as I am. Out of the corner of my eye, Seamus gives me the signal, and I release a breath, my insides collapsing on me.

Curtis comes at me, his fist already flying, aiming for the knockout shot, and he hits my face with precision. My right cheekbone cracks, and my mouth pools with blood. Thankfully, he didn't knock out a tooth, but it doesn't matter much.

My vision sways and pops, and before I know what's happening, I'm going down. Hard. I hit the cement just as the announcer starts to count toward a knockout and my loss.

37

Something is wrong. Something is very, very wrong. Is he sick? Hurt? I don't know, but he was covered in sweat, and his face was all red when he came over to me. He didn't look right. Not like Roman. Even like that, his focus was on me, and when he brushed my finger over where his tattoo is hidden beneath his tape, I decided there's a very real explanation for those pictures.

Roman isn't Adam, who is drunk and belligerent, shouting directives toward this Curtis guy like an angry parent on the sideline of their kid's soccer game.

Roman, my Roman, wouldn't cheat. He loves me. I know he does. That's all there is to it.

But I don't know what to do with this.

Roman is getting the shit beat out of him, and Roman doesn't do that. Is it because of me? Because he wasn't training as hard as he typically would because he was spending so much time with me instead?

Curtis lands another blow to Roman's back, and I let out a cry I can't suppress, tucking my face into Hayes's chest. His arm wraps around me, and he holds me tight.

"It's okay, Brae. He's tough."

I grasp his shirt in my fist. "What the hell is going on? Can they call the match? Make it stop before he gets really hurt?"

"They can't." Forest puts his hand on my shoulder. "Just stay like that and don't watch."

"Don't watch?" I parrot incredulously. Meaning don't watch Roman get knocked around the ring like a rag doll. Jesus. He's done. He has to be done after this. I don't have stuff with me. Just my bag of basics that I always bring to clean up a cut or two. I don't have anything major, and Katy and Bennett have a new baby, so if he needs surgery... if he's bleeding internally... I stop myself there with a sob I bite my lip to suppress.

He's so grounded for this. So freaking grounded. After he explains the photographs, he's going to promise he's never boxing again.

"Fuck yeah!" Adam shouts. "Hit him again, Curtis! Get that motherfucker." How is that the same guy who came to the hospital tonight to get Psycho Stalker Barbie off my back? How is that the same guy I loved and would have married?

Talk about dodging a bullet there.

I pull away from Hayes and turn to Adam, ready to hit him everywhere he's urging Curtis to hit Roman. I start to charge at him when a hand wraps around my waist. Hayes is pulling me back.

"That won't help Roman," he tells me sternly. "If you get into a shouting or fistfight by the looks of you with your ex, Roman will get distracted, and he can't afford to get distracted right now."

Ugh!

"Adam, you're the biggest piece of shit on the planet. Who cheers for someone else to get hurt?"

Adam gives me a look, his eyes all glassy, and his friends around him watching me with equally drunk eyes. How much did he have to drink tonight?

"The ex-best friend of the guy who stole my girl. That's who. I think I'm entitled to my cheering, Braelyn. When will you see that he's bad news? He's going down. And when that happens, there will be plenty of time for us to talk about everything."

"Yeah, not gonna happen."

"He is!" he swears adamantly, but he totally misinterpreted what I was saying. Adam could be the last man on earth, and the survival of humans was in my uterus's metaphorical hands, and I'd sit my ass on a beach with my vibrator and watch the world end.

Hayes gives me another tug, and I willingly go back to him. Adam's not worth my effort. I stand with my back to the ring, grateful I chose this position as another round of jeers and "ohs" hits the air. It smells of sweat and blood and pain, and my insides roil.

Forest and Hayes are tense, their bodies rigid, but they're staying quiet, holding vigil beside me.

The end of the round is called, and I release a breath. I'm shaking terribly, and I spin around, my arms wrapped around my chest while I search and search, but I don't see him. He never takes these breaks. He usually comes over and chats or smiles or makes sure that I'm okay amongst the fray.

But he's not doing that tonight.

Forest locks an arm around my shoulder and holds me close, Hayes tightly against my other side.

"Just breathe, Brae," Forest whispers to me. "It'll be okay. He'll be okay."

"Yeah," Hayes agrees. "He might not be as pretty as he normally is for a while, but he'll be fine."

I'd laugh or smile at that if it were possible for me to.

The next round starts and it's the same as the others with Curtis wailing on Roman, who gets a hit in here or there. I'm not sure how much more I—or Roman—can take. Roman manages to stay up through the fifth, but when the sixth round starts, everything changes.

Curtis comes out swinging, and Roman doesn't see it in time or is too banged up to react as he otherwise would. Curtis nails Roman in the face, and Roman goes down hard. A scream lurches from my throat, and I bury my face in Hayes while clutching Forest's arm. I can't watch. I can't fucking watch.

But I also have to see, and I peel my face away from Hayes's shirt just as the announcer calls out, "One."

Is Roman out? I can't tell. He's on the ground and it's not looking good. Adam is hooting and hollering, cheering and talking about how much money he just won. I can't pay attention to him. I'm too focused on my guy on the ground.

"Two."

Jesus. My heart is pounding so hard, and I don't want Roman to lose, but I also want this to end. I don't want him to get hit again. I can't take it and he can't either.

Just before the announcer calls three, Roman moves and slides himself up to his feet.

"No!" springs from my lips. *No more. Please, Roman, no more.*

Roman staggers a step, and the announcer guy checks him. I can't hear what Roman says, but whatever it is, it appeases the guy because he steps back. Curtis's smug grin slips when he sees Roman back on his feet. He thought he won. He thought that was it.

He squares his shoulders, gives Roman an incredulous head shake, and gets himself back in position to end this once and for all. Curtis charges like a bull, his arm up and fist rearing back. Just before he makes contact, my eyes slip closed, but then I hear a different noise from the crowd. Shock and delight.

"Holy shit!" Hayes yells, shaking me.

I open my eyes to find Roman pounding Curtis's face and stomach. Blow after blow, hands switching off. Fists covered in blood. Muscles moving as if he had never been on the ground or hit once.

"No!" Adam shouts. "What the fuck?!"

Curtis shuffles backward toward the edge of the ring, his hands and arms up defensively, but he can't stop Roman.

There are no ropes here. This isn't professional boxing.

There is the line of the ring and the crowd beyond. This is also Fight Club rules, and they only call you out or stop the match when you're on the ground. Curtis hits the line, and the announcer tells him he has to get back in the ring or he's out.

Curtis sidesteps to his left while wildly throwing a punch to try to knock Roman off him. It doesn't work. Roman doesn't relent. He lands a hard jab to Curtis's side, very likely cracking some ribs, judging by Curtis's reaction, and Roman takes that, rears back with his right fist, and lets it fly. It lands straight into Curtis's face beneath his eyes and against his already fractured nose.

It knocks his feet out from under him, and he drops to the ground in a heap of dead weight, his body hitting the ground with a bounce since he didn't do anything to break his fall. It's horrifying to see. The sound alone is enough to make some-one's stomach turn. But that's it. It's over. Match done.

Curtis is out, and Roman wins.

Somehow, Roman ripped a rabbit out of his hat and pulled off that victory. I have no clue how, but I don't care. I tear myself away from Hayes and Forest and race straight toward Roman just as the announcer declares him the victor. He turns just in time, and I launch myself at him, pressing myself against his sweaty, banged-up, and bloody body.

"Oh my god! What the hell? What on earth just happened?" I pull back. He's a total mess and can barely hold me. "Are you okay?"

"I am now."

I get a crooked smile, and he dips to kiss me. Before our lips make contact, the sound of Adam losing his drunken mind pulls us apart. I twist to see Adam rampaging toward us.

"This is fucking bullshit!" he booms, his arms flying about. "No fucking way you just won that. This is a setup."

Roman doesn't reply. He simply shifts me until I'm tucked under his heavy, sweaty arm.

"You piece of shit!" Adam jabs his finger at him. "Do you know how much you just cost me? You're going down for this. You have no clue. You're going down, and then you're going to die, and I'll be watching the whole fucking time."

"Bye, Adam." With that, Roman walks us to the back room.

"You're dead!" he calls after us but doesn't give chase. "Your life is over!"

For a few minutes, it's just us in here, and I help Roman up onto the table. I open my bag, moving quietly and methodically, my thoughts all over the place. This honestly might be one of the worst, most intense days I've had in I don't even know how long.

Gloves snap onto my hands before I reach for his, pulling them out in front of him and removing the blood-saturated tape. His knuckles are an absolute mess, cut up and split in some places.

I can feel him watching me, and truthfully, I don't want to look at his face yet.

"You can ask," he says after a long, tense beat.

I shake my head, the after rush of endorphins hitting me hard and making me quake.

"Do you want to tell me why you're mad at me then?"

A laugh bursts from me. "This so does not feel like the time for that." I get the tape fully off and move on to his body. His left flank is purple with bruising. Gently, I press in on the spot, and he hisses in a breath and tenses.

"Are you short of breath?"

"No."

"Roman, do me a fucking favor and take a deep breath in, and after you release it, then tell me that."

He chuckles lightly, but I have no humor in me. "Yes, Nurse Fritz."

"Do not try my patience," I warn.

"Are you going to look at me?"

"Not yet."

Dutifully, he sucks in a deep breath, fully expanding his lungs, and releases it slowly. He's in a lot of pain with that, likely having cracked a rib or two or four. But it doesn't seem to be puncturing his lung. At least nothing terribly obvious. I shift around to his back, and there's a large purple and a black welt over his right kidney.

I curse under my breath, but I don't touch it.

"Survey says?"

"Very likely a renal contusion and some fractured ribs. If you're lucky. It could be a lot worse, but I don't have CT vision."

"What about my face, Braelyn?"

A tear hits my cheek. "I'm so fucking mad at you right now."

"I know, baby," he says, his voice soft and tender. "Come here, okay? Come where I can see you. I'm sorry. I know you're upset, but I couldn't say anything, and I can't really tell you more here either."

Jesus. What is going on?

Pulling my big girl panties on, I force myself back around the table to him. Then I slowly lift my chin and bite my lip so I don't sob. Not to be ironic or cheesy or anything, but he looks like fucking Rocky at the end of *Rocky 1* where he's crying for Adrian and his eye is all swollen up and his face is a bleeding pulp of a mess.

Roman's right eye is completely swollen shut, and that side of his face is so bruised, there's hardly any pink skin remaining. He has a gash that's still bleeding pretty heavily, and I feel like a bitch because I didn't look at his face first, and he's been bleeding like this.

I grab some gauze from my bag and press it to the wound, feeling worse when he winces.

"You either have a maxillary or orbital fracture or both." I can barely get the words out. His hand comes to my hip, and he holds me close.

"I know. I felt it when it happened."

My eyes close, and I release a tremulous breath.

He squeezes my hip. "Tell me why you're mad at me."

I shake my head, and he pulls me in a little closer.

"Braelyn, tell me why you were mad," he urges.

I don't open my eyes as I ask, "Do you know any redheads?"

"Redheads?" he repeats as if the word doesn't make sense to him. "You mean other than Quinn? Does she even count as a redhead? Or Keegan and Kenna?"

"Yes, she counts and no, I don't mean Quinn or your cousins."

"Baby, look at me. I know it's not a pretty image right now but look at me please."

My eyes snap open, only to narrow.

His other hand comes up to my shoulder. "Talk to me. I can't fix this if you won't tell me what's up."

"Have you ever hooked up with one of your waitresses?"

"No," he answers quickly, his one good eye on me. "Not ever. I've never touched an employee. Why?"

I shake my head. I really should have known it wasn't what she said. "It's nothing."

"It's something. I want to know."

"Argh!" I take his hand and place it back over the gauze for him to apply pressure against his cheek. Then I dig through my bag until I find those stupid pictures. The ones I crumpled and shoved to the bottom.

He takes them from my hand, studies them, and says, "Where did you get these?"

"Asshole, that's not the response I was looking for."

He shifts, switching hands with the gauze and the images so he can look at it clearer. "This was taken this morning."

And now I'm going to be sick. "I know."

"No, you don't know. Who was following me to take this, and where did you get it?"

"Jesus, Roman!" I spin around, my arms flying everywhere. "You're kissing a woman, and that's your response?"

"Braelyn, I wasn't kissing her. A woman came up to me in the coffee shop, literally blindsided me with a hug before she kissed me out of fucking nowhere. What you're seeing is my hands on her shoulders, pushing her back. She was acting like some deranged fan, and I told her to back off. So again, where did you get this?"

He's telling the truth. It's written all over him.

"Corporate Barbie, who turned into Super Psycho Stalker Barbie. She's been having us all, including Adam, followed. But it all started with a vendetta against me. All of it. Her husband was my patient, and he coded and died, but she heard me tell one of the doctors that I knew he was going to code before it happened. Since then, she's believed I had something to do with his death somehow."

He blinks at me. Well, with one eye. But he's staring at me and blinking. "That's... seriously fucking scary. Are you okay? Did you have her arrested?"

"No. Adam showed up and blackmailed her to stay away from me. She said she was done with me anyway now that she took you from me." I jut my chin toward the pictures.

"But you came here tonight anyway."

"I was angry and hurt, but I knew."

"Knew what?"

"I knew deep down that you'd never hurt me like that."

"Never. Not ever." He sets the pictures down on the table he's sitting on and grabs my waist. "I finally won you after all these years. Do you honestly think I'd ever throw that away? Braelyn, there is no other woman on this planet for me but you. And there never will be. It's you and me, kid. That's how our story goes." He flips his hand over and shows me the infinity symbol tattoo. "This is us."

I sigh and sink into him. He's right. Ours is the sort of story that never ends. It's forever.

A second later, the door opens and in walk Hayes and Forest. I hadn't thought much about the fact that they weren't in here with us until now.

"It's done," Forest announces.

"What's done?" I question.

"Adam," he replies.

EPILOGUE
ROMAN

Sometimes it's good to be a Fritz. But most of the time, in this town, it's good to never have fucked over Seamus O'Brien or have ever tried. That's not to say I was cool with his plan. I wasn't. Not necessarily, and mostly because I knew how it would affect Braelyn.

"I don't trust yer wife's twat of an ex," Seamus said bluntly as we sat in the car in the back of the warehouse.

"I don't either," I agreed. "And that started before he ever tried to get me hurt and then arrested."

"You're gonna have to lose. Or at least make it look like ye are. And yer gonna have to look roughed up before that."

I sat there, my gaze out the window, but I heard him. "So Adam bets and bets hard, thinking you're in on his scheme," I surmised.

"We'll bet hard on ye while quietly spreading the word around the room that you're not in peak form after yer public scandal with your wife. We'll whisper around that you're hurt."

"Adam needs to hear it."

"He will."

I nodded. "I'm not losing. I won't fucking go down, and I won't give him the satisfaction of it."

"We won't profit if you lose, boy."

"This is my last match regardless of anything else. I won't be arrested. That's nonnegotiable. And I want Adam taken care of. I don't mean how you often do that. I mean, get something on him where he's the one who gets fucking arrested."

Seamus chuckled. "Ye think you get to dictate anything?"

I looked at him square in the eyes. "Yes. I do. Because I'm the one in the ring. I'm the one taking all the risk. And I'll give you my winnings when I knock the guy out in the sixth."

He studied me intently. "No charity this time?"

I smirked. "That'd be your call, but I'll put the same amount he offered you on the line. A hundred grand. Those are my walking terms. I'll make it look like I'm losing. We'll feed the gossip mill that I'm in bad shape to start. Then I'll take him down, and you'll get whatever the over-under on me is, plus the parlay since I'll put it on the sixth round for knockout."

"I'll take care of him," he said slowly, with a measured tone. "I don't have to tell ye not to double-cross me."

My eyebrows lifted. "Have I ever?"

"No. Which is why I'm willing to make this deal."

My taking Curtis down in the sixth the way I did earned me two hundred and fifty grand on my one-hundred-thousand-dollar bet. All of that went to Seamus. Incidentally, Adam lost two hundred grand on his bet.

"What does that mean?" Braelyn asks cautiously. "That Adam is taken care of."

Forest comes over with his phone in his hand and plays a video of a wasted Adam, who apparently continued his drinking spree during the fight, getting arrested by the chief of police, who Adam hired to take me down. He's belligerent and barely understandable, but he's threatening to sue everyone and their grandmother. Including mine. Good luck with that one.

"He was part of a sting," Forest tells us with a smirk he's

barely able to contain. "According to the police chief, they'd been tracking him and his egregious illegal betting for a while." He looks at me. "Did you know he'd been placing bets on you for years, though he rarely came to your matches?"

"Yes," I tell him. "I made him a lot of money."

Braelyn gasps. "I didn't know!"

"Well, the cops might have had some help tonight, but they have a very lengthy trail of evidence that he was placing large bets and covering his earnings in multiple ways like calling them work bonuses, corporate expense-earnings, or most of the time, simply not declaring them at all. Except he put the funds into his regular accounts."

I almost choke. If my ribs weren't literal fire right now, I might. "You mean tax evasion and money laundering on illegal bets?"

Forest is almost gleeful. "Yep. He'll go to prison for this."

Braelyn is about to lose her mind. "Can someone please explain this to me?!"

"Not here," the three of us say in unison.

"It's all cleared out," Hayes states. "You two can go without any issue." He extends his fist to me. "Good fight, brother. Glad you're finished."

"Finished?!" Her hands shoot out. "Why does everyone here know everything that's going on but me?"

Somehow, I get myself to stand. "Come on, kid. Let's go home."

She waves a finger back and forth, again, like my grandmother would. "No way, Roman Fritz. You need a hospital."

Fuck. I should have known she'd do that.

"Don't test me on this," she warns dangerously. "You need a chest and facial X-ray, and a renal CT or ultrasound. Plus, a med student to do your facial stitches."

My lips bounce. "A med student?"

"You don't even deserve an intern after the night I've had at your expense."

Damn. "Hopefully, you're into Frankenstein then." But I can't argue with her. The woman handed me pictures of me kissing someone and was being stalked by a woman who clearly meant harm. Speaking of that. "Hey, I need a call with you tomorrow," I say to Forest.

"Sure."

I'm going to have him do his research into her and see what she's up to. At the very least track her to make sure Brae is safe. I don't trust that Adam and his blackmail are enough. We'll make sure she never goes near my girl again.

"All right, Nurse Fritz, take me to the hospital."

SOMETIMES IT SUCKS BEING A FRITZ. Brae takes me to her hospital, which I expected. Except I have about ten thousand cousins who work here, and for those who aren't related to me by blood or marriage or whatever else, everyone knows me.

"Can you believe it?!" Brae is incensed. "It was an attempted mugging in the back alley behind his restaurant. They really got him."

Jack seems to already be in on the ruse, but the nurse helping him isn't. "Oh my gosh. You poor thing. Did you file a police report?"

"He didn't see anything, but yes, we will right after we make sure he's okay."

"Absolutely. I'll get the portable X-ray going, an IV because he looks like he's in shock from the episode, he's been sweating so much, and some labs." She looks at Jack, who gives her a firm nod.

"Yes. Let's get all of those going. I want a CBC, CMP, and let's type and cross him in case he needs blood."

"I don't need a transfusion." I try to hold in my annoyance, but part of me feels like they're fucking with me. It was a boxing match. Not an actual mugging.

"You don't know that," Jack chastises, and yeah, this is going to be a long night with him and Braelyn. Good thing Wren isn't here. That woman is the ultimate ball buster. "I'll be right back. I need to see who's on to do your face."

Jack leaves the room, and Brae turns to the nurse. "I think he needs a rectal for guaiac testing to see if there's any intestinal bleeding."

I tilt my head at my wife. "Nice try."

She gives me the most innocent yet professional look I've ever seen on her. "I'm completely serious. You could have internal bleeding."

"No. That's a hard no."

"Yes, but there are better ways for us to determine that, don't you think?" the nurse questions even as she seriously considers this.

Braelyn sighs in dismay. "I suppose."

Score one for me. For a change. I give her my best attempt at a cocky smile, but she's not having it. Probably because nothing looks cocky on me at the moment. I change tactics.

"Can I go up and see Katy and Bennett if they're awake?"

Braelyn is about to chop off my balls. "Katy gave birth tonight by an emergency C-section, and Baby Callan is in the NICU. They need their sleep."

I hold up a placating hand, realizing I'm already on very thin ice with her. "Fine. I'll visit them another day."

"Good news," Jack announces just as the nurse jabs a needle into my arm to draw my blood and then starts my IV. "We have our best fourth-year medical student to do the sutures on your face."

I cock an eyebrow, which is no easy feat. Hell, I don't even know if it's arching up with all my facial swelling, but I don't care because what the fuck? I can't tell if he's serious or not. He looks serious, but Jack is that kind of guy anyway.

Typically, I'm not vain. I'm not. I box. Let's start with that. I've had multiple fractures on my face before, and my nose is far from perfect. But the gash under my eye is long and jagged, and there is no fucking way I'm letting some pre-doctor hack get at my face.

"No."

Jack laughs. Brae does too. The nurse looks uneasy, but she quickly figures out that they're joking. I hope.

"It's not really your choice." Brae puts her hand on my arm. "We can't let the wound stay open until morning or you'll get a terrible infection. You have to deal with the fourth year."

"Why can't he do it?" I point at Jack.

"He's the attending. Attendings don't suture."

"Braelyn, I swear to god—"

"Actually, I have one of our plastic surgery PAs who will do it."

I keep that finger pointed at him. "Good man. My cousin chose wisely."

"You might not be saying that after we get the films and labs back, but let's get this started."

The ultrasound of my kidneys shows that I'm bleeding from a nasty contusion on my right side, but that it should heal on its own without surgery if I take it easy. My ribs are a different matter, and they want to admit me overnight for observation as one of the fractures has nicked a lung and is causing some bleeding, both internally and into the lung space. They're worried it'll turn into pneumonia or a hemopneumothorax. Whatever that means. They're also worried about my blood count with all of this bleeding.

I decline.

I'm not having much trouble breathing, and I don't feel sick or shaky from blood loss. Plus, I have the best nurse in the world. If I get short of breath or have increased pain or really start to feel like shit, we'll be back. The PA comes in and meticulously sutures my face and refers me to a maxillofacial specialist for my fractures. They're non-displaced, but not great-looking either, and will take at least four weeks to heal.

By the time we leave the hospital, it's the wee hours of the morning. I'm sore as fuck. My face hurts. My side hurts. My back hurts. I need a shower. And I need my girl to completely forgive me because she's still pissed, and I get that.

I'm lucky she's still here with me after those pictures and what I put her through at the match. She could have not come tonight at all and moved out by the time I got home. It wouldn't have been shocking and it would have been justified after what she experienced with Adam. The fact that she trusted me enough to come and to ask me about it and to believe me speaks volumes.

"I can't give you orgasms tonight," I mumble begrudgingly as we get in the elevator and head up to our place. "Or be inside of you."

"Maybe you shouldn't have nearly gotten yourself killed."

Then something occurs to me. "What if you use your vibrator in front of me?"

"You mean like as a form of torture and payback because you can't touch me or come tonight?"

"Yep."

She grins evilly. "I like it."

"Excellent. But first let's shower."

Showering sucks. Everything sucks. I break down and take one of the painkillers Jack prescribed for me because I can't take ibuprofen due to the bleeding. Brae, my lovely nurse and wife, helps me get cleaned up, changed, and into bed. I feel like a baby, and I don't like it. I'm also positive I'll feel worse tomorrow because that's how these things go.

But I'll manage it. Exactly how I'll manage the Adam and

Anne Sharpe situation though Forest is already on it. Either way, it's done. Adam is sitting behind bars and Anne can't get to Braelyn here.

Braelyn climbs into bed beside me, a yawn overpowering her.

"Do you want to just go to bed?" I ask, wishing I could touch her, but I truly can't move all that much. My right side is pretty fucked between my ribs and my kidney.

"There's no fun in that."

"Sadist," I quip.

"Be thankful I'm not tying you to the headboard with rope."

I wince. Just the thought of that sucks.

"I love you. I'm sorry about the day you had. I'm sorry I contributed so much to that."

She rolls over to face me, her brown eyes heavy with exhaustion and her brown curls all over the place. "I'm just glad you're okay. Well, okay enough. We're done with this, right? With all of it."

"Yes. I'll make sure of it. Now take out your vibrator and make yourself come. You've got two minutes because I won't be able to stay awake longer than that."

"Yes, sir." I get a wink, and then my girl gets going with her vibrator, running the long white silicone piece over her clit before slipping it inside. It's the hottest thing I've ever seen and my cock is insanely jealous. So are my fingers and my mouth. It's torture as she said. The best kind, and I alternate watching her face and her cunt until she comes. Then my eyes are glued to hers.

"Will you marry me?" I ask as she's all flushed and sated with a cute little smile on her lips.

"We are married."

"Yeah, but I want you to be my wife. Not fake. Not accidental. Not on a dare. But for real."

She twists and cracks an eye open, peering at me. "You waited until after I came to ask me this?"

"I figured you'd be more docile and less stubborn this way."

Her lips bounce. "Roman, I'm your wife. You're my husband. I don't need another ceremony to prove that. This is us. We're forever, just as we said."

She rolls over and arches up to kiss my lips. I try to deepen the exchange, but she pulls back with a headshake.

"You know that, though, right?" I press. "That there will never be anyone else but you. You're always the one I love, the one I fight with, but most importantly, the one I'm forever fighting for."

"I do and I know we can make it through anything."

"No matter what."

BONUS EPILOGUE

BRAELYN

Six months later

"We welcome you to Monday Night football and the start of a new season here in Rebels Stadium on this cool, crisp November evening. We have two amazing teams going head-to-head tonight."

"Absolutely," the other announcer picks up. *"But the main talk for the Rebels heading into the new season is the coaching change. Famed and beloved Rebels head coach Asher Reyes was promoted to general manager of the team, and he brought in the Rebels' new head coach—"*

"Mute that, would ya?" Forest calls out, pointing at the TV in the corner of the booth that's broadcasting the game.

The sound cuts out, and we all turn our focus back to the field where the lights in the stadium are going dark, and the internal announcer is introducing the team to the field. The glass windows are open, and the sounds of the stadium filter in. It's an excitement that never gets old.

Especially when not one but two of your best friends are on the field now that Quinn is doing part of her residency with the team.

I take a sip of my drink and glance over at Skylar when she accidentally nudges me with her elbow. Poor thing looks miserable, one hand on her large belly, other on her plate that she's balancing on it.

"It's like a tray," I quip.

"It's ridiculous is what it is," she gripes. "I'm too short to be this pregnant."

I laugh. "It just makes you more adorable and round, is all."

I get a half-glare. "I totally might have you strip my membranes at thirty-seven weeks and we won't tell anyone."

My nose scrunches. "I am not stripping your membranes, babe. That's above and beyond the call of best friend duty. Besides, if anyone is to stick their hand up your vagina, other than your husband, it should be Keegan or your OB."

"Ugh. Fine. But I'm so hungry and yet I feel like I have no room for all this food."

"Here." I set my drink down next to my plate, then I remove her plate from her belly and adjust her so she's more upright and less slouched. I grab my jacket and Roman's and stuff them behind her so they're under her lower back.

She lets out a contented hum and nods for me to hand her the plate again. "Much better. Thank you."

A second later, Aston comes in beside her, holding his daughter, Zoey, in his hands. They plop down, and he kisses Skylar's cheek and belly, and Zoey does the same. They're so stinking adorable I can hardly stand it.

"You know," Roman whispers in my ear from the other side of me. "We could get you pregnant."

I throw him a scathing glare, and his hands shoot up in defense even as he gives me a devilishly wicked grin.

"What? I'm just saying it might be nice if our kids are close in age to Skylar and Aston's."

There is some food for thought with that, but I can't even begin to fathom it at this moment. Plus, you know, Skylar can hardly move, and her feet are swollen, and her tits are ginormous.

"No, thanks."

"No little baby Nash yet?" Skylar teases, clearly having heard us.

"Not yet," I assert. "We've barely been married."

Aston throws me a side-eye. "It's been six months."

"Whatever. He's not home a lot right now. All I'm saying is—"

"Hey," Forest says as he and Hayes drop into the seats in front of us, directly in front of the window, but they both turn around to face us since the game hasn't officially started yet. "I just wanted to let you know that Adam will be released this Thursday."

That stops my heart for a moment. I haven't heard that name—or even thought it—in a while now.

Adam did end up going to prison for tax evasion and money laundering. He tried to roll over on Roman, but the DA wasn't interested. Probably because he was as crooked and involved in the underground boxing as it gets. He's also apparently on Seamus's payroll. Welcome to Boston.

In the end, Adam made a deal. White-collar prison for five months. His father was supersonic pissed about all of it. His heir was now a convicted felon, but he stood by him and down-played his crimes and told the world he was set up. Blah. It made back-page news for like a week.

He's not exactly Martha Stewart and people with money don't really care about white-collar crimes. They don't care about the rich trying to make themselves richer, and I wouldn't be shocked if by this time next week, Adam is back at Boston

Nine in the same position he was in before he ever went to prison.

Regardless, I haven't heard from or seen him since that night, and I doubt I will when he's released.

Anne Sharpe was another matter because I had a decision to make.

I debated filing a police report against her, especially with Adam getting arrested and taking away the protective insurance card he promised he'd carry for me. The truth is, despite everything, I felt bad for her. I remember her husband. He was one of those cases that stuck with me because he was so young, and it was so tragic.

She lost her husband, and grief does wild things to people. I get that. I've lived through some of it, and if I ever lost Roman, God help the planet because I'd be losing my mind. I see it every day.

Does it excuse her behavior? Not a freaking chance. But I still get it.

And truthfully, if she hadn't slept with Adam, I likely would have married him and not Roman, and then where would I be? I shudder even thinking about it. If she hadn't stalked me and tried to ruin my relationship with Roman, I might have even sent her a gift basket as a thank you.

I ended up getting a restraining order against her for safety, but I didn't press charges. I left it at that, and she apparently did too, because much like Adam, I haven't heard from her.

Roman healed, but it took him the better part of six weeks before he was fully himself again. His illegal boxing days are over, but last I heard about, Seamus hasn't changed much and is still trying to find another ringer. Whatever. That's his business, and I'm just glad none of us are a part of it anymore.

"Well then," I muse, taking my glass from the narrow table and holding it up. "Here's to Adam. If he hadn't been such a douchebag, I'd never have married Roman."

Everyone laughs but lifts their drinks, and we all clink them together. Roman tosses his arm around me and kisses the corner of my lips.

"If I were really a spiteful dick, I'd send him a welcome home and thank you present."

I can't help the laugh that belts out of me. "You have every right to be spiteful, but it's not worth it."

"Not even a little." He nuzzles me, smelling the skin at my neck. "I have everything I've ever wanted right here."

I lean into him, already missing him. He leaves tomorrow evening for Frankfurt, and in two weeks, I'll join him for the opening of Knockdown. It's been a wild six months with all his travel, but I've joined him a few times and he's been home more than he's been there. He's done two weeks there, three weeks home, and it's worked out better than either of us anticipated, though I miss him like crazy and have no clue how we'll do this for the next year.

Regardless, we will. I have no doubt in my mind we'll manage this and come out even better, stronger, and more in love on the other side.

The door to the suite bursts open and in walks a crew of people, including Katy, Bennett, and their two kids, Willow and Callan, Jack and Wren, Keegan and her husband, Loomis, along with their son, Fenric, Mason's wife, Sorel, and their son Nolan, and Sorel's twin sister Serena. Plus a smattering of other people Skylar and Aston work with at Boston Children's Hospital, who are also Fritz cousins.

Zoey hops off Aston's lap and runs over to play with Willow, Nolan, Fenric, and another little girl as they all take in Baby Callan, who only ended up staying in the NICU for two and a half weeks and was never intubated. He's doing great and is so stinking cute.

In front of me, Hayes freezes and turns back toward the stadium, watching the opening kickoff. I throw Roman a questioning look but immediately get distracted by Katy and Wren coming over to say hi.

The evening goes on, and we watch Crew and Mason light up the other team. Quinn is on the sidelines, and it's fun getting to watch her cheer them on even if she doesn't like working for the team. By the time we get home, it's late, and I'm exhausted.

Roman has his hand in mine as we silently walk up the stairs to our bedroom. "I was thinking about something," he murmurs as we start to get undressed.

"What's that?"

"I don't give as much to charity as I was when I was boxing. I mean, I still give plenty, but it's not the same as it was. It's not enough."

"Okay," I say slowly, watching him as he thinks through his words.

"I wanted to talk with my parents about this, but how do you feel about setting up some kind of charity in Nash's name? Maybe something related to kids with neurological disorders or injuries or something since he wanted to be a pediatric neurosurgeon."

A smile curls up my face, and I walk over to him and jump right up into his arms. He catches me as he always does, and I wrap my arms around his neck.

"I think that's a magnificent idea. I think he'd love that."

"Good. I'll get it started tomorrow morning."

"Perfect."

"Like you."

I roll my eyes, but there's no heat behind it. There's only love and a connection so fierce I'm positive it can never be broken. It'll last us through this lifetime and all the others we find each other in.

His lips come down on mine, and he brings us to the bed.

"I need you," I whisper as I kiss him harder.

"I always need you." He cups my jaw in his hand and

peppers my lips with his. "But does my wife need something extra tonight?"

He pulls me closer, our kiss quickly turning urgent. His arm slides under my ass and he hauls me against him so I can feel how hard he is for me. We make quick work of each other's clothes, lost in the move and slide of how perfectly we fit together.

His fingers loop into the bra straps on my shoulders, letting them fall one at a time. His mouth meets the bony structures of my collarbone where he places open-mouthed kisses along my skin.

My breath hitches and my head falls back as my eyes close.

"You taste sinful. Like lust and endorphins. Like mine."

Reaching around, he unhooks my bra and tears it from my chest, making my tits bounce free. He sucks my nipple deep into his mouth, using his tongue to swirl and his teeth to scrape. My hands fist the back of his hair that's still not long enough to fully grasp.

"Roman," I murmur.

"Yes, baby. Tell me."

His hand slides down my stomach before diving into my thong. He rings my clit with his finger the same way he rings my nipple with his tongue.

"So fucking beautiful," he rasps. "So fucking wet for me."

I moan, arching into him, needing more of him.

"I love you. My wife. My girl. My Brae." He grips my thong on either side of my hips and yanks, eliciting a yelp from me. The satin shreds, leaving me bare and exposed. His hand caresses my smooth pussy as he stares down at it. "God, I fucking love your cunt."

He moves until he's between my thighs, giving me a dirty kiss from my ass to my clit.

I rock into him, wanting his tongue on my clit. Inside me.

"Roman," I whine as he uses a finger to play with my clit without giving me enough pressure. My empty core clenches.

"What, baby?"

"I want you."

"What do you want?"

A blush hits me before I can stop it and of course he catches it.

He crawls up me in an instant and hovers over me. "Tell me."

I reach between us and grip his cock. "I want this."

"You've got that. What aren't you telling me?"

"My ass. I want you in my ass."

His forehead falls to mine, and his eyes close. His cock pulses in my hand.

"Is that your way of saying you want that too?"

He smiles though his eyes are still closed. "Fuck yeah, I do." He opens his eyes and pins me with an intensity that makes me shiver. "You're sure?"

I roll over and climb up onto all fours. My head twists over my shoulder, and I catch him staring at my ass. "You'll go slow, right?"

His eyes meet mine. "I'll go slow. But you have a safe word. Use it if you need it."

"Yes, sir."

I get a smack to my ass, and because I'm already so riled up, I moan and my pussy clenches.

His eyes blacken, and he goes for his nightstand and the bottle of lube he has in there. I watch with rapt attention as he opens the cap and squirts a large amount on his hand. He coats his dick with it, jerking it, making it glisten. His other hand comes to my ass, his slick fingers prying my cheeks open before I feel him at my back entrance.

"Oh."

"Try to relax. I'm just going to play with you first."

He pushes a finger into my asshole while his hand that was jerking his cock finds my pussy. He pumps into me and presses against the back wall while his finger in my ass meets them, his fingers rubbing together, rubbing me, from inside me.

"Shit," I hiss, the sensation forbidden and filthy and yet so fucking good.

"Rub your clit," he grounds out. "Fuck, your ass is so goddamn tight." He inserts another finger into it and starts to scissor them, stretching me, all the while he pumps in and out of my pussy, building me up.

My clit is firm and thrumming with blood and my head bows at the pleasure sweeping through me. I rock back into him, wanting him deeper. I haven't told him this, but I've worked on my ass a bit while he was in Europe. It's going to hurt and I have no doubt he'll be bigger than my toys but my ass isn't quite the virgin he thinks it is.

"Put it in me, Roman. Please. I'm ready."

He hisses out a curse and his fingers are gone, replaced by the blunt head of his dick. "Remember to breathe and relax. And keep your safe word close."

I won't be using my safe word. I already know that, but I nod all the same, knowing he needs that.

Little by little, in and then back out, he pushes into my ass. It's tight, and it burns, but there's pleasure mounting on the other side of that. He's grunting and wheezing, sweat coating his brow. He hits the ring of muscles, the point of no return, and works himself in past them inch by inch. Once he's fully seated, he drags a hand up my spine.

"Breathe."

"Are you?"

He chuckles and groans. "No. I'm trying so hard not to come this second. You have no idea how good you feel. Are you okay?"

I nod, my arms trembling as they hold me up, and I lower myself to my forearms, which makes him groan again.

"Shit. Fuck."

"Don't come in me yet."

"I won't," he grits out, barely holding it together. "But can I fuck you now?"

I glance back at him. "Give it to me and don't hold back."

His black eyes catch fire, and his hands grasp my hips. "Baby, I'm going to pound your ass."

He slides almost all the way out, grunting and groaning as he goes before he thrusts back in as deep as he can go. He does it again, the slide of the lube and the feel of his cock filling me up is better than I ever would have expected. A moan slips out of me, and it sets him off.

"Yeah?"

"Yeah. I want more."

"Christ. Rub your clit again, Braelyn. You're going to come with me in your ass. And the next time we do this, I'm going to put one of your pretty toys in your cunt."

The thought of that turns me on like nothing else, and I push back into him, wanting to take him deeper. I adjust myself so my weight is on one forearm, and my other hand goes to my clit. I rub myself in tight, fast circles, increasing my pace as he increases his.

He uses my hips to pound me on his dick, impaling me with it, stretching me, making me cry out and beg for more. His lips meet my spine, and he kisses a trail up to my ear, his chest to my back. I turn my head to catch his lips. We're sloppy and loud, and the pleasure in my clit and ass builds to a breaking point.

"I'm going to come," I manage, feeling heat crawl through my limbs and tighten my empty core.

"Can I come in you?"

"Yes. Come inside me. I want to be messy with you."

"Jesus fuck. I'm done."

His teeth sink into my shoulder and that's all it takes for me. I come, screaming out my orgasm as it shakes through me. I feel it in my ass, my cunt, my clit. It's everywhere and my face falls to the blanket, my arms giving out on me.

His hips still and he sputters, a bellow ripping from his lungs.

We collapse, panting for our lives. I can feel his cum leaking out of my ass. It leaks everywhere as he gently pulls out of me. I wince, despite the extra lubricant. Roman rains kisses all over me, my lips, my cheeks, my forehead, my shoulders, before he picks me up and carries me into the shower.

We wash off, touching and giggling, before he picks me up and enters my pussy.

An hour later, I'm cuddled up beside him, my eyes closed and my heart happy.

"I have something to tell you," I murmur.

"What's that?" he asks absently, his voice heavy with sleep.

"I have to go to the RMV tomorrow."

I feel him shift beside me. "How come?"

"Because I officially changed my last name to Fritz, and I have to get a new license."

In a flash, he's on top of me, his eyes now bright and open and his smile infectious. "Yeah?"

I smile in return, so giddy I can hardly stand it. "Yeah. I'm Braelyn Albright Fritz."

He takes my left hand and kisses my ring finger before he drops on me, and round three begins. Only this time, we're fighting for each other, and we'll never get knocked down again.

. . .

THANK you for reading Forever Fighting. I hope you loved Roman and Braelyn's story as much as I did. If you haven't read book 1 in the Forever Boston series, check out Forever Undone now. OR keep going in the series with Forever Offsides.